Ulric The Jarl

A Story of the Penitent Thief

by

William O. Stoddard

Double9
BOOKS

Ulric The Jarl
A Story of the Penitent Thief
by William O. Stoddard

ISBN: 978-93-67149-20-1

Published by

DOUBLE 9 BOOKS

2/13-B, Ansari Road
Daryaganj, New Delhi – 110002
info@double9books.com
www.double9books.com
Tel. 011-40042856

ABOUT THE AUTHOR

William O. Stoddard was an American author, best known for his works in children's literature and historical fiction. Born in 1835, Stoddard had a diverse career, including roles as a journalist and editor. He gained popularity for his engaging storytelling and ability to blend adventure with moral lessons.

One of his notable works is "Ulric the Jarl: A Story of the Penitent Thief," which explores themes of redemption, honor, and personal transformation set against a Viking backdrop. Stoddard's writing often reflects his interest in history and human character, making his stories both entertaining and thought-provoking. In addition to his historical novels, Stoddard wrote several books for young readers, emphasizing themes of bravery, friendship, and integrity. His contributions to literature have left a lasting impact, and his works continue to be appreciated for their depth and insight into human nature. Overall, Stoddard's legacy lies in his ability to connect with readers through compelling narratives and relatable characters.

CONTENTS

Chapter I
Around the Viking House-fire

In the Northland were the roots from which grew the great nations which now rule the earth. The tribes were many, but the principal representative and the absorbent of their thoughts and their traditions may receive from us the general name of Saxons. These were the swordsmen of the sea whom the Roman legionaries declared to be the hardest fighters they had met, whether on land or water.

In the Northland were also the germs of political and religious liberty, and here were to be found the first forms of our highest faith.

But the men of the old race sailed southward and then eastward, at the first, taking their gods with them. Not until centuries later did they march and conquer this far western world, but we, their children, still devoutly believe that the great God came with them.

The landward slope of a vast gray granite headland was thickly covered with towering pine trees. Beyond them, inland, lay a snowy valley without woods, and beyond that arose a blue and misty range of mountains. There were no trees upon the summit of the headland; only bare rocks, storm worn and deeply furrowed, were uplifted to meet the bitter wind that swept down over the flinty ice covering of the North Sea from the yet colder winter which was manufacturing icebergs within the arctic circle. Sheer down, hundreds of feet, the perpendicular face of the cliff smote sharply the glittering level that stretched away westerly over the sea to the horizon, while an arm of it pushed in eastward over the fettered waters of a deep and gloomy fiord, rock-bordered.

Here would evidently be a good harbor in summer, when the waters should be free, but now it had a forbidding, dangerous look, and out of the fiord poured continually a volume of roaring sound, the solemn organry of the wind playing upon the icy and rocky reflectors.

There was another gigantic sea cliff at a distance of about a mile down the shore, southerly. Between that and the headland the ice line curved raggedly inward along the lines of a sheltered cove, which might at another season provide a landing place. Midway, and at the head of the cove, there lay, propped up on either side by timbers, the bare hull of a well-made vessel. It was of goodly size, being over thirty paces in length and of full six paces in width at its middle. At the prow and at the stern it was high built, with short decks, under which was room for stowage and for the sheltered sleeping of men. It was lower made amidships, where were both seats and standing room for rowers, and on either side were twenty thole pins. In appearance the hull was somewhat flat-bottomed, but it had a keel. At the center arose a stout, high mast, but upon it there was yet neither yard nor boom nor sail. Both prow and stern were sharply made. Evident was it that she was new and had never yet floated. Her outline was of much beauty, and all her timbers and planks were heavy and strong, that she might battle with rough seas and with the ice cakes of the spring breaking. From her prow projected a beak of firmly clamped and tenoned oak, faced and pointed with iron, that she might break not only the waves, but the ribs of other ships. All around her and in some parts over her lay the white snow, deeply drifted, but wherever the woodwork was uncovered there could be seen much of skillful carving and smooth polishing.

At other places along the curve of the cove there were boats and ships, larger and smaller. All were hauled up above high-water mark, and snow was on them. The larger craft seemed to be stanch and seaworthy, but not any of them were equal in size or in strength or in beauty to the new warship.

Upon a straight line inland a hundred fathoms, as if the iron beak were pointing at it, stood a long, low, irregular building of wood with high ridged roofs, in which were wide holes at the ridges. From these holes, as if they were instead of chimneys, columns of blue smoke were rising to be whirled away by the wind. Stonework or brickwork was not to be seen. Through the strong timber walls, under the projecting eaves, were many openings, equally cut, window-like, for the entrance of light and air on sunny days, but these all were now closed by wooden shutters, some of which were braced from without. The timbers of the house walls were cleanly hewn and skillfully fitted, and they were tightly calked with moss and tempered clay. The roofs were of shingles riven from the pine trees.

Beyond, landward, there were smaller, ruder structures for the shelter of horses, cattle, sheep, and swine, and there were many ricks of hay and straw and of yet unthreshed grain. In either direction around the cove and scattered irregularly up the valley were a number of less extensive buildings for the abode of men. Some of these were mere huts, built ruggedly of timber and unhewn stone. From every roof was there blue smoke rising to testify that there were no empty houses in this seashore village of the vikings. Around the central cluster of buildings there were palisades, but except for these there were no signs of fortifications. It was as if there need be little fear of the coming of any foeman.

Bitter and cold and strong was the windstorm that blew across the icy sea and smote upon the swaying crowns of the pine forest and howled among the bare boughs of the oaks. It came and knocked at the great door in the front of the house pointed at by the beak which was the forefinger of the ship.

The door swung open for a moment and then it closed, but in that moment there rang out loud voices of rude song and the twanging of sonorous harp strings. Also a great blast of fresh, pure air rushed eagerly into the house, where it was much needed. Not but that the vast room, low-walled, high-roofed, was fairly well ventilated in many other ways, but the fire in the middle of its earthen floor was blazing vigorously, and not all the smoke might readily escape at the round gap in the roof ridge over it. Now and then, indeed, the wind blew rudely down through that aperture and sent the smoke clouds eddying murkily among the rafters.

But for the fire blaze and for sundry swinging cressets filled with burning pine knots the great hall would have been gloomily dark, but these lights were enough, in spite of the smoke clouds, to show many things which told of what sort this place might be. So also might be plainly noted the faces and the forms of the men who sat or stood around the fire, or who lay upon the bearskins and the wolfskins that were scattered here and there upon the earth floor and upon the wooden settles along the walls.

A broad table ran across a raised dais at one end of the room, and on this were not only pitchers and mugs of earthenware variously molded, with many drinking horns, but there were also tankards and goblets and salvers of silver, richly designed and graven by the artisans of other lands than this. Of the articles of furniture for different uses some few had an appearance of having been brought from far, but the great, high-backed oaken throne chair behind the long table, at its center, was rich with the grotesquely elaborate carvings of the old North people. On the walls hung shields and arms and armor of many patterns. The steel caps of the vikings hung side by side with visored helmets that told of Greece and Rome and of lands yet further east. There were many men in the room. Some of them were scarred old warriors, but there were youths of all ages above mere boyhood. Likewise were there numbers of women.

As central as was the fire itself were three figures which seemed to attract and divide the attention of all the others. On the side of the fire toward the door towered one who looked a very embodiment of the warlike young manhood of the race of Odin. His blond beard and mustache were full but not yet heavy. His complexion was fair, notwithstanding its weather bronzing, and his steel-blue eyes seemed both to flash and to laugh as he stood with folded arms and listened. His dress was simple. His shoes, that arose above his ankles, were well made. Above them were leggings of tanned leather, and he wore a tunic of thick, blue woolen cloth. He was unarmed except for the slightly curved, broad-bladed seax in its sheath that hung from his belt. Its blade was not more than a cubit in length. It was sharp on one edge only, and it was heavy. The steel hilt and the crosspiece were thick, for a good grip. It was a weapon terrible to meet if it were in the hand of an athlete like this—more than six feet in height, deep-chested, lithe and quick of motion—and already the short seax had won for its bearers, the Saxons, a dreaded name among all the peoples of the south countries to which their swift keels had carried them.

At the left of the fire was a large, high-backed chair made of some wood which had become almost black with age and smoke. It was not now occupied, but in front of it stood the form of a woman, straight as a pine and taller than any of the men around her. Her face was swarthy, deeply marked, haughty, and her abundant hair fell disheveled down to her waist, as white as the drifts upon the mountains. She was clad in a robe of undyed, grayish wool, falling loosely to her feet. On these were socks and buskins, but her lean, sinewy arms were bare as she stretched them out, waving her gnarled old hands in time to the cadence of a semimetrical recitation. She spoke in the old Norse tongue, with a voice upon whose power and mellowness time seemed to have had little effect. Every head in the hall bent toward her, as if her words were a fascination to her hearers, and none willed to interrupt her.

Weird and wild was the chant of the old saga woman, and the fire in her piercing black eyes brightened and dulled or almost went out as she sang on, from myth to myth, of the mystical symbolisms of the intensely poetic and imaginative North. Gods and demigods and goddesses, heroes and heroines, earth forces and spiritual powers, dwarf and giant, gnome and goblin, fate maidens, werewolves, serpent lore, the nether frost fires, the long night of the utter darkness, the twilight of the gods, the eternal hall of the slain, the city of Asgard—long and wonderful was the saga song of the white-haired woman who had, it was said, seen the ice of more than fivescore winters float out of the North Sea.

She ceased speaking and sank back into the chair as if all life had gone out of her. Rigid and motionless she sat, and there was no light in her eyes, but none went near her, nor did any speak. There was indeed a momentary outburst of approval, but it hushed itself. Even a fierce laugh that came to the lips of the tall young warrior died away half uttered.

Almost at the same moment another sound began to fill the hall. It came, at the first, from a large harp that stood a few paces back from the fire. Over the strings of this harp were wandering the long, bony fingers of a pair of gigantic hands, while behind it, on a low stool, swayed and twisted a form whose breadth of shoulder and length of arm were out of all proportion to its height. The head was bald except for a fringe of reddish-gray hair above the ears. The face was scarred and seamed to distortion, the right eye having been extinguished by a sword stroke which, by its furrow, must have half cloven the frontal bone. Age was indicated by the tangled gray beard which floated down below the belt, but not in the powerful, rich-toned voice of the harper, for the smoke seemed to eddy and the fire to dance as the harp twanged more loudly, and then there came to join it a burst of stormy song—a song of battles on the land and on the sea; a song of the mighty deeds done by the warriors of old time; a song of fierce and stirring incitement to the performance of similar feats by those who listened.

The harp grew then more softly musical, for he sang of the blue waves and the sunny shores of the southern seas; of their islands of beauty; of their harbors of peace and their cities of splendor; of temples and castles; of gold and silver and gems; but he seemed to drift beyond all these into a song of something beautiful, which yet was vague and far away and indescribable. His thought and word concerning it became like a refrain, until the minds of all who heard were filled with ideas of the dim and unattainable glory of the land of heroes, the city of the gods, the return of the White One, and the rising of the sun that will never set. Like deep answering unto deep were the last utterances of harp and harper, and as they suddenly ceased the tall young warrior stepped forward two paces and cried loudly:

"O Hilda! wise woman of the hundred winters, if this is indeed to be thy last——"

"I shall go out with the spring flood," she said, interrupting him, "but thou wilt be upon the sea when they lay me in the cleft between the rocks."

"I will go forth as thou sayest," he responded. "Am I not of the sons of the gods? I will sail as my father sailed and as Oswald has sung. I will crush, like him, the galleys of the Romans. I will look upon the cities of the east and of the south. I am of Odin's line. I will go out in the good ship *The Sword*, and will sail until I see the hero god and the city of the gods and the land of the living sun."

Loud now rang the shouts of approval from the bearded vikings as they sprang to their feet and began to crowd around their young leader.

"Go, O Ulric, son of Odin! Sail on into the sunset and the farther sea!" came trumpetlike from the white lips of Hilda.

Ulric The Jarl | 13

Low sounds arose, too, from the strings of the harp, but the door swung suddenly open and upon the threshold stood a man garbed in wolfskins.

"Hael, Ulric the Jarl!" he shouted, and there were many exclamations here and there around the room.

"Hael, Wulf the Skater!" heartily responded Ulric. "What bringest thou?"

"Good tidings!" replied Wulf, joyously, stepping forward. "I came down the mountain slide and across the fiord. No other foot will cross it this season. During days the ice hath weakened and now the wind is changing southerly. There is already a rift in the sky. O son of Brander the Brave, be thou ready for the spring outing!"

"Odin!" shouted Ulric. "Keels for the open sea! Hael to the cruise of *The Sword!* Hael to the bright south! And I, Ulric the Jarl, I of the sons of the gods, I will go out and I will not return until I have looked into the face of one of the gods. And he will know me, and he will take me by the hand, and he will bid me walk with him into the city of the living sun!"

Glad were the hearts of all the vikings as they heard, and with one accord they shouted loudly:

"Hael to Ulric the Jarl! Hael to the cruise of *The Sword!* We are his men and with him we will go!"

Long had been the winter and slow had been the coming of the change for which men waited. Welcome was Wulf the Skater, but Oswald's fingers were slowly busy among the strings of his harp, and they found strange sounds which came out one by one.

"The message of the harp!" muttered Hilda. "It is like the moaning of the sea in the fiord in the long night."

Chapter II
The Going Out of the Ice

Wulf the Skater brought true tidings to the house of Ulric, the son of Brander the Brave, on the day of Saturn. Winter was ending. The word passed on from house to house until all in the village came out and looked upward, seeking for the blue rift in the sky. The wind blew not now as in the morning. The north wind had gone elsewhere, and instead there came up from the south a breathing which was fitful and faint at first. It was cool, also, from having touched the frost faces on its way. Only one more hour went by and the sky was almost clear, so that the sun shone down unhindered and his heat was surprisingly strong.

The south wind grew warmer and more vigorous toward sunset, but with him now came a fog so dense that no man cared to go out into it; for if he did, it was as though darkness touched him. All through the evening the south wind sighed softly among the homes of the vikings, and went wandering up the fiords, and felt its way, shivering, across the flinty levels of the frozen sea, but toward the morning of the day of the sun the breeze brought with it, also, to help it, a copious warm rain. Before the noon torrents were leaping down the sides of the mountains and the sea was beginning to groan and heave and struggle in its effort to take off and put away its winter mail.

"Harken!" said Oswald, the harper, as he sat by the now smoldering fire in the hall of Ulric's house.

"I hear," said Hilda from her place on the other side of the ash heap. "It is the last time that I shall listen to the song of the outing ice, but I shall feel the wind from the sun land and I shall see the grass green in the valley before I go. There will be buds on the trees when I pass down into the earth to meet my kindred. O what a realm is that! The land of shadows. The under world which has the sod for a roof. But the old runes on the rocks tell of wide places. One may travel far in that land, and where I may go I know not."

The gnarled fingers of Oswald were searching among the strings of his harp, but only discords answered his touches.

"I have heard," he said, "that they hang their shields on the roots of the trees, and they see as we see in a twilight. I think I have heard them harping in the summer nights, when the moon was full and the wind was in the pines. I would that my own harp might be buried with me."

"No need," said Hilda. "They have better harps than thine. They will give thee one. It is well that the weapons of a warrior should be placed beside him in his tomb, but they must be marred in token that he useth them no more. He hath left others for his kinsmen. There are many good swords in the old tombs. One day they will all be opened and the blades will be found."

"And also much treasure," grumbled Oswald; but his harp twanged angrily as he said it, for he had ever been a man to hold fast anything in the shape of coined money or of precious metal. Many were said to be the outland coins in his leather bag in his room at the southerly end of the house. He had sometimes shown them to inquiring folk, but grudgingly, and he had always tied them up again tightly, as if he feared that there might be a thief even among the vikings.

Hilda arose and walked slowly across the room to the open door. She looked toward the sea, but the mist and the rain were a curtain.

"Hammers!" she said. "I can hear them. Ulric and his men are at work upon the ship. She will be ready to launch when the ice goeth out. She will sail to the Middle Sea, but when I look for her I cannot see her come again."

Once more she turned, and this time her slow and stately march carried her to the farther end of the hall, on the dais, where many suits of armor were hanging. She went straight to one of these and she touched it, piece by piece, while Oswald leaned upon his harp and watched her.

"When the hour was upon me," she said, "I saw the son of Brander in battle, and the men upon whom his ax was falling bore shields like this. There were dark men with them, wearing turbans. It is well. I think that at the end of this cruise he will come to me where I am. It were no shame to his father's son that the valkyrias, when they come to call the hero to Valhalla, should find him circled with slain Romans. Brander the Sea King took these arms for his trophies in the great fight off the coast of Britain. He drove the Roman galley ashore. He burned it with fire. Not one Roman escaped."

"I have seen Britain," muttered Oswald.

"Brander the Brave liked Britain well," continued Hilda. "It is a fair land, he said. If he could take more men with him, he would drive out of it the Romans and the Britons and keep it. But he said they have no good winters there, and the summers are all too long. It would be no land for me. What would I do in an island where the fiords do not shut up at the right season? I should perish!"

Very thoughtful was the face of the tall daughter of the Northland as she passed along, inspecting the armor and talking to herself about its varied history. Some of it had been won in fights with far-away peoples before she was born, but more of it had been brought into that hall before her eyes, and she had heard the bringers tell the tales which belonged to its pieces and to the swords and spears. Now, therefore, hanging there on the wall, the war treasures of the house of Brander were page-marks for her memory, and she also was a book of the old history of the Northmen from the days of the gods to this hour of her own closing.

Swiftly went by the day of rain and thaw, but their work was tenfold in the night which followed it. The rain fell on the roof in increasing abundance, and the wind threw it with force against the sides of the house. The torrents on the mountains grew into small swift rivers, and they made a continual loud sound of rushing water; but that was not the tumult which so filled the air and smote upon the ear. All other sounds were overborne by the booming and groaning of the ice and by the roar with which its loosened edges ground against the granite cliffs in the fiords.

The day of Saturn had been a day of frost and snow and storm until near its close. The day of the sun had brought the sun's breath from his own land and his smile into the sky, and he had slain the winter at a blow. The morrow would be the day of the moon, and before its arrival came now this night of such uproar that Oswald did not care to touch his harp, and the vikings mended their armor and sharpened their swords in silence. Hilda also was long silent, nor had Ulric the Jarl spoken aught that could be heard by all. When at last his voice arose, and men put by their work to hear, he gave answer to a question of Tostig the Red.

"Aye!" he said loudly, "the ship is ready from stem to stern. We will launch her behind the ice as it leaveth the shore. We will follow the floes as the tides bear them southward; ever do they melt as they go. So shall no other ship sail before us, and we shall be the first of all keels from the Northland, this year, among the islands of the Middle Sea."

Fiercely twanged the harp of Oswald and loud rang the shouts of the men who heard the young jarl speak his purpose, but before the harp could sound again Hilda arose in her place.

"Son of Brander," she said, "thou wilt go. Thou wilt see many things. All day have I been watching thy path, and the clouds are over it. In this thing that I now tell thee, do thou as did thy father: crush the keels of Rome in the seas of Britain and smite the men of Rome on the British island. And in the end of all thou wilt die, as did thy father, at the hand of a spearman of Cæsar."

"So be it," shouted Ulric, with a laugh on his lips and a flash of fire in his bold, bright eyes; "I ask no better!"

He said no more, but seated himself and began to sharpen his seax on a smooth, hard stone.

Chapter III
The Launching of "The Sword"

The day of the moon, the second day of the week, dawned brightly over the village of the vikings. The faces of the cliffs along the shores of the Northland boomed back continuous echoes of the thunderous reports of the splitting ice. The frost had been strong, and the winter mail of the sea was thick and hard, but the sun and the lifting tides and all the torrents from the mountains made a league, and they were more powerful than was the ice. The south wind also helped them.

All the hours since Wulf the Skater brought the news of the coming thaw had been spent by Ulric and his men in getting the good ship *The Sword* ready for the water. No room in her was to be wasted, and her hollow, to her very keel, was now closely packed with provisions, taking the place of other ballasting. There were tightly stowed barrels of pork and beef, and there were bags and boxes of hard bread, and casks of ale and casks of water. Over the greater part of these were planks fastened down like a deck, for the voyage to be undertaken promised to be long, and all except provisions for immediate use must be sealed until a day of need.

The seats of the rowers were all in, and the short oars, and also the long oars, which a man would stand erect to pull with. The small boats were fastened upon the half decks, fore and aft. The mast was now stayed and rigged and the spars and the sail had been swung in their places. Not of woven stuff was the sail, but of many well-dressed skins of leather, that it might toughly withstand any gale.

There were twenty oars on a side, and the crew who were to do the rowing, taking their turns, had been carefully selected during the winter. Their war shields were hung along the bulwarks, and they placed them there with great pride. The chosen men who lived further inland were now arriving, and they were as eager as were the men who dwelt on the shore. Stalwart and high-hearted were all the vikings who were to sail in *The Sword*. Among them were veterans who had fought under Brander the Brave, the father of Ulric, and others were youths who were now going out for their first venture in distant seas. Great store of weapons went on board, for there had been much making of bows and arrows and swords and spears and shields all winter. So the gray-headed and caretaking warriors declared that the ship was exceedingly well provided.

At the dawn of the day of the moon Ulric the Jarl stood at high-water mark looking seaward.

"As the tide turneth I shall know," he said to those who were with him. "The flood hath lifted the ice, but the ebb must lower it. *The Sword* will be launched at the next high tide if the outing is good."

That might be toward the evening, and word went out so that all might be ready.

The ship as yet bore no flag, but on the forward half deck stood a great anvil, carved finely of oak and blackened, and upon the anvil was fastened a massive hammer, made in like manner, that Thor the Great, the god of war, the smith god, might go with *The Sword* into any battle. Now could more fully be seen the carvings and the gildings and the many rich ornamentations which had been lavished upon the ship, and men who now saw her for the first time marveled at her beauty and at the strength of her timbers.

"Larger ships have been," they said, "but not many, nor was there ever one that gave better promise of bearing well the shock of another ship or the stroke of an ice floe."

All day the sound of harping could be heard in the house, for other harpers besides Oswald were now there, and they played and sang in a rivalry with each other. Hilda was not to be seen. It was said that she had shut herself up in her own room and would have none speak with her. Although the house was thronged, there were none who thought well to disturb her. Not many, indeed, were curious enough to pass near the closed door behind which she was believed to be looking into the twilight where the gods live, and out of which come those whose shadows darken the woods at times and whose voices are heard in the night as they talk to one another across the fiords.

The noon came and at low tide the ice edge was out twenty fathoms from the shore, leaving clear water behind it. If it should shove in again, there would be no launching, but as the ebb ceased there came an unexpected help. A mighty drift of snow and ice had formed, in early winter, hundreds of feet above the level, and yet in a hollow of the high mountain at the head of the fiord. Hard and strong was the grasp of this glacier upon the rocks and trees at its sides, but under it was a stream which had been covered, though not entirely closed. Above and beyond was now a lake of melted snow, and the water from it was forcing its way under the glacier by that rivulet channel, mining, mining, mining, until its work was done.

There was a great sound of breaking, a sound that was sharp, rasping, shrieking, as if the mountain uttered a great cry to see the glacier tear itself free and spring forward. The screams of a gier-eagle, startled from the withered pine tree on the summit, answered the scream of the mountain. Down, down, faster and faster, to the sheer precipice at the face of the fiord, and then the glacier itself uttered an awful roar as it leaped headlong from the cliff. A thunderous boom responded from the smitten face of the ice, and through the clefts that were made in all directions the freed salt water bounded high into the sunshine, which it had not seen since it was imprisoned in the dark by the winter. The entire mass went over, and with it went the bowlders, earth, and trees which it had rent off and brought away. The blow which it struck was as a blow from the hammer of Thor, and a vast wave rolled out of the fiord, breaking the nearer ice as it went and splitting square miles of the sea face beyond into floes of a right size for drifting. Out slipped the ice edge at the cove, a hundred fathoms further. In it came again angrily, but only to retreat once more and leave a wider, surer harbor for *The Sword* to dip her keel into when her launching hour should come.

All things were ready, both at the house and on the shore, when Oswald left his harp to go and speak to one of the maidens, of whom were many come to see the warriors depart.

"Go thou to Hilda," he said. "Say to her that shortly she will be needed at the ship."

"Come," said the maiden to other women who were near her, for she cared not to go alone.

Truly it was not far to go and come, stepped they never so slowly, and they soon brought back word that her door was open, but Hilda they did not find, nor did any know whither she had gone.

"So?" said Oswald, thoughtfully. "Pass thou on, then, and tell this to Ulric, the son of Brander, for he will understand. Bid Wulf the Skater and Tostig the Red that they come now to me."

Hastily went the maiden, for of this errand she had no fear.

On the summit of a low hill not more than half a mile from the house was a great heap of stones. Around it, in an oval, standing like watchful sentries, were many great stones, tall and upright. Upon the faces of these uprights were chiseled words in the old runes. A path that led to this hill had been kept open during the winter, and when Hilda left the house, with none to mark her going, she had walked along this path. The snow in it was soft, taking footprints, and Hilda stooped, looking closely at some which were already there. She followed them until they ceased at the heap of stones. She smiled and bowed her head approvingly.

"Ulric hath been here," she said. "He hath spoken to his father at the tomb. The son of the hero will himself be a hero. There is no other like him among the young branches of the tree of Odin."

Strong affection sounded in her words concerning the youthful head of the ancient house of Brander the Brave. A flush came for a moment into her withered face, and she stood in silence gazing at the tomb. Slowly her arms arose, waving, and her lips opened in a recitative that sounded like a song, wherein she was speaking to the father of Ulric and to other names than his, calling them her kindred. Louder, more weird, mournful, thrilling, grew the tomb song of the old saga woman. But it suddenly ceased, for to her came a response from one that stood upon the crest of the central heap of stones.

Not in any human voice of the dead or of the living was her answer, but from the gaunt and grisly shape of a large gray she-wolf, famished-looking, that stood there, snapping fiercely her bloody jaws and gazing at Hilda. Then lifted the wolf her head to send forth a long-drawn, wailing howl.

The long, late winter had been a hard one for all wolves and for other wild beasts, for against them the sheepfolds had been well guarded. And now this hunger-driven monster from the mountains had taken her opportunity to venture in almost to the village, finding this day a flock without a shepherd. She had ravaged unfought, and now she was here upon the tomb of Brander. Her presence there was as if she had been a written message to Hilda.

"Art thou here?" she exclaimed. "Aye! Thou art as I saw thee at the house. Thou art the name of Rome, O bloody mouth! Scourge of the world! Curse of all nations! Hungry one! The swords of the Northmen shall yet smite the cubs of the she-wolf in their own den."

A sharp, harsh bark, another howl, and a snapping of jaws replied to her and then the she-wolf sprang away, disappearing beyond the tomb, but Hilda turned and walked houseward along the path, muttering low as she went.

When Tostig the Red and Wulf the Skater came to Oswald, the harper, he gave them an errand, for they at once went away together to one of the best made of the stables in the rear of the house. They had not yet returned when Hilda walked past the house and on down to the beach. All men knew that the right hour for the launching of *The Sword* had come when Hilda came and stood at the prow of the vessel, laying her hand upon it.

She spoke then but few words, pointing at the heaps of driftwood and loose pieces of timber which were there and giving her commands. Those who heard her began to gather all this wood into a great heap. It was more like two heaps, for there was left a bare spot in the middle large enough for a yawlboat to have been lodged therein.

Ulric, the son of Brander, came and stood by Hilda, and as she looked at him the color arose again into her face and a kindly light kindled in her eyes. He also smiled at her very lovingly. She spoke a word that none else heard, and he blew three long, powerful blasts upon his war horn. From all directions came in haste the vikings and the other shore people and the upland people, both the old and the young, men and women. From the house came all who were in it. Oswald and the other harpers marched to the beach together, bringing their harps.

Now from the stables beyond the house came Tostig the Red and Wulf the Skater leading between them, whether he would or not, the snow-white colt which at two years seemed large for a four-year-old, but which as yet had neither been bridled nor mounted. That was partly because of the spirit that was in him; for none but Ulric or Hilda would he willingly let lay a hand upon him, and his eyes now grew red as if he were fretted overmuch. As he was led along he reared and plunged and snorted furiously, but Tostig and Wulf were strong men and they brought him to the heap of wood and in front of the hollow in its middle.

Hilda had brought with her a long polished staff of ash wood, which had something of woven cloth stuff wrapped closely around it. Now she made a sign to Oswald and he struck his harp. So did the other harpers, following him, and the sound of their music stirred the blood of all who heard, so that the men shouted and clashed their spears upon their shields. Then ceased all the harps but that of Oswald, and he sang a song of war which called upon Odin and all the gods to sail with their ship, *The Sword*, and give her a successful cruise, with many battles and much blood and great plundering and many burnings of the ships and of the strongholds of foemen.

The tide was rising fast, but the ice came no nearer the shore, and it was seen that there would be free searoom for the launching. All things else were ready for this, and the launchers with their hammers and their handspikes were prepared to go to their places. Oswald ended his song and all looked at Hilda. She did not at once speak, and her face grew ghastly as the face of one from whom life had departed. Taller she seemed as she raised her right hand and pointed to the colt.

"Ulric the Jarl," she said, in a hollow voice, but clear, "son of Brander the Brave, heir of the old house of the sea kings, son in the true line of the hero gods and of Odin, slay now the white horse of the Saxons and launch thy keel into the sea!"

Tostig and Wulf forced back the plunging colt into the hollow between the heaps, and Ulric walked forward, drawing his seax as he went. He put his left hand upon the face of the colt and it stood still, looking at him and neighing gently, while at every corner of the heaps torches of blazing pine were thrust quickly in by old women named for that duty by Hilda.

She had walked away to a little distance from the ship, and she stood now between the sea and the land, upon a spot where the sand was dry and smooth. Upon this she drew runes with the point of the staff that was in her hand, all the while chanting a saga which none of those who heard her could understand, except that they knew in it the names of the gods.

"Son of Odin," she shouted, "strike!"

"Odin!" responded Ulric, as he drove his seax to the hilt into the breast and through the heart of the colt.

It gave one cry that sounded like a human voice in sudden despair. It made one plunging struggle, restrained by Ulric, and then the beautiful animal lay quivering in the hollow. At once a heap of fuel was piled in front of it, concealing the sacrifice to Odin, and the long fingers of the fire seized rapidly upon the dry pine and the cedar and the firwood.

Loudly sounded the harps. Loud was the song in which all voices were joining. Out of the fiord came booming a great roar of the sea, for he was smiting his crags and dashing the floes of ice against the granite faces.

"Go forth into the sea, O sword!"

Hilda came again to the ship, unfolding as she walked that which was wrapped around her staff, and the south wind that was blowing blew it out so that all might see. It was a great banner, for a battlefield or for the mast of a warship. It was black, and upon it, fully half the size of the colt which had been slain, was painted the sign of the race of Brander, only to be carried before chiefs of Odin's line, the White Horse of the Saxons. Hilda placed the staff in the hands of Ulric, and he at once sprang on board the ship. He blew a blast of his war horn, and in a moment all the launchers were at their stations. Another blast, and all the rowers came on board and took their seats, taking hold of the short oars, ready to dip them, while tenscore more of vikings, fully mailed and armed, followed and posted themselves fore and aft, spear and shield and ax in hand. Ulric the Jarl stood by the hammer of Thor on the fore deck and raised his horn again. At this third blast, as he blew it, the launchers hammered hard and plied their handspikes and their levers.

"Go forth into the sea, O *Sword!*" shouted Hilda. "Thy beak shall break the ribs of the triremes and thy keel shall plow the seas of the south!"

Out sprang the vessel, so deftly shaped, so strongly made, so well manned, and into the sea she glided, while Ulric, the son of Brander, lifted high the standard and sounded again his war horn. Every harp twanged its loudest, and every horn on board the ship and on the shore, and every voice, joined in the shout of joy that hailed so successful a launching.

The Sword was now upon the sea, floating at the end of her shore hawser, while the crew lowered her anchors from the prow and stern. On the shore the fire flared upward like the streamers in the northern sky in winter.

The pallor on Hilda's face grew ghastlier still, and she walked to the house, forbidding any to come with her. As she went she muttered:

"Beautiful is the son of Brander, my boy! my hero! I love him as if I were his mother. Alas, she is not here to love him! O, I am old and it may be that I see not that which I seem to see when my eyes are opened. Not so! Him I shall look upon no more, nor upon the ship. I go, for I am very old. But I would that the young hero might not go down so soon. I would that he might win love and that he might bring home a bride, lest the race of Brander the Sea King should die with him. The gods be his guard where he goeth and the valkyrias find him not for a season!"

So the lonely old woman went into the house and went to her own room. She had seen the launching of *The Sword*, and the ship was to go out with the outing ice.

Rocking at her anchor lay she now, and all along the shore were men and women who rejoiced to look upon her and to think her the most perfect ship that had ever been built on the coast of the Northland. The fire was blazing high above the sacrifice to the gods, for many hands were ready to put on fuel, from time to time, and all knew that it must burn until *The Sword* should be out of sight.

It was when the sun was sinking, and the waves were washing gently and murmuring low along the beach because of the softness of the warm wind from the south, that Hilda came again, walking hastily. Her head was covered with her hood, and they saw not her face, but she spoke to a youth who stood by a small boat.

"Take thy boat," she said. "Go thou to the ship. Give Hilda's word to Ulric the Jarl. Bid him come to the shore, coming alone, rowing himself. Stay thou there until he returneth. Bid him that not one man of those who are now on board shall come again to the shore."

The youth sprang into his boat and went with his message. The men on the ship were greatly busied with stowing of goods and with other care for the fittings of all kinds, but they saw his coming, and Tostig the Red hailed him:

"What doest thou, coming to the ship? Is it not forbidden?"

Then the youth replied with Hilda's message, and Ulric himself came, but he descended into the boat without speaking while the youth clambered on board. It was for him a matter of pride, and a thing to be remembered in after days, that his was the last foot of any among the shore people to tread the deck of the beautiful ship before she should sail for the Middle Sea, and for the fights in which she was to crush the galleys of those far-away nations.

Ulric took the oars and rowed to the place where he saw Hilda awaiting him, and she was alone. She had her staff in her hand and she was again tracing runes upon the sand. It was the spot where she had stood before the sacrifice was slain, and neither man nor woman would have dared to tread upon it until after the next tide. This, when it should come, would wash out the marks which had been made by Hilda. Ulric stepped out and drew up his boat and walked near her.

"I have sent for thee," she said, "to show thee a thing. Thou art ready, and thy ship. See to it that naught else be sent to her from the shore. None of the men must again set foot upon the land. Sail thou away this night, and linger not."

"I had so ordered," responded Ulric. "The ice goeth out steadily, and we are to follow it. But I am glad to say this last word with thee, for thou art very dear to me."

"More than my son art thou," said Hilda, "because thou art also of the sons of the gods."

"There are gods in the south," said Ulric, thoughtfully. "I have it in my mind that I shall see one of them before I return. I would that I could see him in battle, like Thor, or Tiw, or Odin."

"Be thou thyself like one of them," said Hilda, and she gazed at him lovingly, throwing back her hood.

Very bright were her eyes for a moment and then they grew sad and dim, as if a mist from the fiord had floated into them. Ulric looked upon her withered face as if also it were beautiful to him, and he said:

"Thou art a loving woman and true, and I will keep thy bidding on the sea and on the land."

"I shall see thee not again," she said, "and I willed to look upon thy face this once."

"It may be that thou wilt be here when I return," he responded, but she shook her head.

"Son of Odin, not so," she said, in a low, soft voice, like that of the young who love and are parting. "Me thou wilt not see, and I know not if in any manner I am again to see thee. They of that land into which I quickly go do sometimes see the people of this land, when the gods permit. If so, I will come to thee some evening when there is a silence around thee, and I will touch thee on the forehead, thus," and she leaned forward and kissed him, placing her hands upon his shoulders.

"I will welcome thee!" he said, with a great thrill, and she stood erect, continuing her last words.

"I have this much more to tell," she said. "Thou wilt sail far and contend with many. As thou knowest well, thou wilt meet no foemen like the men of Rome, on land or sea. Thou wilt not tarry long in any place, for thou art a viking, and thou hast no home in the south. Thou wilt go on from place to place until thou shalt come to this harbor, or city." She pointed at the runes drawn upon the sand at her feet, and he replied:

"I cannot read them, O Hilda! They are in another tongue. They are unlike any that I ever saw."

"Neither can I read them," said Hilda. "But note them with care, for when thou seest them upon the ground of any land thy voyage is ended."

So Ulric stooped low and studied well the deeply graven furrows which the saga woman, the seeress, had drawn upon the sand. They were in shape like this:

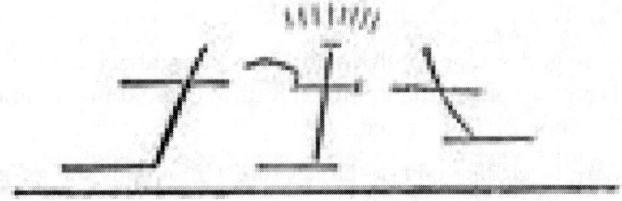

"Thou seest?" she said.

But the runes were close to the water's edge and the tide was coming in. At that moment came a great swell out of the fiord, rising and surging along the beach, and it put out a hand of foam, glittering in the light from the setting sun. Hilda stepped back beyond its reach, and so did Ulric, for a sound came with it. Back fled the billow, breaking as it went, but it left behind it no trace of those strange runes on the sand.

Hilda clasped Ulric in her arms, for a moment, but she did not weep.

"Go thou to thy ship," she said. "I go to my own place."

"Farewell, my best friend," he replied, but she turned and walked away, and all who met her made room for her, for a low voice like a wail crept out from under her hood, and she did not walk firmly, as was her custom.

"Very great was her love for the son of Brander," said all of them; and they knew that this was her last season, for she had told them so, even at Yule.

Ulric rowed to the ship and went on board. The youth returned to the shore with his boat. The sailors pulled up the anchors. Then the watchers on the shore saw the long oars go out, the rowers standing in their places on either side of the ship, while the young jarl, the leader of men, stood alone at the stern, steering with one hand while the other held his war horn. Long and powerful was the blast he blew, for it was a farewell to the Northland and to the people he was to see no more. So sailed away the good ship *The Sword*. It had been a grand launching, but there were those upon the beach who turned and went away to their houses mournfully, even weeping.

In the house of Brander there was silence. Hilda had gone to her own room. All guests had departed. The household folk were for the greater part at the beach, by the fire of sacrifice, and Oswald, the harper, sat in his place with his harp before him, leaning upon it.

Chapter IV
The Ship "The Sword" and the Ice King

The morning of the day of Tiw dawned mistily across the cold North Sea. Everywhere, as the sun looked in through the floating curtains of fog, he could see steel-blue waves wrestling foamily with the masses of ice. Who in this place would imagine that in some other, far away, the same sun had found the bright flowers and green leaves of the fully opened spring?

The wind increased with the coming of the sunshine, as if the additional warmth brought to it better strength wherewith to blow away the mists. One mound of white vapor had been thicker and higher than its neighbors. It had gathered over something that it was hiding, but the breeze blew now a short, sharp gust and the mound was gone. So was uncovered the good ship *The Sword*, and her crew could discern what things might be around them.

Ulric the Jarl was standing in full armor on the fore deck. He had been waiting for this clearing, and now he put his horn to his lips. He blew it lustily, and all who heard him raised a shout, for they knew that no land was in sight and that their voyage had begun.

"We have gone far in the night," said a large man standing near the jarl. "But there is much ice. We can do little more than drift, but we can use the oars somewhat."

"We shall go but little faster than doth the ice," replied Ulric. "But, O Knud the Bear, thou wilt off with that black shirt of thine when this sun is higher."

There was loud laughing at that, for Knud was clad in the warm skins of the bears he had slain. Even upon his head was that which had covered the skull of the largest of them. Good clothing it was for winter time, but it was likely to prove heavy gear for southern wearing.

The jarl gazed southward, hoping to see open water, but only ice fields lay between him and the horizon. The mist was fast disappearing, nevertheless, and those who were watching were seeing further; but now a great cry arose from the stern, where Wulf the Skater was taking his turn at the helm.

"O jarl!" he shouted. "Mark! Seest thou how we are pursued? Come hither!"

Down from the fore deck and quickly along the ship to the after deck went Ulric and those who were with him, and there was no need for any man to point with his hand as Wulf was pointing.

"The ice king!" he said, shivering. "I told thee how I saw him anchor off the North Cape when the leaves fell, and the first freezing put ice around him over the calm waters. He came down from his own place that far last summer. He seemeth to me to be as tall as ever, and he hath many strong floes with him."

Ulric looked, and so did they all, saying nothing at first, for the sight was rare. Not often did any mountain of ice float into that water; and here was a mighty one. His peak arose, they could not tell how high, and the sun was glittering gorgeously among his crags.

"He is moving faster than we are!" exclaimed Tostig the Red. "He will strive to overtake us. He could crush us like a nutshell with one of his crags."

"We will keep out of his path if we may," responded Ulric. "But how is it that he saileth along so well against the wind without oars? There is no tide. If there were any current, it would be with us as much as with him."

"Aye," said Tostig the Red. "But did not Hilda ever tell thee? I have heard her speak of these ice kings. The gods that walk on the bottom of the sea push him along that he may go south and die, for his time hath nearly come. Never, I think, was anything like him seen below the fiords until this day."

Vast, truly, was this ice mountain which was nearing them, propelled by some unseen hand. If there had been a strong undercurrent it would have moved the wonder from the north in precisely this manner. Nevertheless all Northmen of the sea knew that any peak of ice above the surface must rest upon a mass of ice seven times greater.

All the vikings upon *The Sword* watched earnestly for the next sign of whatever was to come, but Ulric took the helm and sent the rowers to the long oars, two men to each oar. Well and vigorously did they row, and the ship was deftly steered into and through one after another of the open channels between the small floes around her. Much distance was gained, but at last the ice fields beyond began to close tightly and the rowing ceased.

"Son of Brander!" shouted Knud the Bear from the fore deck. "Mark! The floes are lifting!"

All saw that it was true. Under all the nearer ice-pack a hidden field, the forefoot of the iceberg, was slipping steadily on unseen until those floes rested upon it. And now there came a grating sound along the keel of *The Sword*, and she too was lifted. The ice arose with her, so that she sat firmly in a great cleft of it, remaining upright, indeed, but as completely out of water as she had been upon the strand before her launching.

Silent and stern stood Ulric, facing the ice king and asking of himself, "My voyage hath but begun, and is it ended? Was my ship built for this?"

Not so was it with the mind of Knud the Bear, for he gazed long and joyously upon the untellable beauty and majesty of the ice king, and then with a great laugh he shouted:

"Sons of the Northland, the gods are with us. They have sent him. Nothing can stay him. He will carry us fast and far. There will be no toilsome rowing, and we need not care for the direction of the wind. The gods of the frozen sea come with him. They would send us south that they may go and fight the gods of the islands where there is no ice, for they hate them."

"So be it!" replied Ulric, gloomily, but he looked again and he said to Knud, "I know not the ice gods, but I think there are friends of thine yonder. Seest thou?"

Every man was gazing, for there was naught else left to do. Around the pinnacles and the cliffs of the ice king there were sea birds flying and screaming. On the snow-packed levels there were brant and geese and ducks and other fowl that should have been at the south by this time, and that would soon, no doubt, be going.

"Odin the Strong!" exclaimed Knud, "I see what thou meanest. I had seen a white fox, I thought, but yonder are the bears of the night country. They are white, that they may see one another in the dark, and there is nothing else that is so fierce as they are."

"Hilda sayeth," replied Ulric, "that all the world north and east of us must forever belong to the sign of the bear. Hast thou ever slain one of these white ones?"

"Never," said Knud. "I have not hunted to the northward so far as to know much of them. Wulf the Skater hath met them oft enough on the north coast, but they go back into the night, for they hate the sun. If it would not anger the ice king, I would go out and slay one even now. But he brought them with him."

So thought others of the vikings, as if the crew of white monsters now clambering nearer over the rugged ridges of the ice were as his own cattle to the mighty gnome who had builded this frozen tower for his castle.

"As many they are," said Tostig, "as the fingers of a hand. I have heard that they have no fear of men."

If the bears had no fear, they at least had much curiosity, and they were coming to inquire what this might be that lay upon the ice with so many men walking around within it.

Ulric went into the after cabin for a heavier spear than was the light weapon he had with him, saying to Knud, "White bear have I never slain. This chance is mine, but the second fight belongeth to thee. I do not rob thee of thy hunt."

"Thine by right, O jarl, is yonder great one," replied Knud. "No man may go before thee unless thou wert hurt or dead. But I warn thee that the long claw, over there, were he to grapple thee, is worse to meet than might be three Romans."

"I would face more than three Romans," laughed Ulric. "But thy pale friend on the floe is a king of bears."

He returned speedily, armed and armored for battle. The spear he brought was long and strong, with a steel crossguard at the heel of its broad blade. It was very sharp, but its weight would have been unwieldly for a slight man.

Twenty fathoms from the stern of the ship stood the great bear growling, and the others walked around at a greater distance. He was a fathom and a half in length and his paws were tremendous, with claws like reaping hooks. No man ever faced any beast more terrible in aspect than was that angry monster from the darkness which broodeth over the forever frozen sea.

Down stepped Ulric, and when he was a few yards from the ship some of the men followed with Knud, but not too near, lest any should seem to help and so should spoil the honor of the fight.

The surface of the ice was broken and there were chasms in it, but it was as firm to stand upon as the dry land. Moreover, *The Sword* was now lying not far away from the mighty perpendicular front of the ice king. None knew yet what might be his aspect looking northward, and there were those among the vikings on the ship who shook their heads doubtfully, considering this matter of the bears.

Stone still stood this bear, growling at intervals, until the jarl drew within six paces, holding his spear leveled. Then, with a loud roar and a clashing of his teeth, the huge beast made his rush, rising upon his hind feet and spreading his enormous arms to close with Ulric. Had he done so his hug would have been speedy death, but the point of the spear met him firmly, with a thrust which buried the blade to the crossguard midway between his shoulders.

"That would slay anything else that liveth," said Knud to Tostig, "but the white ones die hard. Mark! the jarl! The son of Brander! It is grand!"

His comrades answered with a shout and then they were still, and so were all the vikings, who crowded the decks and bulwarks of the ship, looking on.

Horrible was now the roaring of the bear as he struggled against the spear of Ulric, striving to plunge nearer. What tenacity of life must have been his, to fight on with the spear blade in him so deeply! Around swung Ulric on the slippery ice and his whole frame was strained to its uttermost endurance by the swift changes of that wrestling, but the plunges of the bear forced him backward a fathom at a time. His face was now but an arm's length from that of his vast antagonist, and they were looking each other eye to eye. Red and yet full of green fire were the eyes of the bear, and his teeth glistened awfully in their ranges as his wide jaws opened to gnash them. But that the descendant of Odin was many times stronger than other men the combat might here have ended.

"Slip not now!" shouted Knud. "Son of Brander, there is a chasm behind thee. Stand fast, if thou canst! Thou art beyond our help!"

Only his own length from him was the cleft in the ice floe, and it went down to deep water. If he should fall into it in his heavy armor, none might hope to see him again.

Roar—roar—roar—in dreadful wrath and pain struggled the bear, for this was his death throe; but Ulric's foot found a brace—a break in the ice—and he gathered his last strength, the strength of the sons of Odin, the hero might of the old gods.

Snap! The tough ashen shaft of the spear broke at the guard, and both bear and hero fell heavily, but Ulric arose with his seax in his hand. The claws of the bear wrenched away his shield as if it had been a piece of oaken bark, but the seax was driven in to the hilt, and as it came flashing out the life of the bear came with it. Over he rolled with a loud shriek, that was echoed back from the face of the ice king. Then he stretched himself at full length upon the ice and lay still, while Ulric stepped forward to cut off his forepaws for a token.

"Hael!" shouted every voice among the vikings, as the white one rolled over. "Hael to Ulric the Jarl, the son of Brander! The son of Odin! Hael to the first good death and to the long cruise of *The Sword!*"

Chapter V
The Unknown Thing

The ice king had lost only one of his fierce white flock. It had been the largest of them all, however; and in the latter part of Tiw's day there had been a feast of his flesh. Greatly had the crew of *The Sword* enjoyed that feast, and they believed the saying of Knud that there was courage and strength to be gained by such eating after so brave a battle. "The gods themselves eat mightily," he said, "and they have nothing better than this."

During that day a number of the vikings went out to explore the ice fields somewhat, and they captured many wild fowl easily with bow and arrow. They reported having seen in the distance other animals, like great seals or walruses. They also planned to hunt the remaining bears, but the jarl forbade it, being unwilling that they should go far from the ship lest harm should befall them from sudden breaking of the ice.

Nevertheless, to all testing, it seemed to be packing even more firmly. The entire visible mass of it drifted steadily southward, as if the ice king, or the under gods who were pushing him, knew of the channels by which they were to steer him into other seas than this.

Night came, and then the day of Odin. But now the worst foe of the ice king, deadlier than even the sun, was wearing him away with floods of warm rain. There were rivulets pouring down his sides, and some of his pinnacles and crags came crashing, thundering down from time to time. This was, therefore, not a good day for hunting, and the vikings passed it on board the ship, or near it, but not dismally, for there were among them many whose minds and tongues were busy with old voyages and old fights, and the land to which they had sailed. Also there were songs to sing, and there was much ale, and no man was hindered from feasting. It was a time, too, for the remembering of sagas, and many spoke of Hilda, but Ulric did not utter her name, saying rather that it would be well if Oswald and his harp were on board.

These two, indeed, the saga woman and the old harper, sat at home in the house of Brander that rainy day, speaking to one another across the ash heap, on which a slow fire smoldered. Their talk was of many things, but from all it would ever come back to some word concerning the ship and her crew and Ulric. To others Hilda had spoken little, and they noted that she had not eaten since the launching. Oswald was fretful and fitful, and he said that he cared not for harping. In an early hour of the day he had gone out and he had even climbed to the crag on the top of the headland that he might look far to seaward, but he had returned, shaking his head, to say to Hilda:

"All is ice! She is out of sight, but the floes have closed behind her."

"So they close not before her I care little," replied Hilda. "They will conquer the ice, for the sun will help them, and they are sailing nearer the sun."

Oswald was long silent then, and at last he arose and walked out of the hall while Hilda went to the door and gazed seaward. It was to his own room that the harper made his way, leaving his harp near the dais. In a far corner of the house he had been given his place, for he was held in high honor. Nevertheless, it was but small, and bare save for a table and a lamp thereon and a stool. There was, also, a heap of skins for warm sleeping, and from under this Oswald drew out something, stooping and then looking behind him to be sure the door was closed. "What will the jarl bring me, when he returneth from the southlands?" he muttered. "Bright gold, I hope, for there is more to love in the yellow, the heavy, than there is in light silver. The touch is not the same, and gold hath a better ring."

It was a bag that he held, untying its mouth, and his hand was now in it. He drew out pieces of varied shapes, looking at them and rubbing them with his fingers. "The faces of kings are on them," he said. "Runes of the southlands. I can read some, but all I cannot read. May the gods guide the jarl to places where he will find many like these and bring them to me. He careth not for them himself."

Hilda, standing in the doorway, grew sad and wistful in the face. "Gone," she said. "Gone beyond seeing or hearing. And I love him so! He is my hero! My beautiful one! I am old, and I am soon to pass away, and I know not clearly whither I go. Sometimes I would that one of the gods might come and tell what things there are in those countries for such as I am."

Then turned she and went back to her great chair by the fire; but Ulric also was thinking of her and of Oswald, for he said to Tostig and Wulf and those who were with them, under the after deck: "The tongues of the south folk? We do well to talk about them. My father knew many. Oswald, the harper, and Hilda could speak with him in all of them and they had more that he knew not. She hath learned much in her hundred years, and she is not like other women. When I was a child, and afterward, in the long winter evenings, when we had naught else to do, I loved to have them teach me, and they said it would be my need some day. I can talk with a Briton or a Roman or a Greek. But Hilda and Oswald taught me many words of a tongue that belongeth to a people who live on the easterly shore of the Middle Sea. They are a trading folk, and our sea kings found them everywhere. They are not like other folk, and they have a god of their own, but none of them can tell what he is like. I have thought I would wish to see him, but Hilda sayeth that he will not come out of his own country. And that, too, is much the same with our own gods; but I wish they may go with us now, for some of these southland gods are cunning and strong."

"Not as are the gods of the North," said Tostig, sturdily. "I too have heard of these Jews and their god, but I do not care to see either him or any other god. It is more than enough for me when I hear them whispering across the fiords."

"So!" exclaimed Wulf the Skater. "I have been out far on the ice, when there was no wind and there was a bright moon, and I have gone landward with speed lest their voices should overtake me. I heard them loudly once, and that night I was chased by many wolves. I slew some, but I stopped not for their skins, for the rest were an army."

"Glad am I," said Ulric, "that if I meet one of these gods I can speak to him fairly well in his own tongue. How else, for instance, could I question this Jew god? We shall sail all around the coasts of the Middle Sea before we come home."

"What couldst thou ask him?" replied Knud. "And what thinkest thou he might tell thee?"

"One thing that Hilda knew not," said Ulric. "I am curious if the gods of those lands know the gods of the North. I would know if this Jew god hath ever met with Odin and Thor, and whether or not they are friends. If they have fights, as do our own gods, which of them is the stronger? I have thought that if I were a god, I would bring all the others under me. It is not managed well."

"I would not have land gods meddling too much with the sea, save in battles," said Tostig. "It is well as it is. But the Middle Sea is wide; we may not look upon all of its coasts. There are deep bays and many islands."

"They say," responded Ulric, "that there is an open water leading southward, and that if one can find it and will sail into it boldly, fearing nothing, he may follow its leading until he shall find the city of Asgard and the home of the gods. Moreover, there are lands which no foot hath trodden. I would see some of them if they are to be found by sailing not too far."

So said they all, and there were other tales to tell concerning seas and lands.

They still were talking of these things when a loud shout from one of the watchers summoned them, and they rushed out to the gunwales and the decks. The rain was no longer falling and the sky was clear, so that they saw well what was doing. The ice king had not at all lost his grip upon his own floes, but southward was a vast rift in the ice pack. Wide and blue was the open water, but it was not very near them, and as they were looking at it from their icy anchorage the watcher shouted again:

"O Ulric the Jarl, whales! They will come up again from under the floes. I saw them. A great herd!"

Loud voices replied, inquiring, but they ceased, for the herd quickly showed itself. Many and huge were the whales that emerged, and some of them sprang half their length out of the water.

"They are pursued!" exclaimed Knud the Bear. "I have seen them spring in that manner when the swordfish troubled them. But see them flounder now!"

Strange indeed was the confusion and the tumbling about of this herd of the sea. They were beating the waves into foam, and they were plunging hither and thither as if wildly affrighted.

"I think that it is neither the swordfish nor the thrasher," said Tostig the Red, for he had halfway climbed the mast and he was leaning out to see. "O jarl, it is one of the monsters that Hilda hath told us of. She sayeth that only a few are left, for the gods destroyed them lest they should eat up all the whales. Look yonder!"

They were near enough to see, but could not note clearly until a great fragment broke away from the field of ice which carried *The Sword*. Through that chasm at its outer border there came up a shape which was not the head of a whale. It was long, with vast jaws, and in them were pointed saws of long white teeth, with which it tore terribly the side of a tremendous bull whale that was nearest. But the bull whale turned and fought him, and there was a vast whirling of foamy water, as the two sea creatures struggled against each other, beating with heads and fins and tails, but the vikings could none the better discern the form of the whale's enemy.

"He is a comrade of the ice king," said Wulf the Skater. "Never before was he seen in these waters. He is somewhat like a snake, but with a vast belly. I saw his head once before, long ago. Ten more were with me in the ship, and we had been long storm-driven. The old men told me much about him."

"He could upset a ship," said Tostig. "I am glad we are here on the ice. But thou mayest have seen another like him."

"Not so said the old men," replied Wulf. "He is alone. There! He showeth again!"

"I am glad we have seen him," said Ulric. "But I am more troubled concerning the ice king. See ye not that he is fast melting? I have thought that he is beginning to lean this way. We are drifting, truly, but we do not get away from him. We are his prisoners."

They well understood that there might be deadly peril for them in aught that should change the position of the iceberg, but there was naught that they could do, even if sure death were coming. So they preferred to gaze after the herd of whales, and every now and then they thought that they caught fresh glimpses of the monster from the under sea, the terror of all other monsters. Few of them but had heard and could tell old sagas of such creatures, the remnants of the forgotten days, and they agreed that this one was the world-snake that Hilda had sung of as the destroyer.

"He eateth men joyfully," said one, "when he can get them."

"Hilda said," replied Ulric, "that he cometh among men no more. He cannot live in any sea that is plowed by the keels of ships. The gods are against him. But now the whales have fled and he hath followed."

Then turned they to stare at the ice king, and he seemed as strong as ever. Far away at his right they saw the bears, walking to and fro, and the wind brought from them a sound as if they were moaning.

Chapter VI
The Fall of the Ice King

When the sun arose upon the fifth day of the week, the day of Thor, the glittering pinnacles of ice king still towered high above the floes, and these covered the sea as far as the eye could reach. All the white mass was evidently in motion and the drifting was rapid, but it seemed to the vikings as if their danger were striving to push nearer to the ship. She was now lying almost within his reach, if he should choose to strike her—and she was but a very small thing. Her crew, going and coming around her, were but so many specks upon the ice. From her masthead still fluttered bravely out her White Horse banner, and she was yet altogether unharmed, but the rowers were at their places continually.

A prudent captain was the jarl, for, although the men were impatient, he forbade their going far from the ship. He held them back even when the remaining white bears appeared near the feet of the ice king.

Knud was almost angry that he was not permitted to go forth and slay them.

"One man for each bear, Ulric the Jarl," he said. "It is our right. We may not ever meet them again, and the chance for honor were lost. Thou hast won thy pair of claws."

"Thou hast slain bears enough," said Ulric. "Were I to let thee go, thou mightest perchance be left behind on the ice, or under it. Small honor in that. I promise thee the next chance to get thyself killed fairly."

"I obey," growled the grim old hunter, "for thou art my jarl. But when we return from this cruise I will go with Wulf the Skater into the winter of long night and we will find them there. I will not go to Valhalla until I have slain one as large as thine."

"Mind not thy bears now," responded Ulric. "Seest thou not? Art thou blind?"

He blew his horn sharply, and all who were on the ice around the ship sprang on board in haste.

"Mark!" he shouted. "Between us and the foot of the ice king there is a chasm that widens. We know not when the field may break away. Then he will be upon us. Every man at his place this day!"

They who saw could understand, and there was no more talk of hunting. Even when a white fox came and looked at them, within bowshot, no arrow went after him.

"Let him go free," said Tostig. "He hath wild fowl enough for the catching, but he will swim far before he runneth on land again."

It was a time of doubt and of waiting, but the drifting ceased not. There was much discussion at intervals, among even the elder seamen, as to precisely in what part of the sea they now might be, for there were no guidings. Toward the sunset, after long hours of idleness that brought weariness, Ulric went and stood by the hammer of Thor on the fore deck. Tostig the Red came and stood by him and laid his hand upon the hammer, for Tostig was a smith, as had been his fathers before him. Not only could he smelt iron out of the right rock, but he could harden it for cutting and for bending and springing. The secret of that art was his inheritance, and Hilda had said that it was a thing that the old gods who were dead had brought with them from the east before Asa Thor's time. It was from a rising-sun land, but a cold one, that Odin led his children, said some, and there were runes on the rocks to prove it, if they might be read by any now living.

"We go faster," said Tostig. "We have already gone far this day. If the gods were against us, I think they would not so swiftly bear us forward without wind or work."

"Who knoweth the will of the gods?" replied Ulric. "Not thou or I. They puzzle me greatly. I would they might come at times and show themselves. How can one know what to think of a god he hath never seen! I mean to look upon one of them, if I may, before I sail back to the Northland. That were a thing worth telling of a winter evening by the fire in the hall."

"And have all men answer thee that thou wert lying?" laughed Knud cheerily, from behind Tostig. "I believe that Hilda seeth them at an hour that cometh to her, but I would rather let them alone. I will think well of them if they will but shove us along in the right direction. They work finely now, it seemeth, but the sun goeth down. Thor hath been friendly to us during all his day, but I doubt if we are as safe after he is gone. The morrow will be Freya's day, and she meddleth not overmuch with seafaring matters. Ægir is the god of the sea, and of him we know but little, nor of Ran, his wife, nor of his nine daughters. They must at this hour be all under the ice doing nothing."

The saying of Knud was a thing that it was hard to dispute, but it was in Ulric's mind to wonder whether or not he and his vikings were drifting altogether beyond the help of the old gods of the North.

The wind began to blow strongly, and the men listened with eager ears, for they thought that they could now and then hear shrill and angry voices from the neighborhood of the ice king. Some of them were like shrieks, but these may have been made by the gale itself, blowing among the crags and chasms.

"We will both eat and drink," commanded Ulric. "Let every man be hearty, that he may have his full strength for that which may be before him."

After he himself had eaten he went to the after deck, putting his hand upon the tiller. From that place he might best watch the ice king, and there came others to stand with him, waiting.

"He is very tall," said Ulric, at last. "I doubt if we shall ever look upon his like again. But saw ye ever such moonlight? I have known days when I could not see so well as I can this night."

"Aye," said Wulf. "I know this moon. It is not such light as ours, for he hath brought it with him. It is the light which the gods make instead of sunlight in his own place, and it will not go south any further than he goeth. But mark the bears!"

"Something troubleth them," said Ulric.

All could see them plainly, and they were like ghosts wandering to and fro among the rugged heaps of the ice floes. They were much scattered and they moved as if they were hunting for something which they could not find, and they were calling often to each other, moaning as if they were in pain or in great discontent. Sometimes as they did so they lifted up their heads toward the moon, but oftener toward the ice king.

"Look at him now!" exclaimed Ulric. "The moon is shining upon him wonderfully.

"It is so," said Tostig, "but I think not of that. Wilt thou note this, that whenever there cometh a boom of the rending ice the bears call out to their mates? More than we do they know of such matters. All such creatures have gods of their own, and we may have offended them. I like it not."

"The gods of the bears will care for the bears!" said Knud. "They have naught to do with men."

Nevertheless, it was a time for men to speak softly concerning such things when powers whom they saw not and knew not were dragging them and their ship along so helplessly. There are times when one feeleth that he can get along well enough without the gods, but this was a different matter. All the vikings talked soberly and they were glad that their jarl was a son of Odin.

It was a strange, solemn, weird night in spite of the moonlight, what with the peril and the moaning bears and the booming ice. After all, they said, Odin himself might not be with them. There had been places, as all men knew, where all the gods had abandoned even the bravest of the Northmen. Men like themselves had died without a sword cut or a spear thrust. All hope of falling in battle might be lost to them among these treacherous ice floes. It was a short night, if there had been aught to measure it by, but to the men on *The Sword* it seemed long enough. None cared to go under a deck, but there were some who lay down and slept. The moon sank lower and lower and the shadows lengthened across the ice fields, but there was yet a great flood of broken light when Ulric, the son of Brander, uttered a loud cry and put his war horn to his lips. Every man sprang to his feet, for each thought that he had never before heard such a blast as that. A louder sound instantly answered it, but none could tell whether it came from among the ice peaks or from down toward the bottom of the sea.

"The bears are moaning again!" said Knud. He was ever thinking of his bears, but all the rest were hearkening for what might be coming next, and they knew not yet the meaning of Ulric's blast.

"Oars!" shouted the jarl. "Every man to his place! There is free water southerly. The ice king is bowing!"

Loudly moaned the bears, for a moment, and they seemed to be running toward the ship, as if they would come on board; and Ulric blew his horn again with the notes of battle defiance, but then there burst out upon all sides a roaring, splitting, rending sound, such as none of the vikings had ever heard before.

"He hath struck! He is aground!" shouted Ulric. "Hark to his breaking! His hour is come!"

If that were true, so also it seemed as if the hour of *The Sword* had come, and of all who were on board of her. But the gods were with her. If the forefoot of the ice king had indeed caught upon a shoal, checking and breaking him, the shock of that striking had separated the great floe in front of him so that it might move freely. Still it no longer upheld him, and he suddenly began to pitch forward toward the ship. Vast was the roll of the sea that swelled away from his pitching, and powerfully it uplifted *The Sword* in her bed of ice.

"Hold hard, all!" shouted Ulric. "Ready with your oars! Odin!"

Up gazed they then, and the bravest of them shuddered, for the gigantic white head of the ice king was bowing nearer, as if he would cast himself upon them. On rolled the great wave, steadily, and all along the crest of it the ice it carried was rending into fragments that ground angrily against each other. The floe that carried *The Sword* became twain that parted, letting her down and shooting her swiftly forward. It was just then that the ice king fell upon his face, his uppermost pinnacle almost crashing upon her stern.

The foaming water dashed across the deck and drenched Ulric at the tiller. He was wearing no headpiece now, and the salt spray drops glittered brightly among his yellow curls. But they glistened not with moonlight, for while they all had waited and watched the sun had risen and his first rays lit the hero face of the son of Odin as he shouted to his men to row their best, and as he steered the good ship *The Sword* into the open water the White Horse banner of the Saxons floated gallantly from the masthead and men sprang to set free the sail.

"Hael, O Ulric the Jarl!" shouted Knud the Bear. "We have a good sea captain."

So said several of the elder vikings.

"Hael, all!" cheerily responded Ulric. "The ice king hath fallen and we shall fear him no more. The gods are with us!"

Loudly shouted they all, and those who were not rowing clashed their swords upon their shields as if they had won a victory.

"Aye!" growled Tostig the Red. "'Tis a stout ship."

Chapter VII
The Living Sand

It was the time of thaw in the Northland, but the snow and ice go fast when the winter letteth go its hold. Already great reaches of land were bare, but no man might travel far from his own home because of the floods from the melting. All must wait until days should pass, and these were growing longer, but they were full of unrest. Even the cattle in their enclosures lowed impatiently to one another; for the brute creatures know well the signs of the return of green grass to their pastures. In the house of Brander there was no shadow because of the absence of any who had gone, but these were spoken of cheerfully. Moreover, there came boats and larger keels into the cove from other villages up and down the coast and from out the fiords that were opening. Far and wide had been known the building of *The Sword*, and many would have been glad to look upon her. All these were disappointed, but there were wise old vikings and jarls of note who said to Hilda:

"Thy foster son hath done well. It is like his father. Other keels will follow him speedily, but he will be first to strike."

As if she had been mistress of the house was Hilda, and she entertained well all who came. Reverence was paid her because of her high descent and her kinship to Odin the Strong, and because of her hundred winters, but even more because of her learning and her knowledge of the gods. Men asked her questions concerning them, and there were those who believed that she had seen and known more than she would tell.

"I would not like to anger her," said one, "lest she might afterward come to me in a bad hour, for she hath knowledge of charms and of witchcraft and she can write runes."

There was reason in that, said all, but that she was a kindly woman and that she kept the house of Brander liberally.

Much time she now spent among the old armor, the trophies on the wall, and in the study of such things as had been brought from the lands around the Middle Sea. She made Oswald open his bag and she read the many inscriptions upon his coins, and she talked to him of Greece and of Rome, where most of them were made. He also knew about his gold and silver pieces, and there were some even of copper for which he had names and values. What good was there in such things in a land like this, where money was not needed?

"I would that Ulric had them," she said. "He might buy with them another ship, or provisions, or arms."

"Not save of a friend," replied Oswald. "He will need nothing that his sword can win for him. It is not the custom of the vikings to be long in need."

The household knew by her face that her thoughts were not troubling her concerning Ulric and his men.

"She hath had no ill token," they said. "It must be that he doeth well."

They knew not of the ice king, nor how narrowly he had missed his last angry blow at *The Sword*. But that peril was over and the good ship was flying along in safety, driven by strong rowers, who had also some help from the sail. They would have had more but that the winds were variable. Therefore the days and the nights went by before they again saw land, and the older seamen knew by that that they had kept in the open sea and were well advanced in their voyage.

"How fast or how far the ice king bore us I know not," said Knud the Bear, "but if that headland were not of one of the northern isles, we have seen a cape of North Britain."

"Not so far south as that," argued Tostig the Red, "but all these coasts are bad to land upon. There is naught worth the taking away."

"Our errand is not to them," said Ulric. "We will not waste an arrow upon them. I will not let the prow of *The Sword* touch the sand until we see the mid-coast of the British island — —"

"We shall see a storm this night," interrupted an old viking. "The wind changeth to the northwest, and Knud may wear his bearskins. It will be cold."

When the night fell all were willing to cover well; but the rowers might rest, for the ship carried her sail all the more safely because it was not too large and because she was well laden. There was a spirit upon Ulric which kept him at the helm, so that his men needed almost to take him away by force that he might sleep.

"I would I might see Hilda and have speech with her," he said to himself. "I have strange dreams when I close my eyes. She might tell me what they mean. Do the gods come to one when he is asleep? I have heard so. But they have told me nothing—save that I have dreamed of men who wore the armor that hangeth behind the table on the dais. Strong men they were, and dark, and I think they were good swordsmen. Before long it may chance that we shall meet a trireme of the Romans if my dreams have that reading. I must burn one of their ships before we pass these seas."

Heavier blew the gale and higher rose the waves, and *The Sword* sped on as if she were a waterfowl, but all on board were willing to be as well covered as was Knud the Bear. The night was dark and the next morning they saw no land. The storm drove them onward steadily all day, and now and then they saw ice floating, but no sail of any ship. Again the night came, and the moon was out and the wind lulled, but the waves were still rough.

"We will not row," said Ulric, when they inquired of him. "There are coasts now not far away. When the dawn cometh we will seek some bay or harbor. I have heard that there are villages of North folk hereaway, and they would be friendly."

So said they all save Tostig the Red, who laughed somewhat grimly and replied:

"I think there are villages upon many coasts whereof the folk are willing to be friendly to a crew like this. The seax hath many acquaintances who are willing to see him stay quietly in the belt."

"So hath the ax," growled old Biorn the Berserker. It was rare for him to speak, but he was leaning upon the long handle of his weapon, and when he lay down on the deck the ax slept beside him.

It was after the middle watch that night, and Ulric was at the helm. He was steering a straight course southward and the ship was slipping quietly over the waves. He was awake, truly, but somehow he seemed to himself to be dreaming almost, and his eyes were downcast. "The runes upon the sand," he muttered. "I can see them now, before the wave washed them away. When and where am I to see them again, and to know that my voyage is ended? Who shall read runes, and how shall I be sure that I am not mistaken? For Hilda will not be there— —"

Even as he spoke there came to his ears a sound, and he looked suddenly up, gripping hard the tiller.

"Faint and far away," he exclaimed, "but it was a trumpet! There are three in the hall at the house and Oswald taught me their soundings. Up, all! Rowers to the oars! I will send an answer!"

Long and powerful was the horn blast that went out across the moonlit sea. Clearer and louder than before was the trumpet voice which instantly responded from the right—and that was toward the British shore. The men shouted not, for they were listening, and those who knew were telling the younger vikings that the jarl had heard from the Romans. It was good news to hear, after long waiting, and the rowers put out the long oars eagerly.

"The dawn draweth near," shouted Ulric, after blowing his horn again. "We will steer toward yonder trumpet. There will be much music with the sun's rising. We will see if the gods of Rome are better than the gods of the North in the seas of Britain."

Loud voices answered him bidding him lead on; for the blood of the vikings was rising hotly, and Biorn the Berserker sharpened the edge of his great ax while he beat the deck with his feet and out through his thickly bearded lips there poured, low, but swelling, a song of the skalds at the gate of battle.

Red grew the edges of the eastern sky as *The Sword* pressed her iron beak to the crests of the waves and sprang forward. Joyously rang out the war horn of warrior after warrior, for on board were vikings of high descent who would not have chosen for their jarl any of less degree than a son of Odin. They were men entitled to go forward into the feast of swords shoulder to shoulder with kings and with chiefs of renown. Said one of them to Ulric:

"Jarl Ulric, many spears from the stowage. The Romans cast well and their spears are heavy. I mind not their light javelins nor their arrows. Close not with any trireme at the first."

"I will be prudent," replied Ulric; "but bring out the spears. There are arrow sheaves enough and stones for slinging."

"Let them not ram *The Sword*," continued the old fighter. "Her ribs are strong, but so is the beak of a war galley of Rome. Strike her not save amidships."

Well was it for older men to counsel so young a leader, but Ulric had been taught from his infancy not only by Brander the Brave and Oswald, but by all the sea kings and berserkers to whom he had listened while they talked of war around the mid-fire in the old hall. Naught had they said or sung but he had made its teachings his own against an hour like this.

"A trireme!" shouted Knud the Bear as the daylight brightened. "She is of the largest. Helmets and standards and the shields of a cohort of a legion. They are more in number than we are."

"Twice more," said the old counselor, "and her bulk is nearly thrice that of *The Sword*. Beware, O jarl!"

"I see her well," responded Ulric. "She is heavy in the water. I think she is overburdened."

"They are swift also," said Tostig the Red, "but that keel cannot turn as nimbly as can our own. Let us go nearer!"

"Within a spear's cast!" shouted Ulric, fiercely. "We will not pass her without a blow. Wulf, take thou the helm. I will go to the fore deck."

There he stood in the morning light, as the two keels neared each other. The Roman trumpets sounded at intervals, and they were answered by the war horns of the vikings.

"She is a splendid war vessel," said Ulric to those who were with him. "Never yet have we builded her like. Her bulwarks are higher than ours and her sail is many times broader. It is made of woven stuff. Her prow is a ram. We must not let her strike us."

"Neither will we strike her," said Biorn the Berserker, "unless we can hit her amidships. She is a danger. O jarl, beware! I do not think we may take that trireme, but we can get away from her."

So did not think the trierarch and the centurion on board the trireme. He who was captain of the vessel was of one accord with the officer in charge of the legionaries whom she was conveying. If Ulric could have heard them converse as *The Sword* came toward them, he would have learned somewhat of the estimation in which such as he were held by the wolves of Rome.

"A Saxon pirate, O Lentulus," said the trierarch to the man in armor at his side. "It is early in the season for them to be seen in these waters. They are the scourges of the sea."

"And of the shore, friend Comus," replied the centurion. "We will make short work of this one. It is of good size, and it swarmeth with men as with bees."

"Hast thou ever met them in fight?" asked Comus, "or is this thy first sight of them?"

"This is my first service in these waters," replied Lentulus, "but I have heard much of them. I would we had some legions of them to send against the Parthians, or into Africa. Laurentius had a cohort of them with him in Spain. They make the best of gladiators; Cæsar hath used them in the arena. But it is hard to take them. Let us see if we cannot send him a present of these pirates for the summer games. He is ever in need of good swordsmen."

"Little thou knowest of them," laughed Comus. "We may capture a few wounded men. The rest will die fighting."

Even while he spoke Tostig the Red was remarking to his friends at the stern of *The Sword*, just forward of the deck: "A fine stone for my sling is this. I will strike that high-crested one. There is often much treasure on a trireme, if Thor will let us take her. But the men we want not, nor the keel."

"Burn her," they said, "and throw the soldiers overboard; but the Romans die where they stand. We shall take no prisoners but the rowers. The jarl will slay them." So without thought of mercy on either side did the two keels draw nearer.

They were not yet within a spear's cast when they who were with Tostig stood away from him to give him slinging room. "He is the best slinger," they said, "on all the North coast. Let us see what he can do. He is not a boaster."

As the vessel climbed a wave Tostig poised himself, swinging slowly the leathern thong which upheld the square apron in which his pebble rested. Two pounds only in weight it may have been, but it was smooth and round from much chafing on the shore of the fiord with other pebbles as the sea waves had tossed them to and fro in many storms. Over the crest of the wave went *The Sword*, and as she did so the sling began to whirl swiftly in the hand of Tostig. Hand went to hand to give it double force, and then, as the downward plunge of the keel went with him, he gave his might to it and threw.

None saw the stone, so swiftly did it pass, but the trierarch said to the centurion:

"O Lentulus, thou art said to be as good a spearman as Pontius of Asia. Have thy pilum ready and try thy fortune."

"It is too far," said Lentulus, poising his pilum. "I was in battle once with that same Pontius. Hercules! I am slain!"

Loud clanged his brazen helmet and prone he fell upon the deck. He did not move again. The stone hurled by Tostig had left him but life enough for that one outcry as it smote him.

"May all the gods forbid!" exclaimed Comus. "What ill fortune is this? He is dead! Toward the pirate! Strike her through and through!"

Even as he spoke a legionary at his side went down before a second stone from the sling of Tostig, and the shouts of the vikings mingled with the clangor of their war horns.

Deft was the steering of Wulf and the swift rush of the trireme was avoided, *The Sword* passing her stern so near that every spearman might make a cast. But the legionaries, pilum in hand, had faced the further bulwark, thinking their foe came that way, and not so many of them were at good stations. Their bowmen also had been deceived, and their greater number was of no account. Nevertheless, many Roman spears flew well, being mostly of the lighter javelins used by them in the beginning of a fight. Easily were these caught upon the broad shields of the vikings, as if it were in a mere game at home, and no harm was done by them or by the arrows. Closer were they when they did their own throwing, and a hundred heavy spears went hurtling in among the legionaries.

"Follow!" shouted Comus. "Have ready the grapplings! Strike and then board her!"

A good officer was he, and the rowers as well as the legionaries obeyed him angrily, for they deemed the Northmen insolent in assailing such superior force.

"Away!" shouted Ulric. "Hael to thee, O Tostig. Get thee to the stern and pitch thy pebbles among her rowers."

Tostig was toiling hard, and so were other good slingers, of whom the trireme seemed to not have any, but *The Sword* swept on out of range while her enemy was turning.

"O jarl," said Biorn, "she is not clumsy, but her steersman went down. Let us gain what distance we may. That was a good blow, but we may not strike the next so easily."

The older vikings looked watchfully, as did Biorn, and again they said: "Our jarl is young, but this was well done."

"Westward!" shouted Ulric to Wulf. "We must lead them toward the land. I would I knew this coast."

"That do I," said Biorn, "if we are where I think. There are high cliffs, but there is also much marsh land; and off the coast there are great shallows, worse for a ship than any rocks might be. Watch for them."

"They are our friends," said Ulric, "but they are not friendly to a deep vessel like yonder trireme."

"Aye," said Biorn, "it is our old way of battling such as she is, but there is an evil among these shallows. Hast thou not heard of the sand that is alive? There is much of it hereaway."

"My father warned me of it," replied Ulric. "If horse or man setteth foot upon it, it will seize him and suck him down. But it could not swallow a ship."

"Were she a mountain!" exclaimed Biorn. "The living sand would be worse than a Roman trireme for *The Sword* to escape from. Yonder is a land line at the sky's edge, and I think I see breakers."

The rowers were rowing well and *The Sword* had gained a long advantage before the Roman oarsmen had recovered from their confusion. Now, however, Ulric upon the foredeck was measuring distances, wave after wave, and he spoke out plainly to his men.

"Swift is *The Sword*," he said. "I had thought that no keel on earth could be swifter, but we are laden heavily; so is the trireme, that she turneth not nimbly, but in a straight course she is swifter than are we. She hath many rowers and she is sharp in the prow. She gaineth upon us little by little."

"Woe to her," responded the vikings. "She moveth too fast for her good."

"The land riseth fast," said Biorn. "The breakers are not far away. Under them are sand shoals."

"The Roman is but a hundred fathoms behind us," replied Ulric. "Wulf the Skater, steer thou through the breakers. Let us see if she will dare to follow."

Comus, the trierarch, was overeager, or he would have remembered that which he seemed to have forgotten. They who were with him were stung by the death of Lentulus and by the ravages of the Saxon spears and stones. None counseled him to prudence, and he dashed on in the foaming wake of *The Sword*.

"Breakers, but no rocks," muttered Wulf, as he grasped his tiller strongly. "Now, if we fill not, we shall dash through. Pull! For the Northland pull!"

Hard strained the rowers. High sprang the curling breakers on either hand. Loud rang the shouts and the war horns. But *The Sword* rose buoyantly over the crown of a great billow and passed on into smoother water.

"Odin!" roared Biorn the Berserker. "The trireme is but fifty paces—"

"Struck!" shouted Ulric. "On, lest we ourselves may be stranded!"

"Deep water here, Jarl Ulric," calmly responded an old seaman near him. "We have passed the sand bar. It may be the tide is falling. The gods of the sea are against that Roman keel."

"Or they are not with her to-day," said Ulric. "She is held fast. Cease rowing and put the sail up again. We will see if there is aught else that we may do. I like not to let her escape me."

Up went the sail, and for an hour *The Sword* did but cruise back and forth, only now and then venturing near enough for the hurling of a stone or the sending of an arrow. It was then too far for any harm to the Romans, but they could hear the taunting music of the horns.

"Low tide," said Biorn at last, "and she lieth upon bare sand. We are well away. We can do no more."

"Watch!" said Ulric. "They are troubled."

"She lieth too deeply. What is this?" So asked the Roman seamen of their captain as they leaned over their bulwarks and studied that bed of sand. He answered not, but one, a legionary in full armor, stepped down from the ship to examine more closely—and an unwise man was he. In places the sandy level seemed firm enough, and a horse may gallop along a sandy beach after the tide is out and leave but a fair hoofprint. That way armies have marched and chariots have driven. There were other patches, however, whereon the sand seemed to glisten and to change in the sunlight, and here there was potent witchcraft working. At these had the sailors been gazing, but the soldier did not reach one of them.

"Back!" shouted Comus. "It is the living sand! We are all dead men! Back!"

The legionary strove to wheel at the word of command, but his feet obeyed him not. Even the vikings were near enough to see that the sand was over his ankles.

"The under gods have seized him," muttered Ulric. "It is from them that the sand liveth. They are angry with him."

"*Vale! Vale! Vale!*" shouted the legionary. "O Comus, I go down! They who dwell below have decreed this. See thou to the ship and follow not the Saxons."

"Follow them?" exclaimed Comus. "*Vale*, O comrade! But the trireme lieth a handbreadth deeper. She is sinking! O all the gods! Have we come to this ending? Who shall deliver us?"

"None, O Comus," said a man of dark countenance who leaned over the bulwark at his side. "We have offended the gods and they have left us to our fate."

Lower sank the wooden walls of the great vessel, while her helpless crew and the soldiery stared despairingly at the pitiless sand and at the White Horse flag of the vikings dancing lightly over the sea so near them.

"Form!" commanded Comus, and the legionaries fell into ranks all over the vessel. "Put ye the body of Lentulus upon the deck," he said, "and bring me the eagle of the legion. O Lentulus, true comrade, brave friend, we salute thee, for all we who were of thy company go down to meet thee. Behold, we perish!"

Silent sat the rowers at their oars. The standards fluttered in the wind. The trierarch took the eagle and went and stood by the body of Lentulus.

"They are brave men, yonder," said Biorn the Berserker. "They will to die in line. So do the Romans conquer all others except the men of the North."

"They have one trireme the less," replied Tostig the Red. "But they have many more. This is not like burning one. I see no honor to us in this."

"Honor to the gods," said Ulric. "She was too strong for us and Odin destroyed her."

"It is well to have him on our side," said Tostig; but Knud the Bear laughed loudly, as was his wont, and said: "Odin is not a sea god. What hath he to do with sand and water? Some other god is hidden under the living sand. We shall leave him behind us when we go away——"

"Her bulwarks go under!" shouted one of the vikings. "Hark to the trumpets! They go down!"

The trumpet blast ceased and there was a great silence, for the like of this had never before been seen.

"Oars!" commanded Ulric. "We will search the coast. Such a warship as was this came not hitherward without an errand. She may have had companions."

The old vikings all agreed with him, and an eager lookout was set, but behind them as they sailed away they saw nothing but a bare bed of sand, over which the tide was returning.

Chapter VIII
The Saxon Shore

"O jarl!" exclaimed Knud the Bear, in a morning watch, "we have wasted days in this coasting. The weather hath been rough and the men are weary, for we are tightly packed in this ship."

"No longer shouldst thou prevent us from seeking the shore," said another. "I would hunt, and get me some fresh meat." There were also voices of impatience and of discontent among the crew.

The jarl listened, and thoughtfully he responded: "I have not forgotten that the Romans sail in fleets. We are one keel. If now we have avoided any trireme that was company for the one which was swallowed by the sand, we have done well. We will steer toward the shore. My father told me of such a coast as this."

"As the sun riseth higher," said Biorn the Berserker, "I think I can see a low headland. This is not my first cruising in these seas."

"It is well," said the jarl. "We will go within the headland. If we find a good shore, we will land, for I am of one mind with you."

All the older vikings approved of his prudence, for they knew the Romans better than did the younger warriors, full of eagerness. Even now the sailing of *The Sword* was with caution. The noon drew near and they were close to the headland. It was neither high nor rocky, and on it was a forest; but here was a surprise, for the trees growing down to the beach were in full leaf.

"The winter tarried late in the Northland," said the vikings. "We have also been many days upon our way. The summer is near."

They might also discern patches of green grass, and now Knud shouted from the fore deck: "A deep cove, O jarl! It is very deep."

Ulric was at the helm, and he responded: "Thou hast good eyes, O Bear. Watch thou for rocks and shoals and give me word. Let all eyes watch also for boats or men."

The rowers rowed easily and *The Sword* slipped on into the cove. Here was dense forest on either side, and there were rocks, but the trees were large and old and there seemed to be little undergrowth, nor was there any sign of the dwellings of men.

"The Britons," said an old viking, "build not often on the shore. They are not seamen. They have no forts but wooden palisades, and they dwell inland, where they are more safe. They fight well, but they have little armor, and their steel is soft. They are no match for the legions of Rome."

It was exceedingly still as *The Sword* went forward. Away at the left a herd of red deer came out under a vast oak and stared at the newcomers. At their head was a stag with branching antlers.

"Now know we," said Biorn the Berserker, "that no men are near this place, for these creatures are exceedingly timid. But their venison is of the best. In Britain are also wild cattle in abundance, and wild swine. We will have great hunting before we sail to other places."

Swiftly away sped the red deer, for the prow of *The Sword* touched the strand and Wulf the Skater sprang ashore, followed by a score of vikings.

"On, up the bank!" shouted the jarl. "Return and tell what thou seest. All to the shore and stand ready if he findeth an enemy."

"A prudent jarl," murmured Biorn the Berserker. "He will not be surprised."

Nevertheless, the younger men laughed scornfully, for they liked not well the hard discipline of the jarl, and he brooked no manner of disobedience, as was his right.

Back came one from Wulf the Skater. "O jarl!" he shouted. "A fine spring of water. An open glade. Wulf asketh if he shall now cut the saplings."

"I come soon," replied the jarl, "but cut stakes for a palisade leading down to this beach on either hand. Though there be no Romans here, there are Britons not far off."

Axes were plying speedily, and while the first fires were kindling many sharp stakes were driven, to be woven between with flexible twigs and branches. Such was ever the custom of the Saxons upon a new land, for behind such a wattle-work defense a few warriors may withstand many, and light palisades guard well against horsemen. Not all could work in these matters, and twoscore were selected by lot for the first hunting, going out in four parties, with a command not to venture too far. They were bowmen, but they went in their armor. Before the sun set there was a good stockade from tree to tree around the spring, with arms that reached out on either hand almost to the shore.

"We will make it stronger," said the jarl, "but behind it we are safe; for we might also retreat to the ship if there were need."

No red deer save one stag and a doe did the hunters bring in, and there would have been a lack of meat but for the slaying by another party of four black cattle, fat and good.

"O jarl," said the men. "Did we not tell thee? This is better than being packed so tightly in *The Sword*. This is good venison."

Well contented was he also, and he saw that he must humor the men if he were to command them well thereafter. For this reason, therefore, other and larger hunting parties went out the next day, and they came home heavily laden.

"O jarl," said Tostig the Red, for his party, "we have also found paths, but no men. We saw hills beyond, but a river is between us and them, and a great marsh. I think no Britons come hither across the marsh."

"On the morrow I will go," said Ulric. "I will leave Biorn in command of the camp. I have no need for hunting, but I must know the land."

Barrels of ale had been brought to the shore, and that night was a feast, with songs and sagas. After the feast the jarl went and lay down to sleep under an oak, but his eyes would not close for thinking of the Northland, and of the Middle Sea, and of Asgard.

"This landing is well," he thought, "and I am glad to be in Britain. But here I may not linger too long. O Hilda of the hundred years, not yet hast thou visited me. I wonder if thou or the gods could find me this night under this oak tree. Who should tell thee where to come if thou wert seeking me? The gods see everywhere. Biorn sayeth that the gods of Britain are gods of the woods, and we are from the sea. I care not much for wood gods."

Then he rested, but he arose early and chose the men who were to go with him.

"Guide me to the river and the marsh," he said to Wulf the Skater.

"I will, O jarl," said Wulf; "but Tostig saw a wild boar yesterday and he hath gone out after him. A vast one, he sayeth, with tusks like a walrus. He will fight well if they can bring him to a fighting."

"Let Tostig win his boar," said Ulric. "We go to the left and we hunt not. I am full of thoughts about this place."

A score of vikings were with them, and they marched on in order, two and two, as if they had an errand. Grand were the trees, and high, with branches whose foliage made a gloom to walk in.

"Are we nearly at the marsh?" asked Ulric at last. "Here are rocks."

"I know not, O jarl," said Wulf. "We came not so far southerly yesterday."

"Hael, Northmen! Hael! But sound no horn! Who are ye?"

As if he had suddenly arisen through the ledge of rocks before them, upon it stood a tall shape in full armor, spear in hand. From under his helmet tangled white hair fell down to his shoulders, but his right hand, holding the spear, was lifted as by one who giveth a command.

Again he spoke: "I am Olaf, the son of Hakon, of Droningsfiord. Who are ye?"

"Northmen of thine own land," said the jarl. "I am Ulric, the son of Brander. Our ship, *The Sword*, lieth at the shore. How camest thou where thou art, and who is with thee?"

"None are with me," said Olaf, sternly. "We were many, but the Romans have smitten the Saxon shore of Britain and our villages are gone. They have smitten many of the Britons also, and they march to smite them again this day. Tell me, O Jarl Ulric, hast thou seen aught of certain triremes which were to come? I would know if there are more Romans near than I have already counted."

"One hath perished, as I will shortly tell thee," said Ulric. "I have seen no other."

"Good!" said Olaf. "There floateth one in a harbor not far away, but they who came in her are fewer than when they landed. Twain came, with a cohort. One hath sailed. Their force was sent to slaughter the Druids at their great sacrificing, but first they struck our village at our harbor. We fought, but they were too many. I cut my way through the ranks of their lighter spearmen, and they followed me not far because of the nearness of the Britons."

Olaf was now descended from the rock and was become as one of them. Great was his wonder at the story of the living sand and the trireme.

"The gods of the Britons are strong at times," he said, "but they are not to be depended on. They have done this because of the great sacrifice, that the Romans may not hinder it. Therefore come thou with me a little distance and I will show thee a matter. The Romans are tangled in a wood. Meddle not thou and thine, however, for thou hast another work to do."

"I meddle not," said the jarl, "but I thank these Druid gods. We were closely pushed and in peril when they ensnared the trireme with their sand. I will offend them not, but I would see these great sacrifices and I also would offer my token."

"That the Druids will forbid thee," said Olaf. "Follow me quickly to the crown of this ridge, for it is on the bank of the river."

Even as he spoke there came to their ears a clangor of trumpets, as if many sounded at once.

"Romans!" exclaimed Ulric.

"Sounding first were they," said Olaf, "but these hoarse ones, very loud, are blown by the Druids. Hear, also, the harping. Now look thou, for thou art a captain."

The river before them was but narrow, although it might be deep, and on the other side was a broad open space surrounded by a forest with dense undergrowths of bushes, as if it were marshy. In the open was arrayed a cohort of Roman soldiers, well ordered, but beyond and in their front might be seen and heard much larger numbers of such as they were, all disarrayed and scattered by the copses. None assailed the cohort in the open, but all the forest swarmed with half-armed Britons, hurling darts and plying their light blades. Arrows, also, were flying, and there was a great tumult of mingled sound.

"The men in white robes, keeping afar," said Olaf, "are the Druid priests. This is as an ambush, and the Romans are falling."

"Their commander hath some wisdom, I think," said Ulric. "His trumpets call back his men for a retreat. He will escape."

"He loseth half his force," said Olaf; "he will lose more as he retreateth."

Fiercer and fiercer arose the sounds of the combat, the shouting, the howling, the twanging of loud harp strings, and the braying of the trumpets. Hard was it for the vikings that they might not have a part in such a battle.

"The Romans are outnumbered," said Olaf, "but they fight well. Their retreat will be to the river mouth, where was my village. There have they a camp in our own stockade, and they have also increased it with a rampart of earth and palisades. There we must strike them. It is but a little distance. Come and see."

"But first," said Ulric, "I would see the end of this battle, and I would have speech with a Druid concerning the sacrifices."

"That thou mayest not this day," said Olaf, "and the Romans are cutting their way through the tumult of half-naked spearmen. Lo, how they slay the Britons! But the ranks of their cohort will be thin when the remnant reacheth the fort. So hath it often been in their warfare in Britain, but each new commander of legionaries cometh here a proud one, thinking only of easy victory."

"The darts fly in showers," said Ulric, but Wulf the Skater urged him.

"O jarl!" he exclaimed. "The village! The fort! The trireme! Why wait we here? Let us go with Olaf!"

The jarl answered not, but walked rapidly, and the rocky ledge grew higher as they went; but there came an end of it.

"We have walked far," said Ulric. "The way of the Romans was shorter. There come they and their array is not broken. I can see their commander ordering them."

"Thor the Thunderer!" exclaimed Olaf, "what havoc the Britons have made among them! The gods of the Druids have protected their sacrifices."

"Every Roman left behind hath perished," said Ulric. "Only these are alive."

"Not so," said Olaf. "Not a wounded man or one entrapped hath been slain. He belongeth to the gods at the place of sacrifice."

"With them as with us," said the jarl. "That is the old North custom. I have seen men slain at the stone of Odin. He who is captured must lose his head. It is well — —"

"Seest thou?" loudly demanded Olaf. "The ruins of our village are yet smoking, although three days have passed. I saw thy ship on the sea yesterday, but knew not of thy landing. I meant to watch for thee or for the coming triremes after seeing the battle."

"Yonder trireme at anchor," replied the jarl, "floateth well out from the river mouth. She is large. How shall I take her? For there are yet Romans enough to hold her well. I must come to her by night in *The Sword*."

Long and thoughtfully gazed Ulric, studying the position of the trireme and the arrival of the beaten Romans at the fort.

"O jarl," said Biorn the Berserker, "knowest thou not that I am a fish? The trireme is held but by an anchor and a cord of hemp. Go thou and bring *The Sword*. When thou art at hand to strike thou mayest have the trireme drifting with the outgoing tide. Strike not when the tide runneth in?

"Thou canst swim," said Ulric, "and thy seax will sever hemp; but if thou waitest here until I come, how wilt thou know in the dark of my coming, or how wilt thou know where to ply the sharp edge?"

"When I hear thee whistle thrice," said Biorn, "as if thou wert calling thy hawk, I will know of thy coming. If the whistle is from this shore, I meet thee here. If it is from seaward, I swim to the trireme. Thou wilt know the hemp is severed when thou hearest my own falcon call."

"I go with thee, O jarl!" shouted Olaf, eagerly, "that I may be thy pilot."

"Well for thee, O Biorn the Berserker," said Ulric; "thou art of the heroes!"

"Here sit I down," replied Biorn. "It is a pleasant place. I think this taking of the trireme will depend upon thee and thy sword more than upon a man a fish cutting hemp!"

"Haste, now," said Ulric to his men. "*The Sword* is far from us and this is to be a night of great deeds, and not of ale and feasting."

Olaf led, as the guide of their rapid marching, and Biorn sat down upon a rock to gaze at the doings around the river mouth and at the fort.

"There come the Britons out of the woods," he said to himself. "If they had been well led they would have pursued more closely—only that few care to press too hard upon even the wreck of a Roman army. Now are all the Romans within the stockade."

The Britons were many, but their prey had escaped them. The camp fort was too strong for them to storm, and their showers of darts flew over the palisades without much harm to any within. The taunting clangor of their harps and trumpets sounded furiously for a while, and then the multitude swiftly vanished as if it had melted away.

"If these Britons had a captain," said Biorn, "instead of a herd of priests, and if he would arm them well, the Romans would disappear from Britain. But I think Ulric the Jarl will find many swords on yonder trireme. Even now they go out in small boats. Biorn the Berserker will be with him when the Saxons are on the Roman deck!"

Chapter IX
The Taking of the Trireme

The night was at hand when the jarl and his party arrived at the camp, and already all others were around the camp-fires.

"O jarl!" shouted Tostig. "Come thou and see this mighty one! We hauled him hither upon a bundle of branches, and he wearied us with his weight."

"Never saw I such a one!" exclaimed Ulric, gazing at the great boar which lay at the fire by the spring. "Was he for thy spear alone?"

"For mine!" said Tostig. "Now am I even with thee concerning the white bear, for this one fought as did the son of the ice king. He nearly overcame me after he had slain Nef, the son of Ponda, and had rent him in pieces. He had no wound from Nef."

"We did watch them," said a viking, "and to Tostig is the honor. If his spear had broken, as did thine in the bear, I think Tostig would have lost the battle."

"Then had I felt those great tusks," laughed Tostig, "But it will take all the night to roast him well."

"He will roast while we fight," replied the jarl; "and some of us will eat not of him, but in Valhalla. To the ship, all! We go to attack a Roman trireme. Let those eat now who have not eaten, taking their meat with them. I leave not a sword here!"

"He who would stay behind is nidering!" shouted Tostig the Red. "We will follow our jarl to the feast of swords, and they who return may find the boar roasted. Hael to thee, O jarl! Thou bringest good tidings."

Not until all were in the ship, however, did Ulric explain to his men fully and carefully the errand upon which they were going. Wild was their enthusiasm, and once more the young and the discontented were satisfied with their jarl.

"He is a son of the gods," they said, "and he will lead us to victory."

"Or to Valhalla," growled Knud the Bear. "Not all of you will eat the roasted boar's flesh."

The rowers rowed with power and *The Sword* went swiftly. Ulric was at the helm, and Olaf was at the prow sending back words of direction. The distance to be traveled was less on the water than on the land, through the forests.

"I would I knew of the doings of Biorn," said one, as the ship rounded a point and entered the harbor at the river mouth.

The jarl answered not, but shortly he put his fingers to his lips and whistled thrice.

"Row slowly, now," he said, "till an answer shall come. I am glad the moon is not yet arisen. We go on behind a curtain."

The jarl's signal had been heard by a man upon whom was only a belt, to which hung a sheathed seax and a war horn. He stood at the water's edge at the harbor side.

"The jarl cometh!" he whispered, and he went into the water, making no sound. Before that he had crept along the shore, landward, bearing his arms and his armor, and now he had but sixty paces to swim. The Roman sentinel on the deck of the trireme heard only the ripple of the outgoing tide against her wooden walls.

Knife upon hemp cutteth silently, but soon the sentinel turned with a sharp exclamation, for out of the seaward silence there came a long, vibrating whistle, another, another, and then from the hollow of a dark wave near the trireme there sounded a fourth like unto these three. This last he answered with a shout, and he hurled his pilum at that darkness in the water, but the trireme herself responded with a lurch and a yawing as she began to be swept away by the tide. There were rowers on board, and they quickly sprang to the oars, but they were few and there was yet no steersman. There were many soldiers also, but their officer ordered a number of them to the oars, that he might get the ship under control. When, therefore, there came gliding swiftly out of the shadows the unlooked-for warship of the Saxons she was alongside and her grapplings were made fast with none to hinder.

From the opposite side of the Roman vessel, as it were from the water itself, now sounded furiously the war horn of Biorn the Berserker. Full half of the legionaries rushed in that direction and their hurled spears were too hastily lost in the sea. Terribly rang out the war horns and the battle shouts of the Saxons, but the first man of them on board of the trireme was Ulric the Jarl, and down before his ax fell whoever met him. Close behind him were his followers, so that the nearer Romans were not only surprised, but outnumbered.

Up the side, near the stern, climbed Biorn the Berserker, and for a moment he was alone, so quickly had fallen twain who were there. Taking in hand the helm, "Biorn! Biorn the Berserker!" he shouted. "O jarl, I am here! The ship is ours!" Hard fought the remaining Romans, nevertheless, against such odds, but all the rowers were slain at their oars.

"It is done!" said Ulric. "Silence, all! I have called twice for Biorn. Where is he?"

"O jarl, son of Brander the Brave!" came faintly back from the after deck, "hast thou fully taken this trireme?"

"We have her!" answered Ulric. "Thanks to thee, O Biorn! She is thine!"

"Odin!" shouted back the old berserker. "Then bear thou witness for me, at feast and in song, that Biorn, the son of Nar, the sea king, died not by drowning, but by the driven spear of a Roman, in all honor. I go to Valhalla as becometh me. Rejoice, therefore, and smite thou these Romans once more for me. I die!"

There was a silence of a moment on the ship, but then the oldest viking of all blew triumphantly his horn and shouted: "We have heard! Biorn, the hero, hath gone to the hall of the heroes. He died by the spear, and not a cow's death. Good is his fortune. Hael to thee, O Biorn! And hael to Jarl Ulric, the leader of men."

Clashed loudly then the shields and spears, but already Saxon hands were upon the oars and Tostig the Red was at the helm, with Olaf by him. Only it might be a dozen warriors had been named by the valkyrias to go to Valhalla with Biorn the Berserker, but the Romans whose bodies were cast into the sea were ten times as many.

The Sword and the trireme were now going out with the tide into the open sea and into the darkness, but there had been much sounding of trumpets in the camp of the Romans. Few as were the remaining legionaries, they had marched to the shore ready for action. There were small boats at the beach, but it was all too late for any use of these. Those who patrolled and inquired, however, found at the side of a rock a helmet like a bear's head, a shirt the hide of a bear, two heavy spears, an ax—the trophies to them of Biorn the Berserker. These were brought to the centurion in command and he examined them with care.

"The pirates of the North are here," he said. "Woe is me that ever I came to this death coast! Here shall we leave our bones, for the Britons will come like locusts, and we have lost our trireme!"

"Another ship cometh soon," said his friends. "We may hold the fort well until her arrival. All is not lost."

"Know ye that?" replied the centurion. "If the trireme of Lentulus were above the water, she would have arrived long since. He hath never failed an appointment. I think it was his evil demon and not the favor of the proconsul that made him the count of the Saxon shore. The fates are against us."

So darkly brooded the Romans over their many disasters, while Ulric the Jarl ordered the steering of his two ships up the coast and into the cove where he had first landed.

"I would have speech with a Druid, if I may," he said to Olaf. "It is strongly upon my mind that I must see this great sacrifice to their gods. Manage thou this for me. Thou hast been in league with them."

"What I can do in such a matter I will do," said Olaf. "But, O jarl, I have somewhat to say to thee concerning this trireme. Consider her well, for she is a strong warship and there is much room in her."

"Also much plunder," said Ulric; "but that must wait for the day. Each man hath his share, and the shares of the slain go to their kindred when we return."

"So is the North law," said Olaf; "but where shall any man stow that which may be his prize? *The Sword* is but a nutshell. Thou wilt think of this matter, for thou art jarl."

The night waned toward the dawn and all had need of rest. The ships were anchored, therefore, and the cove was still.

The trumpets at the Roman camp greeted loudly the sun's rising. The sentinels were changed and the patrols came in from the edges of the forest to report that no enemy seemed to be coming. The soldiers sullenly attended to the customary morning duties of the camp, now and then glancing seaward as if they hoped to see a sail. The centurion in command walked along the lines of his intrenchments, studying them, but his eyes more often sought the earth. A stalwart man was he, in splendid armor, and his face bore scars of battle. Well had he fought the Britons the day before, but now he loudly exclaimed:

"O my imprudence! I should have waited for Lentulus and a greater force. Will he never come? But, if he come, the fault of this defeat is not his, but mine. He will be acquitted, and I am left alone to account to Cæsar for a lost eagle of a legion!"

He smote upon his breast and again he walked onward, downcast and gloomy. Once more he spoke, with exceeding bitterness:

"How shall I answer for the loss of the trireme here in the bay? Will not all men say that I kept no watch?"

He stepped upon the rampart and stood still. Near at hand were the ruins of the Saxon village, but they had ceased smoking and lay black and bare as witnesses of the ruthless blow which he had smitten upon the Northmen of the Saxon shore. Beyond were fields which would not be cultivated this season as formerly. There were many corpses yet unburied, for the slayers had spared none save boys and girls for the slave market. The very young, the very old, even the middle-aged women, had been slain, and the fighting men had fallen with their weapons in their hands. The prisoners were guarded in a kind of pen at the left, and they were many.

"Petronius," shouted the centurion to an officer of rank, "take with thee ten and slay all. We have no conveyance for them. Let not one escape."

One order was as another to a Roman soldier, and Petronius answered not, but marched away into the camp, seeking his ten who with him were to butcher the prisoners.

"I am dishonored!" said the centurion. "Fate and fortune are against me. I can give no reason for the loss of the trireme. I will go down to the shades."

Slowly he drew his short-bladed, heavy gladius from its sheath. He looked at it, trying its edge, and he said:

"Thou hast been with me through many battles, O sword! Thou hast drunk the blood of more lives than I can count. Be thou true to me now, for all else is lost."

Then he knelt upon the rampart and placed the hilt firmly in the earth, the blade point leaning toward him. He braced himself and cast his weight with force. A gasp, a shudder, a struggle of strong limbs, and Petronius was in command of the Roman camp, for his superior officer was dead.

There were many screams at the prison pen, but afterward all was quiet, and Petronius returned, to be told of this new misfortune which had befallen.

"Keep ye good watch," he said, "lest the Britons take us unawares. There is more than one trireme yet to come. But now we will raise the funeral pile of him who lieth here, for he died in all honor."

Orders were given and the soldiers brought much wood, but they came and went in silence, for their fates were dark before them.

So was it with the camp of the Romans; but at the camp of the Saxons, at the cove and spring, there was high feasting, for they found the wild boar well roasted and the venison was abundant. They needed but harps and harpers, for the spirit of song came upon all singers, and it was a day of triumph. Not even the older vikings could say that they had ever heard of the taking of a Roman warship in this wise.

"Some have the sea kings rammed to sinking," they said. "Some have they driven ashore and some have they burned; but the Romans themselves ever burn any keel that they are leaving. Hael to *The Sword*, the victor!"

"The smiters of my kindred have themselves been smitten," said Olaf, the son of Hakon, but he sat with a fierce fire burning in his eyes and his seax lay bare at his side.

"We have smitten them upon the sea," said Ulric the Jarl, "but not yet upon the land. I may not yet leave Britain. Not until I have kept the counsel of Hilda and my promise to my father at his tomb."

"Do as thou hast said," replied Olaf, "lest evil fortune come to thee. But go thou now and look at the trireme. Is she not thine, to do with as thou wilt?"

"I will go," said Ulric, and with him went only Knud the Bear, by his ordering.

First went they upon *The Sword*, for she was nearer, and she was now lashed side by side with the trireme. High above the low bulwarks of the ship from the Northland arose the strong sides of the war vessel of Cæsar, and her greater force in fight or in rough seas was evident. Ulric looked and he thought of the sayings of Olaf, the son of Hakon, for a shrewd suggestion sprouteth in the mind of a wise man like a seed sown in a garden.

"Truly we were overcrowded," said Ulric, standing upon the fore deck of *The Sword*. "We are thrice too many souls for so small a ship as this. There was too little room for provisions or for sleeping. There is none at all for the storage of spoils. The men will not brook the burning of the shares which may fall to them. They like not my hard ruling even thus far."

"O jarl," said Knud, "what sayest thou? Let us not burn good plunder. What good to win it if we carry it not home with us? I would now go on board the trireme."

"Come," said Ulric, and they climbed up over her high bulwark, noting how thick it was and well joined together. Thus they passed from stem to stern and in and out of cabins, examining all things—the oars, the ropes, and the sails.

"She is provided for a long voyage," said the jarl. "Sawest thou ever such armor and such store of weapons? We may need them in the southern seas."

"That will we," replied Knud; "but I am an old seaman and I was thinking of yonder sails. There are twain. They are of strongly woven stuff—not skins, like our sail. They will save much rowing. There are good anchors also. Thou sayest well, we are too many in *The Sword*."

Yet she seemed very beautiful as she lay at the side of the trireme, and the jarl remembered how his heart had gone out to her while she was building. She had borne him well, also, and she had proved herself. What might he do with the vessel that he loved? He went on board of her again and he stood by the hammer of Thor on the fore deck.

"What thinkest thou?" asked Knud. "What if I—for I am a smith—put now the anvil and the hammer on the fore deck of the trireme? Will she not then be *The Sword*? Will not Thor and Odin go with her?"

"Do even as thou hast said!" loudly exclaimed Ulric. "So the gods go with us what matter for a wooden keel?"

But his heart smote him sorely.

"I would," he thought, "that I might have speech with Hilda. I will go on shore and question Olaf. He is old."

Old was he and crafty, for already he had been saying many things to the vikings. He had told them of keels overwhelmed in the storms of the southern seas, or crushed by the rams of Roman warships. He had spoken of hungers and thirsts because of lack of room for provisions, and of fights lost because there were no more arrows to shoot or spears to throw. The young men heard him eagerly, and even the old warriors listened with care. They also called to mind such things and told of them, and all who chose to look could see the difference in size between the two vessels that floated in the cove.

Chapter X
The Great Sacrifice of the Druids

In the deep forest stood Olaf, the son of Hakon, and before him stood a tall, venerable man clad in a robe of white which came down to his feet, whereon were sandals. On his head was naught save abundant gray hair and a circlet of beaten gold. On his arms were heavy rings of gold, deeply graven, and in his hand was a long white wand, gold tipped.

"Thou and thy Saxon friends have done well," he said in the Latin tongue. "But I like not this message from their jarl."

"He doth but ask of thee, O high priest," replied Olaf, "that he, who is not as another man, but is of the sons of the gods of the North, may reverence thy gods for the aid they have given him by sea and land, and that he may be present at the great sacrifice, as becometh him. If he may so do, he will give thee a thing the like of which thou hast never seen hitherto, and he will smite for thee the Romans."

"Cometh he then from Odin?" asked the Druid.

"From Odin," said Olaf; "and of higher rank than he is none among the Saxons."

"He is not a king," said the Druid, "but I know of jarls and of their pedigrees. The Romans at thy village are this day smitten by the Britons and we need not his sword. Well is it, however, for him to give a gift. Let him see to it that his offering be right precious. It is a day's journey to the sacred place. He may not come down to the valley of the gods, but he may stand upon the hill, among the oaks, and afterward I will receive his token."

"So be it, O high priest," said Olaf, and he turned away, as did also the Druid.

"Cunning is he," muttered Olaf, as he walked. "But in us also is there prudence and the jarl will be guided in the matter. I think he will not fall into this trap of the Britons. They plotted against us before the Romans came, and gladly would they see Saxon blood upon the stones of sacrifice."

So said he to the jarl at the camp late in the day, and Ulric listened, pondering.

"Olaf," he said, after a silence, "Wulf the Skater hath returned from looking at thy place. No other trireme hath arrived, but even while he was watching did the Britons swarm over the palisades. The Romans were too few to guard their lines, and it was in vain for them to resist a multitude. Thy vengeance is complete."

"The gods have done this," said Olaf. "But what wilt thou do in this other matter?"

"I will leave a strong guard with the ship," said the jarl, "but with the greater number I will go to look upon the sacrifices. Thou wilt guide by a road they know not, and we will defeat their cunning."

"They would not strike thee, I think," said Olaf, "until after the sacrifices. This is their reverence to their gods."

"I would I knew," said Ulric, "the name of one of their gods. I will not sacrifice to one to whom I may not speak. He is a breath."

"Thou mayest not enter the sacred valley," said Olaf; "but I have somewhat more to tell thee. Now do I know what is the name of thy captured trireme."

"The hammer of Thor is on her deck at this hour," said the jarl. "She is no longer Roman. But whose is that gilded shape under her beak? It seemeth a woman wearing a helmet."

"The Druid told me," said Olaf. "She is Minerva. She is to the Romans as are the Nornir. She is both wise and crafty, being a saga woman, and there are runes concerning her."

"She is, then, not of the sea," said the jarl. "I think she will not contend with Thor. It were ill fortune to disturb her, seeing she hath delivered to us the ship; but we must give to it the name of *The Sword* or Odin were justly angry, for we gave our keel to him.

"Thou hast decided well," said Olaf; "but if so, then there must remain one keel only, not twain. It was commanded thee to burn one ship in Britain, and thou mayest not break thy word to the dead and to the gods."

"That will I not," said Ulric; "but now we must speedily prepare this expedition."

Wise had been the work of the tongue of Olaf, for now came the vikings to Ulric to speak concerning *The Sword* and the trireme, so that this which was to be done appeared not as by his ordering, but as the counsel of all.

"Thou doest well," they told him, "to yield to us in this matter. We will have a larger ship. We will have room for our plunder. We care not overmuch for thy small keel, and we will burn her at the seaside. Thou art our jarl in battle, but thou mayest not rule in all things."

Nevertheless, they agreed with him all the more readily concerning the sacrifices, and those who were to go and those who were to stay by the ships were chosen by lot lest any should accuse the jarl of unfairness; for it was hoped that here was to be fighting. Not yet had there been any division of the spoils because all agreed to wait until a more convenient season, or even until the end of the voyage.

"They whom the valkyrias do not name," said one, "may apportion whatever may then be found in the ship. There will be fewer weapons, perchance, and fewer men."

In the dawn of the next day did the jarl lead out his men, and in the dusk did the march end. High and round-topped was the hill in the forest to which Olaf guided them, and below was a narrow valley, bare of trees. There was yet light to see that in the middle of the valley were many great stones. Some of these stood upright in a wide circle, like the burial stones of the North peoples, but much larger. Other stones, long and weighty, lay flat, upheld a little from the ground by bowlders under them at either end.

"They are stones of sacrifice," said Olaf. "On them do they slay both cattle and men. But seest thou the cages?"

"Penthouses of wood I see," said Ulric. "Very large, but of one story and roofed flatly. On the roofs and against the sides are heaps of wood. What are these?"

"Wait till thou seest," said Olaf. "Their shape on the ground is as the body and the arms and the legs of a man, and there is a meaning in it known to the Druids. They make this wooden man of sacrifice, and they fill him full of men and women and children that he may feast. They have made many war captives and they have condemned many for evil-doing or for speaking against the Druids."

"Great fires are lighting around the valley and near the stones," remarked Tostig the Red. "I have seen many men slain upon stones. It is the right place to slay them, where the gods can see all. We shall have a rare treat. But there are hundreds of Britons. They wear little clothing."

"They paint themselves blue, instead," said Olaf. "But it keepeth not out either the cold or a spear point."

More and more numerous grew the throngs in the valley, coming out from under the trees beyond. Not among them, but walking through them in a procession, came scores at a time of the white-robed Druids, bearing no arms, but leading with them human beings of both sexes, arm-fettered, defenseless, making no resistance. There was a loud sound of harping and chanting as the processions drew near the flat stones.

Behind each of these stood a Druid with a large knife, and before him, stone by stone, was laid a victim. Then fell the knives in quick succession, with a twanging of harps and a shout, but the Northmen saw no great difference between this offering and such as they had witnessed elsewhere. As the firelight brightened, however, they could discern that the walls of the wooden man in the middle were open, with wide crevices, through which might be seen the naked forms of those who were shut in. They were even crowded, and they uttered loud cries as they saw torches placed against the heaps of wood surrounding the pen.

"Dry wood," said Knud the Bear. "See how it kindleth! A hot fire! These are to be burned for their god? He is a bad one. I like it not. The Romans do well to kill these Druids. I would slay them myself."

So said all the vikings, and had there been more of them, they might have vented their anger at this thing. It was not good, even for a god, but the throngs of Britons were well armed, after their fashion, and Ulric's men were but few in comparison.

"We would not mind four or five to one," he said, "but we could not slay such a multitude. The fires burn terribly! It is not at all like kindly slaying with a sword."

"A cut on a man's neck is nothing," said Tostig. "He falleth and that is an end. I hope to fall by a sword some day."

The shrieks and cries of agony were dreadful, rising above the twanging of the harps and the chanting of the Druids. There was no help for any of these who were doomed. Among them, said some of the vikings, must be all the Roman prisoners if any had been taken. The burning roofs fell in and so did the red blazings of the side walls. Nor did the swarms of the Britons cease to yell with the pleasure of cruelty while they gazed upon the frantic struggles of these victims.

"We have seen enough," said Olaf, at last. "O jarl, we have far to go. I hope we may again strike the Romans shortly, but I care not much if good Saxon spears find many marks among the Druids. It would require a host of Saxons to hold this island, killing them all, but I am one who will go back to the North and come again, bringing stout slayers with me."

"Some of the white-robed ones come in this direction even now," responded the jarl. "Behind them are spearmen. They must not find us upon this hill, but the woods are overdark to march in."

"After we are well covered," said Olaf, "we may kindle torches, but the way by which I lead you is plain and wide, for the war chariots of the British kings have made it in the old days. The Romans now prevent them from having any chariots within their dominions, but there are free tribes beyond their borders. Come!"

"On!" said the jarl. "This hill was to have been their trap. They seek to march around that they may cut off our going. On!"

Swiftly marched the Saxons for a while, but the darkness of the forest was dense, and now they halted to kindle torches.

"The Druids and their men carried many and bright ones," said Ulric, "so that we saw them enter the woods, but we are too far now for them to discern our own."

After this there were pauses for resting, but the vikings marched on until the dawn. Then went they forward again, fasting, but at the noon they were greeted by the shouts of the men who held the palisades at the spring.

"O Tostig the Red," responded the jarl, "hath all been well with thee and with the camp?"

"Hael, O jarl!" said Tostig. "All is well. We have seen Britons at a distance among the trees, but none came near for speech. I think they are not overfriendly."

"That are they not, but treacherous," said Ulric. "But now let there be roasting and eating and sleeping, and then we shall have new matters upon our hands. We have seen things that are worth telling around a fire in the winter evenings. I like not these gods of the Britons. They are evil-minded."

Many were busy at the fires with venison and with fishes which had been caught, but they who had remained at the camp were cooks for the weary men who could tell of this sacrifice of the Druids. As for the jarl, he ate and drank and then he went on board *The Sword* and lay down to sleep upon the after deck, saying little to any man, and Tostig the Red came and sat down by him.

Orders had been given, moreover, and before the setting of the sun both keels were anchored some fathoms out from low-water mark, and only the small boats were at the beach. It was best, the jarl had said, to trust deep water rather than a stockade after the darkness should come. All the fires in the camp were heaped to burn long, and so were other large fires upon the strand. Then came all the vikings on board the ship, and there could be no present peril. It was a night of peace, but the watchers saw both dark forms and white ones by the light of the fires, and knew that the Britons had come.

"The white ones are the Druids," said Wulf the Skater to his companions. "I am not afraid of their gods which have men roasted. I hope the jarl will find us a chance to spear priests before we sail away from this island."

The rest agreed with him, asking him many questions concerning the sacrifices.

"But for the prudence of the jarl," he also told them, "all we who went would have been taken at a disadvantage in the darkness of the forest. There would have been no fair fighting."

"He is a good battle jarl," they said, but it might be seen that among them were some who were not well pleased with his ways.

There, safe from all assailing, floated the two keels until the dawn. Then went some of the men ashore in the small boats, and the fires were replenished for cooking, but none were permitted to wander into the woods. On board the trireme there was much search going on and great was the delight of all over the plunder discovered. Rich indeed was the store of arms, as if it had been intended to refit a cohort or to arm new recruits.

"It is good, too," they said, "to be able to walk around. There was hardly elbow-room on our own keel. But we knew that we must lose some and that there would be less crowding when we came home."

"We can give a man to every oar of the trireme," said Ulric, "and yet leave threescore to the spears."

But he looked over the bulwark and down into the good ship *The Sword*, and his heart smote him sadly, for the very wood she was made of came from his own trees, and she seemed to look him in the face kindly.

Hours went by before there were any newcomers upon the shore, but Olaf said that there must be patience.

"Watch also," he warned Ulric, "and let not any Briton come on board. We will meet them in the small boats at the strand."

So it came to be, for at the noon the woods became alive with men. Foremost came the chief Druid, followed by some of lesser rank and by harpers. With them were chiefs of clans of the Britons, each one calling himself a king, but being really less than a Norse jarl in power, for he was as a slave to all Druids.

"These," told Olaf, "make the laws and enforce them. They alone know the sagas of the Britons and what is to be given to the gods. They sometimes burn a king if he worketh not their will, and they have magic arts which make the people fear them. I would slay all such if I were a king."

He and Ulric were in the same boat pulling to the strand; and the chief Druid was wise, for he came to meet them attended only by two other Druids and by seven of his harpers. Behind them under the trees clustered the British warriors. They formed no ranks, but they wore a fierce, warlike appearance. Among them were some in armor that was half Roman, as if taken in battle. More had Roman swords, but their own British blades were both short and light. All were armed with javelins, but their shields were of all sorts, only that most of them were made of wicker and hide.

"They are brave enough," said Olaf, "but the Romans seek to prevent them from getting weapons. A Briton might become as good a soldier as a legionary, with arms and with training. Cæsar is always cunning in government."

"Hael, O Druid!" shouted Ulric. "I am well pleased to see thee."

"O thou, the jarl of the vikings," sternly responded the chief Druid. "Too many came with thee. My permission was but to thee and to Olaf. Neither didst thou do reverence to my gods."

"O priest," said the jarl, "I came and I returned as I would. I like not thy gods. What is thy errand with me this day?"

The face of Ulric had flushed hotly upon hearing the haughty speech of the Druid, for he was not one to be lightly chidden by any man.

"O jarl," said the Druid yet more sternly, "I have this also against thee, that thou didst promise me a treasure the like of which I never saw before, and thou didst not deliver it. Where is thy great gift?"

"O Knud the Bear," shouted Ulric, "row now to the shore and bring to this priest the token of the son of Odin."

The second of the small boats came to the shore and Knud and eight other of the tallest vikings, ax in hand, bore out and spread upon the earth the tremendous hide of the white bear, the king of bears. From the skull, also, they had reft its whole cover, putting in eyes of bright leather. The hide seemed to be longer and broader than in life, as if it lay two fathoms from tail to nose.

"O jarl of the Saxons," exclaimed the Druid, "what is this? I have heard of these creatures, but never have I seen one."

"Then have I kept my promise," said Ulric. "Thou mayest hang it in thy house or in the house of thy gods, as thou wilt, but never was the like of it in Britain. He was a son of the ice king. He came from the long darkness, and I slew him with my own hand."

Around the jarl stood now a score of vikings; terrible men for a foe to look upon, for they were throwers of sudden spears. Still stood the chief Druid and his fellows and the harpers, gazing at the great skin, and the Britons in the edge of the wood shouted loudly.

"I agree with thee as to this," said the high priest, reluctantly. "I accept thy token, for in it is a meaning that thou knowest not. There is an old prophecy concerning the Northern Bear and Britain. Thou hast done well. My quarrel is now with Olaf, who standeth by thee."

"But for him thou wouldst have slain me and mine in thy forest trap on the hill, at the sacrifices," answered the jarl, angrily. "Thy quarrel is also with me!"

Then came the rush of the Britons from the woods, hurling javelins as they came, but the vikings were instantly in their boats, and the high priest and all who were with him lay upon the sand, so suddenly were they smitten. From the ships came showers of spears, arrows, stones, and the men in the small boats seemed to be unharmed, for their shields were up.

"Thou sittest very still," said Ulric to Olaf. "What sayest thou? Mine eyes were upon these blue ones."

"O jarl," said Knud the Bear, "we lifted him in, thinking there might still be life in him, but there is none. The spear of the high priest was strongly driven."

"Hael to thee, O hero!" shouted the jarl. "Olaf, the son of Hakon, hath gone to Valhalla! He hath died in his armor! Row to the ships. We will go hence and the body of Olaf we will bury in the sea. There shall be no lamenting for the son of Hakon."

Only this harm had befallen the Saxons from the treachery of the Druids, while the slain lying upon the beach were many. Loudly now arose the wailing of the Britons, for they had a strange death cry of their own, long and vibrating, that went far out across the sea.

"Their gods will be against us," said Wulf the Skater. "We may not now linger long in Britain."

"Very soon," said the jarl, "we will sail for the Middle Sea, but not with two keels. We are too few."

The Sword and the trireme, nevertheless, were now going out to sea with all oars, as if to show how many men were needed for this. The jarl was at the helm of the trireme and his face was clouded.

"Not yet," he said, "have I smitten the Romans upon the land of Britain. That must I do, and I know not how or where. The days go by and it will be winter before we reach the Middle Sea. The voyage is long."

Chapter XI
The Passing of Lars the Old

Sudden is the change from winter to summer in the Northland. The buds of the trees get ready under the frost and open to the sunshine as soon as a few days of warmth have told them that they may safely burst forth. No full leaves were as yet, but the grass was greening and the fisher boats were busy in the fiords.

In the hall of the house of Brander there were fewer to gather now, in the lengthening evenings, around the central fire, but Oswald's harp was always there. Hilda, from her chair, would often ask him to strike up, but there was a lack of spirit in his minstrelsy, and even when she spoke to him her voice was weaker and softer than of old. The wrinkles upon her face were deepening, and they who looked long at her said to one another that a light which did not come from the fire played now and then across her forehead and around her mouth. At other times she was shut up much in her own room, and it was said that she pored long and thoughtfully over polished sheepskins and fragments of gray stone whereon were graven runes that none else might read. Some of these, they said, had been brought by Odin's men when they journeyed from the East into the Northland. Who knew, therefore, but what the runes had been written in the city of Asgard by the hands of the Asas? It was not well to question over-closely about such things. They said naught to her of the matters which were her own, and only once did a little maiden yield to her own curiosity and follow the old saga woman when at night she walked out along the path which led to the stones of the mighty dead. Afterward she told her mother, and then all the village knew, that Hilda did but sit down by the tomb of Brander, weeping loudly and talking with him concerning his absent son.

"It is no wonder," said the villagers, "for she loved Ulric the Jarl. It is good for all our men that Hilda should speak to the gods concerning their welfare. She knoweth them better than we do, and she is to go to them soon. She getteth ready daily."

So fared it in the Northland, but many ships were putting to sea, and there was even jealousy here and there that Ulric and *The Sword* should have gotten away so much in advance of all others. But the ships of the vikings would now be so many as to bode ill for the fleets of Rome and for the merchantmen of the Middle Sea unless Cæsar should send force enough to prevent their coming.

"Olaf told me," said Ulric, talking to Tostig of such matters, "that the Romans fear the coming of the Saxons. Therefore against our villages as well as against the rebellious Druids came these triremes at this time. Cæsar's power in Britain groweth. Around his fortified camps are cities springing up, and he fortifieth also ancient towns. We must come with many keels and a great host when we take this island away from Cæsar."

"But I think we will destroy the Britons," said Tostig the Red, "for we have seen that we may not trust them. I like a place where there is so much good hunting."

Ulric had been scanning the shore line, for he was steering, and now he said:

"We will anchor for the night within yonder rocky point. There is a ledge there for which I have been seeking."

All day had the two ships been coasting slowly, and the men had wondered much what it might be that was in the mind of their jarl, for he was moody. He had also asked many questions of the older vikings. The two ships came to anchor not many fathoms out from the rocky point, but all men were forbidden venturing to the shore.

"It is not well," said Ulric to some who would have landed in the small boats. "If ye but look closely, ye will discern the glimmer of fires in the deep forest. Our movement this day hath been followed, and now a small party might meet too many of their spearmen. They are good fighters."

There was much grumbling among the younger men, for they despised this prudence of his which ever held them in and thwarted their hot wills, but they had no choice but to obey him concerning the boats.

More and more plainly through the night darkness might the watchers on the decks discern the fires that were kindled in the woods. The jarl gazed at them long, thinking many things concerning the Druids and the other Saxon villages of the shore of Britain. He slept after a while to the slow rocking of the ship, and when morn came Wulf the Skater stood by him.

"O jarl," he said, "the Britons build fires along the beach. They swim out to us. I have speared four of their swimmers. What do we next?"

Ulric arose and gave orders. Immediately a transfer began from *The Sword* to the trireme of all arms and provisions, and the men worked rapidly.

Only that Wulf worked not, and that an old viking came and stood by him at the bulwark.

"I like it not," said Wulf, "but Ulric is jarl. What sayest thou, Lars the Old, the shipmaker?"

"Thou art a seaman," said Lars. "I am of thy mind. I toiled much in the shaping and the making of *The Sword*. My heart is heavy."

"So is mine!" exclaimed Wulf. "First of all men, after the jarl, did I take her helm. She is Odin's keel. There is bad fortune in leaving her."

"That do I fear," said Lars, "but I leave her not. I was sore smitten in the ribs in the fight with the Druids on the beach. I bleed well now. I shall not sail in this trireme."

"Good is thy fate," said Wulf. "Didst thou tell the jarl thou wert wounded?"

"Not so," replied Lars. "None know but a few of our old vikings. I thought not much of it at first, for I have oft been wounded. But now they will soon burn *The Sword*. I command thee that thou lay me upon the fore deck, where was once the hammer of Thor. That is my death place."

"That will I do," said Wulf. "So will say the jarl."

"So do I now say!" came to them in his own voice, for he also was leaning over the rail and he had heard. "O Lars, I knew not of thy hurt, thinking only of Olaf, the son of Hakon. Him have we buried in the sea this day, and thou shalt have thy will. *The Sword* is nearly emptied. We burn her on yonder rocks at the point as the tide falleth. We will lay thee upon her fore deck with thy arms and armor."

"Do thou thy duty by me," said Lars, "that it may be well with thee. But leave not *The Sword* until every timber shall be burned, lest some part of her shall fall into an enemy's hand."

"She is ready!" exclaimed Ulric. "We will lift the anchors and move both ships. There will be many to see the burning."

Trumpetings and harpings and angry shouts were answering from a throng of Britons gathering along the shore. Not any of them could guess as yet what would be the next move of the Saxons, but great was their wrath that they were able to do no harm.

"They would we might find reason for landing," said Ulric to Wulf, "but I care not to strike them at this place. We would gain nothing."

"O jarl," said Wulf, "Lars, the shipmaker, lieth down. The valkyrias are with him."

"He dieth not a cow's death," said Ulric, "but as a true warrior of the North. It is as he would will, but he still is breathing."

"Yea, but heavily," said Wulf. "I would I were as he is, that I might not leave *The Sword*."

"O Wulf," said the jarl, "thou hast many a feast of swords before thee. Cheer thee up."

"Jarl Ulric," said Wulf, "do I not know thee? Thou too lovest thy first keel. But I think thou doest wisely. The men have demanded this, and they may not be gainsaid. But I would there had been men enough for both ships, and then I would not have left mine own."

On moved the two keels toward the ledge of rocks, and the tide was falling. They would be bare before long.

"Row, now!" shouted the jarl. "Send *The Sword* far up upon the ledge. She must be lifted by the rocks till she is out of the water. There come the Britons toward the point. Be ready to strike them! The Druids have gathered an army!"

No sail was raised upon either of the ships, but the rowers of the trireme paused while those of *The Sword* pulled strongly. She was light now, having no stowage or ballast, and quickly her prow was thrust high up the ledge between two masses of dark gray stone. Then the trireme was grappled at her stern and many Saxons sprang out upon the ledge. There were several fathoms of water between this and the shore.

"Fast falleth the tide," said Ulric. "Lift ye now Lars the Old, the shipmaker, and bear him to the fore deck of *The Sword*. Lay by him his arms and his armor, breaking the sword and the spear and cleaving the shield and mail that no other may ever bear them."

The vikings carried the old warrior quickly, and he uttered no sound. They laid him upon the fore deck and did as Ulric commanded, but the hilt of the broken sword, having yet half the length of its bright blade, they put into his right hand. In the middle of the ship much wood was placed, heaping it, and in this heap a blazing torch was thrust. Then all the vikings left *The Sword*, and the greater part of her was already out of water.

"They come in swarms!" exclaimed Tostig the Red, gazing at the Britons who rushed along the shore toward the point. "Hael! the fire burneth well! They must not prevent it!"

Up leaped the long-armed flames, catching the fagots of pine splinters.

"Burn thou, O *Sword*!" shouted the jarl. "I give thee to Odin in the fire! Thou art mine own, O good ship from the Northland. I would I might have sailed in thee to the Middle Sea and to the city of the gods!"

"O jarl," said Wulf the Skater, "even so would I have sailed. I think we shall never see that city. The gods are far away, and I know not if they have any city. I am dark this day, and over me is a cloud."

The jarl spoke not again, but he looked earnestly at *The Sword* and at that which was threatening along the shore. Still as a stone lay Lars the Old, and some men thought him dead. There were Druids now at the point, and with them were harpers and trumpeters, and the white-robed ones were chanting to their gods.

The chanting ceased and a Druid raised his sacred wand, shouting fiercely. At that word hundreds of armed Britons began to rush into the sea.

"They are too many," said Knud the Bear. "They do but drown each other. These Druids are not good captains. Therefore are they beaten by the Romans in spite of their gods and their sacrifices."

The fire ran everywhere along the bulwarks of *The Sword* and began to climb over the decks. It climbed the high mast and the wind blew it out like a banner.

"Odin!" shouted Ulric. "The Britons are on the rocks! Smite now!"

Fast flew the arrows and the spears, and almost useless were the wicker shields of the Britons. Many of them had none, and their blue bodies were plain marks for shaft and stone. They fell in heaps upon the ledge, but a score of them broke through the flames to the very fore deck of *The Sword*, and here too the fire was blazing hotly. Here before them lay Lars the Old, stretched out as on his funeral pyre. These were of the best armored of the Britons, and one could understand that they had thought to take *The Sword* and push her off, that by her means they might reach the trireme.

No good captain would so have planned, for such a thing might not be done; but these men were brave, for they stood well and some of them hurled their darts vigorously at the vikings, while others strove vainly to shove *The Sword* from the rocks into the sea.

This thing that came not any man had expected. Just as the strong fire in the cabin began to burst up redly through the fore deck, and a fiercer flame mounted the after deck, and all the bulwarks were ablaze, up to his feet sprang Lars the Old, his gray hair streaming in the wind. One blow he struck with his broken sword, burying it in the body of a British chief, and then he began to ply his long-handled ax with the strength of one who is dying. Upon him turned the spears and the swords of the Britons and he was stricken quickly. He did not shout, but he cleft one more while falling.

"The hero dieth!" said the jarl, hurling his spear, and it flew well, but there were not many now upon the fore deck.

More were swimming from the shore to the ledge, but the fire was completing its work, and the plan of the Druids was broken altogether. When once more the wind put aside the black curtain of the smoke it was seen that the entire prow had fallen in and that to the very helm the flames were fighting joyously.

"We will stay by until she is burned to her keel," said Ulric; "but now pull out a little further."

So did they, and the Britons came no more to the ledge, for the prize they had hoped for was a heap of ashes upon the rocks.

"A good ship was she," muttered Knud the Bear. "She fought well against the ice floes and the storms. May all the gods go with us in this trireme. I would I knew her by some name."

"O Knud," loudly responded Ulric, "I will answer thee. This keel that was Roman hath become Saxon, and her name is now *The Sword*. Else we had not burned the other. The trireme shall be to us as if we had builded her on the shore of the Northland. She will sail with the hammer of Thor and the flag of Odin and not with a Roman god."

"I am better satisfied," exclaimed Wulf the Skater. "But many good rowers must take the oars of this trireme in battle. She is heavy."

"I think," said Tostig the Red, "that we are stronger than are the hired rowers or the slave rowers of the Romans. Her beak will break the ribs of another keel and she will do well in storms."

The jarl's eyes were still upon the burning timbers which remained upon the ledge.

"I will take a boat," he said, "and men with me. We must gather all fragments for utter destruction."

Upon that duty he went, and it was made complete before the small boat returned to the trireme. All the while many Britons watched them from the shore, but came not against them.

"Too many of them have been slain," said the vikings. "They like not our heavy spears."

Before climbing into the trireme the jarl made them row to her beak, that he might examine well its form and its power for striking a blow, and that he might also look more closely at the figurehead.

"It is much waterworn," he said. "She is the wise woman among the gods of the Romans. She will care not much that the hammer of Thor is on the fore deck."

The small boat was hoisted to its place and the vikings began to speak more freely of the trireme by her new name of *The Sword*.

"Up with the sails," commanded Ulric. "The wind is fair. We will go southward this night, and we will seek the Saxon village that was described to me by Olaf, the son of Hakon. But we will not go too fast or too far, lest we may pass it in the dark."

"There may be our kinsmen there that need our aid," said Knud the Bear. "Seax in hand it would be a pleasure to meet Romans."

Now did they begin to discover how much more room there was to walk in from place to place around the ship, but the younger men praised their own prudence for this more than that of Ulric the Jarl. Moreover, to please all, he caused to be brought forth many weapons and much armor. These the men handled curiously, trying on the helmets and the mail and testing the weight of the shields. Garments, also, were given as the men would, and they laughed merrily at each other for the strangeness of their changed appearance.

Well out from the land steered the jarl, not knowing the coast, and there was careful watching for breakers which might tell of shoals or rocks. He was learning, also, the sailing of this keel and her manner of answering the rudder.

"She is swift," he thought, "and she rideth well the waves. We build not yet such vessels in the Northland, though we have plenty of good timber. She will carry us safely into the Middle Sea, but there is room in her for more men. She requireth too many for her oars. I will sail rather than row, lest I breed too much discontent."

Far behind him now went out the last burning of the timbers of the good keel he had builded in the Northland, but upon the mast of this which carried him floated still the White Horse flag of the Saxons which had been given to *The Sword* by Hilda of the hundred years.

Chapter XII
Svein the Cunning Jarl

Sailing on in the darkness, over an unknown sea, the trireme, which was now the viking ship *The Sword*, moved toward the dawn. None on board of her knew the low-lying coast which was in sight when the sun looked over the horizon.

"We are nearer than I deemed," said Ulric; but he was at the prow now, and an old Danish seaman was at the helm.

"There are rocks hereaway at the right," replied Tostig the Red, "but I can see houses and lines of palisades. The Britons build not such houses. They are like our own."

"There are fields, also, and cattle," said Knud the Bear. "There are men on the beach. Let us sail in. Hark! War horns! We are waited for."

"It is a good harbor," said Ulric. "There are four keels on the strand, but they are small. And there are boats. These are not Romans."

"They will deem that we are," said Tostig. "Thy horn, O jarl."

"Not yet," said Ulric. "We will go nearer. All rowers to the oars! Let down the sail!"

Then came a surprise to those who were on *The Sword*, so very numerous were the warriors who came down to the shore outside of the lines of the palisades on the harbor side of the village. This, too, was seen to be larger as they drew nearer, and some of the houses were as great as was the home house of Brander the Brave.

"It is as Olaf told me," thought Ulric. "The Romans do well to fear the Saxons of this coast. We will be friends with these men."

The rowers had brought the ship well in and Ulric stood by the hammer of Thor. Three times be blew his horn, standing bareheaded, nor was there any Roman helmet worn by those who were with him. Moreover, the banner on the mast was the White Horse of the Saxons.

Horns answered him, and then there were shouts of greeting, while some of the shore men pushed out in a small boat.

"Come near!" said Ulric to these. "I am Ulric the Jarl, the son of Brander the Brave. We come in peace. Who are ye?"

Upon his feet arose a short, squarely made man in the boat. He wore fine armor and there was a golden crest upon his steel headpiece.

"I am Svein Jarl," he responded. "We are Saxons all, and this town on the shore is Rika. Where didst thou win thy keel? I tell thee we are at peace with the Romans, as we are with thee."

"So be it," said Ulric; but then he told of Olaf and of the Druids and of the triremes and of the Roman camp.

"Strong tryst between me and thee," said Svein. "Thou hast done well. Olaf would never make peace because they slew his father, as did they thine. They would crucify thee because of thy trireme. But word came to me that the Roman consul Licinius is in Britain, and I have sent him bodes, making agreement. We are at war only with the rebellious Britons, not with his own. We are too few to contend with Rome. Land thou and thine if thou wilt, but see that thou sailest away quickly."

"I understand thee," said Ulric. "I am but one trireme against more than one if the consul sendeth them. But we will not land here. I will go to thy house in greeting, but no more."

"Come," said Svein. "I like thy flag, and I was thy father's sure comrade. The son of Brander is welcome to the house of Svein Jarl."

Small boats from the ship were ready, and in one went Ulric to the shore, taking with him many men in the other boats, for he thought: "I know not Svein well, and Olaf spoke ill of him. He is a friend of the Romans."

So said the vikings who remained on the ship, and they kept good watch, saying to one another:

"We like it not that our jarl should thus venture himself. How know we what is behind yonder palisades?"

Hearty and kindly were the words spoken to Ulric and his Saxons by the warriors who met them at the beach. Neither did Svein seem to lack in any wise, but walked on toward the palisades, bidding the newcomers to follow. At the side of Ulric the Jarl now walked a tall man and large, in full armor, but wearing over his shoulder a bearskin.

"I am Sigurd, the son of Thorolf," he said. "I am a Northman, like thyself. The greater part of Svein's men are Danes, as he is. I am not with him, save that my keel was wrecked and I owe him for hospitality. But I am free, having fought for him against the Britons."

"Sail thou with me," said Ulric. "There is room in *The Sword*. Share thou fight and prizes by land and sea. Thou art welcome."

"I will put my hands in thine and be thy man," said Sigurd. "Mark thou this, then. When we pass the gate of the palisades many will come and range themselves with thee and me, for they are as I am and would depart from this place. Thou hast thine ax. Be thou ready to smite with it, as will I and mine."

Then those who looked upon the face of Ulric saw that it became white and that his eyes were fiery, flashing blue light, and they thought, but spoke not. "The jarl is angry! Trouble cometh. We will watch if this is a place of swords."

Then again they looked and he seemed taller and his face was red and his eyes were full of glittering, and some trembled, for they said each to his mate: "Seest thou? It is the Odin wrath! Lift thy shield! War cometh!"

Open swung a wide gate in the palisades and Svein marched in, turning to beckon, while many warriors closed in line with the company of Ulric and his Saxons; but there were others who remained behind and prevented some from closing the gate. Even as Sigurd had said, when he lifted his hand and made a sign forty and four more who were among Svein's garrison walked along, spear in hand, until they seemed of one band with Ulric's.

But a sound came loudly, and then another—and another.

Svein stood still and blew upon his war horn, and it was a command to his Danes that they should form as spearmen. From behind a wide house rang joyously the note of a Roman trumpet, and a line of legionaries, headed by an officer, began to show itself. The third sound was the angry word of Ulric, the son of Brander.

"Svein Jarl," he shouted, "I know thee. Thou art Svein, son of Hedrig, my father's enemy. Me thou wouldst betray to these wolves of Rome, but thou art not able. I will give thee and them to the valkyrias."

"Hold thou, Ulric the Jarl," said Svein. "Thou art caught in a trap. Thou shalt but give them up their trireme. Thou mayest remain with me. Lay down thy weapons. Thou and thine are prisoners. We may deal with thee as we will."

So said the officer of the legionaries, mockingly, coming forward, followed by his force. It was but fourscore of men, and they were the garrison of this village, with Svein and his Danes and his Jutlanders.

But Ulric was a good captain, and he and his Saxons were stepping backward and the gate was still open. Then fell quickly three men who strove to shut it, but they went down by the spears of Sigurd's Saxons.

At that the Romans charged, and their charge was that of warriors expecting to conquer; but Ulric, the son of Brander, was taller by the head than any among them. He waited not, but stepped out and met them in front of the triangle formed by his men, and the flashing of his ax was like the swiftness of the lightning, and his wrath was terrible. Fast flew the spears on either side, but the Saxons threw first, not waiting, and there were quickly gaps in the Roman line.

Now charged Svein and his followers with shouts of victory, save that a number of them were Northmen and had no heart to this work. These fell back muttering, and one of them said, loudly:

"Ulric, son of Odin, win thou this fight. The gods of the North be with thee. I shed no blood in any such quarrel. I am not a Roman."

Nevertheless the Saxons from *The Sword* had been too much outnumbered if it had not been for Sigurd and his sailors, for these fought like men who were to die if they did not conquer.

Wonderful was the havoc wrought by the ax of Ulric, and the Romans fell away from before him. Then picked he up a pilum from the hand of a slain legionary and he cast it with his might. Well had it been for Svein the Jarl if his shield had been ready, for the pilum passed through him at the waist and he would betray no more Saxons. So fell the Roman officer at the hand of Tostig, but the charge had been well made, and only half of Ulric's own men were with him when his triangle was beyond the gate, marching to the shore.

"Odin!" he shouted. "We have slain three for one! Let us burn their keels."

But some of the men who had refused to fight for Svein came around by another way and joined the Saxons. Well was it, they said, that the Roman officer had forced Svein to strike at once, for there were hundreds of Danish warriors in the upland, and if these had gathered, none of the crew of *The Sword* could have escaped.

Even now there was preparation for swift following, but Ulric's men took every boat, and the nearest keels on the beach had already fire in them, put there by Sigurd's men and the other Northmen who had deserted Svein. These ships were also pushed out into the water that they might burn more surely.

Within the palisades every Saxon who had fallen wounded had already been slain by the Danes, but these had been sorely smitten and they had lost their cunning jarl.

Back now were Ulric and his men on board the trireme, and count was made. "Thirteen heroes who went to the land with us," he said, "have gone to Valhalla. With them went six of Sigurd's company. Therefore, we have ninety more strong men to handle so large a ship and to hold spears in battle. The gods are with us, for they have given us a brave combat and a victory."

The keels from the shore were burning hotly, and there might be no pursuit, but Ulric commanded to lift the sail of *The Sword*, the trireme, and to steer for the open sea.

"Now do I know," said Knud the Bear, "that Thor came on board with his hammer. We needed more men for the oars, to change hands when one company is weary. It is good to have the gods with us in such a case."

The wind blew off the land and the ship sailed away gallantly, steering southward, and Ulric said to those who asked him:

"We will not again set foot upon the shore of Britain. Our work here is done. We will avoid all keels, friend or foe, that may come near us. We go to the Middle Sea, and our voyage, thus far, is prosperous."

The sun shone brightly in the Northland all that day, but Hilda sat by the fire in the hall of the house of Brander, and she was shivering. Near her sat Oswald, the harper.

"It is cold," she said. "This fire is but red coals and ashes. Let them bring wood."

So sat she while they went for wood, and she gazed mournfully into the great heap of gray and red, dotted with dying embers.

"I saw not the ship," she muttered. "But I saw Roman helmets. There is Ulric, and the Romans go down before him. Where is the ship? I see her now, and she is burning. How, then, can Ulric sail away? I read it not, save that he is not slain. O that I could look upon his face again before I go! How is it that I cannot see the ship? But I knew that she would never come again. It is well that he hath smitten the Romans so soon. I will go to my room, for I am old and the ice is out of the fiords and the buds are open and I have seen the grass again. I need but the one token more and then they may lay me away as I have bidden them. Ulric, my beloved! Thou art as my son!"

Chapter XIII
Hilda of the Hundred Years

"Hast thou ever taken a keel into the Middle Sea, O Sigurd, son of Thorold?" asked Ulric of his gigantic friend.

They twain stood together upon the after deck and *The Sword* was sailing but slowly, for the wind was contrary.

"More than once, O jarl," responded Sigurd. "I have seen the Greek islands; I went up the Adriatic Sea with Alfkel the Sea King. We had five keels, and we took great spoil, but only three of our ships ever again touched the shore of the Northland."

"What befell the two that returned not?" asked the jarl. "Was it a fortune of the sea?"

"Not so," said Sigurd. "In that sea the triremes of Cæsar are too many. But thou hast need to consider thy present course. Thou wilt do well to coast along the land easterly after thy last sight of Britain. Between these islands and Spain is a great sea full of storms. Try it not with a straight passage, but go from point to point, going on shore when thou wilt."

"I think it is good counsel," said the jarl. "I have heard of that sea. As to the Adriatic, I would enter it in due season, but first I would see Rome itself, if I might."

"Not if thou go to its port in a keel thou hast won from Cæsar," said Sigurd. "That were but to offer them thy head. Thou wilt do better among the islands and toward the great land that is called Africa. There dwell the black men, and in the inland there are giants wonderful to see; and also there are powerful magicians."

"I care not much for them," said Ulric, "although I am curious about giants. Tell me all thou wilt of thy voyages."

Willingly did Sigurd tell, and he had seen many wonderful things in the southlands.

"I shall gladly see them again," he said; and even the next day did this talk go on, for a gale blew and *The Sword* went before it with but one small sail lifted.

Sigurd's men were now as if they had been with Ulric from the first, and by them a matter had been told which was now more fully given by the tall viking.

"Svein concealed it from me," he said, "but an old Dane warned me in private. The Roman officer of that garrison was but waiting for the arrival of more legionaries, for Svein's men might not be depended on in such an undertaking. It would have included thee and thine. All who did not belong to Svein or who were minded to leave him were to have been given up as war prisoners to the Romans."

"That they might lose their heads!" exclaimed Ulric. "I am glad he is slain! It was a dark purpose."

"Thou hast not read it rightly, nevertheless," said Sigurd. "Hast thou not heard of the great games and shows of Cæsar and of his chief officers?"

"Many a thing have I heard," replied Ulric, "but not from any man who had ever witnessed the things he told of. Hast thou seen?"

"No, Jarl Ulric," said Sigurd, "but I have listened to brave men who have looked in upon such things. As to one affair, we learned little by little that the proconsul of Britain desired good swordsmen to contend with his trained slaves and with his wild beasts. It was also for his profit to send Saxons as presents to Cæsar to be slain in the great shows of Rome. For this purpose all we were to be entrapped and caged as soon as their hunting party should become strong enough to take us alive. We were to be set upon unawares. Therefore did we sleep by watches, fully armed, for the thing was to be done in the night. So was the idea of Svein, the treacherous, concerning all thy crew."

"He will entrap no more Saxons henceforth," said the jarl. "As for me, I would gladly fight a lion or a tiger. It would be great sport. I will try if I may meet these wonderful beasts before I return to the Northland.

"Thou wilt meet thy lion with full armor," responded Sigurd, "but it is not so in these games of the Romans. There is no fair fighting. They arm thee as they see fit. Often thou art not matched with one man or with one beast, but with odds, that they may see thee overcome or torn. This is their delight concerning prisoners and malefactors which cost them little. They spare their dens of animals and their purchased gladiators that they may more cheaply see much blood. But there is worse than this among them, for they use the scourge upon us, and a man would rather die ten times than be made to feel the stroke of a whip, as if he were a slave."

"If I were indeed lashed," growled Ulric, "it were well for that man, even were he Cæsar, not to come near me in after time if there were a blade within my reach. There might come a sure cast of a spear, and I throw far."

"This scourging," said Sigurd, "is to break the proud spirit of such as thou art. I think thine or mine would not be so destroyed, but rather a red fire kindled in ashes that would smolder for a time. But they know us well, these Romans. A captive Saxon is chained as an untameable wild beast until they push him out of his cage into the arena."

"So slay we all Romans!" exclaimed the jarl. "We will count them but wolves. But I will see many other cities if I may not go to Rome. The wind changeth and I think a storm is upon us."

Soon fiercely howled around them an angry north wind, tossing the sea in great surges, but the trireme proved herself stanch and well behaved. She held on her way swiftly. Often saw they the land, but after one night more Sigurd called Ulric to a bulwark, at the dawn, and he pointed first westerly.

"Seest thou," he said, "yonder high white cliffs? We are in the narrow sea between Britain and Gaul. We have been driven about too much and we have expended days. Now we may drive southward and we may not meet other keels often. The Britons of Gaul are like those of the islands. They are not sea-goers, and they are all under the rule of Cæsar."

"We have no need to strike them," said the jarl. "They are not our errand. We will but sail on as we have planned. Thou hast taught me many things. I thank thee."

The day went by and *The Sword* drew near the land at times, but it was better to keep well away from an unknown coast. All the crew were pleased to discover how swiftly they might travel and how readily they might turn so large a vessel.

"She will do well in battle," they said.

As to the three banks of oars, the jarl angered some by his urgency in compelling all to practice their use, that they might become well skilled.

"He is a hard master of a ship," said some. "Do we not know what to do with oars?" The older men were better satisfied, and they also studied the handling of a trireme.

The next day *The Sword* was not far out from the westerly shore of Gaul and a thing came to Ulric the Jarl as he stood upon the after deck steering and watching the land. He was thinking deeply, also, concerning the gods, and he was remembering those persons whom he had left behind him in the Northland which was now so far away.

"What is this?" arose a sudden inquiry in his mind. "I am not alone! I think that one sitteth by me. I have felt the touch of her hand upon my hair, stroking it. There hath been no voice, but the hand is the hand of a woman and I know it well of old. I will wait and see if she will speak to me. I have hungered for speech with some whom I may not see. I think that of the unseen ones there must be a great multitude and that their land must be wide, but no man knoweth what it may be like. In it is the city of Asgard. There is Valhalla, and there dwell the heroes from innumerable battles. I shall not ever be fully contented until I hear the valkyrias call my name. But first I would have speech with one of these strange gods of the southlands. The Grecians have many, and so have the Romans. I have willed, also, to look upon the face of the god of the Jews, for he is said to be a strong one and very beautiful. O thou that touchest, I pray thee touch me again."

The wind went softly by him and there came a low whisper in his ear so that he heard it thus, as if it had been a voice:

"Son of Odin, I have passed. Have passed."

More heard he not, nor did he see any, but at that hour there was a great silence in the house of Brander in the Northland.

In her chair sat Hilda, as she was wont, but she was very white, and her eyes were shut. Around her stood the household, save that Oswald, the harper, sat with his head bowed upon his harp. Not many men were there, and the women and the maidens did but look at one another and at Hilda, for they knew not whether she were living or dead, and they feared to put hands upon her.

Then opened she her eyes and her lips parted.

"I have seen him," she said, "but the ship is not *The Sword*. I have been as if I were asleep, but it was no dream. Where my heart is there was I, and I will go to him again. Now, when I sleep again, put ye my veil over my face. Let me not fall from my chair, but place me upon my bier and make ready to carry me to the cleft of the rocks. If it may be, I will speak once more before I go."

So went she to sleep and they covered her face, but now the women wailed loudly and all the men of the household were sent for to come to the hall.

"Hilda of the hundred winters hath seen the last outing of the ice," the women said, "and now the grass and the leaves have come. She goeth down to her own and she will see the gods."

A litter was made and they bore her to her room, for she had given the older women instructions and they knew what to do in such a case. The household men came, but they did not stay in the house, for Oswald spoke to them and they went out with him to the place of tombs.

The low hill on which were the standing stones had a face of broken rock seaward. In the middle of this face leaned a tall, flat stone, a slab of limestone, which had been worked to smoothness on its outer side. Upon this surface were many runes graven, in lines and columns, and some of them were like small pictures, and more were like letters of words that were to be read. The stone was exceedingly heavy, and strong men worked with wooden levers to lay it aside without injuring it. When that was done there could be seen a chasm, as if the rock had been cloven to make an entrance for any who would go in. At this the men looked, but as yet they kept their feet away from it.

All over the Northland there are such tombs as was this of the house of Brander the Brave, the sea king, and in them are the bones of the mighty. But in some, as in this, are not buried the heroes after whose names the tombs are called, for they fell upon far-away battlefields or in fights at sea, but at their tombs were made sacrifices to the gods, nevertheless, and the songs to the dead are to be sung there by their kindred. If any man have a hero son, to this place must he come to speak to his father and to the Asas, or he will be accounted nidering and unfit to be a jarl and a leader of men.

Low had sunk the sun when a procession walked slowly away from the house of Brander. The men of best rank and name were proud to be permitted to bear the bier of Hilda, as if she had been a princess; for she was of the race of Odin and she had talked with the gods for a hundred years. Therefore, also, every man wore his full armor; but of the women there were some who carried goblets and pitchers which had been Hilda's, of pottery and of bronze and of silver and of beaten gold. Others there were who carried her best garments, rending them as they came.

"She is not to be burned," said Oswald. "She is to be laid in the inner crypt, with her feet toward the east. Her coffin is of wood, and it was in her room, but I have brought it. Let her be placed therein."

It was a long box made of planks of the fir tree, and it was large enough. In it did they lay the body of Hilda, taking it from the bier. Then the strong men bore it into the cleft of the rocks, but not many were permitted to follow and see. Three fathoms deep was the cleft, and then it widened, making a small room, and this could be seen well, for some of the men bore torches. There were other coffins, and there were bones and skulls uncovered at the sides and in the corners. There were stones also, set up in the form of coffins, and in them were bones and many good weapons, as if to each man had been given shield, ax, sword, spear, helmet, and mail, and vessels of pottery and of metal, with good garments. But the arms and armor were for the greater part marred, bent, broken, and the garments were rent.

"Speak not," said Oswald, "but put down the coffin of Hilda here. The runes on the rock beside it were graven by herself for the memory of Brander the Brave, for she loved him well."

In the coffin were some things placed. Upon it was laid a plank of fir. On this, then, and on the earth at the head were arranged all other matters brought by the women. Every man walked out then except Oswald, and he stood still and spoke to Hilda, but she answered him not. Again he spoke, calling her by name, and those without, in the cleft and beyond it, heard him, and they listened well, but they heard no other voice than his.

"Hilda!" he said again. "Hilda of the hundred winters, daughter of Odin, what sayest thou to Oswald, thy friend?"

They heard no answer, but Oswald came forth and bade them place the stone.

"Set it well," he said, "for it will not be moved again. The house of Brander is ended. There will be no other who will have the right to be buried behind the stone."

None answered him, but the women whispered sadly to one another: "What of Ulric the Jarl?"

The men followed Oswald to the house, for a feast had been prepared in honor of the daughter of Odin, and the tables were set. Other harpers had come, with chiefs and men of rank, but no other harp might sound until after that of Oswald.

The central fire had gone out, but he had bidden them leave the ash heap. It was high and gray, and he sat down by it, bringing his harp nearer. All who were there had heard him often, but never before, they said, had they heard him touch his harp as he did now. The music was wonderful, and with it arose his voice in marvelous power, for he sang of heroes, and of gods, and of the unseen lands where the gods live. Also, before he ceased, he sang of Ulric the Jarl and of the ship *The Sword*, as if even now he could see her going into battle and hear the warhorn of the son of Brander.

So was the passing of Hilda of the hundred years.

Chapter XIV
The Jew and the Greek

"O jarl," said Sigurd, the son of Thorolf, "many days have passed since we entered this sea. Thou hast pleased thy crew by landings at harbors. They have also smitten quiet people against thy will, and uselessly. They are hard to govern."

"The thirst of blood cometh upon them," said the jarl. "I would not slay any without good need. What knowest thou of this place where we are?"

"It is the gate of the world, O jarl," said Sigurd. "We have passed all Spain and much too long time have we been in our voyaging. This great cliff upon the Spanish shore is the rock I named to thee at the beginning. Southward, across this narrow strait, is Africa. The Romans name this rock the Pillars of Hercules. He is of their old heroes, a strong one, a half god. Not as Thor or Odin. He is of the giants."

Many more things said Sigurd, and the vikings thronged around to hear. Of the older men, also, were many who knew this place and who had words to speak. The younger men were exultant and their speech was boisterous; but the face of the jarl grew harder as he heard them, for they had offended him often by their deeds in Gaul and on the coast of Spain, and by their cruelties to peaceable merchant sailors whose keels *The Sword* had overtaken. "I am made a pirate against my will," he had said of these things. "The greatest of the sea kings are not so, for they have many friends and tributaries among the peoples and islands of the Middle Sea." Nevertheless, he now spoke loudly to all.

"Beyond this cape," he said, "is the Middle Sea, which was from the first the destination of our voyage. Glad am I to have come so far out into the world. From this place onward we are as men who sail into a battle. So will every man bind himself to his obedience, lest his neck shall feel a seax."

This was the law of the Northmen upon the sea, and none might complain; but the jarl's hand was upon his sword hilt, and some of the men turned to look at each other for a moment.

Very smooth was the water, for there was no wind. The air was soft and warm. Only one bank of the oars propelled *The Sword*. She was now in no haste, and all who were on board of her felt their hearts beat with rejoicing. To most of them this was their first long war cruise, and all things were new, so that they watched eagerly for that which might be next to come.

"O jarl," said Tostig the Red, "beyond all doubt we shall soon see triremes of the Romans. Will they not at once inquire concerning us? Wilt thou avoid such a keel or wilt thou hasten into a battle?"

"I have considered well," said the jarl. "Of a merchantman we may exact tribute, but we need not always destroy. It is not the way of sea kings. Prisoners we take not any. A warship of Cæsar we must strike in her middle, without warning, that she may go down speedily and that too wide a report of our coming may not be given to those who would pursue us with a fleet. I know not, after such delays, that we are the first of the vikings this year in the Middle Sea."

"O jarl," said Knud the Bear, "care not for that overmuch. We will but go the farther into the sea. I am with thee in thy saying that we must sail to the eastern shore of all these waters."

The jarl lifted his war horn and blew long and loudly and his face grew brighter.

"To Asgard!" he shouted. "To the city of the gods! And we will smite the Romans."

Shield clashed on shield. Horn after horn was blown. The vikings shouted joyously and Sigurd the son of Thorolf lifted his great voice in a song of war.

"Easterly!" commanded Ulric to him who was steering *The Sword*. "The gods of the Northland are with us and our voyage hath been well prospered."

On floated the good ship, but she seemed to be sailing over a sea of peace, so quiet and so beautiful were both sky and water. An hour went by, and now Ulric, sitting on the fore deck, sprang suddenly to his feet, for there came a shout down from Wulf the Skater above the sail upon the foremast:

"O jarl! A sail! Eastward. And no other sail is with her."

"She is our prize!" shouted the jarl. "We may not fail of taking the first keel that we meet, whatever she may be. A man to every oar! But let those who hold the spears put on Roman helmets speedily. Open the sheaves of arrows. Bring out spears in abundance."

Other commands he gave, and there was no discontented man on board; none who was not willing to do the bidding of his jarl in battle. Then were they glad to be led by a son of Odin; and a hard ruler in a quiet time may be the captain men seek after if an enemy is nearing.

The jarl bade the rowers to row, but steadily, not wasting their strength, while the Roman helmets were brought out from the stores of *The Sword*, and the vikings laughed merrily at each other in this strange disguising.

Very soon they were near enough to learn the kind and the action of this keel which they were to contend with. She was not now attempting to either come or go, but she was drifting along over the calm water with her sails flapping lazily against her mast. The vikings might see, however, that her decks were full of armed men, and that she was a larger vessel than had ever been seen in the seas of the North. Vast was her length and breadth, and she carried five banks of oars instead of three, for this was one of the new quinqueremes which Cæsar had builded for the conveyance of his legions. She was planned, therefore, more for carrying than for speed, although her weight and force might be terrible to crash against another vessel. She was high above the water, like a tower that would be difficult to scale. She had two masts, and on these were bulwarked platforms for archers and slingers. She was as much more than a match for Ulric's keel as had this been for *The Sword*, the first, the low-built ship with which he had sailed from the Northland behind the outing ice, only that the quinquereme was less readily to be turned about.

The officer in command of the Roman warship knew no fear of any foe afloat, so sure was he of the superior strength of his vessel, and now he could have no suspicion that an enemy of Rome had come in at this time of the year through the gates of Hercules. He came to the after deck of the quinquereme when his outlooks called him, and his answer to them was haughty.

"Why did ye disturb me?" he asked. "It is but one of the triremes of Licinius coming back with tidings for Cæsar. We may hail her, in her passing, but we may not hinder her. Cæsar is careful of the bearers of his messages. Men die early who meddle with that which doth not concern them."

No change was made, therefore, in the handling of the quinquereme. The rowers sat idly at their places, ready for any orders which might come, but allowing their oars, longer and shorter, to hang in the water, or to rest hauled inboard.

Now there came wind enough to fill the sail, and she slipped along better, while the sailing master came and stood by the haughty centurion.

"They are in haste," he said. "They row swiftly."

"Well they may," replied the officer, "whether Licinius hath had good fortune or whether the fates have been against him. I would not be sent to Britain. Too many have gone to ruin on that island."

"It is a bad place," said the seaman, "and all those seas are full of Saxons. They are fierce barbarians, but they make good gladiators. I would crucify them all."

"Never spare thou a Saxon," said the centurion. "They are food for the sword. Slay every one thou findest on land or sea. Mars be my witness, I will spare not one."

For life or for death, therefore, was the swift coming of *The Sword*. The Saxons must overcome the quinquereme, or escape her in some manner, or they must die without mercy, and this they knew well.

"A strong force on board of her," said the centurion, as *The Sword* drew nearer. "But I see no standard save an eagle on the fore deck. She hath no officers of rank, and that is strange. I will hail her. Sound thou thy trumpet, trumpeter!"

Loudly rang out the trumpet call, and it was answered by a trumpet from *The Sword*. But here too was a mystery. The viking who blew was better used to his war horn, and he knew not that instead of a peaceful greeting he had sounded the notes that bid a Roman legion close with an enemy, to win or die.

The centurion sprang to his feet, for he had been seated.

"Rowers!" he shouted, "to your places! Here is a strange matter! There is evil tidings!"

Other swift orders followed, and every legionary on board the quinquereme was at his post, for the Romans are not easily to be taken by surprise because of their strict discipline and their rule for perpetual readiness by day or night.

"She is a smaller craft than ours," said the sailing master, "but she is a good one. I know her well, and her sign is Minerva. Who now commandeth her I know not."

In that she was so well known as one of the triremes of the Roman fleet in British waters was now a gift of the gods to *The Sword* and to the Saxons. Not the centurion nor his officers nor any seaman or legionary on board the quinquereme had any thought or suspicion of that which was to come.

Onward flashed the swift, strong vessel, the oars of the Northmen biting well the sparkling sea. Fiercely rang the Roman trumpet, warning them to change their course lest there should be a collision. Hoarse were the angry shouts of the astonished centurion, but vain were his too-long delayed orders to his rowers and his steersman.

On the fore deck of *The Sword* stood now a tall shape, wearing indeed the helmet of a Roman, but putting to his lips a war horn of the North. Beside him stood what seemed a giant brandishing a spear. The blast was sounded and then sped the spear. A hundred more were hurled from *The Sword* at the Romans on the decks of the quinquereme. The viking rowers pulled with their might.

Crash! With a breaking of timbers, a braying of horns, a chorus of mocking war cries, the quinquereme was smitten amidships with a force which threw her legionaries prostrate and sent her rowers from their oars.

The centurion was pierced by the spear of Sigurd. The steersman fell by a heavy pebble cast by Knud the Bear. The sailing master went down twice smitten.

Up to the masthead of *The Sword* shot the White Horse flag of the Saxons, and the good ship sprang backward with a great rebound, helped quickly by the rowers.

"We have stricken her!" shouted Ulric. "The sea poureth into her. Back! Strike not again! It is enough!"

As the lightning from a clear sky, so was the deathblow given to the pride and strength of the quinquereme. As a warrior stabbed to the heart was she as she leaned over, and as the fatal blue tide poured in through the deep wound in her side. There was no stanching it. There was no hope. They who had purposed to slay all Saxons were themselves to die. On the decks and at the bulwarks, amazed, confounded, the Roman soldiers and sailors stood and gazed in silence at their utterly mysterious destroyer. Here was a riddle of the fates and furies which none might read. They knew not even the flag of this strange pirate keel. They only knew that they were going down.

On the stern of the quinquereme stood three men who were not in armor. They were bearded men and they wore turbans, and they spoke to each other in another tongue than the Latin.

"We may escape," one of them said. "The god of Israel hath heard. We are not to be crucified. Let us plunge in and go to yonder ship from Tarshish. Ben Ezra, what sayest thou?"

"Follow me," said Ben Ezra, "ere this accursed quinquereme goeth down bearing us with it. On this side, while the Romans are gazing. Take each two short oars. We have somewhat to bear with us. Get beyond a spear cast as soon as we may."

He was a short man, and old, but his eyes were bright and he seemed a brave one. His two companions were youths. Into the water they slipped silently, as he had said, and they swam well, partly upheld by the pieces of wood.

The Sword was not receding, but her rowers were pulling easily as Wulf the Skater steered her around and past the quinquereme. No more spears were thrown nor did any arrows fly, but there was a sounding of war horns.

Brave must have been the trumpeter of the legionaries, for he lifted his trumpet and answered defiantly, even while the water rushed in through the fatal gap in the wooden wall of his sinking vessel.

"We shall have no prisoners," said Knud the Bear. "I would I knew if they had taken any. What if captured Saxons were on board of her?"

"Not at this season of the year," said Sigurd. "But what are those? Look yonder! The Romans wear no turbans. O jarl."

"Bid them on board!" shouted Ulric. "I would question them. Throw them a rope!"

It was a long thong of twisted hide that was cast out toward Ben Ezra and his companions, but it came too late. In a moment their escape had been seen by the legionaries. They were true to their soldier discipline. They themselves must die, but it was their duty to prevent the departure from the quinquereme of any prisoners. Such as attempted it must be slain. So the pila flew fast and even arrows were sent.

"Ben Ezra, I am smitten!" gasped one of the younger swimmers.

"Thou?" groaned Ben Ezra; but in an instant more, he added: "O God of Hosts! My son also! My only son! My Benjamin!"

"Father!" cried out the second youth, in agony, "the spear of the heathen! I die! I die!"

"My son!" again mourned Ben Ezra. "I care not to live! Let me perish with thee!"

Nevertheless, he had grasped the thong of twisted hide and the instinct of self-preservation was strong enough to make him cling to it. Moreover, he had taken three of the short oars, instead of only two, and on these he was buoying up what seemed a small casket of wood. He was doing so with difficulty, and now he exclaimed:

"The jewels! The gold! I must not lose them. They are priceless. The centurion knoweth not that I have them. Not only mine are here, but the prætor's also. O Jehovah of Hosts! Thou hast smitten the heathen! That spear fell short. Ha!"

A pilum struck the oars and Ben Ezra struggled hard for his treasure, but he succeeded in retaining it.

Down sank the two who had been stricken, and in a moment more a strong hand of a viking grasped the old man by the shoulder.

"Courage! Thou art safe!" he shouted.

"This first!" said Ben Ezra, trying to hand him the casket. "It is worth their quinquereme! Ye are Northmen. I am a Jew of Salonica. The Roman robbers plundered my ship unlawfully, and me they meant to crucify, the better to claim my goods. Help me in. I am faint. O my son!"

They pulled him up over the bulwark with some difficulty, but he spoke not nor did he seem to see anything until he was sure that his casket was in the hands of Ulric the Jarl.

"Open it not now, O captain of the Saxons," said Ben Ezra. "I have much to say to thee. When yonder Roman keel goeth down I am no longer in peril, for I have kept the law. But the Prætor Sergius of Spain and the commanders of the fleet rob whomsoever they will. Praise God, she sinketh fast!"

It was even so. The quinquereme was settling in the water and her crew could cast spears no more. They did but stand still and gaze at the sea and at their strange enemy, but some of them even now called loudly upon their gods, as if there could be any help from them.

She was a splendid vessel, and her figurehead was a gilded Neptune with a trident which looked as if it might be of gold. Rich indeed were her carvings and the very handles of her oars were graven and gilded. She was high at prow and stern, a castle of the sea, and the wonder was that she had been cloven at a blow. A lighter vessel with a ram less sharp would perhaps have rebounded without doing serious harm, but the beak of *The Sword* was like a vast spearhead and it had been driven hard by the strong arms of the Saxons and by the weight of the trireme.

The middle parts of the foundering ship could no longer be occupied, and the ill-fortuned men who were to perish were now crowded densely fore and aft. Even now, however, the legionaries preserved their discipline, and they slew some of the hired rowers who pressed them in too disorderly a manner. These were deaths which were but somewhat hastened, yet military order was restored thereby, for the rowers feared the strokes of the pila and the broadswords.

"They go!" muttered Ben Ezra. "So perish all who afflict the chosen people. Rome will yet fall before the sword of Judah and the spear of Israel. Jehovah standeth for his elect. He will have vengeance upon the heathen. He will smite through kings in the day of his wrath."

"O Ulric the Jarl," said Sigurd, "thou mayest trust the Jew. He hateth Rome as we do."

Then came Ulric nearer, still watching the quinquereme, but he spoke words to Ben Ezra in a tongue that those who stood by understood not.

"Father Abraham!" exclaimed the old man, "where didst thou learn Hebrew? I like thee well for this. After yonder quinquereme goeth down thou hast cause to consult with me. There are matters thou knowest not."

"Odin!" exclaimed Ulric. "Watch! She is pitching forward! They are falling!"

In a mass together, as the decks slanted, plunged the overcrowded Romans. It was of no avail to struggle or to thrust with sharp weapons. Angrily, loudly, in his last desperate valor, blew the trumpeter his final defiance, but as the blast ended the prow of the quinquereme went madly under, lifting the stern out of water for a moment. Then went up a great cry and quickly naught could be seen save a few heads of swimmers dotting the blue water.

The helmets disappeared first because of the weight of armor, but the Saxons cast no spears at any who remained, and some who were bareheaded seemed to be swimming well.

"He hath golden hair," said Sigurd, pointing at one of these. "He is no Roman. I will call to him in Greek—"

"Bid him come," said Ulric, "if so be he is not a Roman. He may live."

Sigurd sent to the swimmer a few words in a smoothly sounding tongue, and the golden-haired youth struck out for the trireme, but he was followed by twain who were dark and who cursed him in Latin. Well for him that he was the better swimmer, for they strove to grapple him that he might die with them. He might not even then have fully escaped but that Ulric knew their meaning and said to Tostig the Red:

"I have no spear! Smite those two Romans and save the Greek."

Not one spear but twenty sped in answer to that command, and the youth came nearer alone, for there were none to follow him.

"He was a rower," said Ben Ezra. "He is a slave of the centurion. He is from Corinth. It is perilous to spare him, lest he might tell of this thy doing."

"What harm?" asked Ulric. "Can the Romans do more than destroy? I will myself tell them that this is the third of their warships that I have taken from them."

"Thou sailest in one," replied Ben Ezra, glancing around him. "Thou and thine are men of valor. But the like of this hath never before been seen. A Saxon crew in a Roman trireme fighting the ships of Cæsar! Mayest thou have a fleet and smite them in the Tiber itself! Now sail thou on, for there is another quinquereme and she may not be far away. Avoid her, lest thou fall into a snare of presumption."

"Not I," laughed Ulric. "We have done enough this day. Come thou and talk with me, and then I will have speech with the Greek."

The young Corinthian was now aft among the men, and Sigurd was talking freely with him. There were others of the older vikings who had learned words of the Grecian tongue, and they, too, were both speaking and hearing.

Into a cabin under the fore deck went Ulric and Ben Ezra, and there they were alone, for none was permitted to follow them.

Chapter XV
The Storm in the Middle Sea

Wide but not high was the space which was inclosed under the fore deck of the trireme *The Sword*. Beneath its floor was much room for stowage. The other decks, also, had under them good cabins, suited to many purposes. The decking amidships, whereon tier above tier were made the seats and standing places of the rowers, had openings covered by hatches. Down through these, by ladders, might be entered a great hollow, and this was for cargo and for sleeping room. Very different was all this from the planning of any vessels which hitherto had been builded in the Northland. In the cabins under the fore deck were bunks for sailors and soldiers, but all the garnishing was plain. Here, also, there were stores of weapons, with boxes and bales of merchandise. The cabins under the after deck were divided and garnished for the uses of officers and men of rank who might at any time be on board.

It was not long after the sinking of the quinquereme that the jarl and the Jew, Ben Ezra, stood face to face in a small room under the fore deck. Steadily looked Ulric into the face of the Jew.

"He is old, but he is not aged," was his thought concerning this man. "He is tall and broad and strong and heavily bearded. His face proveth for him high intelligence, but it hath deep marks which one may read. I think him a subtle man and a keeper of secrets. He is a man of rank among his own people, for common men are not as he is. I am glad of him."

"O jarl of the Saxons," said Ben Ezra, "I have blessed thee in my soul, by Jehovah my God, that thou hast utterly smitten to death these Romans. Thou didst wisely not to spare any, as they would not have spared thee or thine. Thou mayest be sure that if so much as one of them were on board thy ship, he were a danger. I will tell thee of myself."

"Say on," said Ulric, "but speak truly, that it may be well with thee."

"Leader of men," said Ben Ezra, "my life hangeth upon thy life. I am one with thee. I do but take care for myself in that I am truthful. I was informed against in Spain to the prætor because I was rich. I was seized, but I and my son and a Jewish youth, the son of a rabbi, escaped from our destroyers.

My ship was ready laden and we sailed in the night. The quinquereme was faster and she overtook us. All were slain but we three, for they were overfull with rowers and soldiers and cared not for more slaves. Even to have escaped the prætor was to be doomed to crucifixion; but they had not yet scourged us, waiting an opportunity. O my son! My son! That he might have been spared! For they have slain his mother and his brethren. He was my Benjamin! My youngest son! The joy of my heart!"

"He was slain by a spear," said Ulric, to comfort him. "He died not on a bed, that thou shouldst mourn so much for him. Thy god hath done well by thee. I saw him swimming bravely till the pilum struck him."

"And the youth, the son of the rabbi Joseph, of Jerusalem!" groaned Ben Ezra. "What shall I say to his father? A fair boy and well favored! They are merciless, for he had done them no wrong."

"Little careth a Roman for that," growled Ulric. "Who is this Greek?"

"He was a bondslave of the centurion of the band of legionaries on the quinquereme," said Ben Ezra. "His father was a rich man in Corinth, but the proconsul lusted after his goods and he was accused. He was but slain, not crucified, but his older sons went to the arena to feed lions, and this Lysias, for his youth and beauty, was kept alive, if a man be indeed living who is slave to a Roman. Thou mayest trust him that he hated his master."

"For what part didst thou intend to sail," asked Ulric; "seeing the Romans could have found thee anywhere on the earth?"

"Not so," replied Ben Ezra. "I were safe if once I were in Judea or Galilee."

"And where are they?" asked Ulric.

"At the eastern shore of this sea, as thou shouldst know," said Ben Ezra, "is the land of my people. In it are many cities and mountains, and its provinces are under different governors. He who is threatened by one needs but to flee to another if he can take a gift with him. I have a gift for thee wherewith thou couldst buy a consul, if so be he had no opportunity to rob thee. My goods, all but one casket, went down with the quinquereme. In that casket are gems of my own—"

"I want them not," said Ulric. "They are not my prizes. I struck no blow for them. Keep thou that which is thine own. I am a Saxon, not a pirate."

"Thou art a sea king," replied Ben Ezra. "I have had many dealings with such as thou art. They are not like other men, for they keep faith with strangers. But this, also, I tell thee: as the Roman ship began to fill the centurion went mad, it seemed, for he took from his crypt in his cabin his own jewels and some that the prætor would have sent to Cæsar to buy a pardon for some of his offenses. These, also, went into my casket, and he placed it on the deck and by it a small bag of gold. With aid of three oars for floats and with strong swimming I rescued all, and here they are. Even the centurion knew not their value."

"I know what gold coins are," said Ulric, as the bag was opened before him. "Oswald the Harper taught me concerning money. Are these thine?"

"Nay," said Ben Ezra, "they are thine, for they belonged to the centurion. Of the stones I will show thee. That sardonyx is mine. It was graven in Egypt, and on it are words of the wisdom of the priests of Isis."

"Runes like Hilda's!" exclaimed Ulric, gazing earnestly upon the characters which blended with the varying tints of the beautifully polished stone. "Canst thou read them?"

"Not so," said Ben Ezra, "but this sardius, also, is mine. It is a stone of the temple of Jehovah at Jerusalem, and on it is his most holy name. Touch it not, for thou art of the heathen."

"What have I to do," asked Ulric, "with a matter belonging to your god? I have thought that I would like to see him some day. I am sailing to find the city of the gods. He will be there, perhaps, among them."

"He is a great King above all gods," said Ben Ezra, reverently, but his eyes were dwelling upon the glowing, blood-red tint of the inestimable gem which bore the holy name.

"Odin!" exclaimed Ulric. "I think your god would be on good terms with the gods of the North, for I have heard well of him. Thou mayest tell me more about him some day. But now thou mayest tie up thy gems and give me mine. I have the ship to command, and I care not overmuch for stones."

"My sardius alone is worth thy trireme," said Ben Ezra, frankly. "Keep thou thy treasure carefully and a day may come when it will be of use to thee. Divide not with thy men. Give them other matters."

Ulric laughed loudly as he responded: "Good faith is kept among us, O Jew, but my vikings are welcome to all I possess. The ship itself is theirs, if I am slain, and they will carry to my own house anything that belongs to me. We are not thieves, like the men of the southlands."

Ben Ezra looked into his face and said: "Verily thou art my friend! I have not met any like unto thee. I would thou mayest go with me to the city of my God, to Jerusalem. There is his temple and it is the wonder of the earth."

"So have I heard," said Ulric, joyously. "I think I will go and see. But whither shall I steer at this hour?"

"Toward the coast of Africa," said Ben Ezra. "Thither was I sailing. There are old harbors there for which the Romans take no care. In them are pirate peoples, foes of Rome, ancient Carthaginians, Egyptians, Libyans; but thou wilt be friends with them."

"*The Sword* will sail for Africa," said Ulric; "but as for pirates, we will see to that matter."

"Verily there is none like thee!" exclaimed the Jew. "Thou art like Saul, the son of Kish!"

Into a small sack of deerskin did Ulric put his jewels, looking at them one by one and admiring their great beauty.

"Never saw I such before," he said. "They are such as kings wear in the southlands. I think the gods must have many of them. These white ones are pearls, and they are lustrous. The green stones are emeralds."

"They are of great value," said Ben Ezra. "Especially that large, flat-faced one. It is engraven with the sign of the sun, and it came therefore from Persia. Thy pearls are from the East, and they are wonderful, but some of mine are as large."

"I will keep the gold in my belt pouch," said Ulric, "and thou shalt teach me to pay with it."

"Thou shalt not be cheated," said Ben Ezra.

Then he took his closed casket with him and walked to the after cabin, for in that was to be his abiding place, and he said that he would mourn there for his son.

"Southward!" shouted Ulric to the viking at the rudder of the trireme. "We have done well this day, and the night cometh."

A wind had arisen and the sails were full, but the men did not seem to be idle. They busied themselves with the tackle and with the stowing of the ship, but every now and then each one would step out on deck or lean over a bulwark to look long and earnestly across the sparkling sea.

"This water is very blue," said Tostig the Red, "and so is the sky. O Knud, thou hast put away thy bearskins."

"Aye," said Knud, "but how canst thou bear thy mail in such a heat as this? I found this jacket of silk in the after cabin. It is cool and it is fine."

"Red as blood it is," said Tostig, "but it would not keep out an arrow. Thou dost never care much for armor."

"A shield is enough," replied Knud, "and I can catch arrows on my seax. I would not be overweighted. I trust the gods will soon send us another fight. I would get hand to hand with some good fighter. There is more pleasure in killing with steel than with the prow of a ship."

The jarl gave orders concerning many things, and then he spoke to Lysias the Greek. The youth had seated himself in a hollow place between two oar benches and his face was in his hands, for he was weeping.

"Not often do men weep in the Northland," said Ulric, sternly. "I have heard that the Greeks are brave. Why mournest thou? Hast thou not had good vengeance upon the Romans this day? Not one of them escaped. Thou shouldst rather be rejoicing."

"Alas! Alas!" murmured the beautiful youth. "Corinth! My Sapphira! I shall never see her again!"

"She was thy love?" said Ulric, softening somewhat. "I never had a love save Hilda, the saga woman, and she was a hundred years old. I loved her well. Where is thy Sapphira?"

"She was more lovely than a dream!" said Lysias, looking up through his tears. "Her father was Licander, the astrologer, and she was like a star. He knew the heavens and the stars in their courses, and he read their signs. But he foretold to the Romans their Parthian defeat and they slew him for his bad augury. Of his kindred they left not one, and Sapphira they sold for a slave to Pontius Pilatus, the procurator of Judea. I care not to live, for I have been scourged and I have lost my love."

Even as he spoke he threw off a light robe of linen which had covered him, and Ulric saw the half-healed, festering lines of the Roman scourge all over the flesh of Lysias.

"Thou mayest well weep for that!" exclaimed Ulric, "if thou art the son of a free warrior."

"I did stab three in Spain," said Lysias, "and I had plotted to sink the quinquereme, for she had a bad leak which might be opened."

"Get thou up!" said Ulric. "I will gird thee with a sword and give thee a shield and spear. When thy scourgings are healed thou shalt have mail. Thou art strong."

"I have won foot races," said Lysias, rising, "and I can ride any wild horse. I am a bowman and I can cast the javelin far and truly."

"Be more contented, then," said Ulric. "I will give thee chances to strike Romans. There is no need for thee to mourn."

"Thou knowest not love," said Lysias; "but I thank thee, and I would have weapons."

"Come with me," said Ulric, and they went together to the after cabin.

There were doors by which this might be closed, but one of these was open and they went in. Then it could be seen that this cabin space, which was large, was divided into four apartments by strong wooden walls, each having a door and a window, and in the windows were small sheets of glass to let in light and keep out the sea. This first room where they now were had been the place prepared for some person of high rank to occupy, an officer in command of the ship or a high passenger. It was finished in carved wood, with hangings of silk and linen of many colors and of fine needlework. Here, also, were lamps that hung in cressets, and there were fixed tables and soft couches and many fair weapons and pieces of splendid armor. None of these had the jarl worn as yet save a helmet and a rare coat of linked mail richly gilded. Now he selected a good belt, with a sheath and sword, and a long sheathed dagger.

"Throw off thy robe," he said to Lysias. "Put on this tunic and the sandals. Belt thee with these."

So the youth did, and it could be seen that his shape was not only comely, but molded for great vigor. The muscles stood out upon his arms and shoulders and Ulric himself was but a head the taller.

"These will soon heal," said Ulric, examining the lash cuts. "Oil them well. I will aid thee. They are now not deep. Thou art a good swimmer. I noted thee in the water. Here are thy shield and spear."

"They are Greek, not Roman," said Lysias. "I am glad of that. I want a bow and arrows."

"A quiver and a bow are here," said Ulric. "But the arrows are long and so is the bow. See if thou canst bend and string it."

"That can I?" exclaimed Lysias, seizing the bow. "It is from Sparta, for only the Lacedemonians make them of this length. The Parthian bows are shorter, for horsemen, but only a Parthian can bend them—or such as I. We are of the ancient Corinthian archers, and there were none better on earth."

He was bending the strong wood as he talked, and Ulric saw that he did so and put on the string of twisted silk with ease. Then took he an arrow from the quiver and drew it to the head.

"Thou art the captain," he said. "Thy men call thee the jarl and say thou art of the sons of their gods. Canst thou send this arrow farther than I can?"

"I will handle thy bow," said Ulric.

He, too, unstrung and strung it and drew the arrow to the head, but he said, thoughtfully:

"Thou of the Greeks, I understand thy saying concerning skill. I am many times stronger than thou art, and yet I think thee the better bowman. I will call on thee if I would have a sure arrow sent."

Lysias lifted the spear, which was a fathom long, and light, but he looked around the room and found more of the same pattern and made a bundle of them.

"They are well made," he said, "and their points are of good steel. I once threw one like these through the heart of a man from Athens. He was an enemy of my father. I met him on the seashore and I was quicker than he in casting. He should have worn a thicker breastplate."

"Hah!" laughed Ulric. "I am a spearman, but I prefer the North spear and the pilum."

"I like them," said Lysias, "but I know one man that can outthrow thee. He is a Roman knight named Pontius, and they call him the spearman. He is the procurator I told thee of. I would I might live until I can kill him. He liveth now in Jerusalem."

"Thither go I!" exclaimed Ulric. "I have promised Ben Ezra that I will take him to his own, and I must go to that city and see the temple. I have it in mind that I may see his god. They say he is a good god and a great fighter like Thor."

"I have heard much of him," said Lysias, "but he is more like Jupiter. If thou wilt land at the island Paphos, I will show thee his statue and thou canst see what he is like. We shall hear his voice thunder if I read this weather rightly."

"Then he is Thor!" said Ulric, turning to the door. "Come! I know not the weather signs of this sea."

Out they went and Lysias glanced around the sky. His face was brighter now and he stepped firmly like a warrior.

"O jarl," he shouted, "I am a seaman also. Take down thy sails quickly! Put out a bank of oars. Bid thy steersman keep the head of thy keel southward, for from thence cometh a tempest. The sky will darken rapidly."

"The Greek is right!" shouted Sigurd. "I had forgotten the sign of such a storm, but I call it to mind. It is a strong one."

Down came the sails, out went the oars, and the thick haze on the water southerly, which had been sunlit and fair to look upon, shot up toward the middle heaven, blackening as it went.

"O jarl," said Wulf the Skater, "thank the gods! We are to see a kind of storm that we do not have in our own seas."

"Fine storms come to us in midsummer," said Ulric, "and they roar well in the fiords. Will the anger of Thor be louder here? The Greek saith that his Jupiter can thunder, and the Jew told me that his Jehovah is also a thunderer. Are they of kin? They who speak the same tongue are of one house."

The Greek was now standing by the anvil and hammer on the fore deck.

"The sign of this ship was Minerva," he muttered, "but the Saxons have given it to Vulcan. If yonder cloud is indeed of the wind from the African desert we may yet wish that Neptune were our steersman. But what care I for the gods? They were never yet of any use to me. My father made many sacrifices, but the Romans slew him."

There now were sails in sight, but these were fast furling. Most of them were small, but one, at the greater distance, had seemed much wider than the rest.

"I have been watching her," said Sigurd to Ulric, speaking of this craft. "I am not young, but my eyes are the eyes of a falcon. Now that her sail is down her oars are out and she steereth toward us. The storm will give her oarsmen enough to do."

"But we must watch her," said Ulric. "Even a merchantman might seek our company, but she may be a warship."

"So may some of these lesser keels be of the pirates of these coasts," said Sigurd. "They are many, and we do well if we smite them, for often they are good captures."

"Here cometh the wind!" shouted Knud the Bear, exultingly. "The foam flyeth!"

First came a sheeted flash of the blinding lightning, and after that closely followed a deep-throated reverberant peal of thunder.

"The voice of Jah!" muttered Ben Ezra. "He hath spoken from his high place."

"Jupiter the Thunderer!" exclaimed Lysias, still standing by the hammer of Thor as if for protection. "I fear him only at such hours as this; but he is a god of the Romans and I am a Greek. Evil are all gods or I should not have lost my Sapphira. Evil are they and wicked, and they hate men, for they destroy us. There is no man but must die, and if the gods were good, we might live. But these Saxons are brave seamen!"

Little cared they for storms, these sons of the sea kings. They shouted and they sang as if they were in a battle, while the waves grew mad and boiled frothing around the high wooden walls of *The Sword*. Her head was kept toward the wind and she rode the billows like a vast waterfowl, for the Roman shipbuilders were well skilled.

Less easy must have been the course of a keel that strove to cross the surges with her side to the wind, and it now could be seen that the large stranger was laboring and that now and then waves broke over her.

"She bringeth small peril to us," said the jarl. "We will row with but one bank of oars. Let their rowers weary themselves with three. The trumpeter on her fore deck soundeth a signal."

"Of what good," laughed Wulf the Skater, "is the blowing of a horn in such a gale as this?"

"He sendeth us a signal to heave to and wait for them," said Sigurd. "What sayest thou concerning this fellow, O Jew?"

"I think her one of the cruisers sent out by the proconsul of Spain," replied Ben Ezra. "They are all weaker vessels than this, but they are swift. They protect merchantmen from the African pirates to rob all for the proconsul."

The air grew darker, denser, and the salt spray flew into all faces, but the jarl stood upon the after deck and blew upon his war horn a blast louder than that of the Roman trumpet.

"Thy horn be exalted!" shouted Ben Ezra. "It is as the horn of a king! May Jehovah of Hosts be with thee, thou mighty man of valor! Sound again! Let these heathen know that we fear them not."

"But for the storm we might strike them," growled Sigurd. "It is ill to let such a prey go by us."

Now was there also a change in the appearance of Ben Ezra. He stood by the jarl as erect as a pine tree. From the stores of *The Sword* he had provided himself with arms and armor of the best, by permission of Ulric. The visor of his brazen helmet was open and it might be seen that his dark face glowed like youth as he gazed angrily at the enemy.

"He is a warrior!" exclaimed Tostig the Red. "I like him well. I think he might strike a good blow with that long crooked sword which he hath found. I saw it, but I preferred a straight blade. The shield lifteth lightly in his hand and his mail coat fitteth him. He hath put brazen guarders upon his arms and legs. A small man should avoid such as he in the press of battle."

So said others of the vikings, but they were watching more closely the Roman keel.

The trumpeter sounded several times and as often did they send back defiances from their war horns.

"O jarl," said Lysias, "this is the storm which cometh from the African desert. It is not like any other. Not only is there much thunder and terrible lightning and strong wind, but I have felt sharp sand upon my face. It will blow long and hard, and the waves will not go down, but there will be no more rain. The sky is clearing."

"Thou knowest the storms of thine own sea," said Knud the Bear; "but are we far from land?"

"No man knoweth that," said Lysias; "but here cometh the Roman, like a fool. I would thy jarl might strike him. O jarl, may I use the bow?"

"When thou canst," said Ulric, "but the distance is yet too great."

Like fierce and angry music rang out the laugh of the Greek, but his arrow was on the string and he raised the bow.

The Sword sank heavily into the trough of a sea wave and the Roman keel was lifted high upon a surge, just as a long, vivid sheet of lightning seemed to bring her nearer by its brightness. Her steersman was a giant, unarmored, straining hard at her tiller and bracing himself. At him was Ulric looking when suddenly he threw up his hands, letting the tiller go, and the feathered shaft of the young Greek's long arrow quivered against his naked bosom.

"Odin! Well shot!" shouted Ulric, but the bowstring twanged again and another Roman fell upon the deck beside the dead steersman.

Left to itself and to the will of the wind and the waves, around swung the keel of the Romans, while a great surge poured over her bulwarks and her rowers were hurled from their seats. Wild was their shouting and another surge poured in.

"Strike her not!" said Sigurd. "Be thou prudent with thine own keel, lest thou shouldst be in some manner disabled. Let the Greek send his arrows, but steer upon thy course."

Ulric so ordered, but shaft after shaft did Lysias send, not all of them hitting, but not all failing of a mark. Other war horns than that of Ulric were sounding and other bows were also quickly plying.

"I think," said Tostig the Red, "that we have no better bowman than this Greek. He will be a good help in a sea fight. I like well to see his long arrows go so straight to their places. Then the mark goeth down and it is time to laugh."

The Roman rowers were toiling hard to recover control of their vessel, but the Saxons knew little of the astonishment and dismay that reigned on board of her. Her crew had not thought of an open enemy at the first. They had deemed *The Sword* a friend until the sounding of the jarl's war horn. Even then they had expected no resistance, at least no attack, until their steersman fell and a man of rank near him was pierced by an arrow.

Better than a sailing vessel can a rowed keel turn her head to the waves, however, and before long the Romans were once more striving to overtake the Saxons.

Chapter XVI
The Dead God in Africa

Clouds without rain swept fast across the sky and the waves followed *The Sword* as if they willed to overwhelm her. Well was it that her stern was so high and that she was strongly builded. It had seemed, also, that no sea harm had befallen her pursuer, but now the darkness deepened and the watchers on *The Sword* could no longer discern the Roman.

"O jarl," said Sigurd, "it is a time for prudence. This flying sand telleth of some shore, I think, at no great distance."

"It might be carried far by such a wind," said Ulric. "But Ben Ezra told me of great cities in Africa which have been buried by the sand blown from the inner deserts."

"What further counsel hath he?" asked Sigurd.

"Answer him, thou," said the jarl to Ben Ezra.

"O warrior of the Saxons," said the Jew, "thou sayest that thou hast sailed these seas aforetime. Thou mayest know that the presence of one Roman trireme portendeth the speedy gathering of a fleet. It were well to destroy this one if she cometh near us again. But we have now escaped her pursuing. Let her watchers not see this ship again. I would advise that we now go eastward by the stars, for we may note them at times through the rifts in the clouds."

"I will so order," said the jarl. "I were not wise to risk harming my own keel by a battle among these high waves. It is a peril to a ship to be dashed against even one heavy timber where the aim cannot be made certain. Moreover, we have been long at sea and it were well to seek a harbor."

Ben Ezra said no more, now that his counsel was approved. The head of *The Sword* was turned eastward and all the oars were plying. Neither was the wind now so much against her, but the waves were still tumultuous. Fast waned the night, growing darker as it passed, and the jarl himself remained at the helm.

"I go onward into an unknown sea," he thought. "Who may tell what may be before me? Dawn cometh. There is gray light. O watcher!"

Answered him then not a Saxon, but the deep voice of Ben Ezra from the foremast.

"O jarl! A fire! Hold! We near a land!"

"Cease rowing, all!" shouted Ulric. "O Jew, look again. What seest thou?"

"Only a dim fire, far in the southward. It is a guide for us, but we may seek it cautiously. The wind goeth down."

"It is so," said Knud the Bear. "It was a hot wind, and this air is cooler. I thought we were sailing into a furnace."

"The desert is like a furnace, I have heard," said Sigurd. "Men burn up in it and all horses die; but lions live there. How can any beast live in a land of fire?"

"I know not," said Ulric, "but yonder is a brighter streak of dawn. We shall soon know if the Romans are near us. We may slay them if the water becometh smooth enough for a good fight."

"It would be a grief to all men," said Tostig the Red, "if we lost an opportunity. But if this be land, I want some beef."

"Good!" exclaimed an old viking. "We had many cattle on the Gaulish coast, but in Spain we got little but sheep. Hereaway may be found cattle. We may throw a net, and we may find fishes."

The jarl said nothing, for he watched the sea and the sky and he steered the ship.

"Nearer!" shouted Ben Ezra from the mast. "And the daylight cometh. I watch for the Romans. May the curse of Jehovah be upon them and theirs forever!"

Lysias was on the fore deck, and as he heard Ben Ezra he muttered angry words in his own tongue. Then he whispered softly to himself, or to a shadow, and his fair face grew white and his teeth ground together as if he were in agony. So do they suffer who have lost a love and know that it is forever gone, for Lysias had said:

"Worse far than if they had slain her! I would that she were dead and I with her. But I may live to slay Romans. Why did this Saxon jarl spare any of them? But he is captain, and they say he is a wise one."

In the small wooden fort for slingers and archers, high up the stout mast, sat Ben Ezra, and a viking sat with him.

"O Saxon," said the Jew, "would thy jarl spare them if they came with the day?"

"The son of Brander is jarl, not I," replied the viking, surlily. "Speak thou not carelessly of the leader of men. Thou art no seaman. He will strike when he is ready. Let that content thee."

For deep and strong was the hold of Ulric upon his older men, by reason of his skill as a seaman and as a captain and because of his good fortune; for they saw plainly that Odin and Thor were with him and that the gods of the Middle Sea could do nothing against him. Even the ice gods had been his friends and the god of the Druids had also helped him, sending him away from Britain unharmed. It was a great thing to have such a jarl, of Odin's line. They all knew, moreover, that Hilda, the saga woman, must by this time have gone down to the gods and that she willed exceedingly well to the crew of *The Sword* and to her young hero.

"He is truly a leader of men," growled the Jew through his thick beard, "but I would once more smite these Philistines of Rome."

"In that I am with thee," said the viking, heartily. "Thou art a good sword. I would see thee in battle. It is pleasant to look upon a warrior that slayeth zealously. But our feast of blood will come to us. Wait."

Up sprang the sun above the blue waves of the Middle Sea, and all the Saxons shouted joyfully. It was true that there were no enemies in sight, nor present hope of any good fighting, but here was a land that they had never seen before. All seamen know the joy there is in finding a country that is unknown.

"Hael! O land of the South!" shouted Tostig the Red. "Thou hast mountains as tall as are those of the North. But this is a bay, a harbor, not a fiord."

"What sayest thou, Ben Ezra?" asked Ulric of the watcher on the mast.

"Row in!" replied the Jew. "There is no other keel in this haven and it is a good one. I see no sail nor any boat seaward. This is Africa, and a city is on the shore, but the fire was at the head of the bay. There are rocks ahead. Row around them."

"I see them; a great ledge," said Ulric. "Broken and sharp-toothed are those rocks, and they would wreck any keel that should strike upon them. It is a place of wrecks."

The rowers rowed and *The Sword* went on through a wide passage at the right of the ledge. Then she was in a great basin where many keels might ride at anchor, and before her and on either side of her lay the land.

There seemed but a gentle slope at the seashore. Beyond might be a plain for a few miles, and then, lifting their heads so high that they entered the dominions of the upper gods to be capped with ice and snow, were the many mountains. Into that upper land no man may enter, for the ice gods will freeze him and bury him in snow for his insolence.

It was all exceedingly beautiful, but the rowers now rowed slowly and all the other Saxons watched warily as *The Sword* drew nearer what seemed a landing place, a structure of stonework builded far out into the harbor.

"Bring thy ship to yonder wharf," counseled Sigurd. "No men are to be seen, but there are walls and temples and houses. This may be a town of the magicians of Africa. Beware of them, Ulric the Jarl."

"I would I knew who kindled the light," said Ulric, thoughtfully. "If we had sailed toward it in the dark we had perished on that ledge."

"Thereon are fragments of wrecks," said Sigurd. "The breakers there are high."

So said other of the seamen, but *The Sword* was now making fast to the stone jetty, and Ben Ezra was already out upon it walking shoreward, with his scimiter drawn. He seemed like a younger man. But he was not to go alone, for closely behind him hurried Lysias with his bow, and Knud the Bear.

"Here burned the fire," said Ulric, a few moments later, pointing at a heap of ashes near the head of the jetty. "There hath been much burning of wood at this place."

Nevertheless he left it behind him and marched rapidly forward. He left a strong guard with the ship, but he thought it best to enter this strange town with tenscore of armed Saxons arrayed as if they were to be assailed by some enemy.

On went Ben Ezra, but he met no man, and he came to a wall, in the face of which was a ruinous gap where once had been a gate. From this opening it was seen that a broad street led away, bordered by ruined palaces. At its far end arose one of the temples which had been discerned from the ship, as it stood upon high ground.

"Here," said Ben Ezra, "is a city which Jehovah hath smitten for the sins of them which dwelt therein."

But he spoke loudly, in the old Hebrew tongue, and at once a voice responded:

"Who art thou, O Jew, coming hither with a sword? The sword hath departed from Israel, as it hath from Tyre and Carthage. I am Annibaal, the foe of Rome and of Greece, and I am dying of hunger. Come hither to me."

As if without fear Ben Ezra walked toward the sound of that voice not many paces. Then crawled out from behind a fallen column a naked, sun-darkened, very hairy shape of a vast man, larger than Sigurd, the son of Thorolf, but he lay prone upon the sand gasping. Only one eye had he, for the other was but a hollow socket, and he had but one hand and one foot and both of his ears were gone. He was but a mutilated remnant of a strong man, and his only weapon was a long straight sword, very bright and seemingly keen, with a golden hilt, whereon were glittering gems.

"O Annibaal," said Ben Ezra, in the tongue of Tyre, "what is this city?"

"It is the city of the dead," said Annibaal. "I was a chief of Carthage, whereof this was a colony, but some came hither from Tyre, and here were already many from Nubia and from Egypt. First the Greeks of Alexander harmed us in the old time, but after them, in my day, came the Romans. They smote us hip and thigh, slaying whom they would slay, making slaves of many, and of me, a prince and captain, they made what thou seest, leaving me here alone."

Already Lysias and Knud stood by Ben Ezra, and behind them a few paces halted Ulric the Jarl and his men.

"I wonder thou didst not die," said Ben Ezra, "or that the lions took thee not. I see some of them even now."

"I have slain lions," said Annibaal, "but it is now as if I were friends with them and they harm me not. It is their city and we agree together. Yet I had at this time no more food and I perish, but I lighted my death fire to trap Roman ships to my ledge. I have slain many there, and sometimes I have had joy to hear them when the wind brought their cries to the shore. Their bodies float to the strand and the beasts and the ravens feast upon the wolves of Rome."

"He must die," muttered Knud. "He slayeth sailors. It is not good to trap men, so that they die a cow's death. It is wicked to rob a warrior of his right to die in fight or by the righteous breaking up of his keel."

So said other of the vikings, thinking of Valhalla and the gods, for they all were religious men, scorning an evil action. But Ulric had sent in haste for food and for water and for ale, commanding that this man should be fed.

"Ye are too late," said Annibaal. "I pray thee, rather, for thou art a prince, strike me with thy spear."

"That is a just thing, O jarl," said Sigurd. "He hath been a warrior. Thou wouldst ask thy kinsman to make the hero spearmark on thee if thou wert unluckily perishing in thy bed. Send him marked to his gods, that they take him not for a coward."

"Not yet," said Ulric. "Ben Ezra, talk thou with him as thou wouldst."

In Hebrew and in the tongue of Tyre did the twain converse. When the water came, and the food and ale, Annibaal drank a cup of water, but more he could not do, for he was passing.

"I have learned much," said Ben Ezra; "but he dieth. Refuse him not thy mercy, O jarl. He is a prince, and he is worthy of thy hand. Take thou his own sword and smite off his head lest thou fail of a friend in thine own hour. Quick ere he fainteth!"

Ulric took the long, beautiful sword, which had slain both men and lions, and he struck as became him, for he heard murmurs among the Saxons.

Annibaal had feebly lifted his head to receive the gift he had asked for, and it was severed well, falling upon the sand.

"Well done, O jarl!" shouted Knud the Bear. "I liked him not, but it were shame to let a brave warrior die of thirst. Now do I not fear at all to go on into this place, for we have put blood at the gate."

The other Saxons shouted their approval of their jarl's kindness to Annibaal, and they marched forward willingly, blowing their horns and clashing their spears upon their shields, for all this great ruin was very wonderful.

The street was long, and as they went on Sigurd remarked to the jarl:

"Where there are lions there are no cattle. Where the Romans have been there is left no plunder worth taking. We will but use our eyes till we tire and then we will lift our sails and depart."

Ulric answered not, for a strange look was on his face and his eyes were studying the sword of Annibaal.

"This hilt hath many runes," he said to Ben Ezra. "Canst thou read them?"

"Not so," said the Jew, "but one thing the Carthaginian told thee not. I had heard much of this city. It was first builded by the kings of the forgotten ages, whereof there are no writings. Our own writings tell us somewhat of them. The Egyptian priests know more, but tell it not. So did those of Babylon the elder. Here was a great people, but they perished. Even their gods died, being slain by the sword of Jehovah."

"As many gods have been slain by Thor and Odin," responded Ulric. "I like your god, that destroyeth his enemies."

More slowly they walked as they drew near the front of the great temple.

"The stones of it are large," said Ulric to Ben Ezra. "They are greater than the Druid stones that I saw in Britain."

"I will show thee greater stones than these in the temple of Jehovah at Jerusalem," replied the Jew.

"I will go there with thee," replied Ulric. "But these are wonderfully graven. Only a good chisel may cut granite rock."

"Their tools were of bronze," said the Jew, "and none but their priests knew how to make them. Taller pillars are in Egypt than in Greece or Rome, but they are of the old time. No more are set up since the Egyptian gods departed. They, too, were overcome by Jehovah."

"He is a great god," said Ulric, reverently. "I would be glad to see him. Let us go up these steps and look in."

Some of the vikings paused on the steps and would go no further, for a chill was on them in spite of the sunshine. One said to another: "The magicians may still be here, or some of the old gods of this place."

"The son of Odin need not fear them," was answered; "but we are not as he is. Let us wait until he hath gone in."

Great was their faith in their jarl, but they were disappointed that in this harbor they were to obtain no cattle nor any plunder.

First went Lysias, as if he feared not at all; but he had seen many temples, and this was one from which its gods must have gone away, leaving it solitary. His bow was in his hand, however, and suddenly he stood still, putting a long arrow upon the string in haste.

"Strike him!" shouted Ulric. "He may escape if I try to spear him."

"A splendid lion he is!" shouted Tostig the Red. "Thou canst not slay him with thy arrows! Let me go to him!"

Even at that moment they had passed the portal, for at the top of the flight of steps was a level place, stone-floored, surrounded by these vast pillars whereof they had been speaking. Across this level was the portal, but no doors were in it to hinder. Beyond, as they now saw entering, was an open space, a hundred cubits wide and more in length, but it had no roofing. It seemed like a place of assembly, and at its further end was a high dais, whereon was an altar and behind the altar an image. But on the altar couched this lion, tawny and large. His head had been between his paws, but now he arose and sent toward them a roar that was like half-smothered thunder.

The arrow sped and it smote him in the breast, entering deeply.

"Odin! What a bound was that!" exclaimed Ulric, and all the Saxons shouted for the pleasure of seeing the stricken beast fly through the air toward them.

"He belongeth to the Greek," said Sigurd. "Spoil not his sport. He shooteth well. He is a warrior's son."

It had been a disgrace to any viking to interfere, even if the lion should slay the Greek, but Svip, the son of Leiknar went forward wrongfully, lifting his spear. All others did but stand where they were and they called out angrily to Svip.

"He is but a Greek," said the son of Leiknar; but the lion sprang again and he sprang far, with a short roar which was fierce and guttural, taking Svip for his enemy. Brave was the son of Leiknar, but he knew not aught of lions. Upon him fell the mighty beast, beating down the spear with a forepaw. Sharp were the long claws and swift and terrible was the tearing. The shield was no defense and the mail was rent as if it had been leather. Torn into fragments was the strong viking ere he might draw his seax, but the bow of Lysias twanged again and his arrow sped well.

"The lion hath no mark but his," said Sigurd, the son of Thorolf. "Back! This is his battle. Let him win it or perish!"

This was a moment when men look, but do not breathe, for the lion turned upon Lysias and the youth faced him boldly, drawing his long arrow to the head.

"Well shot!" shouted Tostig. "O Greek, thou art a good bowman, but he hath thee!"

The lion had gathered his strength to spring, but the shaft had gone in too far. The roar choked in his throat. His limbs refused to cast him. He rolled over, snarling, and pawing at the pavement.

"I would thou wert a Roman!" said Lysias. "But such as thou art have torn my kindred in the arena."

"Slain!" shouted Sigurd. "Thou hast done well, O Greek!"

"Svip, the son of Leiknar, erred to his death," said the jarl. "The fault was his own. But this lion was first smitten upon the stone of sacrifice. What sayest thou, O Jew; is there in this any offense to the god of this place?"

"There is no god," responded Ben Ezra. "Here are but idols, and upon their altars couch the beasts of the field. We may go forward. Who needeth to fear gods of stone, which are the work of men's hands and which neither walk nor speak?"

"The lions have no god," said Lysias.

"Let him win it or perish!"

"I would not fear him greatly if they had," said an old viking, "but if he were a man, with a sword in his hand, then I would know what to do with him."

Some of the Saxons then declared that they knew what to do with the skin of such a lion, and they remained to take it off rather than go any nearer to the stone god behind the place of sacrifice. Grand and huge was he, the idol of this broken temple of old time. He was the head of a man upon the body of a beast, carved out of more stones than one, and he crouched there, looking at them with a stern and terrible expression.

"I think," said Ben Ezra, "that he is one of the forgotten gods of the Sidonians. They will not set him up in Egypt, but he was like Jupiter."

"There is no hammer," said Sigurd. "It is not Thor. See the jarl!"

They had paused, looking, but the son of Brander the Brave had walked curiously to the side of the god and was studying his marks, for there were many.

"I would," he muttered, "that Hilda were here, for I think she would read. These are like the runes upon the old Odin stone beyond the fiord, and they were made when he came from the East. I think this to be one of the Asas; but how came He to make this temple and place it here? The gods do strangely at times."

By him now stood Lysias, and he said: "O jarl of the Saxons, linger not. The Jew hath found a stone which must be lifted. He waiteth for thee."

No message had Ben Ezra sent, but he was stooping over a flat slab in the place of sacrifice. Upon it there were marks of fire and the stone was crumbling.

"Why lift it?" asked Ulric, drawing nearer. "What have we to do with the secrets of the gods? Why should we anger them?"

"They are dead," said Ben Ezra, "but I think this to be a door of the priests. It is but a broken stone. Give me thy spear."

"Nay," said Ulric, "I can pry with a spear shaft. We will have it up if anything may be hidden here for us."

The fire-broken limestone yielded in several pieces to the prying of the tough spear shafts. As its pieces were lifted, or as they fell away, behold stone steps, from which all shrank back save the Jew and the son of Odin and the Greek. Even Sigurd held back a moment, saying:

"I like it not. It is the jarl's place. Let him venture first. He knoweth runes that we know not. So doth the Jew, but the Greek is a young fool."

Dangerous indeed it was for any man to step into a chamber under the altar of a strange god, but when they went down and entered it and looked around there was but little to see.

"A store of broken weapons and rust-eaten armor," said Ulric. "Some of the hilts and shields are good enough. But there are many skulls and bones."

"A crown!" shouted Ben Ezra, with a round thing in his hand glittering. "Here placed they the ashes of kings from the altar. I know not why they should have buried with one the diadem of his realm. It may be that his dynasty was ended. Many of these stones are rare and precious. Here is gold, also, but the silver is of no great value. Let us bear all to the ship, for the spoil of this sacred tomb of the kings would buy a Roman province."

The vikings in the outer air were summoned, and now they were not unwilling to venture, for the fear of the place had departed when they heard again the voice of the jarl. Neither did they care overmuch to find merely the remains of the dead, and they were greatly pleased with the treasures.

Ben Ezra bore away one shield which was heavy with gold, and in the middle of it was a jewel so like a great red eye that the vikings said it was looking at them revengefully, and they would not touch it.

"This place the Romans missed in their search," said Ulric. "Little reverence have they for the altars of unknown gods."

Even heavy were the burdens carried to the ship, and now all who had been left to guard her were entitled to take their turn in the exploration of the city. They went and they came, but they found nothing to bring with them and they slew no wild beasts. They reported, however, that they had seen a leopard and a number of hideous beasts which Ben Ezra told them were hyenas, which delighted to feast upon the dead of battlefields. Successful fishing had been done in the harbor with the small boats, and there was enough for all, but that night there was much murmuring over the lack of fresh meat.

"Besides," said some of the men, "this strange treasure hath its value, but there hath been no good fighting. When will this jarl of ours lead us to a throwing of spears? The months of the summer are already wasted."

To these an answer was given by Sigurd, the son of Thorolf, that to them was the fault, for by reason of their unruliness had there been needless landings and delays on the coasts of Gaul and of Spain, and idle cruising after fishing boats and empty merchantmen which fought not and paid but little.

"And the jarl forbade us to slaughter their crews," said one. "I would have slain all."

Men who will to find fault may readily prepare a cause. Thus far the voyage of *The Sword* had been even too prosperous, being guided by prudence, and there was lacking the curbing which cometh from wholesome disaster. The weather was all too warm for Northmen, and some few of them had sickened, and of this sickness had four vikings died a cow's death but for the mark of a spear which was given them by the hands of friends. Now, also, the skin of the lion aroused jealousy against the Greek. It was declared that an hour must be found for him to feel an edge of a seax, for he was not a Saxon and there should be no outland men like him and Ben Ezra upon a ship from the Northland. The jarl was too hard in some matters and he was too soft in others. Nevertheless, days went by while all looked at these temples and houses and the mighty fortifications. As for the jarl, he explored somewhat, but he abode mostly with the ship. He was silent and moody, for there were many things upon his mind.

"I have come far out into the world," he thought. "I have seen that which is exceedingly marvelous. I have looked, also, upon the face of a dead god. Now I will go on until I may have speech with one that is living."

Chapter XVII
The Murmuring of the Men

Out of the African harbor sailed *The Sword* with a good wind, and there was no present need for rowing. No longer were the Saxons willing to linger in that place and live upon fishes. Small pleasure was to be had there, they said, save to lie at night and listen to the cries of many wild beasts. They had not hunted at night save that one of the youths of Sigurd's party had ventured beyond the jetty foolishly and had not returned. Blood had been found in the morning, but not any of his bones. It had been better if the weather had been rough or if the men had been at the oars, for in their idleness upon this blue and peaceful sea was an occasion for discontent.

"The jarl must do better than this!" they said to each other, and as they talked of battles the thirst for blood increased among them, for it is as a wild fever when it cometh.

"O jarl," said Sigurd, the son of Thorolf, not long after *The Sword* passed beyond the ledge whereupon so many had been wrecked by reason of the revenge fire of Annibaal, "I think we do well if we steer now eastward. We shall find too many Roman triremes in this neighborhood."

"I would seek them," said Ulric, "if not too many of them were together. Dost thou know of a shore or an island where there are cattle?"

"Verily I do," said Ben Ezra, "but I know not if we may find it easily. We may but sail on. Lysias is with the steersman now, and he is pointing."

Vebba, the son of Uric, was at the helm, and he hated the Greek, but he listened, for he could not despise a good bowman.

"I would carve the blood eagle on thy back," he said, laughing, "but if thou wilt guide to where we may slay somebody, thou art better worth killing. I hate thee."

"So do I hate thee," said Lysias, boldly, "but we may not fight on the ship. I will give thee thy sword play when we get to a good place. But I shall strike thy head from thy shoulders."

"Good!" said Vebba. "I like thee better. But bring us first to some good fighting."

Then went Lysias to Ulric and the Jew, and they conferred somewhat, but Lysias passed from them to the after cabin, and came out bearing something that he took with him to the after deck.

"I saw it there," said Ulric. "It is a harp, not half so large as that of Oswald's. What can the Greek do with it?"

"Wait and see," replied Ben Ezra. "Among the Greeks are those who are skilled in music. Hearken!"

All ears upon *The Sword* were suddenly turned to listen, for the harp was a good one.

"He playeth well!" said Sigurd. "No man shall slay him. We needed harping."

"Aye," replied the discontented men, and then they shouted to Lysias: "Sing!"

Not at once was he ready to sing, and the harp sounded on as if he heard them not.

"Sing! Sing!" they shouted again. "Sing, or we will slay thee!"

"Slay on, cowards!" laughed Lysias, angrily. "What care I for slaying!"

For he had been muttering hoarsely to himself something about Sapphira and there were tears in his eyes.

"Down!" shouted Sigurd, to a viking who was drawing his seax. "Harm him not, lest I send thee a spear! I would hear his harp. Down, I say!"

The spear of Sigurd was a matter to be avoided, and the seaman left his weapon sheathed and sat down. But at that moment arose the voice of Lysias in a grand Greek song, a song of war and of contending warriors.

"Right!" shouted the men to Sigurd. "Thou shalt slay any that shall rob us of our harping. He singeth well."

None would have expected a voice so powerful and so sweet, and they who heard it clapped their hands or clashed their spears upon their shields.

Then the war song ended, and the harp began to send out low, sweet music that made them think of the Northland. They said to one another that now the trees were in leaf, and the grass was green, and the wind was in the pines, and the waves were on the shores, and the voices of the gods could be heard in the fiords. The women and the children, too, were in the houses, or they were caring for the cattle, and the fisher boats were out from all the villages. So they grew quiet and looked across the blue waters of the Middle Sea less discontentedly, and the thirst for blood waned away for the hour. And yet they knew not that now the Greek was singing in his own tongue of

Sapphira the Beautiful, and that he did not at all see the ship, or those who were in it, or the sea, but that his eyes, like those of the blind, were seeking far away for a face and a form that were out of sight, beyond—he knew not where.

His own countenance, with its perfect outlines and its youthful color, exhibited his sadness in keeping with the flowing music of his lyre, but he knew not that the eyes of Ulric and of Ben Ezra were reading him. Unlike the rest of the vikings, excepting Sigurd, they understood the words of the song, which was from one of the old poets of the better days of Greece.

"I have heard," whispered Ulric, "that even as he saith, the young women of his people have great beauty."

"Yea," returned the Jew, "I have seen many of them. I have seen this Sapphira, and she did excel. But no maidens are as those of Israel and Judah, the roses of Sharon and the lilies of the valley. Their voices are those of birds and their forms are of the heaven. Such was the mother of my son in her youth. Such were my daughters. I am glad that they fell by the sword——"

"How were they not captured by the Romans?" asked Ulric.

"Because of the swords of their husbands and their brethren," said the Jew, calmly. "All died together, but the fairest of them needed no sword save her own. She chose to die by her own hand rather than to become the sport of the heathen."

"She did well," muttered Ulric. "She was dark and she was beautiful. She was brave and true. I have never loved, but I would I could find one like her."

"If she were of the race of Abraham," replied Ben Ezra, "she might not wed save with one of her own people. That is our law concerning women."

"It is a good law," said Ulric. "Hilda, the saga woman, told me of it. She said that ye have good sagas of your own and that your runes are ancient. Are there any among you that are descended from the gods?"

"We have but one God," said Ben Ezra, "and all we are his children, for he is the creator and father of men."

"He is Odin, the all-father?" said the young jarl, inquiringly. "Then, when I get to Asgard, I shall see him. I have thought much concerning gods. That was a strange one in the temple in the city of ruins. He gave us much treasure."

"We took it," said Ben Ezra.

"Yea," replied Ulric, "we did so. But the Romans did not find it, nor any others that came, until the god who sat there watching permitted it to be taken. That was but his stone face that we saw. Thou knowest not much of gods, to think that he saw us not. Is thy god blind, that thou canst hide away from him?"

"Not so," said Ben Ezra, thoughtfully. "Talk no more. The Greek hath ceased. I think thy men like him better, but there is a spear waiting at any hour for either him or me."

"So is mine waiting for him who may cast his own unduly," said Ulric, angrily, "and that know they well. But the sun is sinking and a sail is in sight. Sigurd seeth afar. He is coming."

"A small trireme," said Sigurd, as he drew near. "I think we must take her."

"Take her," said the jarl. "Oars, all! Vebba, son of Uric, steer for yonder keel!"

Loud rang the shouts of the Saxons and the discontented became good-humored, but there was little need for fast rowing. The stranger was nearing them at its best speed, and ere long they could hear the sound of a trumpet.

"The grapplings!" commanded Ulric. "If we may not strike her with the ship, we will board her!"

Swiftly the two keels approached each other, and rash indeed were the Romans, for they were arrogant, not knowing with what they had to deal. They saw the Saxon flag on the mast. They heard the war horns. Many men they saw not at the first, for concealment of his strength was the prudence of the jarl, lest his enemy might strive to escape. All the more freely did the fighting men of the small trireme crowd her decks and gather at her bulwarks.

Even from afar did the arrows of Lysias and Tostig and other bowmen and the slingstones of Knud begin to go in among them, angering them as some of them fell, hurt or slain. They, too, had bowmen, but neither good nor many, and their arrows were short.

Cunningly did Vebba veer away *The Sword* at the nearing, that a flight of spears might hurtle among the Roman soldiers, thinning them. Past them shot the swift keel of the Saxons, only to turn again suddenly, crashing back upon their further banks of oars. They, too, had been ready for boarding, but their bulwarks were not so high as were those of *The Sword*. Her grapnels were well thrown, moreover, and the two ships were as one when the legionaries made their brave rush to climb on board their enemy. Well had it been for them if they had been more in number. Well if they had not been so rashly self-confident, and if they had not been half beaten by astonishment at the sudden appearing of the Northmen at the ship's side.

With laughter and with mocking did the Saxons hurl their spears and then follow with sword and ax. Over the bulwarks they went, through the gaps left by slain Romans, and quickly they went two for one, slaying joyously. No Roman thought to surrender, nor was any mercy in the hearts of the vikings, but among them all did none smite more eagerly than did Ben Ezra and Lysias.

"Slay! Slay!" shouted the Jew. "O Greek, thou art too slow. Hew down! Smite under the fifth rib! Let none escape!"

"Good fighters are they!" shouted Vebba from the after deck of *The Sword*. "I will have a fine contest when I slay that Greek. I will fight him fairly. But I must get the Jew before me to see how he will handle that crooked blade. He cleft a Roman to the chin. Hah! I am but steersman and I miss the killing."

So did others of the vikings, for there were not enough on the trireme to put blood upon every good sword or spear. They were all gone too soon, and there was disappointment. Nevertheless, the legionaries had died hard, and nine of the Northern heroes had gone to Valhalla.

"To them the gods were kind," said Sigurd, "but this trireme is a fair prize. There are ten head of small, fat cattle, besides four fresh carcasses. We must have them on board *The Sword*, with the other plunder, before we kindle the fire."

The men were attending to that, for here was their fresh meat without the trouble of landing to find it. All of the slain might be burned with the trireme, with all honor, so there was no more care for that. Some Saxons were wounded, but not so that they might die, and there were no prisoners. All provisions and arms were taken over speedily and the good spirits of the men were returning, for none of them waited for needless cooking of the beef that was ready. Roasting might be done afterward, but the sharp knife could shred, and a viking cared for little more at the end of a won battle.

"Fire, now," commanded Ulric, at the last. "Throw off the grapplings and let her drift away. I would see her burn."

So the rowers pulled to a little distance and paused, letting *The Sword* rock gently over the soft waves while the fire blazed more and more brightly upon the decks and in the waist of the Roman trireme.

"She burneth well," said Sigurd.

"So burn every Roman keel!" exclaimed Ben Ezra. "Jehovah of Hosts hath been with me this day, and I have gotten vengeance upon mine enemies. My sword hath been deep in the hearts of the heathen."

Lysias was silent, but his fair face glistened with pleasure as he gazed upon the mounting flames. His lyre was now in his hand again and his fingers wandered over the strings.

"The harp! the harp!" shouted some of the vikings. "If he playeth not, we will slay him."

"An evil spirit is among them," muttered the Jew. "Whence he cometh I know not. Who shall cast him out? for we have neither scribe nor priest on this accursed vessel. I think that he belongeth to the idol upon the fore deck."

In that he spoke of the anvil and hammer of Thor, for to him the Saxons ascribed the gift of this victory.

"He is a demon," said Ben Ezra, "and he hath entered into these uncircumcised. I would he might lead them to Gehenna."

"The harp! the harp!" again demanded the vikings, and the voices of the rowers were joined to the shouts of those who were feasting.

"The wind riseth well and so do yonder flames," said Lysias; "but they who are dead feel no pain of burning. Within me is a fire which is a continual torment. The harp were a relief, and I will sing."

It seemed as if a strange spirit of wild song had come upon him and his lyre. It mattered not greatly that few of the vikings understood his words, so fierce and so triumphant was the music of his singing. Moreover, they looked upon his face and it gave them an interpretation, for there was a terrible meaning in its expression.

Now the rowers ceased and the sail was up, but the burning Roman ship also felt the fresh wind, and it was as if it strove to keep them company while Lysias sang.

"She will founder shortly," said the jarl. "We are leaving her. I would I knew more nearly whitherto we have come. We are far in the Middle Sea and we should be near some of its islands."

"Thou knowest," remarked Sigurd, the son of Thorolf, "that opposite to the southerly point of Italy there lieth a great island, whereon is a volcano, vomiting fire, for under it is the world which burns, and there do the gods war with one another. I think we are between that island, which is called Sicily, and a part of Africa. O Jew, what sayest thou? Thou hast visited many parts of Africa."

"We have wandered here and there," said Ben Ezra. "The question is difficult. But if yonder haze telleth of the coast of Sicily we may meet another trireme soon. There are many hereabout. They will for the greater part be merchantmen."

Down sank the vessel they had burned, with much loud hissing of fire meeting water, and the clouds of smoke and steam went up while the Saxons blew their war horns and shouted their exultation. They all had feasted well, however, and those who were not on watch were willing to slumber while the increasing gale carried *The Sword* swiftly toward the east.

Another was at the helm, and Ulric, the son of Brander, went and sat down upon a silken-covered couch in the after cabin. He was alone, and he brought out his jewels to look at them. They were many and they were beautiful, and he turned them over one by one.

"Never before," he said, "did I have so good a lamp as this that hangeth here. The oil, too, is perfumed and the room is full of a sweet odor. These are the ways of the Roman captains and rich men. I may not see Rome, for there are too many quinqueremes in the way, too many legions of warriors on the land. We are few. I do not care much for their gods, for I have beaten them. I will go on to Asgard, but I will go first to this temple in Jerusalem. Ben Ezra saith that I can buy both priests and governors with these bright stones. But I may have to slay my own men if they obey not. If I cut down a few of them the rest will be more peaceable. These Saxons that came with Sigurd hardly call me their jarl. If they were dead it would not matter. I will go my own way."

The ruby was now in his hand, the great red stone that was graven with the name of the Hebrew god, and among them all there was no other like this. It glowed like fire in the lamplight, and Ulric said: "It is full of blood. It is a stone of stones. But whence came the blood, and how is it full of fire? Is he angry with me? I think I will carry his gem to him in his temple, and I will tell him I have brought it back. I would not keep from any god that which is his."

So he put it back into the casket and took out an emerald. This, too, was graven with deeply cut runes.

"One of them," said Ulric, "is like the runes that Hilda showed me in the sand by the sea, but it is alone. I care not until there are three. It is green and wonderful. O Hilda of the hundred years, would that I could show to thee this jewel of the old gods!"

The lamp burned low and it was flickering. Without the gale roared loudly and the waves beat against the sides of the ship with a groaning sound. There was no voice but of the wind and of the surges. The curtains in the cabin swayed to and fro, as did the cresset of the lamp.

"Hilda! Hilda!" murmured Ulric, but he saw her not, and even his thought of her was confused in his mind. The saga woman was tall and dark, but not so tall and fairer was this thought which came before his eyes as if he were in a dream:

"So beautiful! So beautiful!" he said. "Her eyes are like stars and her hair is a cloud of shining curls. Her lips are like the ruby of the temple. I think she is one of the Hebrew maidens that Ben Ezra saith excel all others. I will go to that land and find her, for it must be that she also is of the daughters of the gods. And now I can see Hilda, and her hair is white, but her eyes are shut. Therefore I know that they have carried her to the tomb that was made in the rock of Odin. I shall see her no more until I get to Asgard. If this is her hand upon my head, she should speak, for I love her well."

He listened, and the lamp went out, but no voice came; and he lay down upon his couch, but a fire was kindling in his heart.

"Lysias loveth Sapphira," he thought, "but thus did I never feel before. The Hebrew maiden! I would Ben Ezra had not told me of her, for now I can have no other. I had thought that my love would be blue-eyed and a daughter of Odin. Shall I not be content if I find that she is dark, and that she is a daughter of this Jehovah, the god of the Jews? I will go on and I will see what she will say to me."

Then he slept, and *The Sword* swept onward swiftly toward the sunrise.

Chapter XVIII
The Evil Spirit on "The Sword"

Through one day more the western gale blew furiously and *The Sword* was driven before it, for none on board cared for any better steering. Many vessels were seen from time to time, but all were too busy caring for themselves to pay overmuch attention to a trireme that might be fighting the storm as they were. The vikings were at ease concerning the weather, but they grumbled much that the tossing and pitching of their ship prevented them from making fires wherewith to roast their beef or to broil their fish. On board their Roman keel they had found gratings of iron for cooking, better than any of their North making. These gratings were wide, upheld by iron feet, and under them were slabs of stone to receive ashes and cinders. Fire would remain upon them well in any ordinary weather, but in such as this the brands and coals might be cast hither and thither. It was not even a time for the telling of sagas nor for the lyre of Lysias, and again the men grew moody and sullen.

The night returned, and Ulric kept the helm through all its watches, for a heavy weight was on his mind and he had heard from Ben Ezra concerning the evil spirit. "I would I could slay a demon," he had answered, "but of what good is a spear for an enemy thou canst not see? It were almost as if one fought with a god. I have thought I would like to fight with one, but not with Thor or Odin nor with thy Jehovah."

"They who contend with him are broken," replied the Jew, "but I tell thee we are far on our way. I think we are not far from Cyprus. We might safely land in one of the havens of that island."

"We might meet a Roman fleet," said Ulric.

"They have none in these waters," said Ben Ezra. "Their merchant ships of any consequence go and come in squadrons, well protected, and they have driven out all pirates. They will not be watching, I think, for the coming of such as thou art."

"We now are late in the season," replied Ulric. "I had thought to have reached this water before any other keel from the North. We know not what may have called upon the Romans for watching. I am thinking that when this wind abateth I must find the men somewhat to occupy them."

"An evil spirit is a busy one," said Ben Ezra. "All thine would find enough to do in Cyprus."

Afterward many of the men came to the jarl with questionings, and also to the Jew and to Lysias. These were looked upon with more favor for the time, for it was said that they might have some worth for piloting.

A night and a day and a night went by and now the waters were again quieted. They were even too still, for the rowers had to be sent to the oars, and the sun looked down upon them with fervent heat, making their toil burdensome. Once more the ship was floating upon an even keel and the men speedily bethought them of the fire gratings. Twain of the fat cattle were butchered, and the jarl thought well of it, that the men might be kept in good humor. The fires were lighted, and casks of ale were opened, but the evil spirit was, nevertheless, making himself busy among the hearts of the men.

In the trireme *The Sword* itself, when she was captured, there had been a few skins of wine, but it had been red and sour and the vikings liked it not. Such as it was it had long since been consumed. In the spoil of the burned trireme, however, and hardly noticed at the first, there had been found many wine skins. All had been taken with care, and now one of them was opened to find out what it might be.

"Dark and sweet and good!" exclaimed Vebba, the son of Uric. "I will bear a horn of it to the jarl."

Large was the drinking horn, and he filled it to the brim. Sparkles arose upon the surface of the wine, and it seemed to laugh, as if the evil spirit which lived in it were accomplishing his purpose.

"It is strong," said Ben Ezra. "Drink it not, O jarl, for the demon of wine is thine enemy."

But he was too late, for the son of Brander drained the drinking horn as if it had held naught but ale. He felt it from his head to his feet, as if it had been poured upon a fire that was burning within him, and he stood erect, straightening himself and clinching his hands.

"Bring me another horn of it," he said.

"That thou shalt not do," commanded Ben Ezra, sternly. "Thou art the captain. I bid thee drink no more, lest thou lose thy life and thy vessel. The demon is upon thee, O jarl! Resist him, or he will bind thee hand and foot."

Then remembered Ulric a saying of his father and of Hilda, and it was as if he had heard her voice saying: "Son of Odin, beware of the dark wine of the south lands, for in it is death."

"Bring me no more," he said to Vebba, "and let the wine skins be cast into the sea."

But the demon had been very busy and from lip to lip had already passed the goblets and the drinking horns. They had been emptied only to be quickly filled again, and now the Saxons of Sigurd shouted:

"Haha! O jarl! Thou wouldst rob us of our feast? We will show thee a thing."

Sigurd himself went among them, but to him, also, they paid no heed, and he came back again.

"I am sleepy," said Ulric. "Wulf the Skater, these three nights I have wakened. I will lie down for a while. Take the helm."

Then came Tostig the Red and Knud the Bear and four other Saxons of the house of Brander, and they sat down by Ulric, spear in hand, with their axes lying by them. Lysias brought his bow and Ben Ezra closed the visor of his brazen helmet.

"Trouble cometh," he said. "The heathen are full of wine and of the thirst of blood."

There was no quarrel between twain of the vikings that were stepping forth upon the fore deck, but they were berserkers, and their seaxes were in their hands, for they were to fight without mail or shields.

Skin after skin of that dark, strong wine was opening, and the men loved it, but they would see blood, they said, and the two berserkers shouted as they fought.

"Both of them are down!" exclaimed Lysias. "Two more take their places. O that the jarl were awake! But I cannot rouse him. Were the Romans to come, we were all dead men."

Furious was now the drinking, and a man cast a spear at another without cause, laughing to see him struggle and bleed.

"The evil spirit hath entered them all!" groaned Ben Ezra. "This is that which I feared greatly. Every man's sword is against his neighbor."

Terrible was that fighting, for warriors who had lost all skill of warding blows or parrying spear casts were still strong to throw or to strike.

"Where is now this jarl of ours?" yelled a drunken viking. "We will see if he be a son of Odin. We will slay him and then we may sail at our pleasure. He hath ruled us with too hard a hand."

Steady and stern had indeed been the rule of the son of Brander, and he had brooked no gainsaying, but he had been a prudent captain from the first, and there were a full third of the men now to stand by him in his peril. Would there had been more, for on both sides the slain were many. Moreover, when a man went down that was quickly his end, on whichever side he fought, for an enemy came to thrust him.

"Wake, son of Brander! Wake!" shouted Tostig in the ear of Ulric. "Call thou upon Odin, thy father, and draw thy sword."

Waiting for no orders from any man, Lysias was sending his arrows, sure and deep striking, calling out:

"With me be thou, O Apollo, god of the bow! With me, O Mars, god of battles!"

But Ulric opened his eyes slowly and breathed hard. Then he sat up and he saw the men fighting and the blood flowing.

"Odin!" he roared, in a voice they had not heard before; but the weapon he lifted was his pole ax, and he rushed forward to the front of his friends.

"I go with him," said Ben Ezra. "It may be his god hath come to help him. Be with me, O Jehovah of strength!"

"We will guard thee at the helm," said Knud and Tostig to Wulf the Skater. "This will be ended speedily. Look at the jarl!"

"He, too, hath a demon!" burst from the lips of Ben Ezra, as he saw Ulric striking. "They go down before him like corn before the reaper."

Sigurd had been smitten to the deck by his own Saxons, and Ulric stood over him with his ax until the son of Thorolf was hidden by corpses of the slain.

Mad with wine and with the fever of the thirst of blood, the rebellious vikings fought on, nor would they yield to the command of the son of Brander.

"We will die!" they said. "But we will first slay thee. It is a feast of swords."

"I would I could spare enough for rowers," said Ben Ezra, "but their blood is on their own heads. The evil spirit destroyeth them."

"Thus endeth the cruise of *The Sword*!" said Ulric, sadly, when at last he might pause for breath. "Save thee, O Ben Ezra, and Lysias, and these few faithful, there are none living save some for whom the valkyrias are calling. What shall we do? for thou art old. What shall be the end of these things?"

But Tostig and Knud had watched the falling of Sigurd and they were lifting from him the corpses.

"The sail is up," said Ben Ezra. "Steer eastward, for we may not do aught else now than land in Syria. Thou and thine shall see Jerusalem."

"So be it!" said Ulric. "I think we are none of us wounded. I am not."

"Glad am I of that!" exclaimed Lysias. "I feared for thee in that combat. But thou art of the heroes and Jove was thy keeper, with Mars and Apollo."

"A feast of blood!" exclaimed Tostig as he lifted the body of Vebba, the son of Uric, from Sigurd, the son of Thorolf. "The sea king is not dead. He was but stunned."

Slowly arose the old warrior until he sat erect and looked around him.

"I saw them!" he said, huskily. "I saw the Nornir in the air above the sail. I saw the valkyrias, but they looked sternly at me and passed by. Why, I know not, for I fought well. Odin hath taken many this day. O jarl, what doest thou?"

"Eastward!" said Ulric. "Canst thou stand upon thy feet?"

Tostig and Knud aided him, and they brought him a goblet of ale, for wine he would not drink.

"It is well with me now," he said. "My helmet is cloven, but my skull is safe. The ax of Vebba was heavy, but he will strike no more. Sad is it that he and these are slain. Better had they fallen in a fight with the Romans."

"Not so," said Ben Ezra, "for if some of them were living all we were dead. Let us cast them into the sea."

Wulf the Skater had watched the clouds, and now he said:

"Ulric the Jarl, if thou wilt, they should be over the sides speedily, for a wind cometh. We shall use no oars henceforth."

Sad work it was to cast so many forms of dead heroes into the sea, but so had it been foredoomed by the Nornir, and there were some of the wounded who died while the task went on.

Then Ulric sat down by the hammer of Thor and bowed his head, for his heart was heavy.

"I can sing no song," he thought, "over such a fight as this. I think it will now be long before I see the fiords and the hillsides of the Northland. My fate hath changed for me in an hour, and I know not what cometh. O Hilda, was this thy dark saying, that I understood not?"

No voice responded, nor any motion of the air, but he looked upward and he saw birds that were flying eastward.

"So will I go," he muttered, "and they who are with me. There is too much blood upon this keel. I would she were burned with fire, for I hate her. The gods of the Romans have had their revenge upon me. I will never again speak lightly of any gods, for they have ways of their own and they are cunning. Who shall protect himself against an enemy whom he cannot see?"

Well blew the wind, and there was little now to be done save to steer and to rest. All ate and drank, and Ben Ezra seemed to love that dark, strong wine, but he used it sparingly.

"It is made in my own land," he said, "but this came from a Greek island, I think. There is good wine in Canaan. I would eat again of the grapes and the pomegranates of Israel and Judah. O my son! That he might have been with me! O my Rachel and my daughters and my firstborn and his brethren! The curse of Jehovah be upon Rome forever! Amen!"

So the old Hebrew warrior wailed in the bitterness of his soul, and *The Sword* sprang on over the billows, bearing him to his own land, but she was now no longer a warship.

"We will not count the days," said Ulric to Lysias. "We will speak to none that we may pass."

"Pause not!" replied Lysias. "Thou hast thy life yet and I have mine. I have it in my mind that I shall see my Sapphira. I have had a dream in the night and she stood and beckoned me."

Ulric answered not, but that night he slept upon the deck dreaming, and in the morning he thought about his dream also.

"Hilda was there," he said, standing at the helm looking across the sea. "Behind her was the sun rising. Between her and the sun were many warriors, heroes of the gods, armed for battle. There was blood on some of them. But at the right hand of Hilda stood that dark and beautiful one, and there were flowers in her hair, and the flowers were both red and white."

Chapter XIX
In the Night and In the Fire

Days come and go and no man may hinder them. The vikings went to and fro about *The Sword* and she seemed lonesome to them, for they were few and she was a great vessel. From time to time many sails were seen near and far, but none gave chase to *The Sword*. Even pirates and all merchantmen avoid what seemeth to be a warship.

"Winds have been both good and bad for us," said the jarl to Ben Ezra at the close of a day. "What thought is in thy mind as to our nearness to any land?"

"O jarl," said Ben Ezra, thoughtfully, "by the stars that I have watched; by the sun and winds; by the islands which we have passed; by a dim understanding which cometh to a man in such a case; by all the signs which are given me, we are so near to our destination that we may find a shore this night."

"And if a shore," said Ulric, "what shall it be?"

"Even the land that was given to the children of Israel by Jehovah, their god," said the Jew. "It is ours yet, but the Romans have taken the kingdom from us."

"Their gods are very strong," said Ulric, "and they are exceedingly cunning. Else had Thor and Odin saved to us the swords that sailed with us from the Northland. Thy god refused to fight with the gods of the Romans. I think he was wise in that. But he agreed with them that they should not harm his temple, and I will go and see it. I may meet him."

"Thou wilt not see him," said Ben Ezra. "He was seen by Moses, our prophet, but to all others he hath hidden his face."

"I know not that," said Ulric. "They who see the gods are forbidden to tell. Hilda, the saga woman, loved me, but she would tell me naught concerning the dead save that they have a country of their own. There is much good in that country and when I am slain I shall go to it."

"Thou art to die by the sword?" asked Ben Ezra. "How knowest thou that?"

"I am of Odin," said Ulric, "and a cow's death is not for me. There will be blood in the hour of my going. If thou seest me on a bed, be thou a Saxon unto me, and smite me through with a spear."

"So said Saul, our king, to his armor-bearer at the end of a lost battle," said Ben Ezra, marveling somewhat. "I will do as thou sayest; for verily thou art a jarl and of the princes of the North. Never before saw I a man like unto thee for battle."

"Save Sigurd, the son of Thorolf, the sea king," said Ulric, "I have met none that might stand before me. He too, is of one line of the hero Asas, but not of Odin."

Ben Ezra was silent, thinking of these things, and *The Sword* drove onward. He and Ulric were at the prow as the darkness deepened. They could see no more save the stars above and the glancing waves around the ship, but they could hear the music of the lyre of Lysias on the after deck. Knud the Bear was at the helm, and all that remained of the crew were gathered there. They cared not to sleep in the cabins or in the bunks, for some of them said that the dead came at night to look again at the keel from which they had departed and that the evil spirit came also.

"I saw him not," said Wulf the Skater, "but Vebba, the son of Ulric, spoke to me, and I think he said the Nornir were at hand. So sayeth Sigurd, the son of Thorolf."

Greatly dispirited were they all, and the lyre was a comfort, but the song of Lysias was low-voiced and sad and they could not understand the words.

Now from the fore deck came back to them one who had heard from the jarl that they were to look out for a land and be ready to lower the sail.

"Good!" shouted Tostig the Red. "O Sigurd, go to the jarl and ask if we are steering rightly."

"That are we," said Sigurd. "Seest thou not the north star? Go we not eastward? What need to trouble the jarl? I would that they who are dead had obeyed him. Then had we all been more joyful."

"Never had crew such adventures as we are having," said Knud. "I think we may gain some good fighting before long. My hand goeth often to the hilt of my seax and my blood is unquiet."

"A good sign!" exclaimed Wulf the Skater. "I feel better for hearing thee. O Greek, sing us a war song!"

Loudly answered the smitten lyre for a moment, and Lysias obeyed, but quickly came back from the fore deck the command of Ulric, the son of Brander.

"Silence, all!" he shouted. "There is a trumpet, far away southerly. We are too few and we near the land. Hark to the breakers!"

Listening diligently, all ears heard the dashing of that water as if upon rocks, and yet again came up from the southward that distant peal of the trumpet.

"Struck!" suddenly exclaimed Sigurd. "We go upon a shore. Is this thy land, O Jew?"

Not with a great shock, but glidingly and grating hard, did *The Sword* go on a little while the sail was lowering. Then she stood fast, and all on board of her knew that the end of her voyage had come.

Needing no command, the Saxon sailors made ready two of the small boats and prepared to lower them.

"The trumpet is nearer," said Ben Ezra. "But this ledge of rocks cannot be far from the mainland. Thy men seem to know not of fear and they obey thee."

"No Roman arms or armor," shouted Ulric. "We land as Saxons and we will leave behind us no token. Kindle a fire amidships."

To his cabin went he and Ben Ezra, and unto them shortly went Lysias, but each prepared bundles of his own to carry to the boats.

"No man knoweth of thy treasure nor of mine," said Ben Ezra to Ulric. "Let the Greek, too, have gold and silver coins, for he will need them. He hath fought well."

In like manner was every man furnished speedily and the burdens were not made uselessly heavy. Nevertheless, Ben Ezra said to Ulric:

"Never before landed boats of thy people bearing to any shore such treasures as are these. We may buy any Roman governor if in so doing we do not hire him to put us to the sword. We will say that we were wrecked, but we must not be seen on the coast."

Now the boats were lowered and all entered them, but in every quarter of *The Sword* was a hot fire kindled. The Roman trumpet had not sounded again when the Saxons rowed away into the darkness.

"Row harder!" commanded Ulric. "The light of the fire increaseth. We know not how near may be an enemy."

Well had he spoken, for the flames were rising furiously and the light wind fanned them well.

"A shore!" said Sigurd. "A sandy beach!" But all others were looking back at *The Sword*, to see how fast she was burning, and at that moment there swept past her, outside, as if nearing to grapple her, a vast shape of a warship. Then arose suddenly a great volume of shouts in the Latin tongue, and the notes of a trumpet sounding commands, but Ulric said in a low voice to his comrades:

"A quinquereme! And she also is upon the ledge of rocks. What shall save her from destruction by that fire?"

"She cannot escape," said Wulf the Skater. "It is as if we had set a good trap. I think the fire hath already caught her sail. There will many Romans perish this night."

"Pull!" commanded Ulric. "The beach! We are here. Haul up the boats. Out with all cargo and leave them. Hark to the shouts of them who burn!"

Rashly in swift haste had the Roman warship dashed forward to discover what might be this unusual thing, of a light that grew and of a crew that replied not to a trumpet of hailing. Not of any rocky ledge had her steersman or her sailing master been thinking, and her centurion had deemed it his duty to grapple and to board this strange burning trireme. He would yet have passed her once, only studying her case, but his own ship had smitten a sunken rock, which forced her to swerve aside heavily, plunging her alongside of her fiery destroyer.

In vain were then all struggles to release the quinquereme. In vain was any effort to extinguish the swiftly devouring flames. Even of small boats the Roman ship had but four, and there were sailors who secretly, quickly lowered these, dropping into them to row away at once. Of these hurrying runaways there were none but hired Ionian rowers, and they cared for their lives only.

Ill fared it for legionaries in heavy armor, for if they sprang overboard, it was to sink. Sad was the fate of many who went into the water, crowding and clinging, for they perished grappling each other in their astonishment and despair. The Roman warship was on fire from end to end, and the side which was not yet burning was toward the sea. What wonder that all discipline failed and that all thought of obedience was gone? for every bond is loosed by fire.

"If any follow, they must not find us on the beach," said Ben Ezra to Ulric. "I can see that the land riseth high and that there are great rocks. Let us depart!"

"Odin!" responded the jarl. "*The Sword* hath once more smitten the Romans. Every man take up his burden. Follow me!"

"A good captain," muttered Ben Ezra. "I will cleave unto him. But verily our lives are worth but little. I would that we were among the mountains, even in Gilboa or in Lebanon, or in the wilderness of Judea."

"Guide thou after daylight cometh," said Ulric. "I would find crags and trees."

On went they, climbing a steep, and ever and anon they looked behind to watch the awful splendor of the burning of the two ships upon the ledge.

"Here may we halt," said Ulric at last. "We are on a height. It is a forest beyond us. The fire burneth lower. There will be no pursuit."

There they sat down, therefore, wearied with their burdens, putting these aside, and ere long they slept, every man, without fear.

At the ledge of rocks in the sea there was silence, for the two ships burned to the water's edge and there was little left of them. Nevertheless, of the swimmers there were a number who reached the shore, but all were of sailors unarmored, and no officer or legionary was among them. Here at the beach they found the two small boats left by the Saxons, with oars in them, but the four boats of the quinquereme, with the Ionian rowers, had landed further on. There was little to be done by these exhausted swimmers but to lie down and rest, and the Ionians were likewise waiting for day, being full of fear over what they had been guilty of in taking away the boats of their ship. Only the sword could await them if they were found by a Roman patrol of the coast, for they were to be accounted deserters from their assigned posts.

Not long was the remainder of the night. The morn came, and when the sun arose Ulric, the son of Brander, sat upon a rock, under an oak tree, looking out upon the blue waters of the Middle Sea. Beside him sat Sigurd, the son of Thorolf, and scattered around upon the grass were the other Saxons. Lysias stood and leaned against the rock, but Ben Ezra was nowhere to be seen. In the hand of Ulric was the long, straight sword that had been found with Annibaal at the ruined city on the African shore, but it was sheathed, and the jewels of its golden hilt were glittering.

"There are men upon the shore by our boats," said Sigurd. "They are escaped from the burning vessel."

"Look southward!" replied Ulric. "A squadron of Roman cavalry. Let us see what they will do, but let us step back behind trees out of their sight. They are too many for us."

"Worse than that," said Lysias. "Horsemen might carry an alarm and legionaries on foot might hunt us in these forests."

The cavalry rode fast, and the men at the beach looked mournfully into each other's faces, for there was no fleeing from riders. Quickly came these and their officer sprang to the ground, speaking loudly.

The light of the burning ships had been seen from afar, and even now a swift galley had arrived, rowing around the rocks of the ledge, while they who were on board of her studied well the charred fragments.

The officer questioned with care the rowers, and a small boat from the galley came to the shore with another officer.

"Were there other boats than these?" he asked, pointing at the twain left there by the Saxons. "These are from a warship."

"Yea," said the centurion of the cavalry, "and these deserters took away all chance for the escape of our comrades."

"We all swam ashore," they said, "and we found these boats here. Other men than we made off with them, We are innocent."

The two centurions looked at each other and they were of one accord in this matter. At a word of command soldiers dropped from their horses sword in hand. At another word the work of punishment began and the stern justice of the Roman military law was done in utter injustice, for not one of these who were slain had sinned.

"They had done somewhat in other days," said Ulric, "and the vengeance of their gods found them here, bringing upon them a sword. No man escapeth the gods. But I see another man down the beach. He is fleeing as if for his life. I think, therefore, that these were not all who came to the shore in some manner."

Great was the wrath and the dismay of all those Romans at this terrible affair of wreck and fire, but there was no sign to suggest to them the presence of Saxons on the sea or on the land.

Unto the four boatloads of Ionian rowers at their landing place, where they still lingered, came running the one of their number who had gone forth as a scout. Pallid with fear and horror he gasped out to them the thing that he had seen, and he fell to the sand breathless with running.

"To the mountains!" they shouted. "We are slain if we are found on the coast. They now know not that we are here."

Then it could be seen that not only had they taken plenty of weapons even in their hasty flight from the burning ship, but that their apparel was decent. Also their talk indicated that they had many coins of money, and that they knew this country whereupon they had landed. They stood still for a moment, and they swore to one another by their gods that this should forever be a secret, and then they marched away up the steep and were hidden in the forest.

Neither had they failed, in their talk upon the shore, to wonder much concerning the first burning vessel which had been the cause of their own disaster. They knew not of the Saxon boats, but they had said of themselves that they would not willingly fall in with any who had escaped lest their peril might be increased.

"It were death," they said, "and we must at once put any such men to the sword."

The Saxon men, whom they did not know, but of whom they had been speaking, were gathered together on the mountain.

"O jarl," said Tostig the Red, "well that thou didst order us to bring provisions, also, for our first needs. Shall we not now go on into the forest and find a place where we may kindle a fire?"

"O Tostig," said the jarl, "Ben Ezra is our guide. This is his country. What sayest thou, O Jew?"

"Only this," replied Ben Ezra; "that we are upon Mount Carmel, and that the forests thereof are deep. We are safe if we are prudent. It is a wilderness into which not many come at any time, but there are villages and cities not far away."

"Lead on thou, then," said Ulric. "Let every man bring all his burden. We will keep up strong hearts, and we will see to what this strange coming on shore will take us."

They had need of cheerful words from their jarl, for upon them all was a shadow deeper than any of the shadows of the forest. Their faces were dark, but among them all was there no face like that of Lysias, the Greek. There was no light in it, but rather a bitter sullenness.

"Sapphira! Sapphira!" he muttered, walking apart from the rest. "Am I indeed nearing thee? Am I to find thee? Am I, then, to love thee again or am I to slay thee? Thou shalt not live to be the bondslave of a Roman, even though he be a prince and a ruler!"

Ulric the Jarl heard him. It was as if he had been spoken to concerning the Hebrew maiden whom he had seen with Hilda.

"I think that she is somewhere in this land to which I have been guided," he thought. "I will go on and I may find her. This forest is a dense cover of this mountain. I shall be glad to look upon that which is beyond it."

Ben Ezra led onward rapidly, but the way by which he went grew steeper. They came out at last, much heated by their heavy burdens, upon a level place, where were no trees, and here he halted.

"Here let the fire be made," he said to the jarl. "But if thou and Sigurd will walk with me a little distance further ye will see something."

Gladly did the wearied Saxons pause and make their camp, but their jarl and Sigurd followed the Jew. Not far did these go until they came out upon a bold, high promontory of rocks.

"Look!" said Ben Ezra. "The Middle Sea."

There were no trees to hinder sight and the air was pure, so that they saw afar. There were many sails and there were also galleys which might be warships.

"O jarl," said Ben Ezra, "thou art escaped from a Roman fleet. Thou wouldst not have done so but for the ledge of rocks and the fire which destroyed thy vessel. Thou art on the front of Carmel. Now turn thee to thy left. What seest thou?"

"A heap of stones," said Ulric. "They have been shapely, but now they are broken down. Was it one of the altars of thy god?"

"Not so," said Ben Ezra, "but our fathers made that heap for a sign of remembrance. In the ancient days there was on that spot an altar to Jehovah. Upon it the prophet Elijah sacrificed oxen and the fire of our god came down and consumed both the sacrifice and the altar. Here was Jehovah's victory over Baal, the god of the heathen, and here were all the priests and prophets of Baal slain with the sword."

"If thy god is here," said Ulric, "I am willing to remain, for I think he hath befriended us. But I have no quarrel with Baal or with any other god. I think Odin and Thor to be at peace with thy Jehovah, but I like not at all the cunning gods of the Romans."

"Jehovah destroyeth them in the day of his appointing," said Ben Ezra. "They cannot stand against him. He is mighty."

The jarl was silent, gazing out upon the sea, and Sigurd looked around him among the trees.

"O jarl," he said, "I like not this mountain, full of gods. The men have kindled fires. Let us eat and drink and then let us depart."

Chapter XX
Carmel and Esdraelon

"Here are boats!" exclaimed the Roman officer, as he drew rein at the place upon the beach from which the Ionian rowers had fled. "Then there were more of these cowardly deserters. If all these boats had remained with the ships, how many brave men might have been rescued! We will search the mountains for these rascals. If Cæsar hath been robbed of two warships by the fire and the rocks, we will at least avenge the shades of our comrades who were left to perish."

An angry man was he, and with good cause so far as these men were concerned, and their crime was well deserving of punishment. He rode away with his horsemen, but there would soon be terrible hunters for blood among the crags of Carmel. There would, however, be a delay of hours before forces could set out from the war garrisons, and meanwhile the Ionians had been pushing their way into the forest.

They were of one accord that it would not be well for them to continue long in one body, attracting attention, and each man was in dread of all his companions, fearing lest their very number should betray him to the sword. They found what seemed a sufficiently hidden camping place and they slept. At their breaking of their fast next morning, having but little to break it with, they were apparently almost cheerful, chatting lightly among themselves concerning their escape. In that country, they said, were great numbers of Greeks, who came and went unquestioned by the authorities. A few more, if scattered here and there, would go unnoted. Not long time need pass before all of them might be upon the sea again and far away, sailing from the many ports of Syria. Not many of them seemed to be warlike men, but it might be understood, in various forms of speech, that among them was no man who grieved for the destruction of Roman keels and Roman soldiers. Rather did some of them mutter that with their will whole legions had perished instead of half a cohort. They believed themselves to be altogether unobserved, but upon them were now gazing eyes of intense hatred from the leafy ambush of some dense thicket at a short distance.

"O ye who hear me," said one of the deserters, loudly, "know ye this! From the first ship that struck the reef and began to burn did some surely get to the land. Like us they are now in Carmel. What shall we do with them?"

"Slay them!" sharply responded several voices. "Lest they prove our ruin. Slay them without mercy!"

One of them was a tall, gray-haired man, with eyes that were set near together and with a pointed nose. His forehead was high and on it was an iron cap. He said:

"If they be too many, make friends with them at the first, but let none escape. I will attend to that."

They listened as if he might be a man of rank and a leader among them, but hidden by the bushes were ears that understood the tongue in which he and they were speaking, and there were other ears which did not interpret.

"It is of no use to question this Greek of ours, O Knud," whispered one to another of two strong men in the ambush, but his own face and his manner asked a question.

"Be thou silent, Tostig the Red," replied Knud. "Watch him. Do as he doeth!"

For Lysias was muttering low in Greek, "He betrayed my father in Corinth. He would surely destroy me. He is a liar and he must die."

To the head he drew his long arrow, and his companions hindered him not, for his face was burning with wrath, and it pleased them to see him raise his bow.

"He is a young warrior," they thought. "He knoweth what these have spoken."

Truly sped the arrow, and the tall old Corinthian traitor was smitten through the face, so that he spoke no more. Up sprang his companions, wild with fear, but another and another of them went down before they could escape among the trees, for the spears of Tostig and Knud followed the arrows of Lysias and they three followed closely, sword in hand.

"I think," said Knud the Bear when he and his friends returned from a brief chasing, "that too many escaped. I have counted but eleven slain. I will ask the Greek his reasons for this when we reach an interpreter."

"Take all coin from these who are slain," said Lysias, but he made his words plain by action.

"They are Greek and Roman coins," said Knud. "We may need them. I am learning much concerning coins. Oswald, the harper, hath many, but I cared not for them. A sword is better than money."

"Not in a place of buying," laughed Tostig, "and we are not now an army. We must pay."

"I am not a thief," said Knud. "I will pay, but I shall surely be cheated."

"No doubt," said Tostig. "So do we need to take more coins. The Greek is right."

Then they returned to their camp and Lysias stood before Ulric speaking. The jarl listened with care and he became very thoughtful, for Lysias told him all the words of the Ionians.

"So, we are to have foot soldiers hunting in these forests," he said. "I had thought of that. Thou didst well to slay them. But we who are Saxons may not disperse. Go thou and seek thine own safety. Go thou, also, Ben Ezra. Thou art among thine own people."

"Not so," said Ben Ezra. "Let Lysias go, but I remain with thee for a season. Thou needest a guide. It were well for thee and thy men to cross the plains of Esdraelon and get into the mountains of Gilboa. We will go by night, for there is no safety for us in Carmel."

To all the Saxons Ulric interpreted the words of the Jew, and they said to him:

"Thou art the jarl; we will follow thee. But should we not first slay this Lysias?"

"Not so," said Ulric. "He hath fought for us this day."

"Not so!" shouted also Knud the Bear. "He is a good archer. I will cut off the hand that is laid upon him."

"So will I," said Tostig, and his seax was in his hand quickly.

There the matter ended, but Ben Ezra talked with Ulric apart.

"I send Lysias to Jerusalem," he said. "With him I send a jewel to the chief priest and another to the captain of the temple. We will pass over to Gilboa. Thence we will go over the Jordan, at the middle ford. Afterward we will go down to the wilderness of Judea. In that hiding place no search can find us, as I have often told thee, and it is near Jerusalem on the east."

"We are a score of men without Lysias," said Ulric. "Shall we march now?"

"Come thou first with me," said Ben Ezra. "Not with so much treasure may we cross to Gilboa lest we lose it all on the way. I have found a cave in Carmel. Here will we leave the precious stones save a few. I swear to thee by my god that I will keep faith with thee."

"I swear not," said Ulric, "for I know not of an oath with a true companion. Faith of a son of Odin cannot be broken. It is a tryst of blood between me and thee."

"Better than any oath," said Ben Ezra. "Knowest thou not, O heathen jarl, that thou hast covenanted in the name of thy god, whom thou callest thy father?"

"Odin!" exclaimed Ulric. "So it is. He would be angry with me forever if I failed thee in this matter. It is well to beware of provoking the gods. See to it that thou anger not thine own."

They walked away together, none following. Not far to go was it before the Jew stood still and looked around him.

"It is well if we are unseen," he said, "for I have great doubts in my mind."

"I see here a great cleft in the face of this crag," said Ulric. "Like this are many entrances of caves in the Northland. I found some among the faces of the fiords. In them are great bones of men and beasts and store of old-time weapons that are made of stone."

"Thou wilt find bones here," said the Jew, "but I think not many weapons. The cave is dark, and we will have torches."

Exceedingly skillful was he in the kindling of a flame among dry mosses, and Ulric found withered branches of pine full of resin. A torch for each was lighted, and they went in at the cleft, going cautiously.

"In such places as these dwelt the ancient prophets of Jehovah," said Ben Ezra, "but now the caves of the land of Israel are the strongholds of all robbers. I have heard that there are robbers dwelling in Carmel. Turn, now. Let us be sure that no enemy followed us."

The turning was quickly made, for they at that moment heard a sound behind them. Then followed an angry cry and a javelin sped over the head of the stooping Jew to glance from the shield of Ulric. He spoke not, but he threw his spear and drew his seax, for in the cleft passage were armed men. True was the spear-cast and the javelin thrower fell, but over his body sprang Ben Ezra. It was then but a brief struggle between him in his perfect mail and a robber whose garb was but a tunic.

"These were but fools," said the Jew as his scimiter fell upon a fourth of these half-armed men. "I think they are robbers and that they are Samaritans. Accursed are they! I will look to know if there are more of them outside."

He was gone but a moment, and when he returned he exclaimed, hastily:

"Not any, O jarl! We will leave these bodies here for a token. Now we may enter the cave."

"Touch them not," said Ulric. "Thou art wise. I think that any comrade of theirs who may come to see will believe this to be the work of the officers of the law."

"In that were better security for aught that we may will to hide," said Ben Ezra. "Seest thou now, O jarl? This cave is deep. We will go in further."

"There are bones to build heaps with," replied the jarl. "Here hath been a massacre, but these are dry and the slaying was long ago."

Gloomy and terrible was that deep cave in Carmel, with its dark shadows and its whitening skeletons. Among its corners the Jew was searching, holding forward his torch.

"A soft spot in the floor here," he said. "We will dig with our knives. We may come to it again by sure marks, for behind it is the solid rock and at its right a fathom and a half is yonder broken altar."

"Knowest thou," asked Ulric, "to what god belongeth this altar? Was it thine?"

"Nay," said the Jew, "he hath no altars in the caves, but only in the temple at Jerusalem. In the old time was Carmel a stronghold of the Philistines. There have been many gods among these mountains. They were all destroyed by Jehovah."

"I would, then, that he might have a care for these treasures of ours," said Ulric, digging rapidly with his broad dagger. "Go deeper into the earth. Make it wider. Now it is enough. O Jew, if thou and I are slain, no other hand will ever take out that which we will shortly put in."

The casket and some other matters brought by them were now placed in the cavity which the jarl had dug, and the covering was done with care and a removing of surface traces. Then Ulric turned to look upon the altar.

"There are deeply cut runes upon it," he said. "Canst thou read them?"

"Nay, but I know that they are Chaldee," said the Jew. "This altar is exceedingly old. Who shall say what men and what gods have been dwellers in this cave!"

"We may now do no more," said the jarl. "We will return to the men. It is a good prudence, every way, that we leave a mark of blood at the entrance."

"Even so!" exclaimed Ben Ezra. "They were robbers, but also are the Samaritans the enemies of my people. Now am I sure that Jehovah is with thee, and I remember that which is written of such as thou art, that he maketh the heathen his sword."

Ulric was thinking of another matter.

"The burdens of the men will still be heavy," he said, "but not now will they carry any weight of provisions. We will obtain pack beasts when we may. And now we have need for haste lest evil come upon us."

They went out of the cave together and returned to the camp, but Sigurd met them.

"O jarl," he exclaimed. "Lysias hath disappeared and the men are angry. We had thought he would for a while go with us."

"We will guard our own heads, O Sigurd, the son of Thorolf," replied Ulric. "We are better without the Greek. He hath gone on an errand. We will but eat and then we will depart, for the Romans come quickly. The Jew hath a guiding for us."

Nevertheless, the Saxons all were angry, and they ate in silence. Their jarl was too soft with strangers, they said to each other. He avoided too much the shedding of dangerous blood.

He himself was stern and moody, for he was thinking of his lost ship and of the Northland and of Hilda.

"If she knoweth where I am," he thought, "surely she would give me a token. I doubt if she can follow me unto this place. How could she find me in Carmel?"

He stood erect soon, and there was a strong impulse upon him, for he lifted his war horn and blew three blasts, toward the sea, and toward the forest, and toward the great crag that standeth on the promontory of the mountain. The sea replied not, nor did the forest, but from the great wall of rock there came back an answer such as will come in the winter time from out the deep throats of the fiords when the gods are conversing. Once and again it spoke, and Knud the Bear exclaimed:

"Odin is here, or Thor, for that is a war horn of the North answering thine, O son of Brander. It is a good omen. I like to feel that the old gods are with us."

"We will follow thee!" added Wulf the Skater. "Go where thou wilt. I will not again forget that thou art of Odin."

So Ulric took up his spear and shield and Ben Ezra led the way; but the forest was dense before them and it was a long walk eastward before they came out into an open place.

From every lip burst a sudden shout as the Saxons halted to gaze upon that which was before them.

"The valley of the gods!" said Ulric.

"The valley of the slain!" responded Ben Ezra. "The plain of Esdraelon. The valley which is before Jezreel. The valley of Decision. O jarl of the Saxons, it is the place of the meeting of the hosts of kings. Since the world was made here hath been the place of battles. Thereon have fallen more dead than on any other piece of ground. The chariots and the horsemen have there gone down together."

"Here, then, have Thor and Odin contended with the other gods," responded Ulric. "Thy god hath been here — — "

"And all the gods of Africa and all the gods of the East!" shouted the Jew, enthusiastically. "Here the hosts of Joshua contended with the hosts of Canaan. Here have Judah, and Israel, and Egypt, and Babylon, and Nineveh, and Persia, and Greece, and Assyria drawn the sword. In the last days here in Armageddon will perish Gog and Magog, going down before the spear of Jehovah."

"Glad am I to have seen the place," said Ulric, and every viking shouted for joy that he had looked upon the greatest battlefield of the broad world.

Well was it worth coming so far to see, and gladly would they have gone into one of those great combats of the kings; but now they were led on rapidly, for the day was passing. Not long did it take them to walk down to the level plain, but all the while their eyes were busy.

Cities they saw and villages, and many scattered abodes of men. The fields were long since reaped, but here had grown much wheat. There were many vineyards, with groves of olive trees and other fruit trees. Rivers not large but shining. Small hills whereon were towers, as if for watchmen and for garrisons. Names were given to some villages by Ben Ezra, but the greatest town of all was dimly seen, far away across the plain, and he said it was the ancient city of Jezreel. Beyond all, toward the east, arose mountains in long ridges, and they knew from him that these were the Gilboa to which he was leading them.

"O Jew," said Ulric, "where halt we this night?"

"Not on all the plain," said Ben Ezra. "Even now we near the great highway from the south and in it walks a multitude, but I see no armed men. I think that many eyes are already aware of our coming."

That might well be, for the sunlight flashed upon their armor and their helmets and their spear points, but Tostig answered:

"O jarl, what care we for armed men? I think the Jew is right. We must hasten, even if we have to slay a few Romans."

"None are here," said Ben Ezra. "And the people will trouble us not. Pontius the Spearman, the procurator of Judea, hath many gladiators and he hath mercenaries whose speech is strange to the nation. None will question you because ye are not legionaries."

"Well for them that they do not," growled Knud the Bear. "I am no hired gladiator. I am a free Saxon. What sayest thou, O jarl?"

"Nothing," said Ulric, striding forward. "Let us see what this crowd meaneth."

"We have naught to do with them," said Sigurd, "but I am curious to have a look at the people of the land. None of them can say to himself that we came out of the sea on the other side of Carmel."

Every Saxon was as Sigurd in willing to see the people and to know what this might mean, for there were very many in the highway, men and women and children, and there were no horsemen, nor did there seem to be so much as a spear or a shield among them.

Chapter XXI
The Rabbi from Nazareth

Lysias, the Greek, stood in a copse of thick bushes near the forest border and looked out upon the plain, but not toward Gilboa. He had been digging in the earth, as Ulric and Ben Ezra had digged in the cave, but he had not been hiding treasure. He had but wrapped his weapons and his armor in a woolen robe-cloth that he might conceal such perilous evidence from inquiring officials of Rome or of any local authority. Earth and flat stones and sods were over them now, and he had made marks upon trees whereby he might find that place again if he should at any future day will to do so. He now walked out beyond the bushes with no trace upon him that he had been a warrior.

"Well was it for me," he said, "that I found such goodly raiment among the spoils of the trireme. Fewer questions are asked of him who is handsomely appareled. Soon I will procure me a beast and I will go with all speed to Jerusalem. It is a city to which strangers come from all the world, and he who escapeth into a multitude hideth himself in a solitude."

The tunic which he wore was of silk and his robe was of embroidered linen. Sandals were on his feet and his white turban was of a costly silken fabric. If he had retained any weapon, it was now perfectly concealed. To the eye of one who might chance to meet him he would suggest beauty and riches and peace, and not at all an archer whose bow had sent many messengers of death.

"Now must I be careful concerning robbers," he thought. "I have both gold and jewels with me. But to all who ask my errand I shall be but a scholar in the school of Gamaliel at Jerusalem, and therefore I may not enter Samaria, but must pass on swiftly. The Romans themselves favor all such scholars, and I shall have their protection. Their laws are good and my time for smiting them again hath not come. But never will I show mercy to a Roman."

Other things he said concerning the much-vaunted laws and justice of the world's conquerors. Beyond a doubt they not only claimed much in the way of righteousness, and also did many things righteously, but behind this sternly formal justice of theirs, and but little concealed, was a man holding out his hand for bribes, and near him was a place of scourging and the sword of a ready executioner.

Nevertheless, Lysias walked on joyously. Soon he was in a highway, and by it passed through hamlets. He looked inquiringly at all places as he went, but he paused not for conversation with any whom he met or greeted. At last he came to the open gate of a wall, behind which were a goodly house and some outbuildings of stone. In the gateway stood an old man, well appareled, and before him Lysias stood making reverent obeisance, as to an elder.

"I am Simon Ben Assur," said the old man. "Who art thou, O Greek?"

"I am Lysias, the scholar, of the school of Gamaliel at Jerusalem," he replied. "I have lost my beast, for he was worthless and he would go no further. Hast thou a good ass for sale, that will travel swiftly?"

"I see that some one hath sent thee to me," replied Ben Assur. "Thou knowest, therefore, that the beast is a swift one."

"Well with thee," said Lysias. "I would buy him but for thy extortionate price. Wilt thou now give me an honest bidding, that I may pay thee and take him away?"

"Ha!" said Ben Assur. "They told thee my price? There is more which they did not tell thee. The ass is young and there is none swifter than he. He is well trained. The saddle and the bridle are to be purchased with him, as thou needest."

"One needeth them to ride withal," said Lysias. "But every beast hath faults and thine is not worth, upon the market, the half of thy asking. I will but look at him and pass on about my business."

Loudly laughed Simon then, looking keenly into the handsome face of the Greek. He turned and spoke to some one within the inclosure, bidding him bring the ass.

"O youth," he said, "I mind not that thou hast spoken with that evil beast of a Samaritan. Arcas offereth that he will pay me for the ass next Passover week; and I rejected him not, but told him that the price must now be paid to me in five golden pieces. I will say to thee that the pay days of Arcas never come, and wise men deal not at all with him unless he giveth double security."

"I deal not with him," said Lysias, "but I will see thy beast."

And now a serving man led forth to the gate a large and well-shaped animal, upon which were a fair saddle and bridle.

"Mount and try him," said Simon. "If thou canst ride at all, thou wilt ascertain what is under thee; but an unskillful rider may wisely choose another, for he is full of life."

Lysias sprang to the saddle and rode back and forth along the highway.

"He must be mine at any price," he thought, "for in his legs is my safety."

"Wilt thou take thy good bargain, O Greek?" shouted Ben Assur as Lysias returned.

"He is no good bargain at five pieces," said Lysias. "No ass is worth so much. I will give thee one piece—"

"Thou art no Samaritan," interrupted the old Jew. "Thou art not Arcas, to buy of me and afterward to rob me of my pay with false witnesses before the magistrate's seat, proving that thou hast already paid me. Hast thou not two pieces in thy hand? I will give thee a writing of sale lest he be taken from thee in Samaria."

"Two I will give," said Lysias, after again galloping up and down the road. "Make out thy bill of sale to Lysias, the scholar. I now return speedily to Jerusalem."

"I think well of thee!" exclaimed Simon; afterward adding, "I pray thee take my greeting to the great Rabbi Gamaliel. He knoweth me. I deal fairly with thee. I am not ashamed to have thee show unto even him this thy purchase."

Back into the house he went and he soon returned with a small square parchment of a bill of sale. But the coins which he received were heavy coins of Athens and he weighed them thoughtfully in his hand.

"Good youth," he said, "take thou now the counsel of thy elder. Carry not too many of such as these with thee. Open not thy purse before strangers. Thou art overwell appareled. Get thee as far as the gate of a walled town having a garrison before the sun goeth down. Ride fast and far that thou mayest be beyond any who might inquire of thee concerning that which is now under thee. Thou hadst better not enter Samaria."

"Fare thee well," said Lysias, urging the ass promptly. "I take thy counsel."

"Well for him if he so doeth," muttered Ben Assur in the gateway, "since Arcas claimeth the beast as already his own. I will myself now depart for Damascus and the Samaritan devil may seek for his five pieces where he will. I have beaten him."

The thought then in the mind of Lysias did not err greatly.

"Something is concealed from me as to this swift one," he said to himself. "I have no business in Samaria that I should risk being robbed and then imprisoned as a thief. But if I now meet a Roman patrol, no officer will deem me a pirate coming ashore from a burning trireme with a band of Saxons."

Therefore he blessed his gods for guiding him to the house of Ben Assur, and he rode on in safety, but not as yet was there any safety for the others who, like him, had escaped the sea and the fire. Far behind him on Mount Carmel, in a place of few trees, an Ionian sailor fell breathless upon the grass while beside him halted a Roman horseman.

"Get thee up!" he shouted. "Answer truly lest I slay thee! Where are thy companions?"

"Slain by robbers in the armor of Saxons," responded the fallen man, rising. "I will tell thee."

Another horseman came galloping to the side of the first and legionaries on foot might be seen not far away. The wisdom of a commander had sent a band of searchers to the side of Carmel toward the plain rather than among the crags and forests.

Gaining his breath as he could, for he had been running swiftly, the Ionian told all save that he claimed to have swam to the shore.

"Thou sawest but three of these Saxons?" said the officer at last. "I had no knowledge of any such pirate trireme. The Saxons are to be the scourge of the Middle Sea if Cæsar destroyeth them not."

More questions were put to the frightened Ionian, and then he was told:

"I will not slay thee. Thou wilt come with me to Samaria. Thy testimony must go before the procurator that a fleet may cruise against these rovers from the ocean stream. Thy companions that remain must be sought out that they may confirm thee."

Calm and wise was this man, and he at once sent forward, also, swift runners to ask here and there if anything had been seen of a band, or of single men, of the Saxons who had escaped from the trireme.

Now the plain of Esdraelon is wide and the skirts of Carmel are long and rugged. There were none who had seen Ulric the Jarl and his vikings up to the hour when they walked out into the highway. By his directions, as a prudent captain, they marched orderly, two and two, as if they belonged to the auxiliary of some Roman legion and were going by due authority.

"So," advised Ben Ezra, "no man less than a quaternion or a magistrate will run the risk of asking thee a question. No man of the people may demand the errand of a soldier lest harm come to him."

"The multitude hath paused," said Sigurd. "They gather around a man. Let us go see."

Right and left parted the crowd as the Saxon column marched onward, but it halted suddenly, the people closing around and behind it, curiously staring, but not touching nor inquiring whence it came.

There was an open space on the broad highway, and five paces in front of the jarl stood the man of whom Sigurd had spoken. He was of full height and broad, but Ulric said in a low tone to Ben Ezra, in Latin:

"He looketh not altogether like a Jew. I have seen darker Saxons. I think he is a jarl. Such as he might be a leader of men."

Proud was the bearing of Sigurd, the son of Thorolf, the sea king; high and stern was the aspect of Ulric, the son of Odin; tall and powerful men were all the other vikings; but not among them all was there one with the dignity of this plainly dressed Jew rabbi, who stood there unarmed and with only a turban on his head.

He spoke not now to the Saxons, but before him on the earth rolled and wallowed one who seemed in agony. His eyes were starting from their sockets and there was foam upon his lips. A shriek burst from him as his convulsed limbs beat the earth.

"He hath a demon!" said Ben Ezra to Ulric. "The evil spirit teareth him. There are many such. Let us see what this rabbi will do. I think him a learned one. Only the learned may deal with demons."

"Come out of him!" commanded the princely man, stooping to touch the demoniac.

On his face was a kindly smile, nevertheless, but they saw not his eyes, for he was looking downward.

Wild was the shriek that came back, as if in a fiercer spasm of inward pain, but a voice followed it, saying:

"I know thee, who thou art, thou Jesus of Nazareth! Thou holy one of God!"

Again he said, "Come out of him!" and it was as if some unseen being called out loudly in an unknown tongue and fled away.

Then arose from the ground the man in whom the evil spirit had been dwelling, and he stood erect, unharmed, like other men.

"A great rabbi!" whispered Ben Ezra. "One of the learned, from Jerusalem. Thou mayest not speak to him while he is healing."

"He that fled called him a son of Odin," replied Ulric. "He looketh like one."

"He may be one of the gods of this land," muttered Wulf the Skater. "I like him not. He commandeth evil spirits and they obey him. I am glad the jarl is also a son of Odin."

"I am glad to have seen a god," replied Knud the Bear. "He is nobler than other men. Let us see what he will do to that crippled one."

Bent and deformed, as if his arms and legs had little shape left them, was this man whom his friends now half led, half carried, before this rabbi of the Jews.

"Canst thou do anything for him?" asked one. "He hath been thus from his birth."

No answer made the man Jesus, but he laid his hand upon the arm of the crippled one.

"Odin!" exclaimed Ulric. "Look! He can stand upon his feet! He lifteth his hands! Thou art right, Ben Ezra. It were evil for me to speak. The cripple singeth! He is praising his god, and well he may."

"Go thou to the priest at Jerusalem," he heard the rabbi from Nazareth say to each in turn of the men who had been cured. "See thou tell no man."

"What meaneth he?" thought Ulric. "Have not all we seen with our own eyes this which hath been done? I would I were healed of something, then would I know what is this secret between them and their god. He is a strong one. What will Ben Ezra now say about his Jehovah? I think this may be a stronger god, for Jehovah doth not well guard the Jews from the Romans."

But there stood the rabbi, Jesus, and he was saying many things to the multitude. Clear was his voice and deep, and they who were not near him needed not to lose a word that he was saying.

"I understand him not," muttered Sigurd. "I am glad to have seen him, but he is not like our gods of the North. It is time we were marching, O jarl."

"Haste then," added Ben Ezra. "This Jesus is a learned rabbi, and he healeth, but the swords of the Romans are not far behind us."

"I would have speech with him before I go," said Ulric to Ben Ezra. "What is this that he saith concerning unending life? Do we not all die? Do we not all go to the gods? He is lying. It is not good for a son of Odin to lie."

"Speak to him not," said Ben Ezra. "He is touching the sick. Never before have I seen a rabbi like this."

"He is of the seed of David," said a short, dark man who stood near. "He is the Christ that was to come. He is yet to be our King. I am one of his disciples. I shall be a prince when he is crowned."

"Thou a prince?" said Ulric. "Thou lookest not like a captain of warriors. What couldst thou do in a feast of swords?"

The short man shrank away chinking a small bag that was attached to his belt, and his black eyes were glittering with anger.

"If I were a king," said Ulric, "I would find me better captains than he. I like not his face. He loveth his bag too well. Come on, now!"

The order went to his Saxons, but at that moment he heard the rabbi saying: "Let him sell all that he hath and come and follow me. So shall he have treasure in the heavens."

"Where are they, Ben Ezra?" asked the jarl.

"No man knoweth," replied Ben Ezra. "I think they are above the sky. It is the place of our people. Thou art a heathen and they have no part with Israel."

"I go to Valhalla and to the city of Asgard," said Ulric. "To the city of the gods. I want no treasure in any place of the Jews. Thou mayest have thy heavens to thyself. Lead on!"

Nevertheless, Ulric strode forward and stood for a moment before the rabbi looking him in the face.

"O thou of the sons of the gods," he said, "I also am of the line of Odin. I think thou wouldst make a leader of men. I will fight for thee if thou wilt."

"Thou art not far from the kingdom," said the rabbi, smiling wonderfully. "Go thou thy way, for thou wilt see me again. Thou wilt come unto me in the day in which I shall call thee."

"That will I!" exclaimed Ulric with an energy that was sudden. "But I think thou wilt need all the Saxons if thou art to contend with Cæsar. It will be a great battle when his legions meet thee. I have slain many Romans already. I am thy man."

"Thou knowest not yet what thou art," replied the rabbi, "but the Saxons also are my people. I shall send for them."

"That do thou," said Ulric; "and I, Ulric the Jarl, the son of Brander the Brave, the son of Odin, I will lead them for thee, for I am a jarl and a sea king. Fare thee well."

No answer made the rabbi, for he turned to speak to a woman in the crowd, and Ulric turned to walk away with Ben Ezra.

"The Romans will slay him," said Ben Ezra. "Thou wert imprudent. I wonder much. Can this be the Christ that is to come?"

"Who, then, is he?" asked Ulric, and as they went onward the Jew told him many things that were hard to understand.

"It seemeth to me," said the jarl at last, "that thou speakest a saga that Hilda of the hundred years told me in my childhood. Odin is to return bringing the gods with him, and some say he hath returned already and that he who saileth far enough to the eastward and southward may find Asgard. I must see this city, Jerusalem, and its temple, for now I do know that thy Jehovah is a god like Thor or Odin."

"He is the greatest of all gods," said Ben Ezra stoutly, "but this rabbi cannot be the Christ. He is but a healer, and there have been many who wrought cures and cast out demons."

"I would he had been with us in *The Sword*," replied Ulric, "in the day when the evil spirit took possession of my vikings. But he could have done nothing against the Nornir and the valkyrias. Even Odin could not prevent their calling. It was the time for those men to die."

"I heard this demon that was cast out by the rabbi," said Ben Ezra, "but I did not see him. I wonder what he is like?"

"I have heard that such are exceedingly wonderful," said Ulric. "They are of many shapes, but none are beautiful. Some of them are strong and the gods have to tie them up to trees lest they do mischief."

"So have I heard," said the Jew, "only the demons tied up by thy gods are not like our own. We have many, and they seize men by night. They serve the magicians."

"I would slay all magicians," said Ezra. "They interfere with the gods too much. But I see the glint of spears away yonder. I trust there are not too many of them."

They had marched far into Esdraelon and the night was falling. The men were weary and their hearts were heavy.

"Be thou prudent," said Ben Ezra. "If this be a Roman patrol, smite not, but let me have speech with their officer."

"We may not flee," replied the jarl. "Not only are we overworn, but these are in part mounted men. Silence all! They come!"

The Saxons halted, leaning upon their spears, not knowing the purpose of their jarl, but trusting him. On toward them rode but three, of whom one wore a white cloak with a purple border.

"A Roman of high rank," said Ben Ezra. "Slay him not. The band is strong."

Not loudly uttered was the hail of the Roman officer, reining his horse.

"I am Julius, the centurion of Tiberias," he said. "I know ye, who ye are—the gladiators of Caius from Jerusalem for the games at Tiberias. Ye have taken the wrong road. Who art thou, O Jew?"

"I am Ben Ezra, their interpreter," replied the Jew. "Were we not forbidden to go by the way of Jezreel?"

The centurion laughed freely at that.

"Caius is careful of his wagers and would not have thy men seen by the wrong eyes," he said, "but I have had fortune to beat his cunning by this meeting. I will look well at them. They seem better than any that may be now ready to contend with them."

"Study them well," said Ben Ezra, and the centurion rode slowly around the motionless body of Saxons.

"Would I might slay him!" muttered Knud the Bear, but none heard.

"He is a fine mark!" whispered Wulf the Skater. "I could spear him off his horse. But the jarl is cunning."

"Cease," said Tostig the Red. "The legionaries are twoscore and we are weary."

"O thou," said Julius to Ulric, discovering that he was the captain, "thou art a tall one."

"He understandeth Latin," said Ben Ezra. "He is not new, as are the others."

"He looketh a tried swordsman," said Julius, for one soldier judgeth easily another. "Saxon, thou wilt win sesterces at Tiberias, but thou wilt lose some of thy company."

"Not unless ye have better swords than any we have met," replied Ulric.

"Truly!" exclaimed Julius, "this is a deep trick of Caius. He will get no foolish wagers from me. But thou, O Saxon, thou wilt have a Numidian lion to fight, and he is larger than any Syrian beast. What sayest thou to that? Canst thou meet him?"

"Judge thou of that when thou seest him before me," said Ulric. "I would gladly meet thy lion if he is a strong one."

"Hard fighters are the Saxons," said Julius. "I will give thy big Hercules a tiger."

He pointed at Sigurd, and the sea king's face flushed hotly, but he was silent.

"O Jew," said the centurion, "obey thou Caius lest thou get the scourge. Enter not Jezreel. Show not thy gladiators to any. Tell not any man that I have seen them and I will give thee ten sesterces. If thou tellest, I will reward thee otherwise. Go on a little. Camp in the old tower by the highway from Galilee. It hath now no garrison. Thy Saxon wolves are guard enough against jackals and robbers."

"I obey thee, O noble Julius," said Ben Ezra. "Thou wilt answer for us if we are inquired of concerning this tower?"

"I will acquit thee," replied the centurion, and he rode away followed by his own company.

All that had been spoken was now interpreted to the Saxons, and it seemed to them as if a good jest had been made of this Roman. They were glad, also, of a sure camping place, and they marched on in the twilight; but the Jew purchased for them two fat sheep and a skin of wine at a place which passed in going. Then came they to the empty tower at the highway from Galilee, but when they halted Ben Ezra would allow none to enter until he had kindled a flame and had made torches.

"These old towers are abodes of demons," he said, "and the rabbi Jesus is not here to cast them out. This Julius may have played a trick upon us, sending us to contend with evil spirits which have heretofore driven all garrisons out of this place."

"Have thou thy will," said the jarl. "But a son of Odin careth not much for demons."

Chapter XXII
The Tomb Song of Sigurd

The broken portal of the old tower in Esdraelon was as the entrance to a dark cavern, and from it came out a wide-winged owl while Ben Ezra was kindling his flame. Away into the darkness fled the bird of night hooting loudly, and the men said to one another:

"We like not these birds. They are of evil omen. They are friendly with bad spirits and the demons have them for their companions."

Ulric the Jarl stood waiting, and he cared not for the owl, but when a torch was handed to him by the Jew he strode forward, looking warily around him as he went, and others followed him closely.

Naught was there to be seen but bare walls of stone and a flight of stone steps that were builded spirally, leading upward.

"O jarl!" suddenly exclaimed Tostig the Red, going past him, sword in hand, "here, also, are other steps. Look! They go down into the under world. Beneath this tower might be vaults and a prison."

"Such places are ever the abode of the evil spirits," said Ben Ezra. "Go not down this at first. It is likely there have been many men slain here, for this tower hath been a place of defense since the old time. It was builded by the Philistines, but the stonework hath been repaired by the kings of the nations who came after them."

Easy it was to obtain enough of fuel for a bright fire upon the stone floor, and the Saxons loved the light of its blaze, although little need was for warmth. There was a well near by, with a bucket for bringing up water and a trough for beasts to drink from. They who planned the tower had provided wisely, but Ben Ezra said of the deep well:

"Many are the demons which dwell in old wells. They entice men to fall in, and they themselves come out to deal evilly with lone wayfarers. Therefore some who encamp by the wells are heard of no more. Only the very learned of the rabbis know how to cast them out. Let us hope that this fountain hath been purified."

"The water is good," said Knud the Bear, "and I was thirsty. The gods make wells."

They ate and drank, and then Ulric the Jarl knew that it was his duty to further explore the tower. He first climbed the stone stairway to the upper part. Here was no roof, and the walls were notched well for bowmen. There was a place, also, for the burning of a beacon light.

"It is a strong tower," said the jarl. "A few men might keep it against many if the portal had a stout gate with arrow holes. We are garrison enough. I will go down."

The stars above were bright, but there was no moon, and nothing could he discern of the plain or of the mountains. He descended the stairway and went to the downward steps, taking a larger torch but asking no company.

"O jarl," said Sigurd, "have a care for thyself. Thou knowest not who may be the god of this place."

"Odin!" laughed Ulric. "Whoever he may be he hath not hindered our coming in. I will see what is below."

None followed him but Tostig the Red, who was ever curious and who had no fear of demons, thinking them of no account.

"O jarl," he said, at the bottom of the steps, "hold up thy torch. This winding stairway hath taken us down two fathoms or more. There is a bad smell. I like it not. I hear something that moveth."

"Help me! For the sake of Jehovah the Blessed!" gasped a human voice not far away. "I perish with thirst. They bound me and left me here to die."

He spoke in the old Hebrew tongue, not unlike the tongue which was commonly spoken in that land, and Ulric answered:

"Who art thou?"

"I am Abbas, the merchant, of Jerusalem," responded the voice. "Water! Water! They were robbers from Mount Gilboa. I was rash, for I had little treasure with me. They got but my ass and a bag of denarii, and they were wroth to have so little. This was their hiding place, but they are gone out for prey."

Over him stood Ulric, holding the torch, while Tostig with his knife cut the hempen fetters and lifted Abbas to his feet. He was naked save a torn tunic, but he did not seem to be wounded. The Saxons above had heard, and a horn of water was brought down by Sigurd, the son of Thorolf, for Ben Ezra was outside of the tower. Abbas drank, gaining strength, and went up the stairway with little help, while Tostig searched that place in vain for anything worth the taking.

"They take their spoils elsewhere," he muttered, "but we will care little for that if Odin hath sent us the slaying of them. I would be glad to kill some robbers."

"Men in Galilee owed me money for merchandise," explained Abbas as he ate. "I came to obtain it, thinking to return in strong company. The Romans make the highways safe to all, and I had no fear. But this band numbereth a score. I think they will return before the morning."

"Put out the fire!" commanded the jarl. "Every man to his spear and shield. We will not let one of them escape. It is evil to leave a man to die of thirst instead of giving him the sword."

"The Romans will thank thee well, O chief of the gladiators," said Abbas. "They have striven to destroy these robbers of Gilboa, but if these are pressed hardly, they flee across the Jordan. They are from the wilderness."

Ben Ezra heard standing in the doorway, and he already knew all. To Ulric he said in the North tongue:

"Beware whom thou slayest. Thou art but a gladiator in this tower. Thou art not here a jarl, to do as thou wilt."

"Ever am I a son of Odin," said Ulric. "I have sold my sword to no man. Who shall stay me from slaying? I will spare not one."

"If thou slayest one, slay all," said Ben Ezra. "There is danger in the enmity of the men of the wilderness. They forget not, and the next of kin may find thee."

"Not if he be wise," said Ulric, but he bade his men lie down and rest, keeping watches.

Then spoke to him the Jew Abbas:

"I will tell thee a thing. Me they may have thought to ransom. I know not. But they will be here at the dawn to lie in wait for a company that cometh from Tiberias with much merchandise. Thou mayest be sure that, if thou slayest them not, then thou and all of thine are to be slain."

"That I may well believe," said the jarl, "but they who slay Saxons may count their men and we will count how many remain."

"So be it," said Abbas. "Thou art a tall one. But thou, Ben Ezra, come hither and commune with me."

So went they apart and they talked much together in the old Hebrew tongue, and it seemed to the jarl that these two Jews might be of kin to each other, so many names did they speak of men and of women and of places.

"I will trust Ben Ezra," he thought, "but of this Abbas I shall know more at another time. I would see the sun upon his face before I can read its meaning."

Then came around him and Sigurd all the other Saxons asking curiously concerning all these things which had taken place. They asked about the tower and the plain and the mountains until they were satisfied.

"Thou art a prudent jarl," said Tostig the Red, "but I would rather fight lions than to be hidden away among the hills like a wolf. Are there not cities to be seen, and wonderful places? I like not deserts."

"We came out to see the world," said Knud the Bear. "O jarl, there might be excellent fighting if we go in the right direction."

"That would please me also," said Wulf the Skater, "and we may begin with these robbers if they are to come upon us. They may be swordsmen."

Other of the vikings spoke strongly, as became warriors, and Ulric saw that they were in earnest. They liked not Gilboa and its caves. They had been shut up on shipboard long and they were in great wonder concerning this country of the Jews.

"Even so am I," Ulric said to them. "We will go on and see cities, as you desire. We will not be Roman soldiers, but there is no disgrace to a Northman in slaying a fighting beast or a fighting man. Only I will serve no master, even though he be a king. I am of Odin."

"We are as thou art in this matter," said the Saxons. "We will serve none save in thy company, but we pray thee lead us into a better place than this tower or a desert."

Now, also, some remembered to speak again of Lysias, the Greek, wondering whether or not he had escaped and where he might be. "Ought we not rather to have slain him?" they said. "Who knoweth what report he may send out concerning us?"

"He will have good care for his own life in that matter," said the jarl. "He will be secret for his own sake. Do ye not also remember that he is a good bowman?"

"I like him for his archery," said Tostig the Red. "I trust that his gods may be with him to help him slay more Romans."

"That seemeth not to be for us," said Knud the Bear. "We are to be friends with them for a season. But I would see a tiger if I may, and also some of these great elephants, which cause me to think of a whale walking upon the land."

"Thou wilt see them at Tiberias if thou goest there," said Ben Ezra; "but be careful of thy speech, for thou art now in a Roman land and thou art but one man. Thou canst not fight a cohort."

"A warrior may be prudent without dishonor," responded Knud. "I like the Romans better, now I have killed so many of them. They are good fighters and they die where they stand, not running away."

So said other of the Saxons, and all slept but the watchers, and the night passed.

It was in the dull hour before the sun's rising that Abbas, the Jew, came to the jarl and touched him, saying:

"Arise, O captain of the Saxons. The sentinel at the roadside needeth thee."

"Stir up the men," spoke Ulric to Sigurd, the son of Thorolf, "but bid them keep in the tower. Come thou unto me at the road."

So went he out and stood by the sentinel, and with them were Ben Ezra and Abbas.

"O jarl," said Wulf the Skater, "I might not leave my post, but I have slain this man that lieth here. What he is I know not, but he crept near me stealthily and I speared him. It was a cast in the dark. He weareth a turban."

"A robber from beyond Jordan," said Abbas stooping. "He is a bowman. Therefore there are others with him. What sayest thou, captain of the Saxons?"

"Let no man speak loudly," said Ulric. "Bring no light. I hear horses. Be ready. Slay all who come, but give no warning."

So did Sigurd, the son of Thorolf, give direction in the tower, and the men were prudent, waiting for what might come. But Sigurd now stood by Ulric and seemed like a giant in the gloom. By him stood another Saxon quickly, and he was lifting his shield when something smote it, making it ring.

"An arrow," he said, "sent strongly. A dozen men, O jarl!"

"Smitten am I!" shouted Sigurd, but he sprang forward swinging his pole ax.

Upon him darkly, suddenly, pressed hard a swarm of men, and they were as locusts crushed by the foot as his ax fell on them.

Ulric stood fast for a moment, but forward with Sigurd went Wulf the Skater full of war wrath. More than one arrow rattled on the shield of the jarl, but he had cast his spear and he was now swinging the long, straight sword of Annibaal, the Carthaginian, for men were upon him and he mowed them as rushes.

"Back to the tower, Ben Ezra!" exclaimed Abbas.

Past Abbas and Ben Ezra charged four Saxons with Knud the Bear; but the two Jews went back to the tower, for they were cunning and they willed not to be discovered by these robbers whose vengeance is forever.

Men half armored, moderate in stature, not expecting great resistance, were without hope in such a fray as this. They were there to be slaughtered, but at a little distance were others who were on horseback. From among these rode one a little nearer, while the others withheld their archery for fear of hitting their own men.

"O Abbas, of Jerusalem!" he shouted. "Would we had slain thee at once! Thou hast betrayed us to the Romans. I will yet have revenge upon thee and upon thy son. Thou art the father of that Bar Abbas that smote me and mine beyond Machærus. May the Romans crucify him!"

Abbas at the tower heard well, but he replied not, and the Saxons were slaying fast the robbers who were on foot. Not one of them escaped, so swiftly fell the steel of the strong ones from the Northland.

Again shouted the man, the robber chief on horseback, shouting to his footmen, but no voice went back to him. Only a spear thrown by Knud the Bear went through him from breast to back and Ulric blew a blast upon his war horn, for he heard a clash of swords behind him.

"It is naught!" shouted Tostig the Red, from the doorway. "We were three and with us were the two Jews. Some thieves who came here are dead, dying easily. Fight on."

Loud were the shouts of wrath among the horsemen, and one was interpreted by Abbas to Ulric:

"He saith 'a Roman garrison is in the tower.' No robber will venture nearer."

"Woe to thee, Abbas!" came fiercely out of the gloom. "Woe to thee and thine! I curse thee by my gods for ever and ever!"

No word spoke Abbas, but the horsemen wheeled and rode away swiftly, while Ulric stooped over one who lay upon the ground.

"O son of Thorolf!" he exclaimed, "I would thou hadst not been smitten."

"That am I," said Sigurd. "The valkyrias have not passed me by. It was the arrow in the dark, and the bowman was near and it pierced my mail."

"Thou didst fight well, being smitten," said Ulric, "for thou art of the heroes."

"Burn me not," said Sigurd, "but bury me by this tower, in my armor, laying my weapons with me. I may need them when I awake among the gods. I know not much of these matters, but I have great curiosity."

"Aye," said Ulric, "and if thou seest Hilda of the hundred years, thou mayest tell her where I am. Speak thou also to my father, to Brander the Brave, the sea king. Tell him I go on to Asgard, and that I have seen one of the gods in this land and that I seek to see him again."

"I also saw him there in the road," said Sigurd. "I think him one of them by his face and by the word of the evil spirits. If thou meetest him again, greet him for me. Give me thy hand, Ulric the Jarl! The valkyrias! Odin!"

Half sprang to his feet the mighty son of Thorolf and he uttered a great cry. Then crashing heavily down he fell prostrate, his shield and his mail clanging. Silently around him stood the Saxons, and one of them said:

"O jarl, so fall we, one by one. I like it not. We shall never again see the Northland. The gods are against us!"

"He died not in his bed," said Knud the Bear. "It is well with him, Jarl Ulric."

"So die I!" exclaimed Wulf the Skater. "Come! Let us dig, for the ravens must not whet their beaks on the bones of the hero."

Therefore, with knives and spearheads and flat stones the Saxons dug a deep hollow in the earth, and into it the sun looked down when he was risen.

"It will do," said Ulric; "but now we will eat and drink. We have slain eighteen of these robbers. I would we had slain them all."

Many coins had been found upon the dead, especially upon him who had been mounted, and all these the jarl divided among the men, Ben Ezra counting for him their value.

"Keep thou some," said Knud the Bear.

"Not so," replied Ulric. "I have enough. I like not too many coins. Ye may need them to buy with. What have I to do with such things?"

"Thou art jarl," reasoned Knud. "If thou take them not now we will yet compel thee. Thou canst not do altogether as thou wilt. We think thou wilt need many coins. They are the custom of this land."

"So be it," said Ulric. "I am learning much about them. But I would rather be rich in cattle and in horses. I have all the lands of Brander. I think I will take some coins with me when I go, to keep them in a bag like old Oswald, the harper."

"We will pay ours here, I think," said Knud. "But let the Jew make thy bargains for thee; for the sons of Odin are not good merchants."

Ben Ezra spoke then, agreeing well with Knud, but the heart of Ulric was heavy because of Sigurd, for the son of Thorolf had kept good faith with him, and the men who are true to friends are the men who are most missed when the valkyrias come to them.

There were eating and drinking and there was much curious examination of the weapons and clothing and armor of the robbers from beyond Jordan. Ben Ezra and Abbas answered all questions, but they said, also, that there must be no going away from the tower until a messenger should arrive from Julius or from some other Roman officer.

Even while he was saying this to Ulric there was heard from the southward along the highway the sound of a trumpet.

"Whoever cometh," said Ben Ezra, "let me have first speech with him. In slaying these who lie here we have been under the orders of Julius, the centurion, and our official responsibility is to him; but he referreth us to Caius, of the household of the procurator at Jerusalem. We have need of cunning."

The sun was high now, and Esdraelon was exceedingly beautiful between its mountains. It was a plain of brown and green under blue heavens, a place where the gods might walk; but Ulric, the son of Brander, listened to the trumpet and looked from the bodies of the dead to the Saxons, who stood in line on guard at the roadside.

"This is the valley of battles," he said, aloud. "O Jew, I will heed thee. Knowest thou anything of this Julius?"

"Not of myself," said Ben Ezra, "but Abbas knoweth of him that he is said to be a subtle serpent, winning much money on wagers, and that he is cruel."

"Mark thou this, then," said Ulric. "I saw in his face a thing that I read better now that we have lost a brave swordsman. Deal thou carefully with these who come. I like not this place where too many have fallen, and where thou sayest the multitudes are to perish in the latter days."

Dark was the brow of the young jarl, and he went and stood by the open tomb and by the body of Sigurd, the son of Thorolf.

Out stepped Ben Ezra into the highway, and he stood there making due obeisance and uttering a greeting, when a Roman officer wearing a white cloak with a purple border drew rein before him.

"I am Caius, of Thessalonica," said the Roman. "Who art thou and who are these?"

"If thou art Caius, thou art well arrived," said Ben Ezra. "Thy swordsmen rested here at the command of Julius, the centurion, and I have somewhat to tell— —"

"These, then, were hired for me by that traitor Hyles?" suddenly exclaimed Caius, in wrath. "And he sent them on to be murdered by Julius? Thou knowest not that Hyles was slain in Samaria yesterday? Tell all!"

Rapidly spoke the Jew, while other horsemen and four chariots halted near in the highway.

Caius dismounted and walked on to where Ulric stood, and the jarl greeted him, pointing down at Sigurd.

"So! I have lost a good sword by this Julius," exclaimed Caius. "He meant me to lose all that he might win the games. Are any more of thy men hurt?"

"None," said Ulric in Latin, "but this was a chief, a hero, a leader of men. Him we must bury before we march."

"I, too, am a soldier!" shouted Caius. "He was a brave man! Bury him according to thy custom. Thinkest thou I am a dog? I, too, will stand by. Brave men grow scarce. I would that Cæsar had ten legions of such as thou art. The new levies are dwarfs!"

Out went the hand of Ulric freely, for the man's face had scars on it and he was of good stature.

"I will go with thee," he said. "I am Ulric the Jarl, of the sons of Odin. It was promised me that I should have a lion to slay and that I should see Jerusalem. Wilt thou keep faith with me?"

"No!" said Caius. "I will give thee not to a lion; but thou shalt go where thou wilt, and then thou shalt see Rome and fight before Cæsar. Wait till thou hast seen this lion prepared for thy destruction. I am not thine enemy to betray thee to ruin."

"I will wait," said Ulric, but he turned and beckoned to the Saxons.

All came and they took up the body of Sigurd, laying it in the deep tomb.

"Put in stones and earth," said Ulric; but Caius, of Thessalonica, stepped forward and threw in the first handful.

"Cunning is he," whispered Abbas to Ben Ezra. "He knoweth men. He is winning these Saxons for himself. There are no men more cunning than the Romans."

Slowly filled they the tomb, but Ulric stood at the head, looking down, and he said aloud: "Who shall sing the tomb song of Sigurd, the son of Thorolf?"

"Thou, O jarl," said Knud the Bear. "We have no harp nor any saga woman. Sing thou to the hero and to the gods."

Song came upon the soul of Ulric and his lips opened—and it was as if Hilda were with him, for he sang wonderfully. There were women in the chariots and they sat listening to the musical voice of the jarl. The legionaries on the horses sat like statues. The Saxons waited, holding each his war horn in his hand, as did the jarl, until the tomb was filled, and they laid a broad stone thereon from a ruined part of the tower.

Ulric lifted his war horn and all the rest did likewise, answering his blast and then shouting. He blew again and he cried out:

"O Sigurd, son of Thorolf, the sea king, I have done as thou didst bid me. Bear thou my messages to the dead. Tell them I come. Keep thou a place for me in Valhalla, in the day when the valkyrias come for me."

"Thou hast bidden farewell to thy comrade," said Caius, frankly. "What doest thou with the corpses of these robbers?"

"Let the ravens and the wolves care for that matter," said Ulric. "They are not ours."

"It is well," said the Roman, for there was pride in the manner of the jarl. "Such work is for slaves, not for thee. An officer will do whatever is needful. Prepare thee to march for Tiberias. Thou wilt have good quarters, near the amphitheater. No man may molest thee, O chief of the Saxons. I like thee well, and I would thy tall comrade were living. Subtle indeed is Julius, the gambler, but he hath obtained only the slaying of robbers, and the quæstor will but laugh as at a jest."

Well pleased were all the Saxons at the respect shown to them and to their jarl, but they went and looked curiously at the chariots in the highway. They studied well the wheels and the harness, but most of all did they gaze at the charioteers.

"Now," said Knud the Bear, "I believe that which was told me, for I have seen black men. I must slay one some day that I may know the color of his blood and of his flesh. They have strange hair, also, and they wear arm rings of silver and rings in their noses and in their ears."

"Those women are like other women," thought Ulric. "Not yet have I seen her who stood by Hilda in my dreams. She is tenfold more beautiful than any of these."

Nevertheless, haste was made, and when the trumpet sounded the march the Saxons were ready for the highway; but it was after the middle of the day, and Ben Ezra had all directions for the way. On went the chariots and the horsemen, and then Ulric and his men followed, saluting first the tomb of Sigurd.

Chapter XXIII
In a Place Apart at Night

"Halt thou! This is the place provided for thy band."

So said to Ulric the Jarl the Roman soldier who stood in the highway before the inn.

It was near the setting of the sun and the Saxons were weary with the heat. They were thirsty, likewise, and they were glad of a light red wine which was brought to them, but Ulric said to the bringers:

"For me water only. I fear much the evil spirit that hideth in the wine of this land. I think he is mine enemy and that my gods are at war with him."

So he drank only water, but they all went in to the supper which had been ordered for them by Caius. They talked not much with any, for the people of the inn were afraid of them, and men and women and children of the neighborhood who came to gaze did so as those who look but in readiness to run away.

The place was but a hamlet in Esdraelon, and around it were vineyards with many olive trees and fig trees.

There was a spirit of unrest upon Ulric, the son of Brander, and his soul was troubled within him. He remained not in the inn after supper, but walked out alone fully armed. He conversed in Latin a brief space with the soldier on duty there, asking him questions, and the answers did not please him.

"Thou wilt feed the beasts of the circus right well," said the legionary scornfully. "They will be hungry when they are let loose upon thee and thine. Thou art no Roman. All barbarians are fit to be crucified."

Down into his face looked Ulric the Jarl. "O Roman," he said, "I am a match for seven such as thou art. I could lift thee above my head and cast thee like a stone from a sling. Well said Caius that these new legions were worthless against the strong in battle. Thou hast no part in Thor the Hammerer."

The soldier's face was dark with anger, but the jarl laughed and passed on, and neither of them knew that Knud the Bear in the door of the inn had been balancing his spear.

"If he lifteth but a hand against the jarl, I will smite him through!" muttered Knud. "The jarl is imprudent. I like it not."

"Lower thy spear," said Ben Ezra near him. "There will be no harm to thy chief. Thou art overhasty and thou wilt soon die."

"There will be blood at my dying," said Knud. "I will strike for the jarl if all the legions of Cæsar should come."

"Wait," said Ben Ezra. "Thou wilt find a better hour to use thy spear."

"So be it," replied Knud. "Thou art old and thou art wise and thou hatest Romans."

On walked the jarl, but he was thinking, and the thoughts in his mind were heated.

"Where am I now?" he said, but not aloud. "Where is the good ship *The Sword*? Where are my companions who sailed with me from the Northland? Where is Asgard? I have seen one god, but when shall I look into his face again? When shall I find the maiden who stood by Hilda? My heart is on fire when I think of her. None like her was ever seen in the Northland. O Hilda, canst thou tell me does this thy beautiful companion dwell among the gods? Then will I go to them that I may greet her, for she is mine."

Other thoughts came to be uttered, but he spoke them not, and he walked onward into the deepening gloom. Very dark it was until the moon arose, and he knew not that the Saxons at the inn were inquiring angrily concerning him.

"What are we if we lose our jarl?" said Wulf the Skater. "But for him we had been lost long since. We would have no more help of Odin if our jarl were taken away."

Ben Ezra and Abbas pacified them, and Tostig the Red said to the others:

"There are but few Romans near and they are bound under Caius. What danger to the son of Brander were a drove of these Syrian cattle, even if they were armed?"

"The son of Thorolf was slain by an arrow shot in the dark," said a viking, surlily. "The jarl doeth not well to go among arrows. I would see his face again."

Murmurs were many, and they all came out and stood before the inn examining their weapons and tightening their mail.

Ulric walked on, but not far, in the brightening moonlight.

"It is like the North country moon in winter," he said, for the air was clear and many things could be seen as in the day.

Beyond him arose a hill, such as may be in so great a plain, and on it there were ruins, grass-grown and mossy. In the old time there had been here a castle or a pleasure palace, none could tell which, and some of the stones were large, arising as pillars with stones laid across their summits.

"Not a temple," said Ulric, thoughtfully. "I hope not. I would not go too near an abiding place of the dead gods. Oft they come back again to trouble men. So saith Ben Ezra. So saith Abbas. They hate men, for men worship them no more."

He walked more slowly, thinking of the gods and of Hilda and of the strangeness that he himself was here without a ship or a strong company, and not knowing what might be before him on the morrow.

"I am jarl no more," he began to say, but at that moment he was suddenly silenced and he stood still to listen.

Not many paces beyond him was an open space on the summit of the hill and around it were fallen pillars, many and great, made of white stone. From this open there arose a voice and the light of the moon trembled among the white pillars.

"He kneeleth!" said Ulric to himself. "Ben Ezra called him the rabbi of Nazareth. If there be dead gods or evil demons here, he feareth them not, for they know him."

Not loudly but with exceeding melody of voice the tongue of the kneeling man spoke on, and Ulric said:

"He singeth not to the dead of this place. It is not a saga of heroes. He asketh many things, that they may be given him. I am glad of the old Hebrew tongue that I understand him somewhat, but much that he speaketh I do not understand."

So he listened more, and the voice went on and the moonlight fell gloriously upon the face of him who was kneeling.

"I have been gone long from the inn," said Ulric in his thoughts. "I must return, but I have learned a thing. He is not alone here, as I am. The gods are with him, and he talketh with them as one god may talk to another, as friend to friend, right kindly. He is not at war with them, and one of them is his father. I would it were Odin, for I like this god and I like his asking for these things that he needeth. I, too, need many things, but Odin is far away and I know him not very well. The face of a god is very beautiful in the moonlight. He is a tall, strong man, a good fighter. But the gods have a strength of their own, greater than that of men. They can uproot trees and overturn rocks and drive the ice out of the fiords. This god could do a great many mighty things. I will have a talk with him some day, and I will ask him concerning Asgard."

Ulric gazed earnestly at the face of Jesus of Nazareth, but the closed eyes did not open and the wonderful voice continued its many petitions.

"I would I might see some of the other gods," thought the jarl, "but to remain here is not well. He hath come to this place to be alone with his father and his friends, and no brave warrior would be an intruder upon the affairs of others. I will go."

He turned and walked away, but his thoughts were dark and heavy within him.

"This man is of the sons of Odin," he said. "So am I. Therefore he and I are of kin, and I would know more of him. I would ask him concerning Hilda and my father. If he may thus talk with the gods, my right is the same. But he is more than I, for the evil spirits obey him. He is no magician, to be friendly with them, but he was not unkind to the demon whom he sent away. If I were a god, I think I would deal well with demons and make them fight for me."

So he communed with himself, walking, until he was loudly greeted at the door of the inn.

"O jarl," shouted Knud, "thou art safe! I did not know where to search for thee. It is wrong for thee to leave us in this manner."

"O Knud," said Ulric, "I am not a child. The night is quiet. Let us all sleep, for the march on the morrow may be long, under a hot sun."

The others reproved him sharply, but they now were glad to rest, and the night waned.

There was no sound of trumpet at the sun's rising, but a quaternion of legionaries came and the guard was changed. The officer also brought orders from Caius that the gladiators should move on toward Galilee. Also a chariot came to carry for them their burdens and their heavier arms and armor, of which there was too much in weight for those who would march rapidly.

"This is not a country for bearskins," said Knud. "Even Wulf the Skater is willing to take off his mail and his helmet. He never would do that thing until this day."

"There is no fighting to be done among these vineyards," said Wulf, "and I think this red wine maketh one's blood hot. I am thinking that I would gladly see a tiger."

"There will be nothing in this land greater to contend with than was the white bear slain by Jarl Ulric," said Tostig the Red. "The children of the ice king were strong ones. I would rejoice in ice and snow at this hour."

"It will be long before thou art frozen, O red one," laughed another of the Saxons. "I am melting, like the ice king."

"Thou wilt make less noise when thou fallest," said Tostig. "But cause me not to remember too much the sea and the good ship *The Sword*. Such thoughts bring me to hate the land, and I listen for the washing of the waves and for the cries of seabirds. It is not good, for the sea is far away."

Silence came then and the Saxons walked on along the highway, seeing all things as they went, but thinking of the blue waters and of the plowing keels and of the North. Ulric strode on in advance, and with him were Abbas and Ben Ezra, telling him many things that he might not be ignorant in his dealings with that which was before him.

"Caius believeth," Ben Ezra told him, "that thou and thy Saxons were engaged for him by his bondsman and purveyor Hyles, who was slain at Samaria for cheating him. We will have all care concerning that matter, but Julius feareth Caius of Thessalonica because of his near friendship with this Pontius the Spearman, who is master of Judea and Samaria under Cæsar. Win thou the good will of Caius, for he is a man of rank and gaineth power. Only trust not any Roman, for they care not for the life of a barbarian more than of a dog."

Ulric answered little, but he thought, and spoke it not.

"These twain are Jews, but one is as a free Northman, a warrior, and the other is as a slave in spirit, fearing the Romans even more than he hateth them. I like not Abbas. He would sell me and mine as if we were cattle. Ben Ezra proveth a true friend and I will abide by his sayings. Here cometh a party!"

Looking along the highway at that moment, he saw chariots and horsemen, but no flag nor any armor.

"Who are these?" he asked of Ben Ezra.

"Let them come nearer," said the Jew. "It is likely they are travelers of importance. Halt thy men at the roadside and we will see."

At the word the Saxons halted, leaving the road free, and they were all willing to stand and watch this company that came.

Four chariots there were, but the one which came first was gilded and carven and was drawn by four white horses. Over it was a silken canopy, and in it sat three veiled women. Of these two were on a front seat, behind the charioteers. He who drove was black and exceedingly uncomely, and beside him sat a large brown man bearing a spear and girded with a sword. These were turbaned and their apparel was good, but not upon them did the eyes of Ulric linger. On the back seat of the chariot, half reclining, was the third woman, and he said to himself:

"This is the princess and the others are her servants. I would see a princess of this country."

Forward he strode three paces, and Knud said to Wulf the Skater:

"How splendid is the youth of our jarl, with his golden hair and his face like that of Odin! There is none other like him!"

"O companion of Hilda!"

"Beautiful is he!" exclaimed Wulf. "But his face is full of pride this day, and I think he is in anger. Speak not to him."

"The woman lifteth her veil," said Tostig, "and she leaneth forward. Odin! She is wonderful! Her headdress is of jewels. Mark the jarl!"

Dark yet fair, with the red of the new rose in her cheeks and with eyes like the lone stars in a winter night, was the young woman who so suddenly leaned forth to look at Ulric. Into his eyes, also, came flashing a great light and a smile of joy was on his face.

"O companion of Hilda!" he shouted in Hebrew. "How camest thou hither from thy place among the gods? I am Ulric the Jarl, and I saw thee when I was on the sea."

Silent was this beautiful princess for a moment, but she grew pale and then red and she seemed to tremble greatly.

"O maiden," said Ben Ezra, "whoever thou art, drive on. He will not harm thee. He is a prince of the Saxons and thou mayest not have conversation with him. He is not for such as thou art, O daughter of Israel."

"Hold thou thy peace!" came from the maiden, as one of high rank may speak. "Warrior of the Saxons, come thou nearer. Thou didst not see me, for I was never on any ship. What is thy meaning?"

Almost at the side of the chariot was the jarl, gazing into her face, but his voice was as the murmur of a harp in the wind when he replied to her.

"O beautiful one!" he said. "Princess of the light and of the morning! More beautiful than are the flowers and the stars! Thy face was where the gods live and I saw thee in my dreams. I will give thee this token from Ulric, of the sons of the gods."

His hand had passed under the mail of his bosom and the bag of gems was there. Now he drew out his hand and he raised before the eyes of the Jewish maiden the perfect gem of which Ben Ezra had said that it was priceless.

"He must not give her that," whispered Abbas.

"Hinder him not!" said Ben Ezra. "Little thou knowest such as he. Wert thou to interfere now, thy head were at the roadside before thou couldst breathe twice. Leave it upon thy shoulders, madman!"

Abbas shrank back, clutching his fingers and scowling, but the Jewish maiden's hand was already grasping the jewel and her lips were smiling with a surpassing sweetness.

"I am Miriam," she said, "and I dwell in Jerusalem. I shall see thee no more. But I give thee a ring for my token. Never have I looked upon such a face as thine."

From her hand she took a ring, and in it was a large, pure pearl, very brilliant, and the gold of the ring was yellow and heavy.

"O Miriam," said Ulric, in the deep tones of the harp of Oswald, "I will wear thy ring, but not in battle. I come soon to Jerusalem, and I will meet thee there, or I will meet thee in Asgard, among the gods, and I will take thee to the house of my father, Odin. Thou art fit to be a princess in Asgard."

His face was like the sun, but hers grew white again, and she drew her veil over it, for Ben Ezra said to Ulric:

"Let none hear thee, O jarl. I know not this matter. Thy words may bring upon her a peril. Harm her not, but be prudent. Thou art a wise captain. Let her drive on. Forward, charioteer! On thy life linger not!"

"Thou art right!" shouted back the brown man, nodding his head at Ben Ezra. "She is my mistress, but she is willful. On!"

The black charioteer slackened the reins of his prancing horses and they sprang forward, but a great cry burst from the lips of Miriam, and the word of Hebrew that was in the sound of it was:

"Farewell, my beloved! I have seen thee!"

"Farewell, O princess!" but in the voice of Ulric, the son of Brander, was a faintness of strong pain, and he turned upon his heel, bowing his head.

"Speak not to the jarl!" said Tostig, grasping the arm of Abbas. "What hast thou to do with an affair of a warrior and a woman? Wert thou to meddle with me in such a case, I would cleave thee to the jaws."

But the chariots all moved swiftly away, and so did the horsemen who were with them, but none of these were soldiers, and in the other chariots were but servants and much baggage.

"The jarl hath marched on," said Tostig the Red. "Follow and trouble him not; for that maiden was wonderfully beautiful and she gave him a ring of remembrance."

Chapter XXIV
The Passing of Oswald

The Northland under the autumn sun was as the South, with green fields and forests and with glowing blooms upon shrubbery and in the hollows of the hills. The fiords were shadowy, with a coolness in the breezes which breathed among them that was pleasant to the wearied fishermen in returning boats.

Upon the high promontory looking seaward at the north of the cove and of the village and of the house of Brander there were no pine trees. Its bald granite knob glittered in the waning light so that it might be seen from far at sea as if it were a beacon. It was not a place for men to seek having no errand to lead them, and not many feet had trodden upon it since the world was made.

Nevertheless, this place was not at the closing of the day unoccupied, and from it there came a sound which went out over the wide water, and downward that it might mingle with the voices of the fiords, and landward, also, that it might be joined with the soft sighing and low whispering of the forests. Not loud was this sound at the first, but it grew louder, and then with it went forth a voice.

"I think my strength faileth me," said Oswald, the harper, pausing in his song. "The harp was overheavy to bring up the mountain. I grow old and I am alone. Hilda sleepeth in the tomb of Odin's sons, Ulric is afar among unknown seas. Am I to die a cow's death before he returneth? Who is there to make the mark of a spear upon my breast, lest I fail of Valhalla? I have fought in many a feast of swords. Why am I to perish slowly, without honor? Sad is the fate of Oswald if the valkyrias pass him and leave him to die in his bed."

Once more the song arose, but now his voice was stronger and he sang of war to the rocks and to the trees and to the gods among the fiords. The old gier-eagle on the withered pine tree northward listened intently, now and then fanning with his wide wings, until the spirit that was in the harping awakened him well. Loud was the scream that he sent back to Oswald, and he dropped suddenly from the branch of the pine tree, spreading his pinions and floating over the sea in a wide circle, rising as he went.

"He is free to come and to go," mourned Oswald, "but I am bound at home and I shall no more ride the war steeds of the open sea nor hear the clang of shields nor see the red blood flow. Where is the good ship *The Sword* this day? Where are Ulric the Jarl and his vikings?"

Low bowed his head and his hands sought fitfully the strings of his harp, bringing out the notes of sorrow.

"I will arise," he said, "and I will go to Hilda's room. I will play to her there and see if she will answer me. She hath not spoken to me since her eyes were closed. But she is with the gods and she hath many matters upon her mind. She hath spoken to Brander the Brave and to jarls and chiefs and kings that were of old. She hath seen Odin, and she hath heard sagas that we hear not until the return of the gods."

He stood erect upon the rock where he had been sitting, and he was not weak, for he shouldered his great harp and bore it with ease as he went down the rugged side of the mountain. Many saw him come, and they who were near enough greeted him, but he paused not to speak. He went not through the village, among the houses, but along the shore, where the tide was coming in and where the waves called out to him as he passed. He turned to listen to them, but across the water came no other voice, and he shook his head sadly.

"Here was *The Sword* launched," he said, halting at the head of the cove. "Here was the White Horse of the Saxons sacrificed to Odin. From hence the new keel went out behind the outing ice. Hilda of the hundred winters told me that there would be no return. Is it so? Will the young jarl never again put his foot upon this beach? Or did she speak only of the vessel? Who may know the counsel of the gods! For they speak unto all men in riddles and the meaning thereof is hidden from us."

He turned and walked to the house, passing through the great hall, bearing his harp, and he went on to the room of Hilda, looking in.

"It is empty," he said. "No other hath slept therein since she departed."

Bare were the walls, and the floor of cloven pine logs lay black, uncovered by rushes. One small table only remained, and upon this was a Roman lamp of bronze, which Brander, the sea king, had brought back from one of his voyages to Britain. There was oil in it and a wick, for such had been a bidding of Hilda to one of the older women and to the housemaidens. They feared much to let that lamp go without filling, if the oil dried away; but it had not been lighted, although a wick was in it.

"I will bring fire," said Oswald, and he did so, going out and returning. He set the flame of his small torch to the wick and it surprised him, for it would not burn.

"O Hilda," he exclaimed, "what is this thing that I cannot light thy lamp?"

There was no spoken answer, but suddenly the wick took the fire and it blazed up a handbreadth, as if for a token.

"Burn thou, then," said Oswald. "I will sing to her."

Quickly they who were in the other rooms of the house and in the hall heard the sound of harping and the voice of a wonderful song, for it was as a love song sung to the dead, telling her of the living and asking her concerning the gods and of all the places of the gods, where she was dwelling. Men and women listened, looking into one another's faces and whispering low, for the song was very beautiful and the harp answered as if it were alive.

Joyously burned the lamp, with a clear golden flame, as the song went on, but it at last burned lower and lower and there came a red color into the fire.

"There hath been much blood!" exclaimed Oswald. "I would I had been with the jarl in the feast of swords. The battle is ended!"

For the lamp went out and the room was very dark, but he sat in the gloom by his harp waiting for what might come.

"Disturb him not," said all the household. "He ever mourneth for Ulric and for Hilda."

Much time went by and now and then there came from that room harp notes, one by one, very faint and low, but Oswald was saying to himself:

"I have heard and I have not heard. All things are a riddle that I cannot read. Surely she touched the harp and her face was in the shadows. O Hilda, speak to me, for I am lonely! Tell me that thou hast not forgotten thy kindred!"

Then fell he down upon his face in a deep swoon, and they who went in because they heard the sound found, also, the harp lying by him with its strings broken. They lifted him and carried him away, taking, also, the harp, but when he again began to breathe and opened his eyes the words that he first uttered were in another tongue than that of the Northland. They heard the name of Hilda, but even when he aroused himself and talked with them he told them naught of what things had occurred to him in the room of Hilda, the prophetess. For there are secrets in the lives of men wherein other men have no part, and no man openeth his hidden heart unwisely. The thoughts of friends whose bodies are far apart are often apt to draw near and to walk the earth side by side. Oswald, indeed, was sending his heart out after Hilda and after Ulric. If the saga woman had in any manner answered him, no man knoweth. Nor can any say that the soul of Ulric was nearer to that of Oswald because both were thinking of each other and of her who had departed from them.

So may the gods look on from their places and see what men see not, and they may often smile, if they are kindly minded, to see men and women meet and embrace without the touching of the bodily flesh.

Three days went by, and because of a request of Oswald's many messages had gone out from house to house and from village to village, up and down the coast and far inland. To everyone it was told that the hour was at hand and that a token of the gods had come to Oswald, but that he was still living. Upon the fourth day all who were entitled to come, by reason of kinship or of their high descent, had arrived. Many men and many women had gathered, and among them were those who brought harps. These sat apart and they spoke to each other in low voices, tuning their harps and listening to the sounds which answered them from the strings.

"The harp of Oswald is broken," said one. "Who shall take it after him?"

"No man," replied the oldest of them all. "It is a harp which came from the East, in the ship of a sea king, and he gave it to the father of Oswald in the days when Hilda was yet unborn. Upon it are strange runes that none may read."

"It shall rest with him in his grave, then," said another, "but Hilda said that he would need it not in the place to which he hath gone."

"They have both harps and harpers there," said the old man, thoughtfully. "I know not the meaning of Hilda's word. So good a harp must find a player, and I think the gods can mend it. We cannot, for we have no strings like these."

Before them lay the great harp upon the floor of the hall, and one lifted it, placing it before a chair as if it might be played upon. There were yet three strings remaining, and the old man sat down in the chair and put out his hands, touching, also, the strings which were broken. Not from these, assuredly, came the sound which now fell upon the ears of the gathered vikings, but all were silent, for the spirit of song was upon this ancient one whom no man knew. Clear was his voice, but thin, and at times it wavered as if with age and weakness, but he sang the departing song of Oswald and of the old time. Strong were his hands also, for as he ceased he gripped with them and these three strings, also, were snapped asunder with loud twanging.

"Hilda is right!" he exclaimed. "The harp of Oswald is dead. It will never sound again. Build ye a fire, high and hot, and burn upon it this frame of wood. I go to Oswald's room."

Rising from his chair, all saw that he was tall and white-bearded, and none detained him while he went to the room of Oswald.

"Thou art awakened, O Oswald, the harper?" he asked, as he entered the room.

"Waiting for thee, old man," came hoarsely from the lips of him who lay upon the bed. "Now lift me up that I may stand erect, and put my sword in my hand. I will not die a cow's death, and thou art mine enemy, having full right in this matter."

"We burn thy harp, as Hilda gave thee directions," said the old man. "We bury thee in a coffin at the foot of the great stone, thy arms and thy armor with thee."

"Also my bag of coins," said Oswald, "and my cup of silver. I know not if I may need them. They have drinking horns in Valhalla. Smite me in the breast. Let the spear mark be a deep one that I may be known as a warrior."

In the doorway and within the room stood now chiefs and heroes and they had heard, and they said to the old one, "Strike him!"

Deep and kindly was the thrust of the spear that was given to Oswald, and he fell to the ground as if he had fallen in battle, so that all the vikings were satisfied.

"Art thou to be smitten," asked a chief of the old man, "or goest thou hence?"

"I am to see the earth put upon him," said the old man. "I came far for this thing, from my place below the great south fiord, toward Denmark. Ask me not my name lest there be a blood revenge in the mind of some foolish one. Take Oswald to his tomb and smite me there, for we are to be buried together and my harp goeth with me."

All went out of the room and the bearers brought the body of Oswald, the harpers playing and the women also chanting. The ancient one took up his harp, which was not very large, and he seemed joyful as he walked with those who went forth to the place of tombs. The grave of Oswald was deep and by it lay a coffin of cloven pine pieces. In this they laid him, bending his swords and seax and breaking the shaft of his spear. His shield and his mail were broken and all were laid upon the body. Then one placed the bag of coins and the goblet at the head and a jarl of rank covered all with a slab of pine, throwing in handfuls of earth and many stones.

"Art thou ready?" he asked of the old one.

"Not thy spear," he said. "Strike with thy sword; and let it be a blow through the heart. As I cease this song to the gods and to the dead I will lay my harp in the tomb. Strike me then."

Now his voice failed him not and he sang well, bringing loud music from his harp.

"I have fought in fourscore of battles!" he shouted. "I have sailed in all seas! I have spared none in the feasts of swords! I have seen the red blood flow from the hearts of many! I die by the hand of a jarl at the grave of my old foeman. O Oswald, I shall be with thee in Valhalla, and there will we cross our swords and fight before the gods. Strike, thou of the sword!"

Down dropped his harp upon the coffin of Oswald and the sword of the jarl passed through him, flashing and returning. Then the ancient one lay upon his harp and earth and stones were thrown in until the tomb was filled and heaped. All the while the other harpers harped and sang, so that due reverence was given to the passing of Oswald.

"Will he see Hilda this night?" asked one of the women. "I bade him greet her for me."

"They say that one who dieth must walk alone a little distance," replied the other woman, "and then he cometh to a dog; and he shall know then where to seek a house that he may enter."

"I have heard many things," said the first speaker, "but they do not agree. I think we know but little certainly. It would be well if one of the dead were to come back and say what he hath seen."

"I would rather hear a saga," said yet another of the women. "I like not the dead. They are cold and they bring ill fortune. Let them stay with the gods."

So said the greater part, but one woman went away muttering to herself. "The dead! The dead!" she said. "They are of no use to us after they are buried. They care not for us any more. But I would willingly have speech with one of them if he would not be overchurlish. I will go, some night, and watch at the place of tombs. The witches watch at tombs and they see wonders. But it was worth seeing, the slaying of the old one. He was a brave warrior and he died well."

There was a feast that night in the house of Brander the Brave, for his kinsmen and his kinswomen entertained their friends joyfully. There was much singing and harping, and the horns and the cups came and went often around the tables. They drank deeply to the success of Ulric, the son of Brander, and to the voyage of his good ship *The Sword*, and to his return in glory from doing great deeds among the fleets of the Romans and among the islands and cities of the Middle Sea.

"The jarl will come again!" they shouted. "And here will he tell us of the feasts of swords and of the crashing of ship against ship. Hael to Jarl Ulric! Hael!"

Chapter XXV
The Messenger of the Procurator

"Not in Samaria this night," had Lysias said to himself when he rode away upon the swift ass whose ownership might be questioned, "but there are many places by the way wherein a wayfarer may find welcome if he payeth."

Behind the saddle had been fastened the leathern sack which he had brought with him from *The Sword*. It contained changes of raiment, but little else, for his coins and his jewels, which were not very valuable, were concealed about his person. More than once as he rode on he both thought and spoke concerning Ulric the Jarl and the vikings, but always did he seem well pleased that he was no longer in their company.

"The jarl is my sure friend," he remarked, "but some of his tall comrades walk with a hand too near the hilt of a sudden weapon."

It was toward the evening when, after riding through towns and villages, he came to what was evidently a caravansary of good size and cleanly keeping at the roadside.

"Here will I halt," he said. "I am now far escaped from burning wrecks and hasty-tempered pirates. I will have this beast of mine well cared for. He showeth no weariness. I think—O ye gods! I know—I am nearer my Sapphira!"

Ere he could dismount, however, before him stood the keeper of the hostelry. Such as he are ever ready to greet with smiling faces the well appareled, riding beasts of price. "He will have money to pay with," thought the innkeeper. "But the land swarmeth with Greeks."

Loud and friendly was his greeting, and in a moment more he was made to understand that this elegant stranger was Lysias, the student, returning to Jerusalem to the school of Gamaliel from a journey to the Lebanon and to the cities of Galilee. Being a man of Samaria, the keeper was the better pleased that his guest was not a Jew, for of them he spoke with scorn and hatred.

"O youth," he said, as they went into the inn, "thou art fortunate. Thou abidest with me this night and on the morrow thy journey will have goodly companionship. There is here a company from Bethsaida and from other cities near the sea of Tiberias. They are merchants, and among them are a taxgatherer and one who dealeth in slaves. There is neither scribe nor Levite to make thee uncomfortable with his evil speech. May they all perish! It is said that the roads are not entirely safe and the robbers come and go without warning."

"I shall be glad of them," said Lysias, "but I think this village must be safe, for I saw the helmet of a legionary as I rode in."

"Where they are the robbers come not," said the keeper, "but they will not be with thee always on the road."

Then walked he away, and Lysias overheard him muttering curses upon all Romans and contempt for all Greeks.

"I think I heard somewhat else," thought Lysias, "and I will look well at this company with which I am to journey to Jerusalem. There have been innkeepers who had no enemies among the robbers and there have been robbers who paid tribute to all innkeepers. I may not carry a bow, but mine eyes and mine ears may do me good service."

Very good was the entertainment given to him and to his comely brown beast, but the departure was early the next morning. Even more in number than he had expected were these who came out into the road at the door of the inn to go on together.

"They are of many kinds," thought Lysias. "No twain are alike. I will not have much conversation with them, but I will watch, for I think they know this innkeeper exceedingly well."

So did he, and it was late in the day when he halted upon the summit of a hill, looking thoughtfully forward and then behind him.

"O ass," he said, "how fast canst thou gallop if it is to save thy master's throat from cutting? Thou hast robbers for companions, and they do but await their opportunity, which I have not yet given them by the way."

The ass did but pull at the bit and the rein was loosened that he might go. On the northerly slope of that hill, however, the company of men and animals which had seemed but peaceful at the outset had halted for a rest before ascending the steep. There were now Jews among them, and others of whose race and lineage there might be curious questioning. Now, also, there were weapons to be seen, such as privileged merchants might be allowed to carry for their protection, and no doubt they had with them written authority to show to any Roman officer. At the first there had been but a dozen men and the women who were with them, but more had joined at a hamlet upon this side of the city of Samaria, now far behind them. Of these latter was an exceedingly black-browed man, having but one eye, and he seemed to be a sort of leader and commander over the others. To Lysias he had averred that he was a dealer in cattle, having a contract with the purveyors of the Roman garrisons. Thus far he had purchased no beasts, but he had looked covetously at the fine ass which carried the young Greek. At this hour he was saying to another of his crew:

"To-night, then. He hath treasure with him, and the beast will bear me swiftly to the wilderness. We will throw his carcass into the pit near the three palms at the crossroad. None will be the wiser and his friends will in vain make inquiry."

"I will stab him as he sleepeth," replied the man spoken to. "The Romans care little if there be one Greek the less. We will speak softly to him when we catch up with him. I have seen that he hath no manner of unquiet mind as to us."

On went the ass, however, at his swiftest pace, even while they were talking, and a long league of the highway did he pass before the intending stabber rode over the crest of that hill.

"Where is the Greek?" he exclaimed.

"Ridden on a little," replied the evil-faced captain. "Pursue not, lest thou alarm him. He will wait for us. He liketh well to prove the speed of his fine beast."

He had not spoken untruly, for Lysias was gladly discovering for the first time that he had found a treasure with four legs, a swift and tireless runner that took pleasure in a race, needing no urging. Only in hamlets and villages, of which there were many, was the rein drawn, and wayfarers who greeted the rider received but brief responses.

"Here am I safe!" he exclaimed at last, "for yonder on the hill is a fort and near it is a camp of Romans. My thieves are no longer a peril. Glad am I, too, that I am so far from the Saxon jarl and his pirates. Their short, sharp blades are ever too near even to each other, and a spear in the hand of a Saxon is but an eager hunter seeking for a mark. I will rest here, and then I will let this beast shorten the road to Jerusalem."

They who had proposed to take the swift ass from him had also hastened somewhat until they inquired carefully of one whom they met, describing Lysias and his bearer.

"Yea," said the man, "ye mean the hasty messenger. He passed me going like the wind. He who sent the message may be sure of its speedy delivery."

Loud and fierce were the utterances of the evil-faced one and his companions, and they cursed their gods for this disappointment. Also they blamed themselves much that they had not sooner taken courage to slay the Greek. It was for this, their cowardice and delay, they said, that the gods had mocked them.

"Never again," said the evil-faced one, "will I throw away a gift that they have placed in my hand. But they might have allowed me the chance I had chosen this night. I have but small confidence in the gods. They are treacherous."

Strong and well made was the Roman camp at the foot of the hill whereon was the castle. There were intrenchments and a mound and lines of palisades, and before these there was drawn up a full cohort of legionaries. It was an evening parade, and along the glittering line there rode without companions an eagle-faced man, who wore no armor.

"Half drilled!" he muttered, angrily. "It is well we are at peace. Of what good were such as these upon the Parthian frontier? Julius Cæsar would never have beaten the Nervii with these dwarfs to face the stout barbarians. He would but have left them to rot in the wilderness, as Crassus did his Syrian levies. But I think I can teach these fellows that they cannot trifle with Pontius the Spearman."

Backward and all around the cohort rode the wrathful procurator of Judea, addressing no man, and then he wheeled and rode out to the highway.

"O thou upon the swift ass!" he suddenly shouted. "Come hither! I require thee."

Bowing low, but answering not, Lysias obeyed him, awaiting further speech.

"Is thy beast as swift as he seemeth?" said Pontius. "I know a good beast. Is he tired?"

"Never saw I one as swift," said Lysias. "But at the close of a day he were better for a rest."

"He may have a short one," said the Roman general, wisely. "I prepare a message that will take thy head with it if it be not delivered rightly. I have naught here but clumsy beasts that travel a league a day."

Then he turned to summon a servant, to whom he gave direction and with whom Lysias rode into the camp, wondering much at his good fortune at such an hour.

"This is of Mercurius," he thought. "I have ever thought well of him, and my father was once a priest of his temple at Corinth; the god hath now remembered me. To him I owe my prosperity upon this journey, and he did not favor the thieves as is his wont."

The ass had been hard ridden, but seemed not much the worse for it. Water and grain were brought to him, and Lysias, also, ate and drank. More time went by than he had expected before a soldier came to summon him to the camp gate.

"Saddle and mount!" said the soldier. "The hand of the procurator is heavy."

No answer might be made except to obey, and shortly the young Greek was at the gate.

"Kill not thy beast, lest thou fail of thy errand," said the eagle-faced commander. "Take thou this letter to the captain of the Damascus gate at Jerusalem. This also, and this. He will further deliver them. Abide thou with him until he give thee answers. Bring them to me."

Few and brief had been his questionings of the young Greek, the pupil of Gamaliel. He was but a tool, an instrument, intelligent, sufficient, sure to serve well because of the scourge or the sword, or of reward. So rule the Romans, and they who receive orders from a Roman general hesitate not to obey.

Silently sat Lysias until the procurator ceased speaking and motioned with his hand. Then, as if of his own accord, the ass went forward. Therefore Lysias had become a royal messenger, whom all men would be eager to speed upon his way, for the fear of Pontius went with him.

"Mercurius!" he shouted, at a goodly distance from the camp. "Better to me art thou than is Jupiter. Now may Venus, also, be my aid if it be true that my Sapphira was sold into the household of this bloody one. O that I might send an arrow into his heart and a flame into his dwelling! But I will not fail of the due delivery of his messages. Who knoweth to what the gods may have destined me? Soon will all the Saxons perish and no man then will know the manner of my coming into Syria. Sapphira! Sapphira! O swift beast! O Venus, goddess of love! Let me go on to Jerusalem that I may once more look into her eyes and hear her voice and touch her hand. She shall not be for another, but for me, for the gods have favored me greatly!"

Chapter XXVI
The Cunning of Julius

"O Jew, thou hast brought to Tiberias the gladiators of Caius of Thessalonica! Woe to thee and to thy accursed race! But I have orders concerning thee and these. They will give us fine sport before long."

Low bowed Ben Ezra to the Roman officer of the gate and his reverent reply came not fully to the ears of Ulric; but the jarl's face flushed haughtily, for he liked neither the speech nor the manner of the Roman. The Saxons, also, were watching their jarl and their faces also reddened, the hands of men tightening upon the shafts of their spears.

"He will be prudent," they said, "but we are not slaves, to be trodden on. As he doeth so will we."

Unto him now the officer turned as if he were looking at some newly caught wild beast.

"O Saxon," he said, "I have heard of thee. Thou didst well by the robbers, but they cost thy Caius of Thessalonica a tall swordsman. Now thou art to be made food for a lion. I shall see thee torn in the circus shortly, please the gods."

With an effort did the jarl steady his temper, but there was a deepness in his voice:

"O Roman, I shall be ready for thy lion. But if thou hast anything further to say thou mayest say it to Caius of Thessalonica. He is a man and he will answer thee."

"What care I for him?" exclaimed the officer.

"He will answer thee that thing also," said the jarl. "It is between thee and him. I have no words with one who openeth and shutteth a gate."

"I will have thee scourged."

"Silence!" ordered a stern, hard voice behind him. "Thou forgettest thyself, Demetrius, of the gate. The scourging of gladiators is not with thee. O Saxon, thy answer is good. March on to thy quarters."

"O noble Julius, the centurion," replied Ulric, "thy tower was a fair abiding place, and thou wert correct in providing it with a garrison."

The face of Julius flushed somewhat, for the jarl spoke to him as one captain may to another.

"I have an account of that affair," he said. "Keep thou thy speech to thyself. Thou hast but slain a few robbers."

"I have heard of thee," said the jarl, "that thou art thyself a good fighter and entitled to the respect of the brave. Thou hast led a legion to victory in a hard battle. Well with thee!"

There is vanity in all men, and the anger passed from Julius while the haughty mannered jarl of the Saxons ascribed to him this fame.

"I have fought more fights than ever thou hast," he said. "But thou art a seaman. I would put thee upon a ship if I had one."

"I am of the sea kings," said Ulric, "but yonder water is too small for a great battle. It is but a fishing pond."

The ground upon which they stood was the high and difficult hill which ariseth behind the city. This, with its palace gardens, was more than two leagues in circuit if the wall were measured around it from a point on the south shore to a point on the north shore. But part of this distance was of crags crowned with forts, and much of the city was a suburb, having no wall. Within were temples and great buildings, and there was an amphitheater near the shore. The Saxons had wondered at the beauty and grandeur of this place as they drew near. They had marched by way of small towns and villages, but up to this hour never before had one of them seen such a city as Tiberias or such a lake as Galilee.

"Speak no more," said Ben Ezra, "but obey him and march on. Our quarters are in the lower town, near the circus. He giveth orders to the guards at the gate."

Forward strode Ulric, followed by his men, and Julius glanced after them. "Caius hath beaten me," he muttered. "I have none to contend with these. They must be destroyed by tigers and lions. I will not waste an elephant upon them."

Once they were within the wall they could obtain from that height a fair view of the city, and they halted as one man.

"O Jew," said Tostig the Red, "is thy Jerusalem larger and better than this?"

"An hundredfold!" exclaimed Ben Ezra. "This abomination of the heathen is but as a handful compared with Zion, the city of Jehovah, God of Hosts."

"Then, O jarl," said Tostig, "I will not get myself killed until I have seen Jerusalem. Manage thou with care, for I think thou wouldst like to see it thyself."

"So will I," replied Ulric. "But I think we shall suffer no harm in this place. I have not seen any strong men yet except some of these Jews, who do not carry arms. They would make good fighting men."

For he had looked at all whom he met with the eye of a captain, and the rabble of that land did not please him.

"Thou art right," said Ben Ezra. "Thou hast seen men of the tribe of Zebulun and of the tribe of Naphtali and some of Ephraim and Manasseh. They are swordsmen if they had a king. Ere long our king cometh. But these heathen of Tiberias are fit only to be crushed under the foot like vipers."

"Speak not so loudly," said Abbas at his side. "Remember that thou art a Jew, and they hate thee."

"O thou of a weak heart!" exclaimed Ben Ezra. "When shall a money-lender be fit to wear a sword! Knowest thou not that I can lead these Saxons through a host of these dogs of the gentiles? The Romans are warriors, but the rabble of Tiberias are scorned even by the lepers. Let us go on."

Fierce was the countenance of the Jew as they went down the long street, for it was broad and on either side of it were temples and shrines.

"Pollution! Abomination!" he exclaimed. "O jarl of the Saxons, these gods of Tiberias are but of wood and stone, the work of men's hands. This place is cursed because of them."

"I will inquire shortly of what sort they may be," said Ulric. "I grow curious concerning gods. What need of so many? They would all go down before the hammer of Thor. Where is thy god that he permitteth them to be here?"

"This was never a city of my people," said Ben Ezra. "It is a work of the Greeks and the Romans. In Jerusalem thou wilt see only the temple of the living god, and of him thou wilt find no image in stone or wood or metal. No man hath ever seen his face."

"I like that," said Ulric, striding onward. "There would be harm if the gods were seen too often. I will yet look again into the face of one, but I am of their kindred and Odin is my father. Thy god seemeth a good one."

All the while the other Saxons gazed as they went, saying not much, but wondering, and all who met them stepped aside, for their stature was great and their arms were splendid. The jarl had bidden them prepare for this on the previous day, and Julius and the gate guards had seen Northmen appareled and armored as if they were now marching to a feast of swords.

Behind them now came on their baggage chariot, and shortly it was joined by horsemen, servants of Caius, sent by him to care for the guidance and welfare of his gladiators.

Before a palace in the main street of the city, well down toward the sea, sat upon their horses two horsemen from whom others reined aside respectfully. These were face to face and they had greeted one another with all ceremony.

"Thy northern wolves have arrived, O Caius," said one. "But thou art short of a tall fighter."

"So art thou robbed of thy robbers, O Julius," replied the friend of Ulric. "Thy tower was a subtle trap, but it hath not profited thee greatly."

"Ha!" responded Julius, mockingly. "Thou hast lost thy best sword. A thousand sesterces that my Numidian lion slayeth thy Saxon chief."

"Wagered!" exclaimed Caius. "And a thousand sesterces more that thy Hyrcanian tiger shall also be slain by the man I will name against him."

"I have thee!" shouted Julius. "We will write these wagers with care and let thy words be recorded with exactness. If either the lion or the tiger shall be slain by a Saxon, I lose that wager, but if a Saxon be overcome by the tiger or the lion, thou losest."

"Thou hast some cunning of thine own in this," laughed Caius, "but thy sesterces and mine will be in the keeping of Sempronius, the judge of the games. I will trust him."

Each of these carried a tablet of wax and a pointed stylus of steel wherewith they wrote, and the words were compared with care, that they might then be written upon parchments, to be held by the judge of the games.

"What meaneth he?" thought Caius as he rode away from the gate. "I will see the Jew, Ben Ezra, as to this matter. There is a trap. I have not yet seen the laws of this circus, and Julius knoweth them well."

Like an inn, large and well appointed, was the house to which the Saxons were guided, near the circus, and they entered it gladly, for they were as men who were walking on into a new world.

"O Abbas," said Ben Ezra, "come with me to the amphitheater. I would inquire there concerning many things."

"Not so," replied Abbas. "Go thou. I have a friend to commune with and I go to meet him."

"O jarl of the Saxons," said Ben Ezra, as Abbas departed, "it is well that he goeth not with us. Come! Trust him not. He is overfond of money. Thou art a soldier. Thou must see thine enemy. Speak not to any man, but hear well. Who here knoweth thy gift of tongues? I am thine interpreter, and be thou as if thou wert deaf."

Ulric did but bow his head in answer to Ben Ezra, but the other Saxons knew the errand of their jarl and approved of his going.

A high arch of marble was the gate of the amphitheater, and on one side of it, upon the wall, was a broad tablet of wood. Upon this were inscribed many things, and both Ben Ezra and the jarl read them.

"Speak not," said the Jew. "One cometh to lead us to the dens."

Through the portal they went, guided by a soldier of Julius, and he seemed pleased to show them all things. First went they across the arena, and this was a broad place, egg-shaped, with vast tiers of seats arising upon all sides. Under these tiers were the keeping places, and from some of these came cries and roarings of wild beasts and the shouts of men.

"Here are the prisons of criminals and of captured rebels," said the soldier as the guard before a door opened it to let them in, "but thou hast little to do with these. They are to slay each other or to be torn by beasts. There are trained swordsmen for thee and thine."

Nevertheless, he and the jarl and the Jew went into more than one of these prisons, looking well at what they found there.

"Wretches!" murmured Ulric. "Some of them hardly seem like men and women. It is well for such as they are to be slain quickly. The gods care not for these people, and so they are given to the Romans."

Not so thought Ben Ezra, for he beat his breast more than once and he whispered to himself in Hebrew:

"O God of Israel!" he gasped. "Here are of thine own chosen people, also, many scores, taken in the snares of the heathen. Where art thou, O Jehovah, that thou hearest not? Canst thou not see this city of pollution, wherein thy name hath not been written? Unclean! Unclean! Woe is me that I am here! It is as Sodom and Gomorrah, and thy fire lingereth!"

What he meant Ulric understood only in part, but he saw that many of these who were doomed were Jews.

"They are not warriors," he thought, "except that some of them are tall and strong. They must all die and get out of these prisons, but they go not to Valhalla, and I know not where they go. I care not to slay such persons."

Now the guard led him and his interpreter to the dens of the animals and Ulric was displeased that his men were not with him to see.

"The wolves," he said in Saxon, "are like those of the North. I think not much of the hyenas, nor of the small leopards. The great leopards are fierce beasts and so are the bears, but I could meet one of them."

There were four elephants in one den, and he walked around among them, wondering at their size and at their peacefulness, while Ben Ezra told him of their intelligence and of their manner of fighting.

The jarl did but study them thoughtfully, and now a keeper said to Ben Ezra:

"It is known by us that this Saxon is to fight the great lion. Come."

The den was near and in it the lion was pacing to and fro.

"He is almost as large in body as was the ice bear," thought Ulric. "He standeth higher and his head is vast. He is a springing beast. He is stronger than the one we saw in Africa. I think he would fail if his heart were cloven. Now I will see the tiger."

Near was his den also, and he, too, walked to and fro, snarling fiercely, for he was hungry.

"O Abbas," said the keeper of the beasts to Ben Ezra, mistaking him, "thou art for Julius in this matter. What thinkest thou of thy Saxon? If he can meet a lion, can he fight, also, the tiger? How will he not be rent quickly when both are let loose upon him!"

"Silence, thou unwise one!" said Ben Ezra. "Is it for thee to let out this tiger?"

"That is my care," said the keeper. "I stand in this small box to throw open the door, and the tiger will be famished on the day of the games."

"Mark thou this thine instruction!" said Ben Ezra. "Wait thou not! Send out thy tiger when thou hearest the trumpet call for the lion. So shall Julius win two thousand sesterces. Hold not thy door till the lion be slain, lest thou be smitten with a sword. Thy life for it! The beasts go out together."

Ulric heard and he understood, for a fire flashed in his eyes, but he held his tongue. "I am to be torn without hope!" he thought. "I am betrayed by Abbas, but I know the thing in the mind of Ben Ezra. He doeth cunningly."

So they walked on across the arena, and as they went Ben Ezra stood still.

"Here," he said in Saxon, "wilt thou halt if thou art wise. Thou wilt have thy mail on, but only thy sword and thy shield."

"I will wear no armor!" said Ulric. "I will bear no weights. What were mail and shield against these monsters? I will bring with me the long sword of Annibaal. Odin be with me! He who fighteth a lion must spring as lightly as doth a lion. He who faceth a tiger must move as the lightning or he is lost."

"Thou art wise!" exclaimed the Jew. "I have seen no warrior like thee. Verily I am true to thee. Sharpen thy sword and let thy hand and thy heart be strong. I would that Jehovah of Hosts might fight for thee, but thou art a heathen and thou must look to thine own gods, if so be they can do anything in such a case."

Dark was the face of the Jew, but he said no more, and they went back to the house of the gladiators.

Eager were all the Saxons to hear the account of their jarl, and he told them many things, but in the gloom of the evening Caius came and he spoke to Tostig the Red.

"Thou art to meet a black giant with a net and a trident against thy sword and shield," he said. "What thinkest thou, O Saxon? Am I safe to wager upon thy success?"

It was Abbas who interpreted, but the men had already heard much of these nets and tridents and Tostig stood still for a moment.

"I have not seen this giant, O Roman captain," he said. "May I be guided by my own jarl?"

"Verily!" exclaimed Caius. "Do thou as he will tell thee, and I know not what it is. O jarl, can he win?"

"I saw thy giant," said Ulric. "Tostig the Red will slay him for thee. Make thy wagers. I would talk with Abbas."

"So do!" said Caius, for Ben Ezra had beckoned him and he stepped away a little.

"What is it?" asked Abbas of the jarl.

"Only this," said Ulric. "I have seen the lion of Julius. He is a great one. Hath he slain many?"

"That I know not," said Abbas. "Why askest thou? What matters it to thee?"

"Little," said Ulric, "but I was curious," and he asked him other questions, keeping him while Ben Ezra talked with Caius, getting full permission that the jarl should wear arms of his own choosing and not the armor of a Roman soldier.

Caius rode away and many great ones came and went, as they had been doing; for they who were to make wagers willed to see these pirates of Caius, as they called them. Not any, it seemed, went away believing that the jarl could face the Numidian, and they declared that Julius would win his wager.

Then the night passed and in the early dawn Ulric, the son of Brander, sat apart by himself sharpening the long, beautiful sword on the stone which Wulf the Skater had brought to him from the North Cape, at the end of the world. To him came then Ben Ezra, looking like one whose soul is burdened within him.

"O jarl," he said, "the great games are set down for the third day hence. Wilt thou then be rested after thy journeying?"

"Were I to meet the lion this day," replied Ulric, "I am not weary. I care more for the training of Tostig the Red in the matter of this black giant. I pray thee procure for me a net and trident that the thing he is to do may not be altogether new to him."

"That will I do," said Ben Ezra, "but thou canst not instruct thyself concerning lions."

Before the close of that day the jarl and Tostig were in a room by themselves, but they told not to any man what they did with these strange weapons whereby so many good swordsmen had been destroyed. That day, moreover, and the next day and the next the Saxons wandered much around the city of Tiberias, for they were permitted to do so freely, and all the people wondered at their stature and their armor.

"What thinkest thou of all these temples?" asked Wulf the Skater of Ulric. "Would it not be well for thee and Tostig to offer sacrifices to some of these gods?"

"What good?" said the jarl. "I know them not and they know not me. I would sacrifice to Jehovah if he had an altar here, because he is the god of all this land. I heard Jesus of Nazareth praying to him and calling him his father. If Jesus were here I would ask him that Jehovah might be to me instead of Odin, for I think the North gods are far away. Caius may sacrifice to his Roman gods if he will, but thou and I have no business with them."

"Thou art wise, O jarl," said Wulf. "I will waste none of my coins upon these priests and temples."

Chapter XXVII
The Lion and the Tiger

Splendid was the appearance of the Saxons on the morning of the great day of the games at Tiberias, when they marched around the arena with the jarl at their head, for their arms and armor were bright and their bearing was that of warriors accustomed to conquer. They themselves gazed, wondering, as they went, at the throngs which crowded the rising tiers of seats. Among these were many in gorgeous apparel, and the rich women had vied with each other in the colors and shapes of their garments and in the gold and jewels of their tiaras and other ornaments. There was a place on a lower tier for all the free gladiators, and to this the Saxons went after their marching. In it was a covered stairway going down to the door by which any among them might enter a room adjoining the arena to wait for his summons to combat. Each company of the trained ones was by itself and they were not too near each other.

Julius and Caius and other great men, with their glittering women, had a place which was as if it were full of thrones, but in the center of this was one splendid chair in which only a Cæsar or a proconsul might at any time presume to sit. It was this day unoccupied, but against it leaned the eagle standard of a legion and before it were scattered flowers.

The games began with races, both of footmen and chariots, and in these the multitude were interested greatly, but only they who had wagers cared much who might win.

When these were over it was time for the shedding of blood, and a band of captives were driven in, knowing that their fate had come.

"I see no swordsmen," was in the mind of Ulric. "Each of these hath a dart, but he is naked and so are the women and children."

Then uttered he a loud exclamation, for a door under the tiers of seats swung open widely and the den behind it vomited wolves famished with hunger and thirst.

"So many!" said Ulric. "Where got they so many? This is the cruelty of the Romans. I see no sport in this thing. It is but tearing and shrieking, for the small darts avail not."

Nevertheless, many wolves were slain before all the captives were torn down. Men in full armor went out to drive the rest of the beasts back to their den, but it was not difficult, for hunger was satiated and a wolf might carry with him a torn limb or a fragment of raw flesh.

Swiftly a crowd of bondservants cleansed the arena, and the feast of the wolves had not been long in duration.

"There cometh now thy giant with the net and trident," said Ulric to Tostig. "He is very black. He is from Africa. Watch him well, for this thing of his is but a trick of skill. Thou couldst parry that three-pronged spear?"

"That can I," said Tostig. "But the net? Let us see what he doeth with that short-legged brown swordsman in mail and helmet."

Brave seemed to be the brown warrior, but the net flew over him and the negro stepped backward, dragging. Then it was but as a flash and the trident was driven deeply through mail and breast.

Loud were the plaudits of the multitude, for the pitiless black had seemed to show both skill and strength.

The next comer was a large man, and Ben Ezra, sitting near Ulric, ground his teeth.

"A warrior of Israel, from the Lebanon!" he exclaimed. "He will but be netted!"

"Watch!" whispered Ulric to Tostig. "Thy turn cometh next. Mark how he faileth and remember what I taught thee."

"I see his sleight of hand," said Tostig. "I have beaten harder fighters than he is. The Jew is snared!"

Longer this time had been the contest, for the Jew ran, dodging, advancing, retreating, striking, and it was only by his utmost skill that the huge African at last threw over him the fatal net. Even then the trident was parried oft, but it struck and the brave Jew went down.

"Now!" said Ulric to Tostig. "I go with thee. We will show them a thing. Let me see thy seax. It is sharp. It will do. Off with thy armor! Take this heavy shield and see that thou cast it well."

Bare, save a cloth around his loins and a helmet on his head, Tostig went out into the arena, and the multitude shouted loudly, but Julius bit his lip. "Here is something more than the Nubian hath yet encountered," he muttered. "I would I might change my wagers. Yonder Saxon is an athlete for the Olympian games."

Well used were the rabble of Tiberias, however, to see their black favorite net his victims. Neither they nor he expected aught but a sure and speedy victory.

Facing each other at twenty cubits' distance were now the two combatants, and on the face of Tostig the Red was a smile.

"Now do I see more plainly the meaning of the jarl!" he exclaimed. "Let this black one but cast his net. Thor and Odin! What a simple trick is this to be slain by!"

The black uttered a great cry, laughing, as he strode forward, but Tostig made no retreat. He did but stamp with one foot, balancing himself, and loosened the exceedingly heavy shield upon his left arm, to seize it, also, with his right hand.

Through the air swept the net of peril, whistling as it went, and flying, with a wide hollowing, to fall over Tostig as it had fallen over many another. Laughed, also, Tostig, throwing with all his strength, and midway in the air the heavy shield struck into the hollow of the net, swinging it suddenly downward, but it fell also over the points of the lowered trident, tangling it. Around and under the tangle, not touched by it, went the white and muscular shape of the Saxon and the swift seax went twice into the bosom of the African juggler with nets.

"Thy sesterces, O Julius!" shouted Caius. "Thy favorite is gone from thee. What thinkest thou of my Saxons?"

True gamester was Julius, for his face changed not its proud serenity.

"I have but learned how a strong swordsman may overcome the weapons of Neptune," he responded. "My lion will bring me back my sesterces."

"Well for thee, O jarl!" muttered Caius. "My Saxons have a cunning captain. He is a man to win battles. I must keep him. But great is his peril now. Jove guard him lest I lose many sesterces."

The multitude was hoarse with shouting, and now they grew silent, for they knew by the lists that they were next to see a trained swordsman torn asunder by the unconquerable lion from Numidia, the beast which had slain heroes before Cæsar.

The trumpet had not yet sounded when Ulric, the son of Brander, went down the stairway to the room below where waited for him the master of the games, and upon this man's face was a bitter smile, for he was a servant of Julius.

"O Saxon," he said, "the edict forbiddeth thee to wear mail. Thou hast but a sword and buckler. The lion weareth no armor."

"Ulric the Jarl," exclaimed Wulf the Skater, "this is a trick for thy destruction!"

"Wait thou, true friend," said the jarl. "Trust me yet a little. Odin is with me this day, and fear not thou these tricksters."

The master of the games understood not the Saxon tongue, but he read well the fierce eyes of Wulf and he fell back a little, for the Skater's hand was on his sword-hilt and the Saxons were known to act suddenly.

"No helmet!" said the cunning friend of Julius. "The lion fighteth bareheaded."

The sword of Wulf rattled loosely in the sheath as the helmet was put aside, but he obeyed a sign from Ulric and drew it not.

"If the jarl be slain," he muttered, "that dog must die. I will see to this matter."

Knud the Bear had come down, but he was silent and his face was dark. He and Wulf turned and went up the stairs and so did the master of the games, well satisfied.

"Now the long sword!" said Ulric, throwing aside the short falchion provided for him. "O but its edge is keen!"

He heard the trumpet sound and the door before him opened. Then the great multitude shouted with admiration and the Saxons themselves wondered.

"He is so beautiful!" exclaimed Tostig the Red. "O that we must lose him! What shall we do without our jarl?"

"Would that I might die with him!" groaned Wulf the Skater, but Knud was thoughtful.

"Do we not know him?" he said. "Is he not the son of Odin? Are all our gods dead? I think the Nornir are not here and that the valkyrias will not come."

A tower of white stood the jarl, with but a silken garment from waist to knee, and his golden-curled head was a glory. In his hand was the African sword, its bright blade and the jewels of its hilt glittering.

"It is not the sword I sent him," muttered Julius. "That might have broken in his hand, but this will not. He is like Mars! O Caius, what thinkest thou of thy barbarian and of thy sesterces?"

"Wilt thou double thy wager?" asked Caius. "I am pleased with my Saxon lion."

"Nay," laughed Julius, "thou wilt have losses enough. Thou wilt see him torn shortly."

For the trumpet spoke again and the lion sprang out of his cage with a roar like distant thunder. The sun rays fell upon his face, however, and he lifted his head, blinded for a moment. Then he saw the throng and he walked along a few paces, as if willing to spring among the tiers of seats, but they were high and he looked again around the arena. Motionless stood Ulric, watching the lion, and between them now was but half the width of the arena. Men breathed not, but leaned forward in their places, and now the eyes of the great beast perceived the jarl and he roared with the roar of hunger and wrath.

"Now for thy Saxon!" said Julius to Caius. "I think his hour hath come."

"O jarl!" murmured Wulf. "Is it for this thou didst sail to the Middle Sea? Where is now thy city of Asgard!"

"Hark!" exclaimed Knud the Bear. "Another cometh! Here is more treachery! A tiger!"

Not with a roar, but with a snarl that was dreadful did the Hyrcanian monster rush from his den into the arena. He was more terrible to look upon than was even the lion, and he paused not in his going. He seemed to rush along the ground, crouching stealthily, and he looked longer and larger as he went.

"The jarl is lost!" said Tostig the Red. "O to be near with my spear for one cast. This is twain upon one!"

"This was thy bargain," said Caius to the cunning Julius. "Thy tiger was to contend with the swordsman of my naming. I have appointed this chief."

"So be it!" said Julius calmly. "I accept!"

"Wait!" muttered Ben Ezra to the Saxons. "The beasts have seen each other. Mark now the swift movement of the jarl! The lion is about to spring! The tiger! O God of Israel, aid thou, even though he be a heathen!"

The tiger's rush was rapid and Ulric sprang forward as if to meet him; but the lion was in the air with a vast bound, his black mane streaming and his teeth showing in the cavern of his jaws.

Not upon Ulric did he alight, however, for at his spring and roar the tiger turned in his tracks as toward one who would wrest from him his intended prey. Past both of them darted the jarl as the Numidian fell heavily upon the Hyrcanian; then his turning was as the light in its quickness and he thrust with his might upon the beasts as they grappled each other, rolling upon the ground and tearing.

"He hath cut off one forepaw of the tiger," exclaimed Knud. "That thrust was at the lion. Again! Again! Such roaring was never heard."

The wild beasts tore as they roared and the multitude uttered loud outcries, but all of the movements in the arena were untellably rapid, nor might they who were watching separate Ulric from his two enemies. He was with them at every spring and turn and roll. The long, keen sword dripped blood and the white skin of the son of Odin was spattered redly, as if he were sorely wounded.

"If he be slain at all thou losest," said Julius.

"O friend," replied Caius, "be thou contented. Thou must buy thee better beasts than these."

"Mark!" exclaimed Tostig the Red. "That was a thrust behind the shoulder. The tiger falleth undermost. O jarl! Beware now of thy lion!"

Over the dying tiger stood the huge Numidian, panting and roaring, and before him stood the jarl, looking him in the eyes.

"Splendid is he!" exclaimed Ben Ezra. "Jehovah of Hosts, be with him now! It is the last."

Forward went the lion, but not with a bound, and he swerved in his rush owing to his many wounds. High in the air and over him, in a leap for life, went the son of Odin, and as his feet touched the earth he turned, thrusting swiftly, and he sprang again. Wild were the plaudits of the multitude, but the lion was staggering and his roar was muffled.

"One thrust more," muttered Ulric. "I am sorely spent and I bleed. Hael, Odin! I have cloven his heart! He dieth!"

Then turned he and walked steadily to the front of the place of the great ones, while a vast clamor arose in all the tiers of seats.

"O Saxon," said Caius, "art thou wounded?"

"A scratch or two," replied the jarl, cunningly. "Am I to fight another lion this day, or wait I until the morrow?"

"O Caius, the sesterces are thine," said Julius. "Thy barbarian hath won for thee. Never saw I the like of this."

"To thy place, O jarl," shouted Caius. "I come to thee quickly. Be thou silent!"

Away strode Ulric, stepping proudly, but the door of the room he sought opened as he came.

"Enter! Enter!" shouted Knud the Bear. "O our beloved, art thou slain?"

"Water, quickly!" said Ulric. "I would drink. Wash me also. Bind up my hurts and put on my mail. Let no man see these tearings in my limbs. I shall not die!"

"Glory to the God of Israel!" exclaimed Ben Ezra. "I am the physician for thy hurts. Bring bandages. These are not to death. I feared for thee greatly."

"Nevertheless," growled Wulf the Skater, "I will slay that master of the games. O jarl, if we had lost thee!"

So said the other Saxons, crowding down to greet him, but the bandages were made firm, the mail and the helmet were put on, and then out across the arena marched they all, the jarl leading them.

"Truly he is not slain," muttered Julius. "I have lost my beasts and my sesterces!"

At the great portal, however, Caius waited with a chariot.

"Not to thy quarters, O Saxon jarl," he said. "I take thee to Capernaum for thy healing. All thy men will follow now, and a ship waiteth at the seaside. Julius must not see how thou art wounded. Wilt thou live?"

"He will live," said Ben Ezra. "Speak not now. Harm was done by claws, but more by a paw stroke on the head. But for that he had slain them sooner, and he was torn only while he was fallen. A hard battle, O Caius of Thessalonica."

"He and his have beaten Julius for me," said Caius. "They shall fight no more save at Jerusalem and at Rome."

"May we tarry long enough to offer sacrifices to the gods of this place?" asked Knud. "I would leave them in good humor. It is well to be on good terms with the gods."

"What sayest he?" asked Caius of Ben Ezra, but Ulric himself responded:

"Peace with thy gods, O Knud. Let alone. I saw when I was under the tiger's paw. I thought at first of the valkyrias, but they came not. The gods of this place we will leave here. They are nothing to us. Come!"

"So be it!" said Knud. "I meant only to deal prudently. Thou art our jarl. We will come."

They lifted Ulric into the chariot, Ben Ezra and Knud and Tostig entering with him, and the other Saxons followed, led by Wulf the Skater. With them now was Abbas, and he said to Ben Ezra:

"The keeper of the tiger's cage hath lost his head for letting him out too soon, and the master of the games lieth slain under the tiers, no man knoweth by whose hand."

"They who butcher many," said Ben Ezra, "do well to avoid knives. The man with all other men for enemies dieth speedily."

But Wulf the Skater smiled joyously and he said to Lars, the son of Beolf, at his side:

"The Jew is a wise one; but beware thou of Abbas, lest he sell thee."

Lars looked at the spear in his hand and at Abbas, and he answered not.

"We have our jarl!" laughed Wulf as they went forward, and quickly they were at the shore of the Sea of Galilee, and they saw a galley, like a pleasure boat, rowing rapidly nearer to the place where the chariot halted.

Chapter XXVIII
The Jarl and the Rabbi

Softly and easily may a wounded man be borne along upon cushions over smooth water under a silken canopy. There was no further fatigue for the jarl, the victor, that day, and before its close he lay upon a couch in a room of one of the seaside palaces. All men went out from him save Caius.

"O jarl, my friend," he said, "I must leave thee. Gain thou thy strength as rapidly as thou mayest. Thy Jew, Ben Ezra, telleth me that he may not tarry here."

"He is not any more needed while I lie thus," said the jarl. "I would see him. If thou art willing, he may go."

"I consent," said Caius. "Thou art interpreter enough for thy men. I will send him to thee, but now I must return to Tiberias, for I have much upon my hands. May all the gods give thee a speedy recovery, and I promise thee that thou shalt yet fight before Cæsar himself. Thou art worthy!"

So saying, the centurion departed, and in a moment more Ben Ezra came and sat down sadly by the side of Ulric.

"Thou goest from me?" asked the jarl.

"Hardly of mine own will," replied Ben Ezra, "but I must go to Jerusalem, and I will return to thee if thou comest not soon to me. I commit thee to the keeping of Jehovah, my god. Abbas goeth also, and there will be one double tongue the less in Galilee. Fare thee well. I have done for thee what I could."

"O Jew, I thank thee," said the jarl. "Come thou again to me and I will ever welcome thee as if thou wert of my kindred."

Little more did they say, for the jarl was in fever and in pain and the hour was late. Ben Ezra departed, but at the door of the room stood Tostig, spear in hand, although this palace was a place of peace.

"O Tostig," said Ben Ezra. "I go away for a season. Guard thee well your jarl!"

"That will we, O Jew," said Tostig. "There will be swords and spears around him by day and night. Whither goest thou?"

"To Jerusalem," said Ben Ezra, "and I think I may have somewhat to do there for thy jarl. I love him much. I come again shortly."

"The gods go with thee," said Tostig. "I think thee a brave warrior. Art thou sure that the jarl healeth of these hurts?"

"No man knoweth surely," said Ben Ezra, "but see ye to it that he hath quiet."

"We will care for that," said Tostig. "I have been sore wounded myself, and while the cuts were knitting I would fain have cleft the head of any who came near me."

So Ben Ezra departed from Tiberias, taking with him Abbas, and the palace of the friend of Caius by the Sea of Galilee contained now only the servants of its owner and these who were called the gladiators of Caius of Thessalonica. For these there was sufficient occupation of mind at the first, for many came to gaze at them, and men of rank, also, were interested, but none might ask undue questions of men whose speech was unknown and whose behavior was silent and haughty. To them, also, not only were all buildings new to be examined, but there were fruits and wines and strange ways of living to become accustomed to. Boats were there, to be used at any time, and the Saxons talked much of the fiords and fishing of their own land while they were amusing themselves upon the Sea of Galilee. Over it did they go from end to end that they might look upon all things upon its shores, and they wondered much that one small sea should contain such abundance of fishes and have so many towns and cities builded beside it, as if there were no other place for the cities of this marvelous land. Few days went by in this manner, but there were other affairs than those of the Saxons.

Ever is it true that the cunning, who believe their ways to be hidden, are sometimes read as are books in strange tongues read by those who are learned in difficult runes. Julius, the centurion, the chief commander of the Roman forces in Galilee, had other hopes and ambitions than the winning of sesterces in gambling, and he had other cunnings besides his tricks of the circus. At this time Herod, tetrarch of Galilee and loving to be called a king, was plotting to gain for himself the entire realm which had been ruled by his cruel father, Herod the Great. To this end he might require the removal by Cæsar of Pontius the Spearman from being procurator, and the destruction of his own brother, Herod Antipas, tetrarch of the lands northward of Galilee. If, therefore, Herod of Machærus and Julius, the centurion, were working together against the procurator, then the near friend of Pontius was as a spy and an enemy in their camp. Nevertheless, Caius of Thessalonica had been received in Tiberias with all the welcoming due to an exceedingly distinguished visitor, an honored friend. Not that Herod was here to meet him at this time, for the tetrarch preferred the safekeeping of his Black Castle, Machærus, on the easterly side of the Sea of Death, which hath no waves and whereon the seabirds die.

Caius, the centurion, walked one evening alone by the shore of the Lake of Galilee, and he communed deeply with himself.

"Thus far Jove hath been with me. I have escaped the treachery of both the wolf Julius and the foxes, the Herods. I do now know that Herod Antipas refuseth to join them, to his ruin. Why linger I here, where I am not safe for an hour but for the swords of my Saxon gladiators? I trust their jarl, for they are his more than mine. He mendeth but slowly from the tiger's clawing. I would he were able to ride even in a chariot, for my errand here is done. Unless he were with me I could do little with his barbarians. Abbas is a traitor, ready for a buyer, and I believe him already bought. Ben Ezra—he is a Jew, and every Jew hateth every Roman, with good cause. I am glad he hath departed. The barbarians are not so, for they are but gladiators, and this Jarl Ulric is not as a common man. I may trust him."

So spoke with himself the grim centurion, the near friend of Pontius the Spearman, considering the affairs of princes and of kingdoms. He walked on, thinking deeply, and ere long he was at the palace by the seashore. A legionary stood guard at the portal, but no Saxons were to be seen.

If one had walked with these at this hour, he would have been at a place from which might be seen the walls of Capernaum. Along the beach were boats and sailing vessels, larger and smaller, and out upon the sea were many fishermen. At the water side were some who spread out a net to dry, but above them, on the high ground, had gathered rapidly a mingled concourse of people. Said one of the net dryers to another:

"The rabbi of Nazareth is there. He healeth the people. Only John is with him. We ought not to be here. Let us go to him."

"Did he not bid us go a-fishing?" replied another. "We have caught many. It is enough. Let us go."

So left they their net and went up the bank, and as they went they heard the voice of the rabbi preaching to the multitude. They listened, hastening, and they spoke no more to each other. All utterances were stilled save the wonderful voice of the preacher, the music of the waves upon the beach, and the low, painful mutterings of one man who hobbled along upon crutches as if to join the gathering.

"O that I am to be maimed!" he said. "I, Ulric, the son of Brander! That I shall no more walk firmly! The tendons and the muscles of my limbs refuse to heal, as if the tiger's claws were poisonous. What thinkest thou, Wulf the Skater? Shall we not go on and see this man?"

"Thou art faint, O jarl," said Wulf. "It is not well that thou hast walked so far. I fear thou wilt but cure the more slowly. One goeth by us! Look at him! Hear him! He is a leper!"

"Unclean! Unclean! Unclean!" a hoarse and croaking sound came to their ears from the ulcered, shriveled lips of him at whom Wulf pointed.

Behind him were four who carried a sick one in a litter, but they held back, not overtaking the leper.

"Come!" said Ulric. "I would look into the face of this god once more. We may hear another of the demons. I have much curiosity concerning them. Put thy arm around me and aid me on."

"Woe is me, son of Brander," moaned Wulf, but his strong arm went around the waist of his jarl and they walked along.

"Unclean! Unclean! Unclean!" the terrible voice repeated, but on the brow of a little knoll the rabbi of Nazareth stood and ceased not his preaching.

All around him were men and women, the old and the young, but these stepped suddenly away, as if in fear, while the leper came toward them.

"He hath no right!" exclaimed one.

"Touch him not! Breathe not his breath," said another, "lest thou become leprous!"

Down knelt the leper, but the rabbi ceased speaking and looked upon him kindly.

"What wilt thou?" he asked.

"That I might be clean," gasped the leper.

"Be thou clean!" said Jesus.

"O jarl!" exclaimed Wulf. "What is this? He standeth erect! He is strengthening! Would almost that thou wert a Jew, for their god is a strong healer."

"Come!" said Ulric. "He hath cured this leper. I will have speech with him. Nearer! I walk more easily. My hurts cease to pain as they did. O Wulf, aid me strongly, that I may get to him. Pass me on! I breathe more freely! I strengthen! I fail not! Fear thou not for me that this shall do me harm!"

"O thou Jesus, of the sons of the gods!"

"O jarl!" said Wulf. "This is but a sudden strength that cometh to thee. Afterward thou wilt fall!"

"On! On!" exclaimed the jarl. "I have somewhat to say that I had forgotten. I must speak!"

Near were they now, and the rabbi of Nazareth again ceased speaking as he looked upon the white face of the jarl, but the crutches of Ulric had fallen from his hands and the arm of Wulf seemed still to uphold him.

"O thou Jesus, of the sons of the gods," said the jarl. "Sigurd, the son of Thorolf, hath fallen in battle with robbers, many of whom he slew. He bade me that I should see thee again and bring thee his greeting."

"O rabbi of the Jews!" exclaimed Wulf the Skater, earnestly, "it is Ulric, the son of Brander the Brave, of the Northland. His gods are not thy gods, for he is a son of Odin, whom thou knowest not. But he is our jarl and we love him. We pray thee that thou wilt ask of thy god for him that his hurts may be healed and that he may become strong to lead us, for we are but as lost children without him."

As yet Jesus answered not, but the jarl stood firmly upon his feet and stepped one step nearer, Wulf stepping with him, but of the other Saxons was none with them.

"O rabbi," said Ulric, "I was torn by wild beasts in the arena of Tiberias. I slew both the lion and the tiger, while they were tearing each other. And now I shall be no more a warrior, for my sword falleth from my hand." As he spoke he held out the hand which had been so strong, and which was now so weak, and it was touched by the outstretched hand of this rabbi of Nazareth.

"Go, thou," he said. "Be thou healed. And remember thou that which thou hast this day seen and heard. Speak not again now."

Wulf the Skater took up the crutches, but the jarl put them away, saying:

"Hath he not bidden us to go our way? Shall we not now do as he hath said? Come! I walk as if I had not been torn. He is a god!"

"O jarl," whispered Wulf, trembling, "what meaneth he? I understand him not. And what is this strange thing which hath come upon thee, as if thou wert a Jew? I think his god is a good god and very strong."

But both he and Ulric stepped backward and the rabbi and the man who was leprous stood face to face.

"Silence, Wulf the Skater!" whispered Ulric. "The god hath spoken to me as to this one. I have looked into his face. What he hath said I know not, but I go to Caius quickly. Where thou art commanded well do thou obey lest evil befall thee."

"Clean! Clean!" sprang from the lips of the healed leper. "Hallelujah! I glorify the god of Abraham. This man is a great rabbi!"

"He is of the sons of the gods, thou stupid one!" said Ulric. "I am healed. Who but a god can cure the scratch of a lion or a tiger? He is as Odin, and I think they are friends, and that Odin bade him heal me. I will fight for him when he gathereth his army. O Wulf the Skater, come! My arm telleth me that I could cast a spear. O thou of Nazareth, thank thy father for me, for thou wilt see him before I do. When I am slain I shall go to Asgard and I will meet him there, and I hope to meet thee. Also, in thine hour, thou shalt be my captain."

"Go now!" said Jesus, turning to a sick one.

"He meaneth he will send for thee," said Wulf, walking on at the side of Ulric. "But we need more Saxons for his army if he is to overcome the Roman legionaries. He would do well to gather the sea kings and all the men of the fiords and of the forests. Even from Denmark and the islands we might bring to him good fighters. How well could a captain keep his army if he might heal all who were but hurt, losing only the heroes for whom the valkyrias had come."

"I walk more strongly!" said Ulric. "I would be where I may look at myself, for the marks were deep and they ran as sores. We will go with Caius to Jerusalem. I think it well for us that we guard him."

"O jarl," said Wulf, "a friend is a friend, but a Roman valueth a Saxon only for his sword and for his spear. I have thought, indeed, that he might yet give one of us a chance to kill this Julius. I shall not be fully contented until I have seen his blood upon a blade of steel."

As a man in a dream walked Ulric, the son of Brander. With him, looking at him as they went, walked Wulf the Skater, and now other men drew near.

"How is it with the jarl?" asked Knud the Bear. "He hath no crutches this day."

"He walketh strongly," said Tostig the Red. "His face is ruddy and his eye is bright. Thou hast been with him, O Wulf; what is this?"

"The son of Odin hath had speech with this god of the Jews," slowly responded Wulf. "I myself asked for his healing, but the sons of the gods are not like other men. Hold ye your peace, for the jarl was bidden to tell no man."

"Let him alone, then," said Tostig. "It is enough that he walketh so well. But yonder is the centurion, Julius, talking with Caius."

"I am to slay him yet," said Wulf. "Watch ye, for we belong to Caius."

Enough of Saxon knew their master to gather that saying, and it pleased him well, for he turned and saw blue eyes that flashed a little, and dark eyes that seemed to ask his bidding.

"There is truth in these Saxons!" he said to himself. "Were I to command the death of Julius, he were dead this hour."

But at that moment the voice of Julius rose in a sound of chiding.

"O Caius," he said, "I did indeed pay my wagers, as became me, but thy Saxon died and the payment should be restored to me. If the lion and the tiger slew him, the wager is void."

"Justly spoken, O my friend," replied Caius; "but knowest thou this man, or is he dead?"

Then turned Julius, wondering, for before him stood the son of Brander smiling in a mockery, and saying:

"Hael to thee, O Julius, the captain! Hast thou any wild beasts with thee this day? I am Ulric the Jarl!"

Proud and strong he stood, with the sunlight upon his golden curls and the strength of a hero showing in his movements, but the centurions, both of them, stared at him as if they were in amazement.

"Thou art not dead?" said Julius.

"O jarl, let him take thy hand," said Caius. "Let him be sure of thee that thou art well."

"O Caius," said his enemy, "thy swordsman liveth. I have been misinformed. But how were his wounds that they have healed?"

"Scratches!" said Caius. "I have care for my gladiators after a fight that they may be ready again. Hast thou any to put against him for a thousand sesterces, man for man?"

"That have not I!" exclaimed Julius, looking hard at Ulric. "He hath cost me enough!"

Then, also, for he was cunning, he understood the looks of the other Saxons, closing around the jarl lovingly, and he ground his teeth, for the thought in his mind was: "They would slay half a cohort of my dwarfs. They would slay me, if Caius bade them. I would I had such a bodyguard that knew nothing but mine own will."

So thought Caius in his mind, silently, but he said aloud:

"O Julius, now the games are ended, and my mission to thee from Pontius is fulfilled, I will set out on the morrow for Jerusalem. The winter is here. What sayest thou?"

"The gods go with thee!" said Julius. "Also, if thou art wise, take with thee thy swordsmen. Thou wilt be safe by the way."

So he and Caius walked on by themselves toward the palace and the Saxons gathered gladly around their jarl, feeling of his wounds that were healed and wondering greatly at his meeting with this son of the unseen god of the Jews.

Chapter XXIX
Beautiful as Aphrodite

At the Damascus gate of the city of Jerusalem halted a weary-seeming ass, upon whose back was a dusty and travel-worn rider.

"Wonderful indeed is the grandeur of this city," he had said, as his jaded beast toiled up the road from the bridge over the Kidron. "I would willingly have paused longer upon the Mount of Olives, but the lash of the procurator is close behind all who ride upon his errands. Somewhere in this city of the temple is my Sapphira even now, but how shall she be made to know that I am here? Not now, but I will climb over all barriers, even these great walls and forts, until I find her."

At the gate was a Roman guard, and to the sentinel on post rode Lysias, saying:

"O guard! From the procurator to the captain of the gate! In haste! I am Lysias, a messenger, with a token in writing. I may not dismount until he cometh."

The soldier saluted ceremoniously the name and authority of the procurator, but he stirred not from his place. He did but shout loudly, and an officer came forth, to whom the Greek repeated his utterances.

"Sit thou in thy saddle," said the officer. "I may not touch that which is in thy keeping. But the centurion cometh shortly—the captain to whom thou art commanded to make thy delivery."

No word spoke Lysias to the important man when he came, but the subofficer made the announcement and the parcel from Pontius the Spearman was placed in the right hands.

"O messenger," he said, "dismount. Thy beast is worn out. So art thou. He will be kept for thee in the stables of the procurator. Thou, too, wilt have refreshment. Rest thee and be ready when thy return message shall be prepared."

Here ended for the present the dangerous responsibilities of Lysias, but in no manner had he yet escaped from the grip which had been put upon him. The lodgings to which he was speedily conducted were as a jail of secure detention and from them he might not think of going forth, lest evil should befall him. He might but eat and sleep while his next duties were in course of preparation. Nevertheless rest was sweet, and his dreams were free to wander where they would, seeking a fair face and welcoming eyes which might not now be far away.

Early upon the morrow he was summoned to come forth, and he was led to the Damascus gate without having had speech with any save with soldiers who were as his jailers. Here a saddled horse of Arabia awaited him and also a high official, whom he knew not, and the captain of the gate, whom he had already seen.

"Hear thou with care, O messenger," said the latter, sternly, handing to him sealed parchments. "This first to the procurator, from me. These from the high priest and from the captain of the temple. I give thee, also, a spoken message, which may not be written, for thee to deliver and then to forget; for thou art of the household of the procurator, and he trusteth thee. Were another to hear these words, lost were his head and thine. Slain is the secret messenger of Herod, and he went not to Cæsar. Caius of Thessalonica is in Galilee watching Julius, the subtle, who plotteth, also, with Herod and with Herod Antipas. Caius may die there, or ere he returneth, but he is trustworthy. Well were it that the procurator should now leave his inspection of the garrisons and of Samaria until a better day and that he should now return to Jerusalem. Go!"

Words in reply or questioning might not be spoken. Lysias sprang upon the Arabian horse, the letters being hidden in his bosom. Away he rode down into the valley of the Kidron, thinking within himself: "Great is the peril to him who carrieth the secrets of rulers. Sure is my death if I do not this errand well, and yet the very doing of it may bring a sword upon me. And now I am indeed of the household of Pontius, wherein is hidden my Sapphira. Surely Venus and Juno are with me, and Mercurius himself hath given me this fleet stallion to ride. He goeth like the wind."

The remainder of that day went by, and the night also came and went. Not any did the messenger have speech with but seemed ready to speed him and glad to see him go from them, as if in having met him might bide a future peril. It was only in the forenoon of the next day, however, that his Arabian steed was halted in the middle of the northward highway, and before him in a gilded chariot sat Pontius, the procurator, reading slowly and thoughtfully the letters delivered to him by the Greek.

"Thou hast done well," he said. "Thou art a speedy messenger. Was there aught else?"

"Here are ears near thee, most noble Pontius," replied Lysias. "I pray thee bid me be prudent."

Down from the chariot sprang the procurator with a fierce flush upon his face.

"Dismount thee! Come!" he said. "Back, all! I would have speech with this man."

Not far behind the chariot, but not as if they belonged to the same company, rode two men upon asses, of whom one said to the other:

"A messenger, O Ben Ezra. There may be tidings of importance. What sayest thou?"

"Silence! O Abbas," replied the other, "thus far our god hath befriended us upon our way. Trifle not with the business of the great lest the sword seek thee. Thou art overcurious. Let it suffice that we are permitted to travel under guard of the procurator's horsemen."

At the roadside now stood he and the Greek and none dared approach them, for the spear of Pontius was in his hand and his brow was dark. "Speak with care!" he said to Lysias. "Forget not!"

"Thus said the captain of the gate," replied Lysias, "and a centurion who stood by him and who gave me this cornelian for a token, telling me not his name— —"

"Cornelius of Cæsarea!" muttered Pontius, but the Greek spoke on, uttering exactly the words which had been given him.

"It is well," he said. "I have word of Caius that he is wise and that his Saxon swordsmen are his bodyguard. More than one secret messenger hath been slain, saith Ben Ezra, the bringer of tidings from Galilee. Trust him, but not the Jew Abbas who is with him, for he is of Julius. I come to Jerusalem quickly. I will give thee a fresh horse in the morning and thou wilt again return, but thou wilt wait for me in mine own house. Go, now, and speak to these Jews, questioning them. What they say thou wilt tell me. It is well that thou wilt be in the school of Gamaliel and also in the service of the procurator, but let no man know of more than of the school."

The strong man is often in desire of a willing servitor, and it pleased Pontius that the eyes of the Greek brightened with delight. His lips parted also, but the word "Sapphira" that was upon them was not uttered aloud.

The ruler turned and walked away to his chariot and Lysias remounted his weary horse.

"I must be cunning with these Jews," he thought; "and in one of them is my deadly peril."

The train passed on and they were riding at his side.

"Who art thou?" he asked of Ben Ezra.

There was no sign of recognition in the face of his former comrade upon the good ship *The Sword*.

"I am a Jew of Spain," he responded, "and my name is Ben Ezra. I go to fulfill a vow in the temple of Jehovah at Jerusalem. Who art thou?"

"I am a Greek of Alexandria, named Lysias," was replied as cunningly. "I am of the household of the procurator, but I am also a student in the school of the great Gamaliel. Thou doest well to perform thy vows. I am now bidden to be with thee. And who is this man?"

"I am Abbas of Jerusalem," he said for himself, bowing low to one who seemed to be trusted by Pontius the Spearman. "I am a merchant and I have had dealings with the procurator."

"O Abbas," said Lysias, "many have heard of thee. Thou art a lender of money and thou art hard in thy dealings. Why dost thou pretend that thou knowest me not? Hast thou not seen me many times in the markets? I think that thou art never seen in the schools. Tell me, how was it with that trouble of thine that thou didst have before the magistrate? Didst thou escape with no more harm than a fine?"

"Nay! Nay!" exclaimed Abbas. "Speak not too much of that matter. The judge compelled that unjust person to pay me my dues and he was cast into prison. I exact no more than my right."

"Thou art, then, a rare money-lender," said Lysias; but the cunning of the Greek had succeeded and Abbas was ready thenceforth to say to any inquirer that he knew this man well.

"O youth," he said, "I will talk with thee further concerning certain matters when we may have opportunity. Be not thou too much influenced by what thou hearest. Is there any news?"

"Tell us what things have occurred," added Ben Ezra, "for we have been in Galilee. I journeyed thither as interpreter for the Saxon gladiators of Caius, the centurion, of Thessalonica. In his service am I to this day."

"A good man and highly honored," said Lysias. "He is a friend of the procurator."

So they rode on conversing, but in Greek. Nor was it difficult as they went for Ben Ezra, even aided by Abbas unwittingly, to inform Lysias completely concerning the doings of the Saxons.

"The procurator," he said, "calleth the gladiators of Caius his own. Thou wilt soon meet them and I will make thee acquainted with them."

"I will gladly have speech with such strange ones," said Lysias, "but the scholars of Gamaliel may not meddle much with the circus."

Ere long as they rode he and Ben Ezra were able to be out of hearing of Abbas and the others, but the speech of the Jew was brief.

"O Greek," he said, "if thou art imprudent in this matter, for thee is not the scourge, but the sword."

"And for thee crucifixion," said Lysias. "Fear not for me. Thou art as I am, and we are one with the jarl and his company."

The place of the procurator's abiding was at hand. It was an ancient palace, which was also a fort, and they who occupied it were of high degree. Of them the two Jews and Lysias might see or know but little, but they had quarters assigned them. In the morning orders came to Lysias only, and he was quickly in the saddle with a message for Cornelius, the centurion. If he found him not at Jerusalem, he was to ride on after him, even to Cæsarea.

"O to be in the procurator's house!" thought Lysias, "for she will be there and I shall see her."

Even as he rode away from the palace gate, however, bright eyes were upon him from a window above and a young girl said in a low, musical voice:

"O Lysias! Lysias! Do I not know that he is in search of me? Woe to him and woe to me if he should find me! What is this which is come? Am I not happy as I am? Surely I do love him. He is very beautiful. He loveth me. But what have I, the favorite of the wife of Pontius, to do with him? What have I to do with a love that I lost so long ago and that is gone? It were but a sharp peril now. If I meet him, I can but tell him that I am no longer his. He is but a swift messenger of the procurator; a fellow to ride horses and to be scourged if he rideth not speedily. I am one to dwell in palaces, wearing gay apparel and jewels and having the favors of the great."

Full of pride was her fair face as she spoke, and in it was a scorn for any who were lowly. To her the apparel of her servitude was more worth than was the love of a youth who had been robbed of his patrimony and whose rank was lost. She sat at the window watching him as he rode away, and she sighed deeply.

"Yes," she said, "I love him, and it is pleasant to love. He is a good horseman. So are all my Roman lovers. What is he compared with a Roman? Even the Jews, if they are rich and of power, are better than a poor Greek boy, fit only for errands."

She arose and walked away, but a mirror was near and she gazed long at her reflection, admiring it greatly.

"I am as beautiful as Aphrodite, they tell me," she said. "I will sacrifice to her this day, and to Juno. There are no gods upon whom Lysias may call for great gifts. He can bring them no rich offerings, while I can have oxen slain before the altar. Aye, and I have had men sent to prison and to the arena if they offended me. I sent that foolish Jew girl to the lions at Jerusalem. I taught her better than to interfere with me."

Her red lips tightened cruelly, and her eyes were terrible and her movements were lithe as those of a young panther as she walked on along a corridor. But Lysias galloping northward was alone upon the highway, and he shouted aloud:

"Sapphira! Sapphira! My beautiful one! My beloved! I am drawing nearer to thee! Thou art dearer than life and I believe thou art true to thy lover. I will find thee yet, and I will look into thine eyes and I will touch thy hand and I will tell thee all that is in my heart."

Strong is love and wonderful are its follies and its treacheries, for even then his Sapphira sank upon a couch in her own room sighing and murmuring in a low voice:

"Lysias! Lysias! My beloved! If I have any other lovers I will name them Lysias in my mind, for I do love thee, and love is pleasant."

The procurator made no great haste that morning, although he prepared for journeying. He had many affairs and his messengers came and went, and it might be seen that he was a thoughtful governor, attending to all who came, only that he sent out some edicts which were full of blood and vengeance.

Not long was it before he stood in a private place with Ben Ezra questioning.

"O Jew," he said, "now thou hast told me how Julius plotted to destroy the Saxon guards of Caius, thou hast told me enough. But for this tall jarl of thine and his pirates I should never again meet my friend. He may give them to me and I will not waste them in the arena. I know of a place to which I may send a good sword and where I may not send a legionary."

Low bowed the Jew and the unspoken word in his heart was bitter.

"Do I not know thee?" he thought. "Thou treacherous one! Thou wilt send a Saxon to do a deed, and when it is done for thee thou wilt slay him and clear thyself. This is the cunning of the Romans. I will beware of thee and thy errands, but I care little for my own neck. O that the Messiah, the Prince of Judah, were even now smiting thee and thine from the earth! He cometh soon, I think."

So, bowing as became his station, but guarding well his face and letting his eyelids fall over any glitter that might betray him, Ben Ezra went out of the palace and was joined by Abbas.

"O my friend," said Abbas, "why linger we?"

"We may not linger," said Ben Ezra. "We depart, but thou wilt travel alone. I have commands from the procurator. See to it that thou art quickly in Jerusalem."

"Whither goest thou?" asked Abbas.

"Art thou mad?" said Ben Ezra. "Or dost thou know but little of Pontius? Keep thy questions to thyself and tarry thou not, for I think thou hast a spot on thy name. Beware lest it turn into red on thy garments."

Very pale was Abbas, but his face was that of a fox with a wolf for his father.

"O Ben Ezra," he said, "thy counsel is good. But be thou careful of thine own head. I can tell much concerning thee."

"In the day that thou chatterest unwisely," said Ben Ezra, "thou wilt spread thy arms upon a piece of wood and thou wilt hear the sound of hammers. Then thou wilt be set up at a wayside for men to mock thee. The Romans hesitate but little concerning such as thou art."

Ghastly was now the face of Abbas.

"O my friend!" he exclaimed, "I meant no evil! I will be true to thee!"

"Thou wilt remember this thy warning!" said Ben Ezra, sternly. "Thou wilt not sin against thine own life. If thou shalt at any time err, it is no fault of mine. Thy blood is upon thine own head."

They parted one from another, and then came to pass a strange thing, for a servitor led Ben Ezra to the armory of the palace. Here he remained but briefly, and when he came out he was armed from head to foot in the panoply allotted to the Jewish servants of the temple under its Roman captain. So arrayed he might ride as if he were a Roman under the sure protection of the procurator. A horse was ready for him and he mounted, riding to the palace gate. At this place was now the procurator in his chariot.

"Go thou speedily as thou hast said," commanded the procurator. "Be not overhasty, but prudent. If it prove as thou tellest me, well with thee."

"On my head be it," said Ben Ezra, and he rode away northward.

"I have purchased him with a price," he said to himself, "but I will deal truly with the jarl. If some of his treasure and some of mine must be paid as tribute to this Roman governor, all that remaineth—and it will be enough for us—will be kept for our own uses. Now for the cavern in Carmel, and the journey will be neither long nor unsafe for a man traveling with the seal of Pontius."

As for the procurator in his chariot, he, too, had a thought upon his mind, and it made his face brighten.

"The gold is well," he thought, "but the jewels! There is naught else for which Cæsar hath so great a lust. I care little for such things. Of what value are bright stones except that they will sometimes buy more than will gold or silver? Let the Jew bring his gems and with them I will defeat Herod and Julius."

Far on along the southward highway rode Abbas, having a pack beast with him and two fellow-travelers. The Jerusalem road through Judea was accounted safe unless one rode alone or unarmed. Still was his face turned backward now and then as that of one who feareth lest he may be followed, for the words of Ben Ezra had been severe, and Abbas knew that he who uttered them had been much in conversation with the procurator.

"He is deep as a well!" he thought. "Can he know anything of my dealings with Herod? Even now I must go to the ford of the Jordan and to Machærus before I go to Jerusalem. Alas! The Black Castle! How many have entered it who never were seen again! Well is it set so near to the Sea of Death! I am a Jew! I hurt not my own people! But it is righteous to profit by the dissensions of the heathen. If Herod and his brother Antipas and this Pontius the Spearman were to slay one another, what harm to the children of Abraham? Ben Ezra doeth not well to keep faith with a Roman or an Edomite. They have defiled even the temple of the Most High."

Chapter XXX
The Javelin of Herod

The Saxons and their jarl in the palace by the Sea of Galilee were now more impatiently awaiting the orders of Caius of Thessalonica. It was at the close of a day that he came to have speech with Ulric, the son of Brander, and to wonder again at his swift healing. He examined the scars, touching them, and asking many things concerning this learned rabbi of Nazareth and of his marvelous cures, for these were things which no reasonable man might easily believe.

"Thou hast thy strength again," he said at last. "Never have I thought much concerning the gods, but I shall deem it prudent to make sacrifices to such as I think may aid me. I have never found them profitable. Take now thy weapons and walk out along the shore with me, for I am restless. I linger here too long on thy account. Come!"

"I shall delay thee no longer, O noble Caius," said the jarl, "but well am I assured that thou doest well to wear mail and to have thy good sword at thy side. Put on thy helmet."

"So do thou," said Caius. "But what said to thee the Jew, thy interpreter? Was it aught more important than thou hast told me?"

"Not so," said Ulric, "but the keeper of the tiger's den told much unwittingly. The beasts were prepared to win more than sesterces. Had I been slain, and Tostig, thou wouldst now have less perfect guarding. I will tell thee, O Caius: I like thee well and I am jarl; not another will my men obey. I think thee a good fighter, and such as I am agree not well with cowards or with those who deal in subtleties."

"O jarl," said Caius, "speak not of Julius, the centurion, as if he were a coward, but he is exceedingly deep in his counsels. There is more than thou knowest in this matter. Thou mayest yet have a chance to use thy long, sharp sword again."

"That might please me well," said the jarl. "I like not to leave a blade too long in the sheath lest it might rust. But glad am I as we walk to feel no more any hindrance from the work of the tearing claws."

"Well with thee, O jarl!" exclaimed Caius. "And now look without looking and mark well without seeming to mark. Seest thou the men in armor who have landed from yonder boat at the shore? They walk not overrapidly, but they aim to come between us and the palace. Canst thou read a riddle?"

"I had noted them already," said the jarl. "Men have told me that the other shore of this Sea of Galilee belongeth to Herod Antipas, the brother of the Herod who ruleth here under Cæsar. I have heard that men who are hated by the Herods die at distances. But thinkest thou that either of them would dare to send a sword against a Roman, and such as thou art?"

"Consider, O jarl," said Caius, calmly. "Who then would know concerning the sword or him who sent it if thou and I were slain upon this beach and our bodies conveyed in yonder boat to be sunken in the sea? Would not the thing be well hidden if the doers of it were shortly also slain by Herod Antipas or by his brother, whichever sent them?"

"Great would be the inquiry," said Ulric.

"Thou art young!" said Caius. "Cæsar might demand my blood of him of Machærus, in whose land we are, or even of this Julius. What if Antipas thus plotted harm to both of them? He could strike them no deeper stab than this! Thy spear, Saxon! O for my shield! I was imprudent!"

"Take mine!" said Ulric, casting his spear. "I need it not. There are now but four. Ha! A javelin! I caught it! Out with thy sword!"

Even while talking had they permitted the five men from the boat to draw much nearer and as if unobserved. Sudden and fierce had then begun this assailing. The javelin had been well aimed, but the quick sword of the jarl had parried it. These were men of war who were coming and they had deemed themselves sure of victory, for one had said:

"On! With him is no one but his tiger-torn gladiator. He hardly may stand erect. The centurion is at our mercy. End him!"

"Use well the shield," said Ulric. "Thou art thyself a good swordsman."

Now he who seemed the leader of these murderers drew back astonished to see how this Saxon, whom he deemed crippled, sprang toward him with a war cry. He was no match for such a one, and his next comrade, turning affrighted to see him fall, left his own neck unguarded against the sword of Caius. What then were the two who remained against two mighty men of valor?

Ill advised had been he who had sent them upon this errand, for the jarl laughed exultingly to find how well his strength had come back to him.

"O noble Caius!" he shouted. "Thou art a good swordsman. They are all down. But these fellows are Jews. How is this?"

"None the less are they from Antipas," said Caius. "I can read his cunning. He will say they are but robbers from the rebel bands beyond the Jordan. Therefore I may bring no accusation against him. But I think thou art enough for five such as these. Well is it for me that thou art healed. Now will I send word to Julius, and his servants may have the care of this carrion."

Ulric was silent, looking down upon the slain. "Jews?" he said. "I think now that they are not so, but they are like them. What is thy thought, O Caius?"

"Samaritans!" suddenly exclaimed the centurion after a closer examination. "Not from Antipas. Here is a deeper treachery. These are from the elder Herod, the fox of Galilee. O jarl, haste! To the palace! We will make ready for our journey. But know thou that our road to Jerusalem passeth through Samaria, whence these came. Verily I have a new tale to tell the procurator."

"And I have a new thought concerning the keeping of thy life," said Ulric. "But there will be more than one round shield with thee in Samaria. A man needeth to have many eyes in this land."

At that moment, while they still gazed down at the dark yet pallid faces of the dead, they heard near them shouts of angry chiding, but the tongue was not the tongue of that country.

"O jarl!" shouted Lars, the son of Beolf, "we saw thee afar! We came in haste! What doest thou here with thy sword in thy hand—thou that wert torn by the Roman tiger?"

"Woe to thee, O jarl!" shouted another. "Thy men should have been with thee!"

"O Caius," exclaimed Tostig the Red, "thou didst fight for our jarl? Then will we fight for thee. Thou hast made good friends this day."

Sufficiently well did Caius understand Tostig and the others who now came running to see how it might be with the son of Brander, and it pleased him greatly.

"I may now depend upon these wolves of the North," he thought, "and sore may be my need of such as they who think not but strike, knowing only a friend and a foe and taking no account of numbers against them."

The jarl explained the matter and he seemed to be forgiven, but he and the centurion returned to the palace surrounded by spears ready for the casting.

"It is well, O jarl," said Caius. "Let all be ready to depart upon the morrow; but I may not go in unseemly haste as in fear."

"Thou wilt go as becometh thee," said Ulric. "He who fleeth unduly from a sword loseth the regard of brave men. We will be ready."

Nevertheless, Caius of Thessalonica rode swiftly to the house of Julius at Tiberias and was himself the bringer of this tidings.

Julius listened to him in a white wrath. "O thou, my friend!" he shouted. "Seest thou not that this thing is aimed at me as much as at thee? If thou hadst thus been slain, it had been my utter ruin. Woe to these Herods! They shall both fall by the sword of Cæsar. The gods be with thy Saxons. Thou needest them. Commend me unto Pontius and say to him that thou and I are henceforth one in all these matters. The Herods now seek to stab him also. Let him guard well his head."

So talked they long together in a nearness which they had not known before, finding themselves in the same peril from the serpents which bite in the dark.

From the gate of Tiberias on the morrow went out a company worth the seeing. Not without armed Roman escort and many bondservants might the chariots of so important a man as Caius of Thessalonica set forth. When to all these were added the vikings, in their best armor and well mounted, it was as if a small army had been ordered southward. To the place of parting and of farewell came, also, Julius and many men of note to do all honor to the friend of the procurator.

"O Caius," said Julius, "I already have a swift messenger from Antipas. He hath sent his horsemen to search the hills beyond the sea and Tarichæa. They will ride with all diligence, and beyond doubt they will find some to slay, but thy shield must be nearer to thee than is the Jordan."

"It will be very near," said Caius, smiling, for near him rode Tostig the Red watching all keenly, and his spear was in his hand.

This, too, saw Julius, and he laughed.

"O my friend," he said, "it is even so. Fare thee well; but they who come to meet thee should have due warning, for thy protectors are no respecters of persons."

All then rode on, and the Saxons talked much among themselves concerning the things which they had already seen in this land. They had visited all towns and villages around the sea, but none of them were more splendid than Tiberias.

"I would have visited Capernaum," said Ulric.

"There is no great thing there," said Tostig the Red. "What hadst thou in thy mind?"

"Only this," said the jarl: "that this son of the old god of the Jews, this rabbi of Nazareth, dwelleth there at times. I owe him thanks and gifts for my healing. Also I have it in mind to ask him questions concerning my father, and Hilda, and Valhalla, and Asgard. Hilda I have not seen but in my dream on *The Sword*."

"One was with her, I heard thee say when thou didst meet her. It was well to give her thy ring. I would have done so. But what would this god of the Jews know concerning thy maiden? The gods care not for such things. She was fair to look upon. But, O Ulric the Jarl, I would I were on the sea again!"

So said all the vikings many times, but they told the jarl that not in any of their goings to Capernaum had they seen Jesus, the rabbi. They had heard of him, that he was away in other places, here and there, teaching and preaching and healing many and casting out evil spirits.

"It is good that he so doeth," said Lars, the son of Beolf, "and that he healed the tiger scratches upon the jarl, but what good is it for him to sing sagas to these people of no account?"

There was none to answer him, for even Ulric himself was silent. Nevertheless, the son of Brander had many thoughts which he did not utter and he forgot not any of the words which he had heard spoken by this one who had healed his hurts.

"I understand them not," he said to himself. "He bade us think of the gods, and that I do. Even now I am seeking their city and that I may get acquainted with my kindred. How shall I do so completely before I am slain? And he who dieth a cow's death, so say the sagas, shall not enter Valhalla, but shall find his place in Hel. I would join the heroes of the old time and dwell with Thor and Odin. I think I shall know more after I have seen the city Jerusalem, which Ben Ezra saith is like Asgard. At all events I will sacrifice horses and oxen and sheep in the temple of Jehovah as if he were Odin himself, for he is the chief god of this wonderful land."

More and more wonderful indeed did it seem to the Saxons as they rode onward all that day, for it swarmed with inhabitants and the villages and towns were many in number.

It was at the gate of Jezreel that their company halted, at the setting of the sun, and Ulric sat upon his horse looking toward Carmel. Behind the city arose Gilboa, wooded and craggy. Before it stretched Esdraelon.

"O Wulf the Skater," said the jarl, "do you bear in mind the things which were said of this city and plain by Ben Ezra and Abbas?"

"More was said to thee than to others," replied Wulf. "It is a city of sieges and a plain of many battles. I can see the blue ridge of Carmel and beyond is the Middle Sea. I would I might see waves this hour and smell the salt air. This is a woeful land, where never is good ice or deep snow. We go on into the winter and we may yet see a snow squall if we are fortunate. But Knud will need no bearskins and Wulf will need no skates—and I sicken when I think of such a winter."

"The great battle of the end of the world and the twilight of the gods!" exclaimed Ulric. "O ye! If Ben Ezra's Jewish sagas lie not, here shall we witness the greatest of all the feasts of swords. Here shall we have for our jarl a god, the son of a god, and there will be gods and heroes to fight with. I, the son of Odin, will be here! Hael, Odin!"

"I will be with thee, then," said Knud, "but if it is soon to come, it were better for some of us to go back to the Northland and return with many keels full of men like ourselves. This god will need Saxons if he is to fight Romans. These Jews will go down like wheat before the sickle, for I have been looking at them and at the legionaries."

"Thou art right!" exclaimed Tostig the Red. "But there is room on this plain for great armies to meet. They will come from many places, Abbas told me, and among them will also be black and yellow men, and there will be great beasts, and the eagles that are wide-winged, and creatures whereof he could not tell me the shape. They may be like the one we saw come up from under the ice to tear the whales, only that such as he do not come out upon the land."

"No man knoweth from whence these will come," said Knud, "but some of them are as great serpents with wings. I like not to think of them, for they are full of fire and sulphur, and who can fight well in a smoke that choketh him?"

After this they entered the city of Jezreel, and they wondered greatly at the strength of its walls and towers, but they saw not many soldiers.

"The land is at peace," thought Ulric, "and garrisons may be small. I am learning something of war cunning from these Romans. What they take they will hold until a stronger people shall come against them. I know of no such people except in the Northlands."

Yet another thought was in the mind of the jarl, and his eyes wandered anxiously wherever he went. In all towns and villages and whenever companies had been met by the way he had seemed to be searching, and a sadness of disappointment was growing upon his face.

"I heard her say she would see me at Jerusalem," he told himself, "but now the time is long. She may have come hitherward. Of these damsels whom I have seen as I came many are fair to look upon, but none are as beautiful as Miriam. Cannot Hilda lead me to her? Shall I indeed not see Miriam until I meet her in Asgard? I would that Caius were in greater haste. We travel slowly."

If he had looked upon fair faces inquiringly with his sad blue eyes, also had all the Saxons laughed to one another quietly to note how many women put aside their veils a little to turn for another look at the face of the jarl.

"Never before have these seen any like him," they said. "They will not see him again, and he careth not for women save for the one to whom he gave a token. He will forever keep his troth with the dark one, the beautiful one, in whose hand he put the ring of the bright red stone as we came through Esdraelon."

Good welcome was given to Caius of Thessalonica and his company by the governor of Jezreel, but the vikings went to their quarters listlessly, for they had all looked across the plain toward Carmel, and the thought within them was that beyond Carmel was the sea and that upon the sea were ships.

Chapter XXXI
The Places of Sacrifice

Questions which are asked by the heart of a man may go far. It is as if they were winged and flew on to a chosen place of alighting, as do the messenger doves carrying letters homeward. One of the birds set free by the ever-beating heart of Ulric the Jarl found a wonderful resting place.

It was in a house in a great city, and upon all the earth was nothing more magnificent than this house of houses. Upon the top of a high mount in the city was a vast space girded with white walls and towers, so that of this whole area was made a fortress of surpassing strength. Within these walls were great buildings not a few and porticos and separated courts for varied uses.

There was one building which was greater than any of the others, and to this as to a center all the many structures related; for the arrangement and the architecture were everywhere exceedingly harmonious and convenient. To this greatest building there were several approaches, but the main entrance was by an ample ascent of broad stone steps. Beyond the level at the head of this stairway were mighty doors whose surfaces were covered with beaten gold and many designs of golden ornamentation.

Within the doors, if one might enter—for here stood ever armed guards—they who went on might see yet more splendors of carven stonework, whereof some of the stones were rare and precious, and of golden and brazen ornament. Here in high places were altars which smoked with almost unceasing sacrifices. Serving at and about the altars were numbers of robed priests with their assistants, and often these were chanting the sagas of their worship, but not in all this place was there any image whereby a stranger might obtain information concerning the shape or person of a god. It was as if he were worshiped in ignorance, none having at any time seen him to make a sculpture or a painting of his likeness.

In this inner space or court where were the altars there stood this day a multitude of men with covered heads, and they now and then uttered loud voices in unison, which were responses answering the sagas of the priests.

Here were no women, but at the right was a portal and a passage leading into another court, which was also large and splendid. This was the court of the women, of whom a large number were present, both of the young and of the old.

This was the temple of Jehovah, the God of the Jews, in the city of Jerusalem. To him only were any sacrifices offered upon the altars, and the sagas were chanted that he might hear them if he would, but none could tell whether or not at any time he might be listening. So many of the sagas formally besought him not to remain at a distance, but to come to this place and listen and do the things asked for by those who brought to his altars these sacrifices.

Sad and sorrowful, yet full of strange music, was the sound of this singing, while the smoke went up from the burnings and while the censers were swung to and fro by the priests to send out upon the air their clouds of sweet odors. Sad and sorrowful was the pleading, for there cometh a heaviness of soul to him who calleth in vain upon a god who is far away, who is unseen, and who answereth not by voice or sign.

On the stone pavement, near to a pillar of bright bronze-work and somewhat apart from any of the groups of the other women, knelt one who was veiled and whose voice arose in low murmurings as of a recitation and a prayer. The hand which drew her veil more closely was well shaped and white and upon one of its fingers was a golden ring among other rings less beautiful. So deep was the red light of the ruby in this ring that its glow seemed hot like fire, and it throbbed as if it had pulses at the movement of her hand changing the light upon it. Also her bosom arose and fell and there were tremors in her voice, and she said, whispering softly in the old Hebrew tongue:

"O thou who art God over all gods, I have sinned to look upon him, for I am a daughter of Abraham and he is one of the heathen. O that he might also be one of Abraham's children and serve the living God, even our God. I have sinned, O Jehovah of Hosts, but I have made my sin offering and I have made an offering of atonement also for him."

Then the gem flashed a great light, but her hand fell and her veil slipped away and the marvel of her face was seen for a moment. Upon it was a smile and a light, and her eyes were closed, but her lips were parted.

"Have I indeed been spoken to?" she whispered. "I have been told that an angel cometh oft into the court of the women. Never have I seen an angel. Who knoweth that one might not come to me? Would he be fairer to look upon than was he whom I saw at the wayside? If this be truth, then do I know that my offering hath been accepted and that it is no longer a sin for me to remember him. Woe is me, then, if I am to never see him more! O he was beautiful! Exceedingly! And I have brought into the house of Jehovah this token which he gave me. But what is this which hath come to me?"

Her eyes were opened, looking downward, and the red glow of the ruby answered them as if it were speaking to her of love. Then she arose, covering with her long silken veil, and she walked out of the court of the women; but a dove, escaped from the cages of the offerings, flew over her head and went out above the great gate and the wall, flying swiftly until he disappeared over the Mount of Olives.

On walked the young woman beyond the temple walls and the sacred mount, going until she came to a street of palaces, ascending another mount. Here shortly she disappeared, but she was more beautiful than any palace and in her light stepping there were both gracefulness and a great pride of manner, as if she were of high degree.

Now at that hour of the evening sacrifice the city was exceedingly still, for men and women everywhere paused in whatever they were doing and turned their faces toward the temple. Horsemen drew rein and chariots halted, and there were many who knelt even in the open streets. But of these were none but Jews and Jewish proselytes from other nations, and there were those who were worshipers of other gods that were sufficient for them. Roman soldiers who were marching halted not, and of these a body of a hundred spearmen passed out at the Damascus gate with an officer at their head.

"O captain of the gate," he shouted, "yonder cometh a messenger. I will await him."

"Hinder him not!" replied the keeper of the gate. "He is known to me. It is the swift messenger of the procurator."

"Am I not captain of the temple?" shouted the officer so loudly that he who came heard him.

"If thou art he," was uttered, hastily, "I pray thee come to me!"

For the messenger halted, not dismounting.

"Dog of a Greek!" exclaimed the captain of the temple, haughtily, "shall I come to thee?"

"There are men with thee and in the gate, O captain," said Lysias, reverently. "I pray thee permit me to obey the procurator and speak to thee only."

"Ho! Thou art right. I come! Hast thou a letter from Pontius?"

"This little script only," said Lysias, handing him a parchment, "and these words — —"

"Utter them quickly!" said the officer.

"'Pontius to the captain of the temple: slay the messenger of Herod Antipas and let the spy from Machærus not live to sail for Rome. Speed this Lysias to Cornelius, the centurion, and keep him afterward in my house safely until I come. Let him have speech with no man and let no harm come to him.'"

"Even so!" said the captain of the temple. "Yonder road along the valley of the Kidron bringeth thee to the Joppa gate. From thence is the Joppa highway, and thou wilt find Cornelius at the harbor fort if he hath not departed for Cæsarea. I will give thee a fresh horse. Tarry not in Joppa or in Cæsarea, but return quickly to me."

"But not to speech with the high priest," said Lysias, "nor to any from Herod."

"I will see to that," laughed the captain. "Thou art careful of thy head. Wert thou unmindful of the commands of Pontius, thy shoulders were bare quickly. Thy fresh horse cometh. Mount and ride on."

Without more words Lysias obeyed, but as he rode on along the brook Kidron he said aloud: "Well for me that I took rest and food while I could, that I fall not from my horse. I can reach Joppa in due season, but what will yonder captain of the temple do with me when I return? I have heard that the messengers of Roman governors are changed like the changing of guards, and that they who are released go sometimes upon errands from which they do not return. I will sacrifice to Mercury!"

Whether or not he were weary, Lysias rode well and his fresh horse was swift. It was but little to reach the Joppa gate, and the sun was but setting when he turned into the highway leading toward the sea. It was broad and well kept, for chariots and for marching cohorts. Looking back, Lysias saw that the gate was closed and none was in the road behind him. Looking forward, he saw no man, but there were houses on either side of the way except at one wide, open space which arose at the left in a small hill. Bare was this ascent and he wondered at it, saying to himself:

"So near the gate and no building thereon? It were a place for one of these outer palaces."

He had paused to fasten the buckle of his bridle and he looked again upon the hill, and now shriek after shriek of utter agony came to his ears from beyond the crest of the ascent. Voice answered unto voice, and he shuddered as he heard, but a man in armor came slowly down the slope.

"In the name of the procurator!" shouted Lysias. "Is this the Joppa road?"

"Art thou of his messengers?" said the soldier. "If thou art, thine ears will tell thee that a score of his enemies are on the wood. This place of skulls will soon smell but badly under this hot sun. Ride on, for this is thy right road."

"This, then, is the hill of crucifixion?" asked Lysias.

"Any place will do," said the soldier, "but the procurator humoreth the Jews and will set up no crosses in the city. The day may come when we will nail them in their temple and set up there an image of Jupiter. They troubled Pontius mightily when we did but carry our eagles to the temple gate, as if one god were not as good as another. What care I for gods!"

Loudly rang again the piercing shrieks while he was speaking, and his hard face widened into a grim smile, as if the sounds pleased him. But Lysias shuddered and his blood ran cold, and he wheeled away to gallop out of hearing of those terrible outcries.

"No Roman may be crucified," he exclaimed. "These are not Romans. To them all other men are less than brutes. I will watch that captain of the temple; but whither should I flee from the pursuit of a procurator's executioner?"

Under such fear as this dwelt all who were governed by the servants of Cæsar, and yet it was said that the common people were more sure of justice than from any other rulers if they remained quiet and paid all taxes without murmuring.

"I will risk all!" shouted Lysias, "if I may but once more look into the blue eyes of my Sapphira, for I know she loveth me!"

The sun went down as he rode, and the shadows came, and through the shadows he galloped on, but now and then it seemed to him as if the shrieks from Golgotha were ringing warningly in his ears.

Chapter XXXII
The Mob of Samaria

The city of Jezreel was for Caius of Thessalonica and his train but a resting place for a night. After leaving behind its towers and the valley of battles, at the side of which it seemed to be posted as a sentinel, Ulric the Jarl himself was satisfied with the speed of the going which brought him to Samaria.

Here, also, as they drew near, the Saxons noted well the fortifications.

"These walls are old," said one. "Those of Tiberias are newer and better. I care not for walls. Better is it to fight in the open field, where swordsmen may come together, shield to shield, in a fair combat."

Tostig the Red heard, and he shouted loudly:

"O jarl, not walls! Rather would I have a good keel like *The Sword* than any fort. Towers and walls rest where they are builded, but a ship may sail into new seas. I am hungry for the sea!"

"I like not the land at all!" said Knud the Bear. "Never again may I be found so far from the rush of waves. I am minded to seek me a keel ere long. I think we shall all die if we may not again see the Northland."

He did but speak for all. While they had been inactive on the shore of the Sea of Galilee, and even more after setting out as if to find new adventures, the vikings had returned in their hearts to their old manner of living. They had thought continually of the sea and of ships. They had talked together of the cruise of *The Sword* and of all the strange things which had befallen them by the way in which they came to this country. They had also told many tales of the great deeds of sea kings, but there had been no minstrel or saga woman with them to sing them a saga or to play for them upon a harp. Often, also, did their conversings deal with the Northland itself in its summer beauty. They longed for the high mountains and the shadowy coolness of the fiords, and for the faces of men and of women and of children on the shores and about the houses. There is ever a kind of sickness which cometh upon brave men in the thinking of such thoughts and in the talking of such remembrances afar. So these vikings, who were all that remained of the mighty crew of *The Sword*, were not only weary at heart, but almost sick in body.

"A keel?" said Wulf the Skater to Knud. "Thou wilt find thee a keel? Wert thou in thine own seas now thou wouldst find them closed against thee. Beautiful would be the ice to look upon. But I think I could make me good skates and reach the fiords over the floes."

So said other Saxons, and they did but look listlessly at the walls of Samaria.

"O jarl," said Caius from his chariot, "come thou hither to me. I have a word for thee."

Ulric rode to the side of the chariot.

"What aileth thy men," asked the centurion, "that their faces are so cloudy? Are they discontented?"

"Not with thee, O noble Caius," laughed Ulric, "but they are ill at ease on horseback and in peace. They would rather fight for thee than travel like pleasure-seekers. One man is ever afraid that, if this continueth, he may die in his bed and go to Hel instead of to Valhalla."

Stern yet pleasant was the countenance of the centurion.

"I understand thy men," he said. "Let them be posted in the doorway of the house where I abide this night. I have no others here whom I may trust, and this is a city of the enemies of the procurator."

"Thou mayest sleep safely," said Ulric. "I will myself keep that house."

"Thy men could not be bribed," said Caius. "I know that of them."

"They have too many coins already," said Ulric. "But I bade them keep all and spend them at Jerusalem. No man need offer them any more. As to treachery, let thine enemy speak of that to Tostig the Red, but first let the seax of Tostig be taken from him."

"I will leave it at his belt," said Caius, "and he may strike with it in such a case. But be not thou overhasty with a man of rank, for thou wilt be held accountable."

"I will be prudent," said Ulric; "but how is it with thy legionaries? If they are on post, is it not life and death with them?"

"Men have died suddenly," said Caius, "with a legionary motionless at the outer door. He stirred not, being as a pillar of wood. Thy men will be free, and will act as if they were hunters of game instead of statues. Thy head is as good as thy hand."

"I will keep thee," said Ulric, "and I would that the men might have a chance to draw a sword or throw a spear."

"They will not," said Caius. "There are no men in Samaria who would trifle with such a guard as thy Saxons. Think not but what I will remember thee for this matter."

The jarl reined away his horse, thinking deeply.

"O Caius, do I not know that thou art as other Romans? So soon as thou art done with us thou wouldst give us to the lions and look on while we were torn, being amused. Soft words are well enough, however, and thou art better than are some of thy people."

For the jarl grew crafty under the burden of leadership, and he seemed older than when he stood with Hilda on the shore of the North sea looking at her runes upon the sand.

A large house like a castle near the eastern wall of the city was assigned to so great a man as Caius, but he went the next day to a feast, being entertained by the governor and other notables, among whom were certain lords of Herod's household.

"It will be late when I return," he said to Ulric at his going. "I will send for thee."

"Not so," said the jarl. "I will come without thy sending. There have been tumults in Samaria since the sun's rising. There will be good spears around thy chariot."

"Do as thou wilt, O jarl," said Caius. "I fear no tumult and I have good attendance."

"Hast thou indeed a guard, and is it not from this man, the governor?" said Ulric. "Leave thou such matters to me, I pray thee, that thou mayest at all reach Jerusalem."

The chariot of the centurion rolled away from the palace gate, and with it rode a score of mounted soldiers sent by the governor as a guard of honor for his distinguished guest. Hardly were they out of sight, however, before the Saxons sprang to their feet at a sudden summons.

"Spears and shields!" commanded the jarl. "Let every man look well to his weapons and to his armor. Be ye all ready to march, but first let every man come to me and report whatever things he hath heard or seen this day."

One had this thing to speak of and another that thing, but for the greater part it all seemed to be of little worth. Their eyes, too, had been better than their ears in a city of an unknown tongue. Nevertheless, the jarl said to Wulf the Skater:

"Thou hast scented this danger, then, thou keen old hunter? So is it with me, only that I better understand sayings uttered in my hearing, and some who spoke believed that I was as a stone wall, having no ears. They were, therefore, careless. I will say to thee that the soldiers who are now with Caius are all from this new legion wherein Julius was for a while the chief officer. It is for our interest that Caius may suffer no harm. Moreover, we may have some good fighting, and that is worth while."

"Thank the gods!" interrupted Knud the Bear. "Now may I the more comfortably eat my supper. It is well to have a thoughtful jarl."

A city by itself was Samaria, as it had been during long centuries. They who called themselves Samaritans bore deadly hatred to all Jews, but could not prevent them from entering the city and transacting business there, although they could have no dealings with the Samaritans. All other nationalities came and went freely, and here was a gathering of the offscourings of the earth. The Jews risk all perils for the sake of traffic, and they had in this matter the protection of the Roman laws. Nevertheless, these hatreds were the root of many troubles, and from time to time there had been bloody riots to be suppressed by the legionaries with but small care upon whom their swords might fall. It might have been trusted that a Roman of rank like Caius would be as safe in Samaria as in Jerusalem or in Rome, and so he would have been but for the intrigues of those who were greater than he. Herod Archelaus, to whom Judea and Samaria had fallen by the will of his father, Herod the Great, had forfeited his realm to the Romans and it was now ruled by Pontius the Spearman. Both the Herod of the Black Castle, whose legacy had been Galilee and some provinces beyond the Dead Sea, and Herod Antipas, who had inherited large districts at the north and east of Galilee, were plotting to overthrow Pontius and also to defeat each other. The favor of Cæsar was the path to increase of power not only for them, but for Roman plotters such as Julius, and there were intrigues against them all at Rome itself. The strifes of those who fought continually for the spoils of Roman conquests were ever records of bloodshed, and no man's life was safe. To be a great Roman was to walk on toward destruction.

Splendid was the feast to which Caius went at the palace of the governor of Samaria, but he was wary and he did not become drunken. Long reclined the guests on the couches at the tables, to be served with all the delicacies of the earth. Also there were dancers and mimes and musicians. But the end came. Some were to abide in the palace, some were to go to their houses near, in the city. The chariot of Caius waited for him, but as he and his slaves walked out at the main portal they heard a sound of trumpets and great outcries of a multitude.

"It is nothing," said Caius. "I heard that the rabble had risen against the Jews. Let the legionaries form in the road. Drive on!"

He spoke scornfully, but the outcries were near, and now came a great rush of men, of whom many were armed. In front of the governor's palace was an open space, into which the multitude was pouring, but from the opposite direction came forward another throng of men. In the foreranks of these was a small man in armor, with the visor of his helmet closed.

"Yonder is the chariot of Caius," he said. "Wait only till the Iberians charge. Then slay him and flee. Let the blame fall on the Jews and the Samaritans."

Two score were the legionaries, and it was the governor, standing upon the steps of the palace portal, who shouted to them:

"Charge ye the mob lest they hinder the going of my guest. Slay them! O most noble Caius, I send out also quickly my own guards and servants. Thou art safe!"

If this were indeed the craft of the governor, it was well hidden, for the soldiers went forward smiting all in their way, and armed men from the palace went also. By this very charge, however, the chariot would have been left alone save for Caius and his charioteers and a few mounted bondsmen. Not in the silken robes of a man at a feast was the centurion at this moment, nevertheless. The robes were to be seen in the light of the torches, but they covered good mail and armor, and suddenly upon his head was a helmet and in his hand a pilum.

"Treachery!" he shouted. "The jarl was correct! O for my Saxons!"

"Here, O Caius!" loudly responded a voice from among the shadows of the palace front. "Halt not thy chariot, but drive slowly. We have abundant javelins."

The torches held by the bondsmen flared in swinging, more being lighted, and past them seemed to go dull red flashes, but these were the bright blades of Syrian darts obtained by Ulric for this business. Strong were the arms hurling, and the darts were better than arrows at so short a distance.

"Jupiter Tonans!" roared Caius. "I have a sheaf of them here in the chariot, for myself and my charioteers. Wise is the Saxon, and he provided them for me!"

A good thrower was he, and some who had stealthily crept on too nearly were smitten as they sprang forward. Then came the charge which had been purposed across the open space, but between its front and the chariot was a wall of Saxons, in full armor, shouting with the fierce joy of battle.

Down went the small leader, cloven to the jaws as if his helmet were of wood. Down went his companions rapidly, while the battle laughter of the vikings rang derisively in their ears.

The other multitude the legionaries were slaughtering pitilessly, but the command of the governor had been to follow, and the soldiers came not back at once.

"Slay! Slay!" shouted Caius. "I come!"

"Come not!" replied Ulric. "Abide where thou art and press on to thy house. We will keep these wolves at bay."

"A fight and I not in it?" said Caius, angrily. "Commandest thou me?"

"In the fight I am jarl!" said Ulric. "I am answerable for thy head. Drive on!"

"Thou art right!" said Caius, justly. "On, O charioteer! Obey thou the Saxon. I forgot that he is a prince and a captain among his own people. I will make him a Roman yet. He should not be a barbarian."

Hardly might any less than a king, nor even a king except at great cost and for policy, obtain Roman citizenship, but this was the meaning of the words of Caius.

Then an arrow flew and struck him upon the left arm, wounding him; but he mentioned it not, for he saw that the charge was broken and that the Saxons came to march with the chariot.

"Not one of them is missing," he thought. "So much for broad shields and good mail. The rioters had weapons, but no armor, and they were slain as cattle. This arm of mine is but scratched."

"On!" commanded the jarl, to his men. "I heard the centurion say he is wounded. O Caius, how art thou?"

"A sting on my arm," replied Caius. "We shall soon be at the house. This is naught."

"Let me see it speedily," said Ulric. "I have picked up an arrow with a grooved head. Thou knowest what that meaneth."

"Haste! Haste!" shouted Caius. "This thing is of Herod, the jackal! I am lost."

But the tumult had been stricken to quiet and the ground was strewn with the dead. Now as they went there came swiftly armed horsemen of the governor and behind these marched the Iberian legionaries. No visible fault might be charged by Caius upon his host of the feast. Not far was it to his place of abiding, but when the chariot halted there he sprang down and entered in a gloomy silence, followed by the jarl.

"Home, now," commanded the officer of the legionaries. "Our duty is done."

Back with them went all servants of the governor, but Caius was in an inner room removing his armor.

"I wore no armlets," he said, "lest the governor might see them. The arrow went past my shield while I threw a spear. Thou hast done well, O Saxon chief. But for thee I had been murdered. This is a small wound."

"I will suck it for thee before I bind it," said Ulric. "Then watch thou if it beginneth to burn, but set thou out hence before dawn."

"That will I this hour," said Caius, and orders went forth.

Great was the declared wrath of the governor of Samaria, for he came himself to inquire concerning the welfare of his guest. Not to him was anything said of a groove in an arrow wherein might be pressed some deadly juice, and he returned to his palace a seeming friend of Caius, complaining bitterly of the Jews and Samaritans, more of whom he threatened to slaughter for this night's business.

Ulric cared for his men. They had cuts and bruises which they made light of, but among them was no arrow wound. So light a missile would have been stopped by a leathern hauberk, and all their mail was of the highest temper of steel.

"We will ride soon," he told them. "Be ready to mount and leave this place of thieves."

"I like it well!" exclaimed Knud the Bear. "It was not a hard fight, as if these fellows had been Danes or Northmen, but I cleft many skulls and I think Wulf the Skater killed a score of them. Tostig was unlucky, and Ven, the son of Gerta, slew more Samaritans that he did."

"He did not," said Wulf. "Thy counting is not good. And I slew two men in armor also."

Chapter XXXIII
The House of Pontius the Spearman

The road from Samaria to Jerusalem hath many windings and there are hills to weary the wayfarer. Climbing one of these slowly was the chariot of Caius of Thessalonica. He was lying heavily upon the back seat, as one to whom this journey had become an insupportable burden.

"This long day draweth to its close, O jarl," he said to the horseman nearest him on the right. "The roads are worse to pass than were those of yesterday. We are now on the level near the ridge of the Mount of Olives. Soon we may see the city. My arm burneth and it is swelling."

"I would we were already with thy learned physician," replied Ulric. "Be of better cheer. I know little of such matters, but I think thou doest well. I will offer sacrifices for thee in this temple of the Jews. Hast thou ever done aught against their god? He is revengeful."

"I have not harmed him," said Caius. "I have not slain Jews. Do as thou wilt, for at this time there is no other god in Jerusalem. I will pay for thy oxen and Pontius will command the priests to offer them upon his altar. Thinkest thou, O Saxon, that any god hath power to heal the wound made by a poisoned arrow?"

"That I know not," said Ulric. "I have often wondered much what the gods may do. One of them healed me of my hurts from the tiger of Julius. Such a god might cast out a poison. He casteth out demons and he healed a leper. He opened the eyes of a blind man. I would that he were now in Jerusalem and that thou mightest look into his face. Also I must offer sacrifices of thanks for that matter. It is not right to obtain a gift from any god and then not to keep faith with him. A god should be dealt with as if he were a brave warrior."

"Well for thee!" exclaimed Caius. "I would indeed that he were here instead of in Galilee. No god may heal aught so far away, and as for this god of the Jews, they will not that a Roman enter his temple."

"Ben Ezra told me of the temple," said Ulric, "that a court is prepared into which all may come. There only will I enter. It is not well to anger priests in their temple, for they know the ways of their god and we know them not."

"Thou art young, but thou art cunning," said Caius. "But I have a great fear concerning this wound in my arm. It is not like any other, and I have been wounded often. A strange thing is poison. I have considered why the gods make such a thing and why they put it into the teeth of serpents. They are evil!"

"A god may need a serpent as thou needest a spear," said Ulric. "It is plain to me. If I were a god, I would make what I required for my errands. So do they work with winds and seas and rocks, and with thunders and with plagues of many kinds. No man getteth away from them if they have aught against him. Anger not the gods, for they are powerful and they are cunning."

"As thou hast said," replied Caius, gloomily, "I have spoken against them at times, and now they have reached me with this Syrian arrow from the quiver of Herod the jackal."

"Odin!" suddenly exclaimed the jarl; for the overwearied horse under him stood still without a pull of the rein, and before the eyes of the Saxons was the City of the Great King, the Holy City, Jerusalem the Beautiful.

Deep is the valley of Jehoshaphat, through which runneth the brook Kidron under its many bridges and between its gardens and palaces. Beyond this valley, as the whole company stood still to admire, they saw the mighty walls of the city, high and white, and the castles and the towers, but beyond and above all these, in the bright light of the declining sun, they saw the glories of the temple which was accounted one of the seven wonders of the world.

"It is Asgard!" said Ulric, thoughtfully, "and I see the temple of a god that hath power on earth to heal wounds and to give sight, and to whom demons give obedience. I think he is not as are the gods of the North, and I will ask this son of his more about him."

But the Saxons who were halted with him said one to another:

"We have come out into the world far enough. We will see this one city and we will do somewhat of fighting perhaps. But then we will find a keel, or take one, and we will return to the Northland, whether the jarl goeth with us or not. The winter of this land is warm, not cold, and we may not abide it. We will go into our own fiords as the ice cometh out, seeing we may not get there sooner."

So strong is homesickness, and so it will change the hearts and the wills of brave men.

At that hour a youth sat in a vaulted chamber of a great building upon one of the hills of Jerusalem. Around him the furniture was good, but somewhat plain, and there were weapons and armor of many kinds scattered here and there. In a corner was a couch, and there were chairs and tables, and on the tables unlighted lamps.

"I do know," he said, "that Pontius the Spearman is in the city. Why doth he not send for me? I am not in a prison, yet I am not permitted to go out into the city since I returned from Cæsarea. The procurator cannot think that I know aught more than my messages, nor fear lest I should betray him. Why, then, am I shut up in this chamber of the castle?"

Little remembered the haughty procurator of so small a matter as a young Greek messenger for whom he had no present need. Somewhere among the household this Lysias was sure to be awaiting a summons, and there were weighty matters on hand. One was before him pressingly in the hall of audience, for he himself stood there angrily reading a written scroll which had been brought to him.

"The high priest and the eagles once more!" he exclaimed. "This god of the Jews! What is he to me? I anger him not. Little he careth for the standards of the cohorts. Go thou! Tell Caiaphas it shall be as he willeth, and I will send him oxen for his sacrifices. The tribute gatherers have brought me even too many horned cattle, and his god may have them."

A dignified man, long-robed, gray-bearded, solemn-faced, who stood before him, bowed low, responding:

"I hear thee, most noble Pontius. I will bear to the high priest thy answer. It shall be to us as a promise from Cæsar. May the blessing of Jehovah of Hosts be upon him and thee."

"Go!" said Pontius, petulantly. "If he cannot do better for the Romans than he hath done for the Jews, my oxen are but wasted."

Lowly bowed the Jewish noble, but there was pride in his obeisance, and as he went out at the gate he muttered:

"The gift of Jehovah to these heathen would be the coming of Messiah the Prince and the slaughter of their legions in the valley that is before Jezreel until the blood should be as a river to wade horses in."

"What thinkest thou, Cornelius," said the procurator to a soldier of noble presence who stood near him; "must we yield to these dogs forever, with their continual turmoil?"

"They have their god," said Cornelius. "I have read much about him. He is gone from them for a while, but he hath promised to come back again. I think we should make him one of the gods of Rome and set up his image in the Pantheon with that of Jupiter."

"That were good policy," said Pontius, "and it would leave these priests of his nothing more to complain of. They are a pestilent nest of fault-finders and some of them get to the ear of Cæsar, doing us mischief; for they are crafty serpents."

"I fear God," said Cornelius. "We are but men and we see but little, while the eyes of God are everywhere."

"Go thou to Joppa, then," said Pontius, "and let no man pass out of the fort without thy knowledge. Thou keepest the gate. Keep it well."

Soldierly, friendly, was the parting word of Cornelius to his commander, but he was a free Roman and there was no servility in his courtesy, nor was there any fear.

"Him, also, I may trust," said Pontius, "but O for the coming of Caius of Thessalonica! I will see, also, Lysias, the Greek, and I would that Ben Ezra were returned from his cave in Carmel with his treasures. I will let him keep a part of them because I have further use for him before he dieth."

In the strong inner chamber of the procurator's castle Lysias walked slowly up and down chafing at his imprisonment, but his eyes glanced hither and thither and they were watchful.

"What!" he suddenly exclaimed, low-voiced. "Is the corridor door ajar? Would it be my death warrant to look out into the corridor? I am under no command not to look, but I may well be prudent where there are so many sharp swords."

The door was but slightly opened, as if he who last passed through had shut it carelessly; but there are traps in prison houses, and Lysias hesitated, going to listen at the narrow crevice, but not laying a hand upon wall or door.

"No sound," he thought. "I may open and close again. Who knoweth what may be here? I offend no order of any officer."

Nevertheless, he trembled as he obeyed the strong impulse that was in him. A step forward and he was in the corridor. It was lofty, its floor was of pictured tiling, and it was lighted by windows at each end. Into it came another vaulted passage three fathoms away, and he went swiftly to that opening.

"Vast is this palace," he was thinking, but at the next beating of his heart he went forward with a great bound, for the music of a woman's voice in a gay song fell upon his ear.

"She is here!" he exclaimed. "Now I care not if I die, so I but see her."

Wide open was a door into this second passage and through it poured the song, accompanied by the touching of a small harp. It was a love song, and he heard:

> "Now cometh he, my love,
> From the land beyond the sea,
> And the fair wind blowing knoweth,
> That it bringeth him to me."

"Sapphira! O my beloved! I am here!"

She sprang to her feet and the lyre fell from her hand. O she was beautiful, in her sudden astonishment and fear, but he who came toward her with open arms seemed even more beautiful than she, for his face was radiant and his eyes were a flame of fire.

"Sapphira?"

"O rash one! Thou art lost! What am I to thee any more? Am I not the slave of the procurator of Judea? Thou art not my Lysias; thou art but a rider of horses."

In her face was a great struggle of pain, nevertheless, and in his was a whiteness, for he fell upon the floor and lay there moaning.

"Foolish boy!" she said, stooping over him. "I love thee, but I am not now thine, nor can I be. The past is dead, and the gods have bidden us eternal separation. Destroy me not and destroy not thyself. Go lest the sword find thee here! The scourge is close to thee, and sudden death both for thee and me."

"I care not for the scourge or the sword," said Lysias, slowly rising and gazing at her. "I care only for thee, O false one! Hast thou utterly changed away from me?"

"What I was that I am not," she said. "What thou art thou knowest. Art thou mad, also, to cast thyself against the power of Pontius? Leave me lest I call for help! I will not die on thy account. I love life, and life is full of love for such as I am. What need have I of thee, O lost lover?"

Anger was in her eyes now, and greater fear, for that which she said was true.

"Kiss me!" he said, faintly, "and I will go. The gods have abandoned me!"

Then stepped she forward and kissed him on the lips and a spasm shook him from head to foot, shaking her also.

"Let thy love die within thee," she said, "and trouble me no more, for I live happily in this palace, where all are my friends. Make me not thine enemy, for in this thou art a robber."

"That am I," he murmured. "I will go. I came far and risked all to see thee. I knew nothing concerning women. Now that I know thee, what thou art, I have no need of thee. Love will die, for all else is dead. Sing thou thy song, but be sure that all thy roses will wither on thy bosom."

"Cursest thou me?" she exclaimed. "Beware what thou sayest! I have power!"

"As a caged leopard hath power, so hast thou," said Lysias. "I leave thee. Be thou a slave, for that is all that is in thee"—and he was gone.

She stood and looked at the doorway by which he had departed, and her lips were without color and her hand was on her bosom.

"What is this?" she asked. "Did I love him better than I knew? Was I too much in fear that I sent him from me? One cometh who would slay him. It is best that he should go lest he should die. Women must be prudent, but this pain is great. I did love him. O that he had not come again, for before he came I was happy. O ye gods, what shall I do? O beautiful Aphrodite, help me, for thou knowest love!"

In the corridor lingered Lysias listening, and then he walked on, staggering as he went.

"O woman! woman!" he whispered. "What is woman and what is man? She is changed and I change not. I cannot hate her, as I thought I could, now she hath spoken. I will wait cunningly, for I am sure that in this palace is one who calleth for my knife or for a spear thrust. I will find him."

In a moment more he was in his own place, still leaving its door ajar, as at the first, but he began to search among the weapons and the armor in the room, finding a small, sharp blade with an ivory handle, and hiding it in his bosom.

"It will do," he said, "but I would I might wear mail."

At that he was stooping over some fine steelwork and he heard a step behind him. It was a crafty thought which bade him continue his speech.

"The procurator knoweth me only as a postboy," he said. "I might serve him better in mail. He hath not many who would be true to him as I would. There are those who are false, but I could bring him a good sword in a hand he might surely trust."

"O Greek!" said a deep, stern voice. "What is this that thou sayest? Put on the mail!"

"O most noble Pontius!" exclaimed Lysias, turning, but lifting the armor. "Thou didst not send for me, therefore I came not."

"Speak not," said Pontius, "save to tell me all that thou hast seen and heard here and at Joppa and at Cæsarea. I have a work for thee."

Lysias told all save his meeting with Sapphira, and the procurator listened.

"Thou hast ears and thou hast eyes," he said at last. "I set thee free of all other service but this that I now tell thee. Thou wilt have another abiding place than this, but thou wilt come and go freely among my servants, being known to them as my messenger whom none may hinder. Now hath one come from the Damascus gate saying that my friend Caius of Thessalonica draweth near, and with him his Saxon gladiators. He is wounded, and my physician meeteth him. Go thou. Hear all. See all. Report to me of his swordsmen.

"Now hearken! Among the female slaves of my wife is one in whom is a peril, for she is fair. For women I care not, but there are men who are fools before bright eyes. In the banquet room and in the balconies get thou speech with this Sapphira. She will be spoken to by my wife that she may hide nothing from thee lest she die in the arena. Judea and Samaria are worth more to me than is the blood of one fair serpent. Come!"

Lysias now stood before the procurator in mail and helmet, girded with a light sword and bearing a silver-gilded buckler. It was the arms and armor of the Syrian mercenaries of Pontius, but as of an officer among them, ordered to duty at the palace.

"Thou wilt go on foot to the Damascus gate," said Pontius. "The physician waiteth Caius at his house. Deliver this scroll to Caius and remain with his company until thou canst bring me exact tidings concerning his wound."

"O most noble Pontius," said Lysias, "I pray thee permission to say this word."

"Say on!" said the Spearman.

"Only in being true to thee have I any hope of life, for thy enemies are my enemies. I also will at times to attend at the school of Gamaliel, as I told thee."

"That is thy value to me," said Pontius. "Wert thou any man's bondservant, or wert thou other than a youth, a scholar of Gamaliel, I would have no use for thee. All they of his manner of teaching are handicraftsmen, even if they are rich. What is thy work?"

"I am a shaper of arrows," said Lysias, "and I know the making of a bow. Thou mayest yet require to have a sharp arrow sent surely to a mark of thy choosing."

"Say thou no more!" commanded the procurator. "Thou art wise to preserve thy head. Only a fool throweth away his life. Go!"

For they had walked out along the passage and before them was a gate of the palace. It was not the great gate, but even here were armed legionaries, and their officer and others with him took note of Lysias and of the manner of his sending.

"He is the trusted messenger of the procurator," said one. "I heard of him from the captain of the temple. When he hath borne many messages we shall cease to see him."

Lysias passed on down the steep street in his brilliant armor as one having a shadow of authority, but his heart was bitter within him.

"I am to see her again," he murmured. "I would she were dead and I dead with her. I will but live to strike this unknown one, even if I stab him with a blade of Pontius. But I must be cunning with these Saxons. Do I not know what manner of pirates they are? Not among any other crew, I think, shall I find men so tall and so strong as are my old comrades from *The Sword*. Their jarl would be a prince of gladiators, but I am not glad that he and his come now to Jerusalem."

Away behind him in the palace, in the room where he had met her, sat Sapphira.

"What is this?" she exclaimed. "Did I not see him walking with the procurator as one walketh with a near friend? Is he, then, more than a horse boy? Is he an officer of the palace, and greater than I? Now am I indeed in pain, for I have need of friends. O love! Why was I cruel to thee? Come again, O my beloved! My Lysias! I will tell thee that I am not changed! Will he return if I call him? He will, for I am beautiful. I am favored by Aphrodite. She will make him bend to me as I will. It was but for a moment, and I was in fear. None must see me this day. I will go at once as if I were summoned by the wife of the procurator. Woe to any who shall hinder me."

She caught up and threw over her head a veil and over her body a flowing robe of silk embroidered with needlework. Then, as if fear hastened her, she flitted away along the main corridor and disappeared.

Chapter XXXIV
The School of Gamaliel

With all honor did the captain of the Damascus gate of Jerusalem receive Caius of Thessalonica, the friend of Pontius the Spearman. The chariot halted before the gate and in it sat the stern Roman centurion, giving no external token of a wound or of suffering.

"O noble Caius," said the captain, after his first greeting, "I have this, also, for thee from the procurator, that his physician, who is also thine, hath gone before thee to thy house. May the gods give him both skill and success."

"I thank the procurator and thee, also," said Caius. "I will now drive on."

"A moment, O most noble Caius," interrupted the officer of the guard. "A messenger even now. He is from the procurator."

There was no stir among the mounted swordsmen who rode before and behind the chariot, but they sent quick glances to each other as their eyes fell upon this messenger.

"Silence, O jarl," he had said in Greek to Ulric as he drew near him. "I shall go with thee speedily. I thank the gods that I now see thee again. I can do many good things for thee and thine. I pray thee bid them, also, to be as if we were strangers."

"They need no bidding," said Ulric. "Hael to thee."

No further word did either of them speak, but Lysias waited at the side of the chariot while Caius read the parchment epistle. It was but brief, and when it was ended the centurion said to Lysias:

"Go thou and come again. I will answer for thee to Pontius. Say that I bid him be with me within the hour lest evil come. Haste! On thy head! O charioteer, drive to my house! On, O jarl!"

"Behold," thought Lysias, "I am in a sore strait. Pontius will scourge me! But I will run."

A swift runner was he, even with the mail upon him, and at the gate of the procurator's palace he halted to draw breath.

"In! In!" exclaimed the officer of the portal. "I will announce thee. The procurator giveth a feast, but I may go to him. This must be some strange errand!"

"The gods be with thee!" said Lysias. "Tell him!"

It was but a few terrible moments, full of fear for the young Greek, and he stood in an anteroom before the stern Spearman.

"What did I bid thee?" he demanded.

"Slay thou me if thou wilt, most noble procurator," bravely responded Lysias, "but Caius of Thessalonica sendeth thee greeting and these words: 'Be thou with me within the hour lest evil come.' I beg thee, O Pontius, let me say this much more: for I heard him whisper, 'Lest he give his power into the hand of him of the Black Castle and his neck to the headsman of Cæsar.' I have not at all disobeyed thee, O Pontius. He bade me return to his house for another commandment."

"Be thou there on his arrival and I will count it thy strict obedience," said Pontius. "Thou art not a legionary, nor under the law of the legion. I think thou servest me well."

Away ran Lysias murmuring: "So narrow is the measure between Roman favor and Roman vengeance! He may die ere I risk his wrath again."

Nevertheless, it is not easy for one of the great to depart from a feast whereat governors and senators and princes are reclining, and Pontius went in to pay the duty of host to his many guests, so that Lysias was in no peril concerning his errand.

The chariot had reached its halting place and Caius had walked into his house, upheld somewhat by his pride, but more by the arm of Ulric, the son of Brander.

Already the physician had examined the wound made by the Syrian grooved arrow.

"O Saxon," he asked, "thou didst suck this poison well and quickly?"

Ulric did but nod his head.

"Then know thou, my lord Caius," said the man of skill, "that but for thy swordsman thou wert already dead. I will do what I can for thee, but it will be long before thou wilt bear thine armor. This wound must be neither bandaged nor closed, but washed only and kept open. Saxon, give me thy sharpest blade."

"It is my seax," said Ulric, drawing it. "What am I to do?"

"Cut into this hard swelling," said the physician. "Cut the depth of two finger breadths and withdraw thy blade."

"Cut!" said Caius. "Am I afraid of an edge?"

"So bidden, I will cut," said Ulric, and the sword point went into the swollen arm.

"I thought so," said the physician. "With that green corruption spurteth out much evil. Widen the cut. Caius is saved. I will put into the gash an ointment that I will bring. It is well for thee, O Caius, that thy strong swordsman is thy trusty friend. I go."

Behind them, by express authority, now stood Lysias, listening, and he said:

"Most noble Caius, this is my command from the procurator. I must go to him."

"Tell thou him the saying of the physician," said Caius. "Tell him, also, that I change not my greeting. He must come."

Again went Lysias, and again he stood before the procurator telling all that he had heard and seen.

"Pause thou here a moment," said Pontius. "I would have speech with my wife."

Still as a statue stood the young Greek, and none who came or went dared ask him whence he came, but suddenly an arm was around his neck and a kiss was upon his cheek.

"I am here, beloved, but I may not linger. I will see thee often. I am still thy Sapphira."

He stirred not, spoke not, nor did he turn to see, but there was a grating of teeth.

"O Lysias! O love!"

"Speak not of that which is dead," he said to her. "Go thou thy way. This is no place for the foolishness of unfaithful women. I will indeed meet thee again, but thou art a slave and I am a free warrior. Go!"

White was now the face of Sapphira and her lips were quivering, but she whispered:

"Scorn me not! I was frightened, and so I was cruel. I do love thee; and thou wilt need me in this place, which is as a spider's web. I go. Follow me not!"

"Follow thee?" laughed Lysias, scornfully. "I did follow thee from far, but now I am as a weapon in the hand of the procurator. I shall serve not thee, but him."

"Ha!" muttered one who heard. "This is, then, the trusted one. Him we must slay."

Well for that speaker if his lips had been closed, for in the shadow behind him stood Pontius the Spearman.

"They who will not betray me must die?" he thought within himself. "Then do I now know one mark at which my Greek may send his sharpest arrow and be guiltless. He may slay this Iberian swine with his own hand."

For the mutterer was a guest who had risen from a table, and he was one who had been an officer of Herod's household, but was now pretending to be an enemy of the cunning tetrarch, the jackal of the Black Castle.

The guest returned to his reclining, and Sapphira had vanished as a lamp that goeth out, but the procurator came forward.

"Say to Caius that I come. Abide thou in his house this night and on the morrow until I send for thee, save that thou mayest go in the morning to the school of Gamaliel. Hast thou money for thy uses?"

"O most noble Pontius," said Lysias, "the swift ass that was mine own is in thy stable. All baggage of mine is in the armory room where thou didst find me. I have gold and silver pieces enough in my pouch for this present. I am not poor, so that what I have be not taken from me."

"I will give orders in these thy matters," replied Pontius. "He who serveth me well is rich enough. Thou shalt have thy swift ass and such other beasts as thou wilt. Go now. I believe thee brave and prudent. Thou art young, too, and the girl is fair. Youth is the time for trifling. Provide thee soon a good bow and arrows of thine own choosing."

"Thanks, O noble Pontius! Thanks! I will send sure arrows at thy bidding!" So saying, the young Greek departed.

Long was the conference that night between the Saxons and Lysias.

"We are little surprised," said the jarl, "for we knew thou wert going to this place. Thou art a good fighter and thou hast rightly taken the procurator for thy captain. I have heard that he casteth the pilum even better than do other Romans. I could follow such a man into battle, knowing that he is fitted to lead. Hast thou found thy Sapphira?"

"Speak not of her, O jarl," said Lysias. "Ere long thou mayest thyself look upon her, but there is a peril in her name at this hour."

"I read thy face," said Ulric. "Keep thou thine own secret. But thou mayest say to Pontius the Spearman that he hath no surer friend than Caius of Thessalonica."

"Even now they are together," replied Lysias. "The procurator will know all that is known to thy friend, but I fear the careless tongues of thy Saxons. They speak to one another concerning triremes and old fights at sea. I would they were in their North country."

"So would not I," said Ulric, "unless I were to sail with them. I may not now leave this city of Jerusalem, and to sail to the north were to sail into ice fields. We must wait until the spring."

Not so thought the homesick vikings in their comfortable lodgings in the house of Caius. Even now they were talking of the sea.

"It is but a few miles to this seaport called Joppa," they said. "We will learn somewhat concerning the road thither and the shipping. We are free men, with the Middle Sea so near at hand."

Caius of Thessalonica slept well after his long communing with the procurator, and when he awoke the jarl sat near him.

"Thou art watchful!" exclaimed Caius. "But in Jerusalem I am safe. I have to tell thee, however, that thy gladiators may not abide within the walls. The quarters for such as they are out in the valley of Jehoshaphat, near the amphitheater. No games are going on at this time, but there will be abundant sport in the days after the Passover feast, when Herod cometh."

The jarl's brow darkened, but he said only: "So be it. I will guide them to their place. I myself will inspect the city and the forts and offer sacrifices, as I told thee. But this know thou, O noble Caius, that not in this city nor in any other is treachery dead. I fear for thee. How is thine arm? I would see it."

"Thou hast knowledge of wounds, but not of poison," replied Caius. "Uncover it."

The jarl did so, and he looked thoughtfully at the sore and then at the feverish face of the noble Roman.

"This man will die slowly," he thought, "but he will die, for this wound healeth not. I will not be here when he dieth, lest I be deemed by others only fit food for wild beasts. So will I say to my companions."

"It changeth little," he said aloud to Caius. "Who shall read a thing like this? I will go and return, but I would my sword might be near thee if there is need of it."

"Go, O jarl," said Caius. "I will send for thee if I require thee. Fulfill thy will concerning the city, for all men may come and go. Only that thou must leave thy weapons from thee or the legionaries will disarm thee. The Jews, also, go unarmed."

"For that I have no care," said Ulric, "but it were a sore thing for Tostig the Red, for instance, to have no hilt near his grip."

"March them away quickly!" exclaimed Caius. "While thou art known to be with me as a guard thou mayest wear thy sword and thy mail. The rules go no further, for there have been many tumults and much bloodshed in Jerusalem."

The jarl answered not to that, but took his leave, and not at all as a servant. Rather did it seem as if the centurion were under his command. He went to his men, and well pleased were they to find their quarters were to be without the walls.

"O jarl," said Wulf the Skater, "this is much better. I would thou wert able now to show us our way to the sea. We have learned much from Lysias and from others. There is good shipping upon the coast and the right keel might be found by brave men."

"Also triremes of Cæsar," replied the jarl. "The coast is well guarded. We will wait a little."

Out into the streets they marched, with him at their head, and many turned to look upon their array as they went on to the gate. The dwellers in Jerusalem were accustomed to seeing various kinds of armed men, but these were unlike any others. Nevertheless, there were devout Jews who lifted hands to curse them in the name of Jehovah, as heathen gladiators whose presence was a pollution of the city of God.

The amphitheater, when they came to it, was found to be larger than that of Tiberias, with more dens for wild beasts and with a better and longer course for the running of races.

"I have been told," said the circus servitor who guided them, "that Herod the Great delighted much in horses. Also that one value of the circus was as a place of execution for tribes who had rebelled against him. His horsemen on the frontier scouted far and wide for captives and his cages here were ever full."

"I care not for circuses," said Wulf the Skater. "I have seen enough of them."

"And I," replied Tostig; "if I might kill an elephant, it would please me. I have a curiosity to know how long it taketh so huge a beast to die."

"Thou wilt see elephants enough," said the servitor, "but they do not often spend them upon the games. They are costly, and they come from far. Men and women are plentiful, and they make as good sport in the killing."

The buildings prepared as quarters for trained gladiators, not slaves, were rude but spacious, and here did Ulric leave his friends while he returned to the city, but he remembered the saying of Caius concerning his armor.

"I may wear a tunic and robe only at most times," he said to himself. "But under the tunic may be a coat of fine mail and hidden by the robe may be a seax. I will not be defenseless altogether where there are so many secret daggers as I hear of. I would have speech with Lysias, if I may. I trust him not entirely, and I forget not that he is now of the household of the procurator."

Not justly altogether was he thinking of the young Greek, for Lysias was a man walking among perils and having a wounded heart under his bright mail and his gay apparel. It was but the next day when he made his first entrance at the school of Gamaliel. Celebrated over the inhabited earth was this academy, and many came from distant lands to hear the teachings of the great and learned rabbi. Among them, also, were those whose real purpose was to obtain for themselves the reputation of scholarship through the name of Gamaliel their teacher, and they were even as Lysias in that matter. In such a company, however, small attention was paid to one more young Greek, who seemed to be rich, save that none questioned him unwisely after being informed that his protector was Pontius the Spearman. Moreover, if there were those who bowed and made way for him on that account, there were others who bent their brows and drew aside their garments that he should not touch them.

"Thou art imprudent," said an elderly man to one of these. "Restrain thy zeal, I pray thee."

"He is a dog!" growled the zealot. "His heathen master slew my father causelessly in the temple, mingling his blood with his sacrifice to Jehovah. I am of Galilee."

"I will ask thee, then," said his adviser, "sawest thou ever this Galilean prophet who cometh from Nazareth? It is said that he worketh many wonders."

"I have seen him," said the zealot, "and wonders he doth work. Hath any other rabbi raised the dead? Who else cleanseth a leper or openeth the eyes of the blind?"

"If thou liest not," was the surly response, "he is indeed one of the learned. I will hear his teachings when he cometh to Jerusalem to the Passover feast. But he will work no wonders here."

"Knowest thou that?" sneered the zealot. "But this thou knowest from the law, that it is not well for thee to speak evil of a rabbi. He who revileth one of the learned goeth to Gehenna."

"I reviled him not!" exclaimed the adviser, as if in sudden fear. "I am a Pharisee of the Pharisees. I am a keeper of the whole law. Verily I will hear thy rabbi when he speaketh. But beware thou of offending the procurator!"

"Messiah cometh!" said the Galilean fiercely. "He bringeth a sword! He will make his garments red in the blood of the heathen!"

"Let not the priests hear thee!" sharply responded the Pharisee. "To them only is given the discerning of such matters. Thou wilt yet be cast out of the synagogue."

The angry Galilean walked slowly away. "What know the Pharisees and the priests concerning Jesus of Nazareth?" he muttered. "I think of him that he is a more learned rabbi than any here in Jerusalem."

Now Lysias heard these men, and already had he learned from the Saxons in what manner their jarl had been healed of his hurts in Galilee.

"This prophet!" he thought. "I will see him if I may. Alas for me, there is no temple here to Mercurius or to Apollo! I have great need to offer sacrifices. No! not to Juno nor to Venus! They have not dealt well with me. I think I shall now hate Sapphira when I see her. How is it then that I also love her, seeing that I would slay her if I could? This is that strange thing between a fool and a woman."

Chapter XXXV
In the Court of the Women

It was still the winter time in the Northland, but in Judea the spring had returned. In the lowlands there was already much heat and a swift growth of all fruits of the earth, but in a high place, like Jerusalem upon her hills, the days were cooler and oft the nights were frosty, so that men builded fires in their braziers.

"This is not according to nature," said Lars, the son of Beolf, among his companions. "We have had no snow save a few flakes, and there hath been no ice thicker than the blade of my seax. I weary of this land!"

"Hael to the Northland!" exclaimed Tostig the Red. "Hael to the driving storms and the glittering ice, and to the frost and to the snow!"

"I will not stay here," said Knud the Bear. "I will depart from an accursed country wherein there is never good winter. But didst thou hear the keeper? He saith that ships at Joppa dare not put to sea because of the rough weather. What seamen are these!"

"O men!" said Wulf the Skater. "By Odin! If vikings were at the oars and if I were at the helm, a keel would seek the open sea."

"We will even go to Joppa when we may," said Tostig. "But our errand will be to the Northland, that we may bring back fleets, and in them Saxons, to march with the jarl into the great battle in Esdraelon. We are too few."

"I am with thee," said another tall viking. "I have considered this matter, and I think it is also the mind of the jarl. He may not go with us, but his secret will is that we go speedily without him. Then will he truthfully say to the Romans that he did not command us to go. I will no longer be shut up in this place as if I were one of the beasts in yonder dens waiting for my turn to be made a bloody show of. I am a free warrior, not a caged wild creature. I will go to the sea."

Other voices were raised in strong accord with his, and their talk went on until their minds were on fire and their purposes had become firmly fixed, for they were men of experience and of great courage. The jarl came not among them at this time, for he was even then at the temple gate inquiring as to the right method of obtaining cattle for his sacrifices to Jehovah. A servitor went into one of the inner courts and brought out a dealer who had bullocks at hand, and this man began to name prices, counting them in shekels of the temple.

"What know I of shekels?" exclaimed Ulric.

"Thou dost not need to know," broke in a voice behind him. "O jarl, I am here. He asketh thee too much. Let me attend to this matter. Well for thee that thou hast it in thy mind to offer sacrifices to the living Jehovah!"

"O my friend!" exclaimed the jarl. "Glad am I of thy coming! This charge is thine."

"Who art thou that meddlest with another man's affair?" demanded the dealer angrily.

"Silence, thou!" was the peremptory reply. "I am Ben Ezra, the interpreter of Caius of Thessalonica, and this is the captain of his guard and of his Saxons. Beware that thou deal not fraudulently with any of his people lest I have a hand laid upon thee. I am in my right in this matter."

"That do I now admit," replied the dealer in a changed manner, "but I charge him not too much. Come thou and see the cattle."

But the prices he shortly named were less than the half of his former asking.

"Pay him, O jarl," said Ben Ezra. "It is well. Offer thy burnt offering, for thou hast great need of the favor of Jehovah in that which cometh upon thee. I will remain with thee, for I also offer sacrifices. O dealer, I will buy of thee. Let the beasts be without blemish. I will have, also, a lamb and two doves and wine for the oblation. Pause not, for I have conferred with the high priest and he knoweth my matter, and this is of his direction."

But for the guiding of Ben Ezra the jarl had been dealt with as an ignorant man, a foreigner having money, but now all things were accomplished with order and rectitude. Nevertheless, the jarl was displeased that he was compelled to remain without in the court of the heathen, not going near the altar whereon his offerings were burnt.

"They would prevent such as I am," he said, "from drawing too near their God and getting acquainted with him. I would both see his face and hear his voice. Evil, evil, is this manner of the Jews! Are they of higher degree in the sight of their God than am I, the son of Odin?"

Nevertheless, from the place assigned him he might see all, and there he stood watching the manner of the slaying of his bullocks and the going up of the great smoke and the swinging of the censers. He listened, also, reverently to the chanting of the priests and the Levites and the responses of the Jewish congregations in the other courts.

"Ben Ezra," he remarked, "might enter the inner court, going where he would, for he is a Jew of high degree. He told me, also, that over yonder is the court of the women. I have offered my sacrifice. Why do I linger here?" For his face grew suddenly pale as if he had been stricken through with a spear, and he exclaimed again, "The court of the women."

Loudly swelled the sonorous chorus of the many chanting voices and there came back strange echoes from the inner walls of the temple. The majesty and the splendor of the temple service were unspeakable, but the jarl turned away from it and strode swiftly out of the court of the heathen. He walked on until he might stand in a place near the broad passage by which the women worshipers, veiled or unveiled, were continually coming and going.

"O Miriam!" he thought. "My eyes have sought thee as I have walked the streets of this city. Hilda cometh not any more to counsel me. I am dark in all my mind. If thou art not here what do I any longer in Jerusalem? It is not Asgard, and here are no gods at all. It is but a city of men like myself, and the women are as other women, and the Romans have the rule in spite of this Jehovah."

His thoughts were burning within him and he felt the sickness of disappointment and failure, and his eyes were dull with longing as he gazed upon this procession of Hebrew women. Suddenly his heart gave a great leap, but he stood still, for he heard a voice saying:

"Miriam! Thy veil! Cover thyself! Yonder Roman stareth at thee!"

"I will cleave him to the jaws!" exclaimed Ulric, turning quickly.

But before he could move a pace or discern one man from another whom to strike a hand was upon his arm and he heard a whisper which thrilled him from head to foot.

"I am Miriam! I am now veiled! Harm not thyself nor me. I think he heard thee not. Strike not a Roman lest thou be crucified. Follow me, O beautiful one. Follow not too nearly, but mark well the house into which I go. The woman with me is my aunt. The Roman of whom she warned me is but a dealer in slaves—but he is a Roman. Come!"

"I follow thee, O my beloved," whispered the jarl, "but if he toucheth thee, he shall die if he were Cæsar!"

Sunken-eyed, hollow-cheeked, with a forehead low and sloping, was the dealer in human cattle who stood shortly at the street side without the portal. His lips were moving with an evil expression upon them, and his eyes had seen too well the exceeding beauty of the Jewish maiden.

"A thousand sesterces for her at Rome," he muttered. "How shall I obtain her? Pontius hath bidden us beware of angering the Jews."

Then he came forward a pace and spoke aloud, with small ceremony, to Ulric.

"She spoke unto thee, O gladiator. Who is she, and what doest thou here?"

Even for the sake of Miriam was the jarl somewhat calm in his manner and cunning in his speech, but his voice was unpleasant.

"O Roman," he said, "art thou unwise? Seest thou not that I am a sword? One greater than thou art will answer for my going and coming. I but do his bidding. When thy head passeth suddenly from thy shoulders thou wilt ask no more questions concerning a damsel who is guarded by the strong and high one. I will watch for thee henceforth. I am one who needeth not to be commanded a second time concerning a sword cut."

"Aha!" snarled the dealer. "I have seen thee heretofore. Thou art captain of the gladiators of Caius of Thessalonica. I quarrel not with him."

"Nor dost thou need any quarrel with the procurator," said Ulric. "His arm is longer than thine. Keep back thy foot from unknown ground lest thou shalt meet a man coming unto thee in sudden haste."

No word came back, but the man's face darkened venomously, for a Roman liketh not a rebuke from a barbarian; but there was fire in the eyes of the jarl and his right hand went under his mantle, and the dealer understood well the meaning of the movement. Nevertheless, a mere trafficker in the flesh of men and women may not wisely stir the wrath of a centurion or of a man in authority. A Roman may not be scourged or crucified, but he may die suddenly as well as another. So turned he sullenly away about his affairs, and the jarl went on his way.

The streets of Jerusalem are narrow with the exception of the broad thoroughfares which lead to the outer gates and the main approaches to the temple. It was a narrow passage between high palace buildings into which Miriam and her aunt hastily turned their feet not long after, escaping from observation by the cruel eyes of the dealer in slaves. No word did they utter, and those whom they met spoke not unto them, for there are laws of privacy and due reserve among the Jews relating to the public greeting of women. He who annoyeth them transgresseth and is liable to be called to an accounting. They walked onward rapidly, and now the way led along the side of a mount beyond which was the valley which divideth the city into, as it were, two cities. Ever at a little distance behind them strode a tall shape which did not manifestly appear to pursue them, but for which all other wayfarers made room on approaching.

"The gladiator seemeth to be in wrath," said one who looked upon him. "Beware of the anger of these wild heathen, for they are even as tigers, and they know no law."

Light was now in his eyes, nevertheless, and his stepping was that of a stag upon the hills.

"I have found her!" he muttered, joyously. "I have fulfilled the token that was given me by Hilda in my dream upon *The Sword*. Now shall I not soon see Hilda herself? Hath she not guided me in this, and is she not now with the gods? This may indeed be the city from which I shall pass on into Asgard. I am glad that I offered sacrifices in the temple this day, for at once have I received this answer from Jehovah that he hath shown favor unto me. He is indeed the chief God of this land to this day, for he hath not permitted the Romans to destroy his temple nor to slay his priests. I think that if they were to do so, he would be angry and he would surely take his revenge upon them. That would I do if I were a god."

The door of a large house swung open as of itself before Miriam and her companion, but Miriam paused upon the threshold. Turning and glancing quickly up and down the street, and seeing no peril, she raised a hand and beckoned. Ulric came quickly, but Miriam's aunt was already within.

"Think not to enter with me now," said the Jewish maiden, hastily. "But tell me quickly, what art thou in Jerusalem? Why art thou here? What doest thou in Jehovah's temple?"

"O Miriam, the beautiful!" he responded, gazing upon her joyously, "I am even as I said to thee in Esdraelon. I am Ulric, the jarl of the Saxons. I am of Odin's line. Of the sons of the gods. I offered sacrifices in the temple of Jehovah asking for thee, and thou seest that he granted my petition."

Even as he spoke she stepped back within the doorway, and he also entered with her, but as yet the door closed not behind them.

"I understand thee partly," she said, trembling greatly. "Thou art a prince among thine own people. O that thou wert a son of Abraham! O that thou wert not a slayer of men in the circus!"

"That I am not!" exclaimed Ulric. "Such business is not for me. I am a free warrior. I go not again into the circus. I am with Caius of Thessalonica for a season, for I am his friend and his guard. I came out from the Northland into the world that I might seek for the city of the gods, that there I may meet my kindred. But I will ask of thee, O beautiful one! O Miriam! how knowest thou Hilda of the hundred years?"

Her eyes burned earnestly upon him while he was speaking and her face was as the dawn of a new day, for in it there were many changes, the color coming and departing and the lips quivering.

"I know her not," she said; and now they had drifted on into a small anteroom near the door, her veil, also, having been put aside more perfectly. "Who is this Hilda, that thou askest of me such a question?"

"Surely thou knowest her?" he said. "She is a saga woman of the Northland. She is learned in all the old runes that are written on the rocks and on the tombs, and she talketh with the gods in their places. I know that it is now many months since she hath been laid in her own tomb in the cleft of the rocks, but I saw her with thee, speaking to me in a dream, when I was on the sea in my ship. She bade me sail on and find thee, and this I have done. Therefore I am glad that I offered sacrifices to thy God. Henceforth he shall be to me as Odin, the God who is over all the other gods."

She listened as if his voice were music and as if she willed that he might not cease speaking.

"Thou hast said!" she now exclaimed, and a voice behind her, deep and sonorous, added:

"Amen! A great King is he, above all gods. He is the God of gods, and beside him there is no other; for Jehovah, our God, is one God, and there is none like him. O heathen man, thou hast well spoken. This day hast thou become his servant, for he hath sent unto thee his commandment in a dream, and thou hast obeyed him. Also thou hast done well in offering thy burnt sacrifices."

"That did I according to the directions given me by Ben Ezra from the priests," said the jarl. "But who art thou?"

"I am Isaac, the aged, the kinsman of this maiden," was the response. "O heathen man, I am glad that thou hast powerful friends, for at this hour we are among perils, both she and I—and all our house. I will tell thee, for one Abbas—accursed be he of Jehovah!—threateneth us with destruction."

"Do I not know him!" exclaimed Ulric. "But surely he is nidering! He is a weak man, and a traitor and a thief. If this be so, his blood be upon his own head, for he must die. I have a matter concerning him that he knoweth not. O Miriam, I am a leader of men, and I am not imprudent. Evil is he who is careless concerning such as thou art. Tell thou me, that I may have strength to obey thee, do I now remain here longer, or do I depart?"

As a man wrestling with himself was the jarl, and her face grew wonderfully kind and sweet as she looked upon him; but Isaac now stood by her gazing at the jarl, and the wrinkled features of the old man were full of fear and trouble.

"Depart!" she said, softly. "It is enough that I have seen thee again. Fail not to return, but when thou comest to the door ask only for Isaac. O that thou wert of my own people!"

"I care not for that matter!" exclaimed Ulric. "It will not be long before I come — —"

But his eyes were looking down, for upon his own broad, powerful hand came, gently alighting as a bird, a whiteness which was lighted wonderfully by the red glow of the ruby in the ring. But the hand of Miriam lingered not, flitting coyly away as if the bird were frightened, and in the fingers of the jarl, the son of Odin, there was a strong tremor.

"Ulric," she said, pronouncing his name for the first time, with a great sigh, "God hath sent us this promise of deliverance from our destroyers. Thy Hilda was in the Northland?"

"An hundred years old was she," said the jarl, "when I bade her farewell. I loved her more than aught else upon earth. She was a princess, and her hair was as the snow, and her smile was exceedingly dear to me. Didst thou ever know and love such a one?"

"I think she is as Hannah, the prophetess of my people!" exclaimed Miriam. "But she, too, hath departed. She was a mother in Israel!"

"Haste!" interrupted Isaac. "Let the young heathen go his way! This is unseemly for a maiden of Judah! He may not remain. But, O youth, if thou canst do anything, withhold not thy hand."

"Fear not!" said the jarl. "I will quickly attend to Abbas and to whoever worketh with him!"

But his eyes were gazing deeply into the eyes of Miriam, and it seemed as if in this manner they were speaking to one another.

"Go!" she whispered. "Have I not thy ruby? Keep thou, also, my token. I am thine!"

"O Miriam," whispered back Ulric, "I think thee also a daughter of the gods. I go!"

The door closed behind him and he strode away, but immediately Isaac spoke chidingly.

"Thou art mad!" he exclaimed, "O foolish daughter of Israel! O unwise damsel! What is this stranger unto thee?"

"O Isaac, my kinsman," she replied, "this matter concerneth both thy life and mine. Did he not fulfill the law of sacrifices? I will go to my chamber, but I enjoin upon thee that thou greet him kindly when he returneth."

"That much I will do," said the old man as one who prudently considereth a difficult affair. "Am not I a man of understanding? If Jehovah hath sent us a sword for our protection, blessed be his name! Even this day hath Abbas been with me, and he hath afflicted me sorely."

"What said he?" she inquired.

"More than I may wisely tell thee," said Isaac. "Only that he again hath demanded thee as the bride of this Tyrsus of Chronea. If thou shalt refuse, he will surely bring thee and thy household before a judge with whom is a gift and in whose hand is destruction."

"Tell thou that to Ulric the Jarl!" she said, vehemently. "Where is now thy wisdom? What more, then, hast thou to say? Is not this the spoiling of thy goods? If I were given to Tyrsus wouldst thou escape the greed of Abbas?"

"Father Abraham!" groaned the old man. "We are in the power of the heathen. Do as thou wilt and I will speak well to thy swordsman."

Far down the street, not knowing or caring whither he went, was Ulric the Jarl, but one who stood at the wayside watched his coming and put out a hand.

"Halt, O jarl! Go no further. Such as thou art have need of caution. At yonder turn into the valley there are Roman guards and they will arrest thee as a gladiator escaped from the circus. Enter not a difficulty."

"O Ben Ezra," exclaimed Ulric, "what sayest thou? Am not I a free warrior?"

"Not long wilt thou be free at all," said the Jew, "if thou wanderest imprudently. The edicts have been strengthened. The master of the games is a hard man and subtle. Go thou rather to the house of Caius or out into the valley of Jehoshaphat."

"Thou art my friend," said Ulric, "and I will ask thee of an important matter. Knowest thou of the doings of Abbas?"

"He is in the city," said Ben Ezra. "What is thy need of him? He is evil."

"I require of him nothing but his blood upon a blade," said Ulric. "He is a plotter against both Caius and the procurator."

"Come thou with me to thy friend's house," replied Ben Ezra. "I know this to be true, but Abbas may not be slain openly."

"If Pontius will command me," said Ulric, "I will bring him this serpent's head on the morrow. Otherwise I will guide my own doing. It is but a stroke of a sharp sword."

Little said they after that until they were in the house of Caius, but when they were there it was Ben Ezra and not the jarl who was summoned to confer with the centurion. Not long was he absent, but when he returned his face was dark.

"Trust not a Roman," he whispered to Ulric. "To them all other men are but as cattle. Thou art only a swordsman in the eyes of this Caius. Slay not Abbas lest thou anger him. He is thy friend truly, but it is a Roman friendship, with a dagger in it. Go thou to thy men. Would thou wert on the sea! Thou hast no right to sell them to the circus."

"That will I not!" said Ulric. "But I will confer with them speedily."

So went he away, but he went with Ben Ezra.

There are many cunnings among those who struggle in the net of power, and a great subtlety had been born in the mind of Lysias. "If the Saxons remain," he had thought, "I am lost. It is long before they may be slain in the arena. I will go and talk with them again. This galley that, is to bear the messenger of Herod lieth at Joppa."

Therefore, even while Ulric had offered his sacrifices, the young Greek was among the Saxons telling them many things.

"This is no merchant craft," he had told them. "This galley of Herod is small, but strong for a rough sea. Ye are crew enough."

"That are we," said Tostig the Red. "But the jarl might forbid our going."

"If ye go not," said Lysias, "ye will be penned as dangerous beasts. The jarl only is secure among the great, his friends. He cannot protect you from the master of the games."

"That dog was here to look at us to-day," said Knud the Bear. "I like him not. I will wear no fetters of his clamping. O ye sons of the free vikings, I go to the sea. Who will go with me to take this keel of Herod?"

"No man will remain behind," said Wulf. "The night shadows come. There are horses in the stables. Every man to his armor, and let us take our treasure with us. We will slay as we go and leave behind us a good mark."

Nevertheless, they were prudent, as became warriors who were few in number, and the guards of the circus had as yet no command concerning them save to let them come and go as they would for a season. The stables were near and the horses were many, and with these were only slaves who feared to speak to a swordsman. Therefore, if a Saxon came to look at beasts or to examine saddles and bridles, no man hindered him. It was but thought that he had curiosity as to trappings which he might use in the games. He did well to take thought concerning his own business against the hour when he must slay or be slain. But all the while a fire burned more hotly in the hearts of the men, for the words of Lysias were in full accord with many sayings of the jarl.

"He hath been troubled in mind concerning us," they said. "He knoweth not what to do. We will take away from him this burden, for we are men and we may save ourselves. It is not meet that we should encumber our jarl unduly. He hath done well with us. He would not have us linger to be slain."

Nevertheless, the dusky hour was at hand and Ulric came not to them, as he at first thought. From the house of Caius he had been silently led to the house of Ben Ezra, his friend guiding him as a man who is in deep thought. The way seemed one which led toward the valley of Jehoshaphat, through many streets, but they came to a door before which Ben Ezra paused and turned to the jarl.

"I will trust thee," he said, "for it is needful. This is the house of my abiding."

"Not large," said Ulric, "and the front of it is dark and ancient. I will go in with thee."

"In it dwelleth no other beside myself," said Ben Ezra, opening the door with a key. "But he who knoweth of this place knoweth of death. It is a hidden thing in Israel, and I charge thee by thy gods and by the wrath of Jehovah, my God, that thou make thyself as one of us to keep well a thing that is shown unto thee in secret."

"I am a keeper of faith," said Ulric. "I will call it a secret of the gods, as if it were the tomb of my father. But in this chamber which we have entered I see nothing save plain and simple matters."

"Come further," said Ben Ezra, "for thou hast taken upon thee thy oath. Did I not tell thee that I had been to the cave in Carmel and that I had made thy treasure secure?"

"It was buried well," said Ulric. "I think no stranger could have found it."

"Neither would it have been of any use to thee or me," said Ben Ezra. "Couldst thou strike with thy seax if it were buried in a cave in Carmel? It is better at thy hand."

"I understand thee," exclaimed Ulric. "At this hour, here in Jerusalem, I have need of money. I was never so at any time. It is true that gold coins may be good weapons. I will be glad of them and of the jewels."

"O jarl," said Ben Ezra, "already have I paid much to Pontius the Spearman and to the high priest and to the captain of the temple. Greedy were they, but I have satisfied them. Of thy share in the matter they know not. Thou hast no need to go to thy men this night, for the morning will do as well, and thou canst plan how they may escape to their own land."

"So will I do," said Ulric. "I will abide with thee. But this seemeth to be as other houses."

"So hath it seemed to any who dwelt here," said Ben Ezra, "unless they were as I am. Is not this back wall strongly made of well-fitted masonwork?"

"A well-made wall," said Ulric. "None may break it through. The stones are very large."

Far back from the street were they now, and the house which had appeared small was seen to be of great extent, as if builded down a steep slope. Suddenly the jarl exclaimed:

"A door of a stone! O Jew, how is it that this great marble turneth at thy pushing?"

"See thou," said Ben Ezra. "It is set into the wall upon pivotings. Therefore it is as firm as the rest of the wall unless it shall be tried by one who knoweth the catch-pin at the side. Even then a weak hand moveth it not. I will show thee, and then do thou make trial for thyself."

The jarl watched and understood.

"A marvelous trick!" he exclaimed, opening and shutting the secret door and finding that much strength was required. "O Jew, beyond is a corridor of stone, and I see steps which go downward."

"Before thee is a great deep," replied Ben Ezra. "Thou art trusted as to this thing in the name of Jehovah. Go in, O jarl of the Saxons. Thou wilt go down into the secret chambers of Jerusalem with me."

Chapter XXXVI
The Secret Messenger

Lysias, the Greek, stood reverently before the Roman ruler of Jerusalem, and the dark, piercing eyes of Pontius were watching his face intently.

"O most noble Pontius," said Lysias, "I have done as thou didst order. All these were the words of Ben Ezra, nor have I failed to tell thee every saying of Abbas and of him who was with him. The messenger from Machærus goeth swiftly to Joppa and the galley of Herod waiteth for him."

They were standing in the small chamber near the banquet hall, and the voice of Lysias was hushed and tremulous, for the brows of the procurator were knitting and the veins in his temples were swelling.

"Well for thee, O Greek," he muttered, hoarsely. "But now it is as if Herod himself were to be with Cæsar, bringing gifts. The very gods are against me!"

"O most noble Pontius," said Lysias, raising his head courageously, "bid me depart and it may be that neither galley nor messenger shall cross the sea to Rome."

"I may not hinder a royal messenger," said Pontius, gloomily. "To do so were sure destruction. Thou canst do nothing."

"But if," whispered Lysias—"if Herod, the tetrarch, might know that his galley had departed, and if afterward no man came to tell him of her voyage?"

"A man may hear good tidings," said the procurator, with a dark smile dawning in his face. "But be not thou at any time the bringer of news concerning this galley. Thou hast a letter to bear for me to Cornelius at Cæsarea. I bid thee to go by way of Joppa and to return. I now write the parchment. Ride thou thy own swift beast. Whoever may be traveling upon their own errands at this time, I meddle not with their affairs."

"Thanks, noble Pontius," said Lysias, "but I will give thee a token. A man will come to thee in haste shortly from the keeper of the circus. He will know nothing of the galley of Herod, but he will tell thee of her departure from Joppa and of her crew. So shalt thou be sure that I know not aught except my errand to Cornelius."

Hasty was now the going and the returning of the procurator, but Lysias had now a small tablet and not a parchment to put into his pouch, neither looked he upon the writing on the tablet.

"Go!" said Pontius. "I will wait for thy man from the circus. Tell me no more!"

Then passed Lysias out into the corridor and the eyes of Pontius followed him.

"Subtle are the Greeks," he muttered. "Already yonder youth knoweth enough to kindle a fire that would burn to Tartarus. Let him do this one thing and I will give him a gift which he hath never yet received."

Not far had Lysias gone along the corridor when a hand withheld him and there was a whisper.

"Lysias! Love! Whither goest thou?"

"Sapphira! O beautiful one! I may not linger. I ride swiftly to Cæsarea. I will return to thee. Wait thou for me!"

"O Lysias! Favored of Aphrodite! Go and return to me. I shall then have many things to tell thee. Then shalt thou know I have loved thee."

Her arms were around him, her kiss was upon his lips, and she was gone. He, too, went on in haste, leaving the palace, but she had retreated into an inner chamber, luxuriously furnished, wherein a lamp was burning.

"I will wait here for my mistress," she said. "A strange thing is love, for it may be lighted like this lamp. It may go out and it may burn again if one willeth. I think I must put out this love of mine for Lysias lest it should burn me. Alas for him or for any who may be made the bearer of secret messages! And I? O Lysias! Well for thee that thou knowest not this change which is in store for me. And thou, O beautiful Aphrodite, be not angry with me that I am to become also a Jewish proselyte and offer sacrifices to the God of the Jews. My mistress hath bidden me to become free and to wed Ananias. It is better so than to be a slave, or to throw myself away upon a Greek youth who must shortly disappear. I love not ruin. I am to be rich and I shall be the favorite of more gods than one."

She spoke with a triumph upon her face and with exultation in her voice. Then she reclined upon a couch, with the light of the lamp shining brilliantly upon her goodly raiment and her beauty, and so she awaited the coming of the wife of the procurator.

Through the Damascus gate passed Lysias, and not long afterward an ass halted near the amphitheater, further down the valley. A slave came out to attend to the ass, and was followed by the master of the games.

"Who art thou?" he demanded, surlily.

"See that thou hinder me not," said Lysias. "Look well upon this signet."

"I obey the procurator," said the master of the games. "Do thou his bidding. But I will see nothing that thou hast in thy hand by any commandment from him. Hold thou thy peace, O messenger. I meddle not."

Lysias had dismounted and, without more words, he passed on into the quarters of the Saxons. Excepting themselves, no others were present to observe or to hear, but he did not find men who were taking rest. Some were making up packages for carrying, some were examining carefully their arms and armor as if about to go into battle, but they greeted the Greek heartily. He looked around him for a moment, not without an understanding of this which they were doing.

"I am in season, O Tostig the Red," he said altogether as if he had been expected to come. "But put ye on Roman helmets, every man. Ye are to ride fast to Joppa this night. Right glad am I to be your guide, for the roads might prove misleading."

"Hael to thee, O Greek!" exclaimed Tostig. "Even now are the horses nearly prepared. We will mount at thy bidding. But hast thou at all seen the jarl?"

"By the will of the gods, and not by his own, he may not now come," said Lysias. "Were he here, he would say that ye go forth at once and that ye ride well. Mark this saying, however, that there will be one at the shore who must by all means enter the galley, but who must not travel far in her."

"It is but a spear thrust," said Knud the Bear. "We will attend to his case."

Silently all, but openly and boldly as by men who obeyed a high command, were the horses led out and mounted. There were also led horses for the packages and for changes, and there was no Roman officer of rank at hand to call this doing in question.

"Ride!" said Tostig. "Odin! It will not be well for any who shall cross our path!"

None was likely to do so. The Romans held Judea by garrisons in forts and camps, and not greatly by moving forces. The highway to Joppa would be deserted after nightfall. Who should rashly interfere with mounted spearmen, whose very helmets were as a sharp warning to the imprudent?

"Swiftly! Swiftly!" exclaimed Lysias, before long. "We now pass the hill of Golgotha. On that mount have many been crucified. Make thee sure that ye get well away with this galley of Herod and that no man may find you upon it in after time. I tell you truly that if ye are now taken prisoners ye would but climb yonder Hill of Skulls."

Silent were the Saxons at that hard saying, but the horses under them appeared to spring forward as if with one accord.

It was at the foot of a steep declivity that the galloping ceased for a brief resting of the horses, and Tostig exclaimed:

"O Knud the Bear, this is well. We have gone far. But I like not this manner of departing from our jarl. I think I should have seen his face and heard his commandment. Were he to need my sword on the morrow, I would be at his side."

"I also," responded Knud. "We are his own men and he is ours. It is in his heart that we may return to the Middle Sea with a hundred keels. What, then, would we care for Roman triremes? We could slay all the legionaries in Judea."

"If we might indeed land here again," said Wulf the Skater, doubtfully. "At all events we have no more upon our hands this night than to take the keel which is prepared for us and to put to sea."

So said they all, and again they pushed forward, but after a while the road by which they traveled was no longer so rugged and so hilly.

"We shall kill the horses," they said, "but we may reach the sea before the dawn."

So did it prove, for more than one horse gave out and his rider mounted another from those which were led without any heavy burden. It was yet dark, at the last, when Tostig exclaimed:

"O Greek, I hear the sound of waves upon a beach. Are we now near Joppa?"

"Too near," replied Lysias, "for into the town itself we may not safely go. We will turn here by this road at the right. If we encounter guards or a patrol, let there be no report made of our passing."

"Halt!" rang out in the road a little ahead of them. "The password! Who are ye?"

It was a legionary at his post, a sentry on guard, and to him rode Knud the Bear.

"I am this," he said. "Take thou my token!"

Down fell the soldier, speared through the face, so that he spoke not again, and on rode the Saxons toward the sea.

"We have now only starlight," said Lysias, "but yonder at anchor floateth the galley of Herod, the tetrarch. This is according to the saying of the procurator. All is well, for he who cometh hath not arrived. There are boats; take them. But here do I leave you, for I have a further errand. Fare thee well."

"Success to thee, O Lysias," said Tostig. "We are thy friends henceforth. Haste thee about thy business. We can care for ourselves now that we see keels and waves."

Many voices bade him good speed, and the strong ass appeared but little wearied as he sprang away northward along the beach.

"Glad am I not to be in Joppa this day," said Lysias. "If I am heard from next at the house of Cornelius at Cæsarea, no man will accuse me of having too much acquaintance with the doings of the gladiators of Caius. I did but bring to them an order whereof I knew not the meaning. I am but a messenger, carrying letters to and fro."

Nevertheless, his heart was full of great anxiety and he remembered how dark had been the hard face of the procurator.

The fishing boats were many, but only two large ones were taken. Into these the Saxons put their baggage of all kinds, but they drove away their horses to a good distance down the beach. Then they took the oars and in a short rowing they were near the galley.

Over the bulwark leaned an armed man as the boats touched the side.

"Whence come ye?" he demanded, but he spoke as to friends, for he was at that hour expecting such an arrival and he saw the Roman helmets.

For a moment no voice replied to him, but the Saxons went quickly over the bulwark.

"Slay now, but cast none overboard!" commanded Tostig. "Here are soldiers sleeping."

These who slept were not many of them Romans, but more were soldiers of Herod, Jews and Arabians and Edomites. They died speedily under the swift thrusting of the Saxon spears, but the watchman had fallen first.

"Spare the rowers in their places," said Wulf the Skater. "We will use them."

But these rowers were all slaves, in chains, and they looked upon the slaughter in silence, as if it were no affair of their own.

"Be ready, all!" suddenly commanded Tostig. "Utter no sound! A boat cometh from the shore, as Lysias gave us to expect. Not from this beach, but from a pier in the harbor. In it are but few men. In the prow is some great one, but he weareth no helmet. Let them come on board with all safety, but none in that boat may return to Joppa."

For a cause known to themselves not one of them had any purpose of at once returning. They came swiftly to the galley and all climbed eagerly on board, casting adrift their boat to float where it would.

"Away!" shouted he who seemed their leader, as if speaking to sailors who were under his own direction. "Row out of the harbor quickly. Speed, or a scourge for every back!"

Saxon hands were already raising the anchor and the rowers put out their oars as they were bidden.

"O all ye gods!" suddenly cried out the great man, stumbling over a fallen soldier. "What is this? O my destruction! The hand of Pontius the Spearman is here! I perish!"

Then fell his head upon the deck at the stroke of Knud the Bear, and shortly all his companions went down in like manner, for they were astonished and they did no fighting.

Being in fear of death, the rowers rowed with great vigor and Tostig was at the helm.

"She is swift!" he exclaimed. "She is a good keel and she rideth well the waves. We are upon the sea! Hael to the Northland!"

Loudly shouted all the vikings, clashing their shields, for it was a joy to feel the lifting of the long billows and once more to wipe the salt spray from their faces. They rapidly examined the ship from stem to stern, but there was much which required more thorough searching.

"O that the jarl were here with us!" groaned Tostig. "The day is here. We, his friends, have escaped from the Romans and from the circus, but our jarl is on the land. It is evil! How shall I answer concerning him when I am inquired of at his own house? Will not some men say that I am nidering?"

Long leagues were rowed and then, for the wind was now right, the sail was lifted.

"We will cast overboard these who were slain," said Knud. "We will weight them, that they may sink. So shall none tell a tale of us to any who may follow. We do as the jarl would have bidden."

"Thou art prudent," said Tostig. "So much for the secret messengers of Herod. We have shed blood upon this ship and the gods of the North are with us. Only let us with care avoid all triremes, for we do not need to be inquired of by a stronger force."

"This is now the spring," said Lars, the son of Beolf. "If we pause not needlessly, we shall soon reach the fiords, but there will be no ice in them."

"It is a good cruise," said another. "We may take much plunder by the way. Let us now search again the cabins of this galley."

Much that astonished them had been found with those who came on board in the boat that they might be slain. More was now discovered in secret places.

"Odin!" exclaimed Knud, examining these matters. "Here are many coins of silver and of gold and a number of bright stones. I think these may have been gifts from Herod, the king, to Cæsar at Rome, but he will not soon see them."

"There are also fine weapons and garments," said Wulf. "It is a very rich galley."

The sun was unclouded, the wind blew fairly from the east, the galley sped forward gallantly, and the rowers rested upon their seats, but now Tostig the Red stood upon the after deck with all the Saxons around him.

"I have heard ye all," he said, for they had been speaking many things. "We are of one mind. But if it be your will that I shall now take upon me the command of this keel, put ye your hands in mine and give me your oath to this saying, that we will be satisfied with this great plunder which we have already taken; that we will keep the open sea, not landing save for food or water; that we will care to take no other keel but this; and that we will sail on until we see the house of Brander the Brave upon the shore of the Northland. After that we will come back to the Middle Sea with many swords and we will seek for Ulric, our jarl, until we find him."

"So will we do!" shouted Knud the Bear.

One by one did the Saxons then step forward and put their hands between the hands of Tostig, and the oath was an oath.

Nevertheless, they were as men who had sailed away forever, unless the gods should see fit to accomplish this their purpose of coming again with a fleet, and with a host to follow Ulric the Jarl and his captain into the great battle in Esdraelon.

Well was it for them that they had thus escaped the sure perils of the circus if they might also escape the many perils of the sea. They might indeed avoid the triremes of Rome, and little cared hardy vikings for rough weather, but the voyage would be long and they were not many spearmen. The slave rowers, however, were sturdy fellows, well selected, and these were likely to be better contented with masters who flogged them not unduly and who thought it a shame that even a beast, being their own, should not be well fed and cared for.

As for Tostig the Red, he had become stern and moody, smiling not at all, and he told the rest of the vikings that Ulric, the son of Brander, was still his jarl, and that as Ulric, to his thinking, would have directed in any case, so would he order.

"That will be well for us," they said.

"I have been troubled in my mind," he told them. "I think that I may yet slay many Romans at the side of the son of Odin. I myself saw that Jewish god of his that healed him of his hurts. I heard his words and they were good to hear, although I understood him not very well. If he is to be the captain of the host, over the jarl, I am contented. But never yet did I see a better sword than is our jarl."

"Nor did we," they answered him. "We will surely return with thee to the Middle Sea, and our treasure shall go with thine to the making of many great keels and the gathering of the swordsmen of the North."

All things seemed going well with them, but there was, nevertheless, a shadow upon the ship, and when the sun was setting Tostig the Red sat upon the after deck sharpening his seax upon a stone and now and then gazing backward toward the east.

"Would I were with him this hour," he said in a low, sad voice. "How shall the years go by with me henceforth if I am never again to see the face of my jarl?"

Chapter XXXVII
The House of Ben Ezra

In the house of Ben Ezra, at the head of the flight of stone steps in the secret passage, Ulric the Jarl stood looking down into a great darkness. But now Ben Ezra came to him, having lighted a large brazen lamp which swung like a cresset at the end of a wooden rod a fathom long. The flame of the lamp was very brilliant, but the smoke thereof was unpleasant to the smell because of some strange oil which burned in it. Such a lamp might not be lighted at a feast or in the dwellings of men.

"Follow me, O jarl," he said. "This is the underworld and thou and I are alone in this place. But not all the swords of Cæsar could find thee if thou wert hidden here. It hath been a refuge for some who fled from a destroyer."

"O Jew," said Ulric, "I will cover this thy secret. May I fail of Valhalla, dying as a cow dieth, if I betray thee!"

"Come!" said Ben Ezra, and they went on down the stairway together.

At the foot of it was a low chamber, the air of which was heavy, but Ben Ezra turned to the left, and as he lifted his lamp there might be seen a narrow cleft in the masonry. A little inside of this cleft there was a barrier of iron-bound woodwork.

"Lift it away by its hand pieces," said Ben Ezra. "Thou art stronger than I."

Very massive was the wooden barrier, but it might be dragged forth and laid upon the floor, and at once a current of cold, damp air poured through the opening, bringing with it a smell as of earth.

"I will go in first," said Ben Ezra. "Now will I show thee my crypt."

In a moment more they were stooping over an open coffer, and he said:

"Here are my treasures and thine, and somewhat which belongeth to thy men. I would they might have it, for we need not any goods but our own. Thou shalt take away at thy will whatever is thine own."

"I may not remove it now," said Ulric, "save a bag of golden coins. But I would ask of thee, if thou wilt tell me, what is this place that we are in and how is there such a cavern, with masonwork and corridors and pillars and cunning doors? Are we to go on into it?"

"Thou wilt go no further lest thou lose thyself as in a wilderness," said the Jew, pointing down the passageway.

"It is like a cave," said Ulric. "I never heard of caves under a city."

"Behold," said Ben Ezra, "the secret of Jerusalem. It is from the earliest time. There was a fort here in the days of Adam and here the giants had their dwelling. There are no writings of those ancient days. But on these hills and in these valleys city after city hath been builded and destroyed. For those walls and buildings much masonry was needed. There were vast halls and hollows made in quarrying stone during ages. Afterward these openings were sealed and made of the secrets of priests and kings. They will not be opened until Messiah cometh."

"He is to be thy great king," said Ulric. "What need hath he of caves?"

"Not any," said Ben Ezra, "but he will know in what hidden depth he shall find the treasures of Adam and of the giants and of the old kings and of Solomon, for all are yonder, where none but he may lay a hand upon them. Let us go."

"I have seen a wonder," said Ulric following his guide. "But if this god from Nazareth is to be thy king, wilt thou not thyself inform him of the way through thy house into his hidden places?"

"He will have no need," said Ben Ezra; "but if I saw that he had the right to know, I would tell him. Messiah knoweth all things. As for this rabbi of Galilee, he cometh to Jerusalem even now, for the Passover feast draweth near. I would gladly hear him again. During years that are gone there have been many sayings concerning him."

"I know that he hath healed my hurts," said Ulric. "He hath also done in like manner by many another. I think that I shall yet be a captain of men under him, and the great battle cometh."

They were now in the upper room and the stone door had been closed behind them, swinging upon its pivots.

"Am I to abide here this night?" asked Ulric. "I have an errand of mine own in the morning. After that is done I must go to my men. They will surely need counsel and ordering."

"I will now show thee thy chamber wherein thou art to sleep," said Ben Ezra. "But, I pray thee, do not too many errands within the city walls, and neglect not to visit Caius of Thessalonica lest thou lose thy strong friend. It is needful for thee to be seen much at his house."

"I will truly care for him," said Ulric. "It is my duty. But I have a great concern as to my companions. O that they were even now upon the sea and utterly escaped from the circus!"

"Else they will surely all be slain," said Ben Ezra; but he led the way to a place for sleeping and the night closed over all.

When the next morning came the watchmen upon the walls of Joppa took note that the swift galley of Herod, the tetrarch, had already departed. So sent they in their due report, but already had it been discovered that whoever might now be in her had left behind them strange tokens. In the highway north of the tower came a company of legionaries to change the sentries, and at the turning of the road they found but a dead man, slain by a spear thrust through his head. Who could have done this deed in a day of peace they guessed not at all, but their officer spoke of the Jackal of Machærus. Not long afterward a horseman in bright armor rode along the beach seeing empty boats that were cast up by the waves, and also the empty place where the evening before the galley had been anchored.

"I am too late!" he shouted, angrily. "The traitor hath escaped to Rome! What answer shall I give to Herod Antipas? His brother hath again outwitted him and I think he is in league with the procurator."

Further up the beach men led along many horses, saddled and bridled, which they had found astray and ownerless, and this thing also was a riddle.

The governor of Joppa was quickly informed of all, that he might make his report to his commander; but at that hour Pontius the Spearman was sitting in the seat of judgment thinking not of Joppa, and before him came not only his own officers, but Jews, also, and people from the towns and the provinces. Suddenly, however, he turned from aught else to look into the face of one who came in haste, seeming to be greatly disturbed in mind. It was the master of the games who now stood opposite the chair of judgment, and at a sign of the procurator's hand he spoke rapidly until he had told his errand, speaking low that none else might hear.

"O thou," said Pontius, calmly, "go back to thy affairs. I care not greatly what Caius hath done with his gladiators. If indeed they have rebelled and if they are in Judea or Samaria, I will retake them for him in season for the games. The fault is not thine."

"O most noble Pontius," said the master of the games, "what sayest thou of the Greek? He came unto them, as I testified."

"What is that to thee?" responded the procurator haughtily. "Care thou for thy beasts and thy cages. See that thou speak not at all to him of this matter when thou seest him. Go thy way!"

The master of the games trembled somewhat as he went forth and Pontius followed him not with his eyes, but muttered to himself:

"The Greek hath made good his token of a man from the circus. I will now wait for a word from Joppa, but I will not question him imprudently when he returneth from Cæsarea."

Heavy matters were now coming before him, and among them all was none which seemed to trouble him more than did certain testimonies concerning the evil deeds of robbers from the wilderness of Judea.

"O ye Jews!" exclaimed the angry magistrate. "How shall I execute justice when so many of you are in league with these evil-doers? In this city is the refuge of these wicked men. Who will capture for me this Bar Abbas that I may crucify him? He hath kindred among you and ye shelter him!"

Loud were the indignant protests which replied to him from scribes and rabbis and rulers, but far back, near the entrance of the hall of judgment, were twain who listened eagerly.

"Father Abraham!" hoarsely whispered one of these. "I may not upon any account bring my matter before him. Even now is my son at my house and he brought much profit with him. He is worth more to me than are all the robbers of Gilboa or the tribes beyond Jordan. He must not fall into the hands of these Roman heathen lest I also be destroyed. The God of Israel be my protector against the enemy!"

Searching eyes were upon him, but the thought in the mind of Ulric, the son of Brander, was: "Well for me that I fell in with him as I left the house of Ben Ezra. Well that I followed him even here. Now will I not cease until I know his abiding place."

Cowering and hiding his face, did Abbas hasten away, hardly daring to look behind him. Many were coming and going, however, and the guilty dealer in stolen goods might not take warning of the manner in which he was followed vengefully from street to street.

"I may not smite him now," said the pursuer, "but he and another will shortly be touched by a sharp edge. There entereth he a door and I will leave him for this time. Now must I see Caius and then I go to my companions. Would that they were on their way to the Northland. Woe to me if I bring harm to them!"

Nevertheless, even before going to the house of Caius, the jarl did one thing which relieved both his heart and his hands from a heavy weight. He went to the door of a house and he was admitted, but he tarried not there, and he came out again, going on in haste, but with less gloom upon his face.

"She will think well of me!" he exclaimed. "I might not have speech with her, but she will look upon my token and she will bless me."

In the house from which he had departed, and in an inner chamber of it, stood the Hebrew maiden, and before her was Isaac, the aged, her near kinsman. He placed upon a table a heavy bag and he essayed to speak, but his lips trembled and his voice failed him.

"O Isaac, what is this?" she exclaimed. "Where didst thou obtain money, seeing the manner in which we are hindered? Hast thou indeed betrayed me again by thy weakness?"

"Nay! Nay! It is thine!" shouted Isaac. "Thy heathen prince came to the door. I saw him, but he lingered not and none other had speech with him. 'This is for her,' he said. 'Tell her I watch and I return, but that she may not go forth, not even to the temple.' So I brought the bag to thee, wondering. Count it, for I have not counted."

He himself untied the bag and poured out the coins upon the table, counting, while Miriam watched as one who seeth dimly in a dream of the night.

"Ulric, Ulric," she muttered, "thou art more to me than are these. I think of thee that thou art pure gold, but who may weigh thee in the balances? Come to me, for great is my need of thy counsel!"

"Of Rome and of Greece and of Judea are these coins," said Isaac. "They are thrice our present requirement. Jehovah hath turned to thee the heart of this idolater and thou doest well to make him serve thee. Thou hast the understanding which is given to women. We will pay our oppressors. We will give a goodly gift to the judge and to the chief priests. We will offer a sacrifice of burnt offering of a sweet savor. And God, even our God, will yet deliver thee also from the hand of this heathen gladiator."

"Isaac," she exclaimed, "peace! Speak not of him unduly! Would that a false judgment concerning money were our only peril."

"O Miriam," said the old man, putting the coins in again and tying the bag, "that also hath been provided for. In this house we may not safely remain, but a sure refuge hath been offered and we shall be for a season as if we were hidden in a well. One cometh shortly to be our guide, and it is needful that thy heathen prince, also, should have information, for he hath more gold than this and his hand is now open."

"Peace!" she again exclaimed, but Isaac went out with the bag, saying:

"Great are the gifts of Jehovah of Hosts! Would that he might now send the sword of this Philistine who loveth her upon the necks of our enemies!"

"I will wait," she was whispering, "until I see him."

Long was the remaining of Ulric the Jarl at the house of Caius of Thessalonica, but afterward he went out at the Damascus gate purposing to visit the amphitheater. He went on down into the valley of Jehoshaphat, walking slowly, and he came to the bridge over the brook Kidron, by which he was to pass.

"O jarl," said a youth who waited at the bridge, "a token from Ben Ezra!"

"None heareth," replied Ulric. "Say on."

"Thy men are not at the circus, he bade me tell thee, and no man knoweth whither they are gone. Go thou not thither now, but let the house of Caius be thy refuge, for there will be an inquiry for thee."

Still as a stone stood the jarl while one might breathe three times.

"I thank thee and him, O youth," he said then. "Go thou to him with his word only, that neither he nor I need any to tell us whereunto the sons of the Northland have departed. I will do as he hath said."

The youth went from him running, but Ulric did not reenter the city by the Damascus gate.

"It will be safer to choose another," he said. "I was seen by the guards when I came forth. They may by this time have some evil commandment concerning me."

So therefore he made a great circuit of the walls, going far, and even after he selected a gate by which he might prudently go in he seemed to have another matter upon his hands. The hours went by, one after another, and it was long after the sunset before he was known to be in the house of Caius. Then speedily he was sent for and he went in to what was now the sick chamber of the centurion.

"O jarl," said he, "how is it with thee?"

"O most noble Caius," replied the jarl, "I am well, but I am alone in Jerusalem. All of my companions have returned to their own land."

"Well for thee," said Caius. "Of that I had been informed. A swift messenger from the governor of Joppa brought strange news to the procurator. What sayest thou if thy men have been hired to serve upon a ship by Herod, the tetrarch? Would they not guard well?"

"O Caius," said the jarl, "thou knowest them and I need say no more, for I am ignorant of all this matter save that they are gone."

"I find no fault with thee," said Caius. "The messenger was sent to me and I have fully questioned him. Also word came from the procurator that I trouble thee not, for Herod must be allowed to direct his own affairs. If he have hired good swordsmen, surely his galley is in safe keeping."

Ulric looked at him darkly, for the voice of Caius was as of one who mocketh bitterly.

"O Caius," said the jarl, "if thou wilt hear me, I have another affair upon my mind. I like not the appearance of thy sore."

"Jarl of the Saxons," exclaimed the centurion, "I seem to myself to be rotting away. I am as one who hath the leprosy. But what knowest thou of any healing?"

"Only this that I have heard this day," said Ulric. "I would have thee live until the arrival of this Jesus of Nazareth. He cometh now to the feast of the Jews. He is of the sons of the gods. Did he not heal me? And may he not also do something for thee?"

"O that he might come quickly!" said Caius. "But the gods can do little for such a torment as mine. There are many things which are too much for them. But I will see him when he cometh. I would make him rich with gifts if he would heal me."

"I will watch for him," said the jarl. "I may not go again to the circus——"

"Go not!" exclaimed Caius. "Remain much with me. O Saxon, when this fire burneth within me I would gladly fall upon my sword but that it would please my enemies. But if thou goest out now, return quickly. Of this be thou sure in thy mind, that I will not permit thee to enter the circus. Thy sword will have better business. I will speak of thee again to the procurator. A messenger from him hath arrived. Leave me with him."

More words might not be spoken and the jarl went out, but it could be understood that with difficulty did the centurion restrain himself and conceal from all the extremity of his suffering from that deadly thing.

"I will go to the house of Ben Ezra," thought Ulric. "Already have I made sure that there are fewer enemies to bring peril upon Miriam and her people. I will see if the Jew hath well attended to his portion of her business. But unless help cometh to him speedily, Caius will surely die."

Chapter XXXVIII
The Son of Abbas

Long and thoughtfully and with many questionings did Ben Ezra listen to the jarl in an inner chamber of his house. "Thou hast done well," he said, at last, "but trust thou not too much the favor of the great. Neither be thou too sure concerning their power. The leaves fall from all the trees in due season. Full of jealousy and of suspicion and of murder are all they who prosper under Cæsar. In the day and in the night is there a weapon not far from any of them. So deal they with others. A Roman friend is ever also a Roman enemy holding a knife, and by the hands of their friends do men die continually at Rome."

"That do I believe," said Ulric. "I will be exceedingly prudent. But, O my friend, what hast thou done concerning Miriam?"

"I have done all thus far," said Ben Ezra. "I did but need to buy the good-will of the judge and one peril passed away. To him and to another I could both pay more and promise more than was in the will of Abbas. But thou, O jarl, hast thou seen the face of this Roman dealer in slaves?"

"That peril also hath departed," said Ulric. "I am told that a man in haste met him in the valley of Hinnom. The patrol found him there in their passing, and his head lay at six cubits' length from his body."

"He had many enemies," said Ben Ezra, thoughtfully. "One may even have followed him from the city. I have now another word for thee concerning Abbas, now that thou hast heard the procurator upon the judgment seat give authority to all such as thou art concerning the taking of his son. The robbers are a power in Jerusalem and the sword of Bar Abbas is against thee."

"I have never seen him," said Ulric.

"Then will I tell thee of his face," said Ben Ezra, and he minutely did so, line by line.

"Fear not," said Ulric. "I would now know that man if but half his face were shown."

"He is said to be cunning in disguises," replied Ben Ezra, "but his best keeper is the fear of men that by denouncing him they may bring upon themselves secret daggers and a vengeance which faileth not."

"No fear have I," muttered Ulric, "but how am I to find him!"

"I trust that thou wilt be prospered in that matter," said Ben Ezra, "but I have this much more for thee. It behooved me to bring both Miriam and Isaac to this house, that I might cover them until this peril pass. Roman eyes that thou knowest not may have looked upon her. We must wait. The slaying of one slave dealer may but make needful the hiring of another by some great one. The house in which Isaac dwelt was but hired, and another taketh it, that he and his may be thrust out. The net is a wide one."

"Evil! Evil! Evil!" exclaimed Ulric. "This city is full of injustice! No such thing could be among the North peoples. I saw no thief ever, nor a purchased jarl or judge, until I came southward."

"So doth the whole land groan," said Ben Ezra. "So doth the blood of the innocent cry out unto Jehovah."

"Why, then, answereth he not?" shouted Ulric, vehemently. "Surely the god of a people should come to their help in such a distress, else they will surely say of him that he is no god at all."

"So have said many," groaned Ben Ezra, "and I grow weary in heart waiting for a Messiah who doth not come. O that our King were already here. Peace, now, O jarl, concerning him. But I will tell thee of Miriam that thou mayest not have speech with her this night. Be thou not also her enemy, to do her harm."

"Where is indeed thy god," said Ulric, "if any hurt may come to such as she is?"

"O jarl," said Ben Ezra, "all Jerusalem hath heretofore been heaped with the slain, and the maidens of Zion were led away captive, because of the anger of Jehovah. Dost thou not understand? We do suffer for our sins and for the sins of our fathers."

"I think the gods do not well in such matters," said Ulric. "They are not just. Surely justice becometh well a brave god. He should not strike down the innocent ones with those who are guilty of evil."

"I know not the counsel of the Most High," said Ben Ezra. "His judgments are a great deep, but they are just and righteous altogether."

"No man," said the jarl, "findeth fault with a stroke of a sword fairly given, since he who dieth in battle goeth to Valhalla and hath attained his inheritance from his brave ancestors. I myself wait for the valkyrias, and I am often weary thinking of the gods and of Asgard. Who would avoid a sword if it were in the hand of a brave warrior in battle? Not I, Ulric, the son of Brander."

"Thou art a mighty man of valor," said Ben Ezra. "I have thought of thee that thou art almost as a son of Abraham. Go thou to thy sleeping, for this house must be even more thy abiding place than is the house of Caius now thy companions are departed."

Sleep came as to one who is weary both in mind and body, but early upon the morrow the two friends were together again taking counsel.

"O Jew," said the jarl, "I am ill at ease concerning my men. Would that I might see them this day and make sure of their welfare."

"So often doth one think of those who are departed from him," said Ben Ezra; "but have thou a care that thou inquire not imprudently. All that I may learn I will tell thee when thou comest again. It is well for thee to go now."

Out walked the jarl, going along a corridor which led toward the door into the street.

"Very wonderful is all this," he thought. "A strange place is this city of Jerusalem, with its many rulers and its secrets of the gods and of the old time, and with these things which are done here. Of what good is it that it hath so great a temple and so many priests?"

At that moment there came to his ears a beautiful, low music murmuring through the cool air of the corridor.

"Ulric, art thou here?"

"Miriam!" he exclaimed, turning to listen.

"O, I thank thee that thou hast come," she said. "I have had such fear upon me! Much rather would I die. One moment I must see thee and speak to thee! Tarry a moment!"

"More I may not do, O Miriam," he said, with a great light rising in his eyes. "But I have given my promise to Ben Ezra and to thy God concerning thee that no harm shall come upon thee. I will but look upon thy face."

"Thou art wonderful!" she said, and then they saw not aught of all the world except each other for that breathing space.

"O thou," she whispered, "I know not if thou art of the heathen or if I am of Abraham's seed. O what but death should part me and thee!"

"I think not even death," he said, "seeing that we go to one place after the sword cometh. But if indeed thy Jehovah be a god and if he have given me to thee, I will offer to him many sacrifices. I must go forth now, for I have many things to do for thee and for a friend. If this Jesus of Nazareth arriveth, I must have speech with him. I have told thee how he healed me."

"So must I see him," she said. "I listened to him many times in Galilee. He is a very learned rabbi and I would hear him again."

"He is more than a rabbi," said Ulric. "He is a god—and he knoweth the other gods. I would ask him concerning Asgard and Valhalla and concerning thee. Thy slave dealer is dead, O Miriam, and soon will I deal justly with this Abbas and those who are with him."

"Thou art my warrior!" she exclaimed. "Thou art as one of the heroes of Israel. I trust thee!"

"Farewell!" he said stepping quickly away from her, but no word escaped her lips. She did but seem to hold back her hand from its purpose of detaining him, and her breath came and went rapidly as he passed out at the door. Then her voice came again and she said, looking upward:

"O thou Jehovah of Hosts, my God, hast thou not made him also? How am I better than he that I should be withheld from him? Do I not love him?"

The feet of Ulric went but slowly from the house of Ben Ezra, and he paid little heed to their guiding, but they brought him to the house of Caius of Thessalonica and the warder of the portal stood before him.

"I have a word for thee, O swordsman," he said. "Thou art well arrived."

"Say on," said Ulric.

"Even now, O Saxon, the procurator himself is with our master Caius and with them is the governor of Joppa. Thou mayest not go in. But pass thou to the Damascus gate, for Caius would know of the arrival of this Galilean healer. It is reported that he is near at hand. Also the procurator would have speech with thee when Caius will send thee to him. These are thy commands and thou wilt do them."

"Say thou, O warder," replied Ulric, "that I go as I am bidden. Well for thee and for us all if the centurion were cured of this evil. Thou wilt fall into no better hands than his if he dieth. I am his friend, and he suffereth."

"Go! Go!" said the warder, earnestly. "All the gods forbid that he should die. If this same Jew rabbi will not heal Caius, it is thy duty to slay him with thy sword."

"Speak thou only good concerning him," said Ulric, sternly. "What hast thou to do with a sword? I go."

The warder stepped backward a pace, for not many men willed to stand before the jarl when his hand seemed to be seeking for the hilt of his seax.

"A sudden man!" he muttered, as he watched his going. "And they say he hath cleft both a lion and a tiger in one combat and that he would wear no armor. A man's head might go from his shoulders as if it were but a flower from a stem. His eye is a fire!"

"I would I better knew the streets," said the jarl, as he strode swiftly onward. "I learn them but slowly, for they are very many and they are crooked and the city is great. Whither, now, shall this one lead me?"

As in an unknown path, therefore, he went on, thinking of many things. The way led him over a hill and through a valley and to a gate in the outer wall that he knew well. Here were Roman guards standing at rest, hindering none, and Ulric halted near them. "Many go out," he thought, "but a multitude cometh yonder along the road across the Mount of Olives. I will wait and see."

Nearer and nearer along the broad highway poured a vast throng of people, while through the gate passed on a tide which went to mingle with them. Many of those who were coming bore in their hands branches of palm trees and they were shouting joyously.

"What is this which they sing?" said Ulric. "What is the meaning of 'Hosanna in the highest,' and who is David, and what is his son? It is a saga of the Jews. The whole city is stirred up behind me. This is a wonder!"

Across the valley and then up toward the gate came on the multitude. Among them were some who took off their outer robes and cast them upon the road before an ass and before his rider, shouting and singing.

"I have heard them say 'a king,'" said Ulric. "But here is no king. None of these men are armed. What saith the procurator to this business?"

"O gladiator of Caius of Thessalonica," suddenly responded a legionary of the guard of the gate, "thou art but a sword. What careth Pontius the Spearman for a mob of women and children? We know thee that thou art accounted trustworthy, and thou doest well to inquire concerning any tumult of the Jews, but this is no affair of either thine or ours."

"I meddle not," said the jarl. "I am under orders from the centurion and from the procurator, but I may watch this matter."

"Watch," said the officer. "Thou art in thy duty. We hinder thee not. But who art thou?"

The man whom he now addressed was plainly a Jew, in sordid raiment, tall and strong, but who was eyeing the jarl with an evil eye, and his manner was insolent.

"I am a servant of the high priest and I am here by his command," said the Jew. "There is an order for the arrest of this gladiator."

"Let no accursed Jew take upon him that business," laughed the officer. "Thy high priest hath enough to settle with the procurator. But whither goest thou from hence?"

"I go to the gate of the valley of Hinnom," replied the Jew, "and thou mayest not detain me."

"O officer," said Ulric, who had been searching the Jew with keen inspection, "I have an errand to that gate and know not the way overwell. I pray thee that thou command him to guide me after I have seen this present matter."

"I object not to that," said the Jew, with a fierce glitter in his eyes, "so that he touch me not to render me unclean against the Passover feast."

"Curse thy uncleanness!" said the Roman, haughtily. "Thou needest not to touch him; but I would he might have a commandment to touch thee. O gladiator, I am told that thou art a sure blade, the slayer of the great Numidian lion. I hope to see thee slay another yet in the circus, but take not the head from this worthless one until thou art duly bidden to smite him."

"As thou doest so do I," said Ulric. "Shall a soldier question his captain?"

"Not if that commander be one Pontius the Spearman," replied the officer, "or even Caius of Thessalonica. Thou art right, O gladiator. None will interfere with thee and thy sharp edge."

"Stand by, thou," said Ulric to the Jew. "I will be with thee presently."

But now the man became seemingly cringing and friendly in his deportment, bowing low and standing in silence awaiting direction.

Nearer and nearer came the multitude along the highway and toward the gate. Ulric heard many of them shouting:

"This is Jesus of Nazareth, the Prophet of Galilee! He is the son of David! He is the King of Israel. He is the one who was to come! This is the Messiah, the deliverer!"

Others there were who loudly gainsaid these acclamations, protesting indignantly; but Ulric's thoughts were full of astonishment.

"I see that the man upon the ass is Jesus. I know that he is of the sons of the gods. This is a wonderful affair. But why cometh he now without an army into a fortified city which hath a Roman garrison? Odin! There is no prudence in this coming! They will slay him before he hath opportunity to gather men for one good legion."

So pondering in his mind, he watched until the ass and his rider passed by him through the gate and into the city.

"I have again seen his face," he said. "I may not have speech with him at this time. But I will take upon me this other errand and see unto what it will lead me. O thou, my guide, we will depart."

"Come, O gladiator," said the Jew. "It is well for thee to have me with thee among so many crooked streets. Touch me not. But what are thy commandments?"

"Hold thou thy peace concerning them," replied the jarl. "Lead on!"

Hot wrath burned for a moment in the face of the tall Jew, but he obeyed, girding himself and striding forward, but the officer of the gate laughed derisively.

"The dog Jew," he said, "will do well not to stir the temper of a Saxon. His head were loosened from his shoulders too quickly. I will not fail to see that fellow in the circus. It mattereth not to me what work there may be for his blade in Hinnom."

"Dost thou not bear in mind," said one of the legionaries, "a certain slave dealer and the loosening of his head? This same gladiator was seen that day at the Hinnom gate, but the guards were bidden to forget him."

"Thou thyself rememberest too much," said the officer, sternly. "Forget that thou hast seen him here this day. But it is good sport to slay Jews. I would there might soon be another tumult. I have made the floor of the temple red with the blood of Galileans. The procurator may have a sharp teaching for more of them during this Passover gathering."

So talked the soldiers of Rome, but the jarl was silent and moody as he walked until he and his guide were drawing near to the southerly wall of the city. Then he spoke quietly, as a man may speak to his friend, one whom he hath known well aforetime.

"O thou," he said, "when hast thou seen thy father, Abbas, and what did he give unto thee concerning me?"

The guide turned suddenly, scowling and trembling, but he responded:

"How knowest thou me? The guards knew me not, nor did any other, for I am changed for that reason. What hast thou to do with Abbas, and what is thy purpose?"

"Thou art but a fool," said Ulric. "I read thy name in thy face. Thou art Bar Abbas. I have known thy father many days. Did he not tell thee how I rescued him in the tower in Esdraelon that he died not? But I have thought him a prudent man. How is it that he hath permitted this folly?"

"O gladiator," said Bar Abbas with a deep, dark smile, "it is no folly. They who would slay me seek me in the wilderness, not in Jerusalem. A man who waiteth within the gate among the legionaries is hidden from the hunters among the hills. I have seen my father and now I go to meet him and his friend the master of the games in the valley of Hinnom, as I believe thou, also, art informed beforehand."

"Then thou hast delivered to him thy spoils?" said Ulric. "But canst thou give me a reason why I should go to meet him in Hinnom?"

"That I know not," said Bar Abbas. "But the master of the games is thy master also. He will give thee thy direction."

"Nevertheless, thou and he are unwise," said the jarl. "I would thou wert armed."

"Save my dagger, I am not," replied the robber, "and thou hast no weapon."

"A warrior is always armed," said Ulric. "But now we are at the gate and here is the officer. Be thou silent."

"Whither goest thou, O gladiator?" demanded the sentinel. "This is forbidden thee. Thou art too far from the circus."

"Dost thou indeed not know me?" responded the jarl. "Or knowest thou not this signet of Caius of Thessalonica?"

"I do know thee, who thou art," said the officer, "and I know the signet."

"By commandment of Pontius the Spearman, the procurator," said Ulric.

"I hear," said the Roman.

"Bind thou this Bar Abbas, the robber, and take him to the prison and report to the procurator that I have done as he did give me instruction. This thing is upon thy life!"

Forward sprang Bar Abbas dagger in hand, but the strong blow of a soldier smote him to the earth and he was bound with cords.

"O man," shouted the captain of the gate, coming hastily, "do as he biddeth thee. We also have full commands concerning Bar Abbas. Well do I know that this is of the procurator."

Then turned he to the jarl.

"Thou hast more to do, O gladiator?"

"I may not answer thee," said Ulric, respectfully. "But now do I go out into the valley to meet one who cometh, and my duty is in my hand. I will return unto thee shortly."

"Thou hast no weapon," said the Roman; but upon his face was a look of understanding, for he was a man of experience and he had been scanning carefully the raiment of Ulric. "What if an evil person were to meet thee?"

"O captain," said Ulric, "he who obeyeth a command doeth well. But if I return not with due speed know thou that I am slain, and inquire into that business."

"That will I do," said the officer; "but they who slay thee may indeed need an inquiry. I think it will not be entirely well with them."

The jarl answered not a word, but he had now upon his mind the things that had been told to him by Bar Abbas on their way, and he went down into the valley, walking rapidly.

"Before me is a trap," he said, "although it was not set for me, but for some other. I will now fall into it, and glad am I that I am so well prepared. This heavy, sharp-edged gladius is better than my light seax."

Even then the captain of the gate was replying to a question from the quaternion.

"The gladiator unarmed?" he exclaimed. "Do I not know how a sheath will cause a wrinkle of a robe to enlarge and stiffen? They who sent him are responsible, not thou or I."

The jarl went on a mile, it might be, and around him was the smoke of the everlasting burning of Hinnom and the smell from the untellable pollution. Here and there, also, he saw heaps of half-consumed offal in which many worms were crawling. This place was to all Jews the picture and symbol of the punishment of the wicked after death. Not many wayfarers were at any time to be encountered here, for all men knew that it was a favorite haunt of evil spirits, of demons, and of robbers.

Nevertheless, as the jarl looked forward through the unpleasant clouding of smoke he exclaimed, aloud:

"They come! Yonder is Abbas himself, and with him are four men. They ride horses. I will wait until they dismount, but woe to me if so much as one of them shall escape."

He stood still, making sure of the hilt of his weapon, but the horsemen came near and at once sprang to the ground, coming forward.

"Knowest thou me?" said the foremost man. "Thy fellows have escaped me, but thou shalt not. I will feed thee to the wild beasts!"

"O master of the games," replied the jarl, "I am of the household of Caius."

"And I am from Pontius the Spearman!" shouted the master of the games. "O ye of Ethiopia, bind him fast!"

The three with him were black slaves, armed with shields and short swords and jereeds, but they were naked to their waists.

"Yield thee, O Saxon," cried out Abbas, mockingly. "I have thy Miriam securely and she will soon belong to my friend."

Now the master of the games was in full armor, but he had turned a moment for the ordering of his slaves. He stooped a little, also, to loosen a coil of cordage that was in his hand for the binding of the jarl, supposing him to be unarmed and helpless against five armed men.

Then swiftly flashed the bright gladius in the hand of Ulric and the head of the master of the games fell to the earth.

"Thou hast sold Miriam?" heard Abbas, a hoarse whisper, but he heard no more, for the sword had flashed again.

The light shaft of a jereed snapped as its blade struck upon the hidden mail of the jarl and the black striker fell across the body of Abbas. His next companion was as a defenseless man before the angry might of Ulric, and hardly was he down before the slave to whom had been given the holding of the horses lay among their hoofs.

"Sure am I that Abbas is dead," said Ulric, stooping over him. "Not one of the others liveth. The horses must now go back at speed. I would not have them seen from the gate."

He pricked them sharply so that they ran in fear. Then he wiped the gladius clean, concealed it well, and walked back to the Hinnom gate of Jerusalem.

"Hast thou accomplished thy command?" asked the officer. "The time hath been but brief."

"Else were I not here," said Ulric. "There were those who came by appointment and one of them was the father of Bar Abbas. The others were but robbers like him."

"O gladiator," said the officer, "so will I report well of thee. I think thou art a sure messenger for an errand of blood."

Questions might not be pressed in such a case, but soldiers were at once sent down the valley to make due inquest.

Onward went Ulric through the streets of the city.

"O Miriam!" he groaned. "Would that I might live for thee! But for this day's deed I think that I may soon die. I will now go to the house of Ben Ezra and I will tell him what hath thus been accomplished for him and for her."

Even as he went his haste was hindered in a narrow street by a great procession which seemed to be one of rejoicing. Maidens came first, with clashing of cymbals and with singing. Behind them were other musicians not a few and many men and women. Then walked lightly on a veiled one in bright robes that were adorned with jewels. Attending her and following joyfully was the remainder of the procession.

"Wilt thou inform me what this may be?" asked Ulric of one who stepped apart from the others for a moment.

"O gladiator," replied the Jew, "this is the wedding of my kinsman, Ananias, the son of the money changer of the temple. He marrieth the Greek proselyte, Sapphira the beautiful, the freed woman and favorite of the wife of the procurator. She hath become a daughter of Abraham. She now goeth to the house of the bridegroom to meet her husband. There also is to be the wedding feast."

"I thank thee," said Ulric, but he walked on muttering doubtfully: "Sapphira? Of the household of Pontius the Spearman? I remember well. That was the name of the beloved of Lysias."

Chapter XXXIX
The Passover Feast

"O jarl," exclaimed Ben Ezra as they stood together in the house, "would that thou also wert a son of Abraham! But thou hast done a deed for which thou wilt be held to answer. O mighty man of valor, I fear that thy life is forfeited to the law."

"Thinkest thou, O my friend," replied Ulric, "that there is now any more peril to Miriam?"

"Not any," said Ben Ezra, "save that all dwellers upon the earth are ever in peril from the evil. Every payment hath been made. Her enemies are slain with the sword. She may dwell in peace for a season. But if harm cometh to thee——"

"Then," interrupted the jarl, "thou knowest that whatever of mine thou hast in thy keeping belongeth to Miriam. See thou to that!"

"Before Jehovah!" said Ben Ezra, "that will I do. The jewels and the gold are hers. But what doest thou now, seeing that the officer of the Hinnom gate will report thee?"

"I sleep this night," said Ulric. "After that I purpose going to the temple to hear the words of this son of the gods from Nazareth. I will speak to him concerning Caius. As for this affair of the valley of Hinnom, it is no secret, and I may not hide myself."

"I also will hear the rabbi from Galilee," said Ben Ezra. "Yesterday he did boldly cleanse the temple of such as were there contrary to the law."

The jarl listened in silence while the Jew told him many things rapidly, but then he said:

"He is brave. I would I had been with him. I will ask him if he needeth now a good sword. I will do as he shall command me."

But now a servant of Isaac came to summon Ben Ezra, and Ulric was alone.

"Would that I might see Miriam!" he murmured, slowly, and a delight spoke laughingly in the soft tone of his voice.

"Ulric, thy Miriam is here! Art thou in any peril? Wilt thou not save thyself?"

She stood at his side touching him, and his strong arms opened and he uttered a great cry, for she glided into them and they were closed around her.

Who shall hear or tell the words that are uttered at such a time, seeing that they are a thousandfold more than words? He who would strive to repeat them is a foolish one, as if he would echo the far-away music of a song in the night.

"Thou art safe!" he said at last. "That is enough for me. Trouble not thy heart overmuch. Only the gods may see that which cometh to us on the morrow. Go thou to thy chamber and thank thy God for me, telling him that I will offer him a great offering and that henceforth he shall be my God also for this thing which he hath done for thee and me."

So she departed as one who must, but who willeth not to go, and the night hours came upon all the city of Jerusalem.

Now at an earlier hour of that day there had been standing in the private room of Pontius the Spearman a tall and stately matron attired in costly garments, and before her stood a youth whose face was full of great agony.

"Be thou silent!" she commanded. "This was my doing. Questionest thou me? What is my freed woman unto such as thou art? Thou hast naught to do with Sapphira! Speak not of the matter to the procurator! I do counsel thee well. Thou art but a youth, O Lysias, and in youth there is folly!"

Low bent his head and his bosom heaved with pain, but he was silent. The face of the matron was noble in shape, and not unkindly, but in it was great haughtiness, for the wife of the procurator was as a queen and no man might question her will. She looked now at the young Greek, pitying him for a moment, and then she went from the room, saying no more, for the matter was ended, and he yet stood there alone.

"All the gods have forgotten me," murmured Lysias. "I will but make my report to the procurator and I will depart—I care not whither."

Even as he spoke the ruler of Judea entered the room, striding as if in haste.

"Thou art here?" he said, and his face was red, as if in hot anger. "Speak on, O Greek! Tell me of all thy doings, from the first to the last, beginning with Cornelius at Cæsarea."

"O most noble Pontius," said Lysias, "from the centurion, this parchment, sealed. He gave me no words to utter."

"I will read," said Pontius, but the epistle may have been not only brief but troublesome, for his face darkened yet more angrily.

"Speak on!" he commanded, and his messenger told all, to the place where he had parted from Tostig and the Saxons upon the shore of the harbor of Joppa.

"More than this is already known to me," said Pontius. "Hast thou spoken at all of this matter?"

"Not to any ear but thine, my lord," said Lysias. "I have been utterly prudent. Even the master of the games cannot know concerning thy dealing with the secret messenger of Herod."

"Thou knowest?" almost gasped the procurator. "Very great is thy knowledge. Thou hast done well in this affair. I will give thee now another errand. Call unto me the sentinel in the outer corridor."

Quickly Lysias went and returned, bringing with him one of the trusted legionaries of the palace guard who had been on duty.

"Take thou this youth," said Pontius, "and lead him to the fifth chamber of the lower corridor. Summon thou to that room one whom thou knowest. Say to him that I will see him again without delay. Then return thou to thy post."

"Follow!" said the soldier to Lysias. "I am bidden to show thee a certain matter."

Lysias obeyed, but with a faintness coming coldly upon him, but as he went there was a sad thought weighing upon his heart.

"O that I might but see her! Did she indeed wed him of her own free will? My beloved! O my Sapphira! O my beautiful one! I found thee but to lose thee!"

There was a stairway, and at the bottom of that there was a long passage. It was gloomy and dingy as of a prison, with closed cages on either side. Here, also, one shortly came and walked with them, a short, broad man in armor, who spoke not.

Lysias himself counted the doors.

"The fifth," he said. "It is open."

"Enter!" commanded the soldier, but he followed not, and the short, dark man went in behind Lysias.

The door closed clanging, and then there was a silence save for the feet of the departing legionary and a sharp sound of a cry from that fifth chamber. A minute passed and then another, and the short, dark man came out alone.

"The Greek," he said, "hath accomplished the errand upon which the procurator sent him. But there is blood upon my hand, and I will wash well before I report to the Spearman lest he inquire of me."

At that hour there was joyous feasting at the house of the father of the Jew Ananias. The bridegroom welcomed his kindred and his friends and the red wine was plentiful. In the apartment of the women sat the bride arrayed in her jeweled robes. All the women who looked upon her praised her, wondering at her great beauty. They said that Ananias had won the pearl, the pearl of pearls, the ruby of rubies, the rose of Sharon and the lily of the valley. Very joyful, also, was Sapphira, for her triumph and her happiness had come to her; but there came a moment when she suddenly put her hand upon her bosom.

"Lysias!" she whispered. "Did I hear him speak to me? Again! It is gone! Thank Aphrodite and thank Juno. It is better to be a wedded woman, a proselyte of the temple, than to be a bondwoman of the procurator."

The days of the wedding feast were to be cut short by the coming of the Passover, for only by express permission of the rabbis had the command of the wife of Pontius been obeyed at such a time. It was well, they admitted, to change a law to obtain a proselyte from the household of the procurator. The next day, however, would not be altogether sacred, and the wedding feast might go on, but it might be extended no further lest there should be a grievous sin against the counting of days. When the next day came, therefore, all things belonging to it followed in their order.

There was a great gathering in the court of the women in the temple, for here had come the prophet from Galilee, and he was not only preaching, but healing also. In front of him where he stood there was seated upon the pavement a closely veiled one, whose head was bowed. It was as if she might also be praying silently.

The sick and the maimed and the blind and many who were in tribulation came and stood by her for a moment to be touched by the rabbi and to make room for others to be healed in like manner. These fell away full of joy over that which had come to them, but the veiled one moved not, nor did several of the other women who were near. Once only did she lift her head, drawing aside her veil, and her voice was low and sweet.

"O Master, what shall I ask of thee concerning Ulric? Canst thou do aught for him?"

"Be thou contented," he said. "He followeth me." He stooped and put his hand upon her head and turned away, for he was departing from that place to the court of the heathen. So she covered her face with her veil and left the temple.

In the court of the heathen was a gathering that was dense for multitude, and here, also, were many who asked for healing. Near to a pillar by the outer portico stood twain who had just arrived.

"O Caius," said one, "hast thou strength to stand upon thy feet for a little?"

"Hardly, O jarl," said the centurion. "But I am a Roman. What part have I in this Jew rabbi and his god?"

"Nay, but stand thou here," said Ulric, "while I go and ask him."

On pressed he through the crowd until he stood before the prophet of Galilee.

"O thou of the sons of the gods," he said, "wilt thou heal a Roman, standing yonder, as thou hast healed me, who am a Saxon? I pray thee have mercy upon him, for he is my friend."

Now he had thus interrupted men of dignities and learning who were standing there asking questions of Jesus and gainsaying him, and these rebuked the jarl angrily.

The reply of Jesus was to them in words, but Ulric fell back thinking within himself: "His face hath answered me. I know not what this is. I will have speech with him at another time. O that I may be with him in the day of the great battle!"

Slowly through the throng he went back to Caius at the pillar against which he had been faintly leaning.

"O Caius," he said, "I did ask him. Thou wilt yet speak to him for thyself."

"Jarl of the Saxons," exclaimed Caius, "I go now to my chariot. Speak not. Seest thou not that I am standing firmly? The pain of the hurt hath departed! But here came one with a commandment from the procurator bidding thee to his house with speed. Delay not thy going, and deal with him as thou wouldst deal with me. I thank thee and I thank the rabbi. Go!"

"O gladiator, come thou in haste!" said one in the raiment of a bondservant who stood near. "The thing is important!"

"Tell him I come," said Ulric. "Wait not. I go not in thy company. But glad am I, O Caius, my friend, if thou art healed of the poison."

"That I know not," said Caius; "but the burning ceaseth. Return thou soon to me."

"O most noble Caius," said Ulric, "I think this matter of the procurator is already known to me. If I see thee not again, may all be well with thee!"

His countenance was bright and his step was firm and he turned away from Caius, going toward the outer entrance of the court of the women. The distance was but short, and here under the portico waited the veiled one.

"Art thou here?" she said. "Hast thou indeed seen him? I spoke to him concerning thee and he told me thou wouldst surely follow him."

"I know not that," he said, "but lift thy veil, O Miriam, that I may see thee—this last seeing. I go hence to death, but O that to thee might come life and joy forever!"

Her unveiled face before him was white with terror and with agony.

"O my beloved, what sayest thou?" she exclaimed. "To thy death?"

"I will wait for thee in Valhalla," said the jarl. "I will have a fair house for thee in the city of Asgard. There thou shalt live with me among the gods. I think this Jesus of Nazareth will also be there, for he is a Son of God and he is my friend and thy friend. Go thou to thy house. Fare thee well!"

Strong and brave grew her face and her form was erect when she responded: "O my beloved, if thou art indeed going now to thy death, then will I also wait and I will come unto thee in thy high place, as thou hast said. From the prophet of Galilee have I heard a new thing concerning those who die, that they have a better country than this and a better city to dwell in. I had not known——"

"O Miriam," said Ulric, "it is not new to me. So say all the old sagas of the Northland. This have I been taught by Hilda from my childhood. She also will be there, and all my kindred, with thee and me."

None saw, but a swift kiss fell upon her lips and then her veil was drawn, but Ulric went from the portico joyously, exclaiming:

"I care not now! She may bring me my ruby in the city of the gods, and I, the son of Odin, will keep tryst with her whom I love. O Pontius! O Spearman! O procurator! I will show thee how little a Saxon jarl careth for the edge of a sword."

Nevertheless, from that hour onward none saw the jarl, and two days went by. These were days of sorrow and of doubt for Miriam, waiting lonely in the house of Ben Ezra. She indeed went forth veiled to listen to the preaching of the prophet of Galilee, but ever her eyes were searching among the throngs of hearers for one who came not. "O that he might have heard these things also," she said within her heart. "Did not Ulric himself say that this is the captain who is also his king? How shall he now follow him into any battle? O that it might be!"

So thought Miriam, praying and weeping, and around her were many other women. "O weeping one," said one of these, "knowest thou not? The Master himself hath said to us that he is to be crucified!"

"Crucified!" exclaimed Miriam.

"Yea," said the other, "but that in three days he will arise from the dead and that then he will take the kingdom. It is a hard saying."

"That the dead rise we do know," replied Miriam, "but none hath ever seen them after their resurrection. I think this saying is like the words of my beloved concerning the city of the gods where I am to live with him. And he—O God of Israel! Where is he now and what hath befallen him?"

The evening of that day was set apart for the feast of the Passover. Many were gathered to eat of it at the house of Ben Ezra, for the kinsfolk of Isaac came also to partake of it. The Scriptures were read and hymns and psalms were sung, and they communed sorrowfully concerning the present desolation of their people, the terrors of the Herods, the oppression of the Romans, and their fears of the things which were yet to come upon them. After this some of them slumbered, but not all. There were those who waked and watched, for through all the city had gone a saying of Jesus of Nazareth that he was the Messiah, and that his kingdom was at hand.

Even the Romans had heard of this saying, but Pontius the Spearman had laughed, for he thought of his forts and his legionaries and he troubled not his mind concerning some unarmed mob of Jewish enthusiasts.

Chapter XL
"A Little While"

It was toward the morning of a new day that one came knocking loudly at the door of the house of Ben Ezra.

"What wilt thou?" asked the porter, partly opening the door and looking forth.

"Tell thou to those who are within," was responded, "that the Romans and the chief priests have taken the prophet of Galilee by force. He is now at the palace of the procurator and a great multitude gathereth. I am a kinsman of Isaac, the aged."

Several were within hearing and the message passed quickly throughout the house. There was then hurried girding of robes and putting on of sandals.

"We will go forth," said Ben Ezra. "I would see what this thing meaneth. He hath done nothing for which he might be taken, either under the law of the Jews or the law of the Romans."

Some said one thing and some another, and so it was over the entire city, for great was the tumult which was arising in Jerusalem. It was said that Jesus had been arrested in the night upon the Mount of Olives, beyond the brook Kidron, after he had eaten the Passover in the city with his disciples. Neither he nor they had fought save for a blow or two, and no man had been slain. Jesus had been taken before the high priest and before Herod, the tetrarch, and before the procurator, by whom he was now to be judged, the others not having due authority. The tetrarch was in the city at this season by reason of the Passover, although it was known that he was at enmity with Pontius the Spearman.

There were many rumors, nor was it easy to determine what report to believe, but when Ben Ezra and Isaac and their company came to the palace of the procurator they saw a strange matter. Outside of the palace was a place which was called the Pavement, and to this, and not into the house, the strictest Jews might advance and not become unclean, to be afterward unfitted for the Passover worship in the temple. Out of this place had been brought a throne chair of the procurator, and in it he now was seated for judgment, surrounded by armed legionaries and men of high degree, as if some matter of importance called for his decision.

Before him, as one who is accused of some crime and is awaiting decision, stood Jesus of Nazareth, but not as any had ever before seen him. He had been both stripped and scourged, and the soldiers of the procurator, besides beating and mocking him, had derisively arrayed him in a purple robe of royalty; but the crown which they had put upon his head was a torture crown, plaited of thorn-tree twigs.

The procurator himself now spoke, not to the prisoner before him, but to the surging mob of Jews upon the Pavement and in the street.

"Behold the man!" he said.

Then arose an angry roar of many voices, among which the loudest words were:

"Crucify! Crucify! Crucify!"

"Take him yourselves and crucify him," said the procurator, "for I find no crime in him."

Then said one to Ben Ezra: "Already he hath been tried and condemned before Herod, the king. Also he hath been well examined and scourged duly by the procurator. Let him die!"

There were many who responded in divers forms of speech to the utterance of the procurator, but a ruler among the Jews shouted loudly:

"We have a law, and by our law he ought to die, because he made himself the Son of God."

When Pontius heard that he arose and went into the palace for a little space, taking the prisoner with him. What further examination was made thus in private the multitude knew not, but when again the procurator came forth, having Jesus brought also, he said to the Jews:

"Which of these twain shall I release unto you, Bar Abbas, the robber, or Jesus who is called the Christ, the King of the Jews?"

But they all answered him with shouts of "Bar Abbas!" for among the rabble were many priests and scribes who were stirring them up to do this thing. Other things were said, both by the procurator and the accusers, but it seemed that he would willingly have refrained from doing any further violence to this man.

"Behold your king!" he said, at last.

"Away with him! Crucify! Crucify!" came back the tumult of fierce voices.

"Shall I crucify your king?" he asked.

"We have no king but Cæsar," responded one, and another added: "If thou spare him, thou art no friend of Cæsar."

Then a servant of the procurator brought out to him a basin of water, and in this he washed his hands, saying to them: "I am innocent of the blood of this righteous person. See ye to it."

"His blood be upon us and upon our children!" roared the mob.

Then Pontius reentered the palace and the soldiers led away the prisoner, for his crucifixion had been commanded, and there is never any great delay in the performance of a Roman execution.

"Let us follow, O Isaac," said Ben Ezra.

In the shadow behind him stood Miriam. "I also will follow with you," she said, "for Jesus of Nazareth is my King."

Within the palace shortly after this, and in the small chamber near the hall of judgment, stood twain who seemed to be having earnest words with one another.

"O Caius, my friend," said the procurator, gloomily, "am I not in a strait place this day? I have heard thee. Gladly would I grant any request of thine, as thou knowest. I may not hear thee as to this King of the Jews. As to thy gladiator, I would give him back to thee if it were possible, but his evil deeds are too many. Without warrant or command he slew my slave dealer in the valley of Hinnom. He slew the master of the games who was over him, and with him also three slaves and the Jew merchant Abbas. Moreover, I have word from the proconsul of Spain that Saxon pirates under this Ulric the Jarl destroyed two of Cæsar's triremes in the British seas. More things than these are justly charged to his account. What say est thou?"

"Thou art justified," said Caius, reluctantly. "I may urge thee no more. But I would gladly have saved him. This matter of Jesus of Nazareth would indeed be brought against thee before Cæsar. It is well for thee that thou art at peace with Herod, the fox."

"I did indeed strive to save the Galilean rabbi," said Pontius. "I will tell thee a thing. My own wife had a dream concerning him and she warned me not to condemn him as of myself. To me, also, he declared himself to be of the gods. I meddle not with them, for little do we know of the gods. But I have this to ask of thee, that thou wilt be my witness of this crucifixion, that I may truly know of whatever shall there occur."

"That will I do!" exclaimed Caius. "I also would see how he dieth, for I have heard many strange things. It would be a rare thing to see a god upon a cross. Where, now, will be his kingdom and who shall do him reverence? I know not, surely, that it was indeed through him that I am healed of my hurt. So say a great many others who are cured. Their evils have departed from them, they know not how. We do know that no man hath such power as this."

"How did he deal with thee?" asked Pontius.

"Not at all," replied the centurion. "I stood at a distance when he looked upon me, and I felt the blood changing in my veins. He did not touch me. How, then, was the healing?"

"This is wonderful," said the procurator. "I will hear thee again about that matter. Go, now, I pray thee. With him and with thy Saxon there will also be crucified a strong rebel from the Lebanon who was captured in Judea. Upon his hands is the blood of many. For this consent of thine I thank thee."

During this time a long procession, accompanied and followed by a mixed and growing multitude, was passing slowly through the streets of Jerusalem. At its head, although many marched on in advance, were a quaternion of legionaries and their officer. Close by these were functionaries of the high priest and rulers of the Jews, with zealous scribes and Pharisees and officers from the household of Herod, the tetrarch. Next in the procession walked three who bore upon their shoulders heavy beams of wood. All three were suffering from the lacerations of the Roman scourge, and one was so far weakened that he fell under his burden.

"Bring me hither that huge Jew!" said the Roman officer in command.

"I bring him," quickly replied a soldier. "He saith that he is one Simon of Cyrene."

"Let him carry the cross for Jesus of Nazareth," said the officer. "We may not be delayed. Scourge him forward!"

So again the procession moved on toward the place of execution.

Upon the bosom of each of the condemned ones, to be afterward affixed over his head upon his wood of torment, swung a wooden tablet inscribed with his name and with his crime. Of these tablets the first was written in Latin only, and it told of the rebel of the Lebanon. Upon the second was written:

"Ulric, the Saxon Murderer."

Upon the third, a larger tablet, was inscribed, in Latin and in Greek and in Hebrew:

"This is Jesus of Nazareth, the King of the Jews."

Of this rather than of the others the rabble shouted mockeries as they read, for here, they said, was a king upon his way to die as a common malefactor, and for him there was no salvation.

Silent was Ulric the Jarl, even when his eyes met those of Caius of Thessalonica, but the centurion drew near to him and said:

"O jarl of the Saxons, I did what I could, but it was beyond my power to rescue thee. Thy sword hath fallen upon too many and thy condemnation is just."

No answer made Ulric, and the centurion turned away his horse.

The gate had been passed and now the low hill of Calvary, or Golgotha, was at hand. The multitude grew as the rising tide of the sea, for all Jerusalem was stirred by this affair and the prophet of Galilee had friends as well as enemies, and many who came were weeping bitterly.

"In a strange manner," thought the jarl, "have the valkyrias come for me and for him. Where, now, is his father, that he hath thus deserted his son in such a place? Are the Romans more powerful than the gods? It is but little that we must die. Shortly I shall be in Valhalla, and I think Hilda will come to meet me at some place that is appointed. There, also, I will wait for Miriam until she shall come. I am glad that I have smitten down her enemies, giving my life for hers, and that I have made provision for her welfare."

The summit of the hill was level, and here a space was kept clear that the multitude might not hinder by pressing. Here were three holes in the earth already dug to receive the long timbers after the crosspieces and the victims should be spiked upon them.

The raiment of the condemned was the execution fee of the Roman soldiers, and there was a stripping done, but the tunic of Jesus was gambled for by them because it was of one piece, to be spoiled by dividing.

The three crosses now lay upon the sand and Ulric looked earnestly upon them, for a strong and sudden memory came into his mind.

"The token of Hilda!" he exclaimed, but in a whisper, hoarse with pain. "These are but as the runes that she showed me upon the sandy beach of the North coast before I sailed thence in *The Sword*. Now know I that my voyage is ended, and I die, as she said, by the hands of the soldiers of Cæsar. But I had not thought of such a death as this!"

First of all did the soldiers seize rudely upon Jesus, scoffing at him, and terrible was the swiftly performed work of the driving of the spikes, but there was not heard by any a cry of pain.

"Brave is he!" thought Ulric. "I also will hold my peace."

Firm, also, was the courage of the rebel Jew from the Lebanon, and the multitude wondered greatly at the fortitude of these who suffered this horror silently.

One by one did the soldiers and their helpers lift the crosses, fixing them firmly in the earth, and a loud shouting of the rabble arose at the lifting, but there was also weeping and wailing and beating of breasts among the multitude.

At the foot of the cross of Jesus now knelt women and men to whom he spoke, and he also uttered words to some who were not so near.

In front of the cross whereon the jarl was nailed there came for a moment a veiled one, putting aside her veil and gazing wistfully into his face.

"O my beloved, thou!" she exclaimed.

"Miriam! Loved one!" he groaned, being in great agony, "tarry not here! Look not upon me! Thine eyes are more than I may bear! Go to thy house!"

Her lips parted and she strove to speak, but a great tremor shook her, and no voice came from her lips except a low, hard cry, having in it what seemed the name of her god. Then turned she away and she had fallen but that the arm of Ben Ezra went quickly around her, and he compelled her to go away a little space that she might kneel and wait.

Time passeth slowly to one who hangeth upon a cross, desiring the coming of the end. The sun beat down hotly. The multitude came and went, and all the open space, to the highway and beyond, was a dense throng.

"I heard him," thought Ulric. "He hath spoken to his father more than once. If I speak to the gods, are they now near enough to hear me? I think not; but I shall see them shortly."

The man upon the third cross turned now in his writhing and he said to Jesus:

"Art not thou the Christ? Save thyself and us!"

Jesus answered not, but the jarl cried out:

"Dost not thou fear God, seeing thou art in the same condemnation? And we, indeed, justly, for we receive the due reward of our deeds; but this man hath done nothing amiss." Then he said to the Christ: "Jesus, remember me when thou comest in thy kingdom!"

Unto him did Jesus make answer: "Verily I say unto thee, This day shalt thou be with me in the Garden."

Then followed a stillness, but the jarl thought of the word which was given him. "I knew not of this garden. There it is that I am to be with him and with the gods. There, also, I shall see Hilda, and Miriam will dwell with me in the garden. It is enough! I am content!"

Great was the cruelty of the Jews and of the rabble, and the hatred of some for Jesus was exhibited in mocking speeches. It was as if they took pleasure in the tokens of his sufferings.

It was now afternoon, and for some time Jesus had been silent, but suddenly and with a loud voice he cried out:

"My God! my God! Why hast thou forsaken me?"

To that utterance the Jews replied in a manner which Ulric did not understand, but again Jesus cried out, saying:

"I thirst!"

A horrible thirst cometh upon those who are crucified, and a drink of vinegar and myrrh with other bitterness is always provided for them by some who are merciful. One ran and took a sponge, soaking it with this provision, and lifted it upon a reed to the lips which were burning.

At that moment Jesus uttered an exceedingly great voice of pain, and instantly it was seen that his soul had departed from his body. He was dead.

"Would that I were as he!" thought the jarl, "that I might be free of this agony and pass on to Valhalla and into this garden to which Jesus hath gone before me!"

The multitude were not gazing as before upon these who were crucified, for now the light of the sun was withdrawn and a great gloom was over all things. The earth quaked under their feet. Great rocks were rended. Fear fell upon men and women, and with one accord they fled away toward the city, beating their breasts and mourning.

Caius of Thessalonica stood watching these things, and other Romans with him. "Certainly," he exclaimed, "this was a righteous man. Truly this was the Son of God!"

But the Jews had taken thought beforehand for yet another matter. The next day would be their Sabbath, a holy day, and by their law it was not well for one to be left upon a cross over the Sabbath. Therefore they had obtained from the procurator an order that the deaths of these three might be hastened by the breaking of their bones. For this business came soldiers with clubs, but they struck not any limb of Jesus, who was already dead.

"I have no mark of a spear," thought Ulric. "It is not well. I die without any wound except of these spikes."

Near to him then were these soldiers, but he saw one of them thrust a pilum blade into the side of Jesus, making a wound from which poured both blood and water. Quickly, now, came merciful relief to the two others, for the soldiers made an end.

Afterward were all the bodies taken down from the crosses, as was required by the law of the religion of the Jews, and the friends of any man were permitted to do their will concerning him.

The sun had long since set, and the darkness was over the earth, when a little company of men and women entered the door of the house of Ben Ezra.

"O Miriam, my daughter," said Isaac, the aged, when they were within, "thou mayest mourn, but be thou comforted. We have buried him in my own tomb. And didst thou not hear what was said to him by Jesus of Nazareth? In him do I now believe. He is God!"

"O my beloved!" wailed Miriam, and she said no more for weeping.

"Miriam," continued Ben Ezra, "I also believe; trust thou, concerning thy husband, that it is well with him!"

"Ye are my friends," said Miriam. "I heard the saying, faintly and far. They are at this hour in the garden, do you say? But I am here and I am alone, for my love hath been taken from me. Nevertheless, I will be patient. It is but for a little while; a little while!"